The French-Czech novelist Milan Kundera was born in the Czech Republic and has lived in France since 1975. He is the author of the internationally acclaimed and bestselling novels *The Joke, Life Is Elsewhere, The Farewell Waltz, The Book of Laughter and Forgetting, The Unbearable Lightness of Being, Immortality*, and the short-story collection *Laughable Loves* – all originally in Czech. His more recent novels, *Slowness, Identity*, and *Ignorance*, as well as his non fiction works, *The Art of the Novel, Testaments Betrayed, The Curtain*, and *Encounter*, were originally written in French.

also by Milan Kundera

Fiction

THE JOKE

LAUGHABLE LOVES

LIFE IS ELSEWHERE

FAREWELL WALTZ

THE BOOK OF LAUGHTER AND FORGETTING

THE UNBEARABLE LIGHTNESS OF BEING

IMMORTALITY

SLOWNESS

IDENTITY

IGNORANCE

THE FESTIVAL OF INSIGNIFICANCE

Theater

JACQUES AND HIS MASTER

Essays

THE ART OF THE NOVEL

TESTAMENTS BETRAYED

THE CURTAIN

ENCOUNTER

MILAN KUNDERA

The Joke

FABER & FABER

First published in the USA in 1992 by HarperCollins Publishers Inc.
First published in Great Britain in 1992
by Faber & Faber Ltd
Bloomsbury House, 74–77 Great Russell Street,
London WC1B 3DA
This paperback edition published in 2016

Originally published in Czechoslovakia by Čescoslovenský
Spisovatel, 1967, under the title *Žert*

Printed and bound by CPI Group (UK) Ltd, Croydon, CR0 4YY

A CIP record for this book
is available from the British Library

ISBN 978–0–571–32626–6

FSC
www.fsc.org
MIX
Paper from
responsible sources
FSC® C013604

4 6 8 10 9 7 5

Contents

Introduction

The best things in life and love are often accidental. I came to publish Milan Kundera's first novel, *The Joke*, in a roundabout route, via his third, *The Book of Laughter and Forgetting*. Here, at the outset, I must confess that when, some time in 1980, I was sent an American translation in galley-proof, I knew of Kundera by reputation, but was otherwise – shall we say? – pretty unfamiliar with his work. In this respect, at least, I was at one with most UK booksellers. In the early 1980s, the British reading public was utterly in the dark about the genius of this modern European master.

Anyway, I read *The Book of Laughter and Forgetting*, a novel set in Czechoslovakia before and after the Soviet occupation, was seduced by Kundera's gravity-defying seriousness and infectiously ludic sensibility, and swiftly acquired the rights for Faber. From memory, we published it to much acclaim in the spring of 1982.

By now, a lot of things seemed to be happening at once. Milan and his wife, Vera, came to London, and we met for the first time, an encounter that quickly blossomed into friendship. Almost simultaneously, Aaron Asher, one of the finest post-war American editors, began communicating his own excitement about Kundera's fiction, and the scandal of his neglect by a succession of English and American publishers. Did I, asked Aaron, know anything about Kundera's first novel, *The Joke*? (Well no, not really.)

Kundera has already (see pp. 319–323) described the history of this novel's aborted UK publication. What I quickly discovered from my research in the British Library was that a 1969 edition had already been published by the now defunct Macdonald imprint in a translation which, on even the most ignorant and cursory reading, was a travesty. Still, despite the massacre of Kundera's prose, it was possible to discern signs of life. The comic premise of Ludvik's postcard to his over-serious girlfriend, Marketa ('Optimism is the opium of the people! A healthy atmosphere stinks of stupidity! Long live Trotsky!') was at once witty and captivating, qualities with which I will always associate Kundera.

We did well with *The Book of Laughter and Forgetting*, both critically in the press and in the trade. Meanwhile, the contractual tangle surrounding a new English-language version of *The Joke* was slowly unpicked. By the mid-1980s, I had signed up with Asher for an Anglo-American co-edition of a fully revised new translation of *The Joke*, superintended by him, and sat back to await the results. (It's at such moments that publishing seems like one of the best jobs in the world.) And then, I think in 1989, the translation arrived. With my inner eye, I can still see that typescript in a distinctively American typewriter font sitting in its box on my desk in Queen Square.

What did I find? There are, in addition to the postcard, many kinds of joke locked up in Kundera's narrative. For example, Ludvik loves to poke fun at people, especially Marketa. She has no sense of humour, and Ludvik, an inveterate seducer, gets bored. But the joke turns out to be on him when his seduction of Helena misfires. More jokes abound in the lives of Kostka and Jaroslav, the two other main protagonists.

For me, then and now, the deeper joy of *The Joke* lies in Kundera's juxtaposition of high-spirited sexual intrigue with cold war politics and the frozen, grey, repressive world of 1960s Czechoslovakia, as it was. Kundera whirls the narrative along from four principal points of view in a seven-part sequence. (The number 'seven' has special meaning for the author, and recurs throughout his work.)

At this distance, what else do I recall? We certainly scored some rave reviews. In the *Observer*, Salman Rushdie, a highly influential literary-critical voice, declared that it was 'impossible to do justice to the subtleties, comedy and wisdom of this very beautiful novel'. Kundera, he went on, in words of thrilling affirmation, 'is clearly one of the best to be found anywhere'. *The Times* concurred.

Kundera, wrote its critic, 'is the saddest, funniest, and most lovable of authors'. Our many readers agreed. This fifth translation of Kundera's first novel quickly went through successive reprints.

That's a long time ago, a lost world now. Before our reissue of *The Joke*, we had also published *The Unbearable Lightness of Being*, which for some heady weeks in 1984 became a national bestseller. I remember wandering round Waterstone's in Southampton Row in a daze, looking at the piled hardback copies and reflecting on the accidental ways of literature, and the luck that Faber was enjoying. Kundera was everywhere, it seemed. When President Reagan held a summit with Mikhail Gorbachev in Moscow in 1988, he even quoted Kundera on 'totalitarianism'. Sadly, when I met the now ex-president in London a year later, under the auspices of the English Speaking Union, it was not really the moment to exchange any literary-critical appreciation, even supposing Mr Reagan had known what I was on about.

At Faber, we were now fully committed to a programme in which we republished all Kundera's work, including his play *Jacques and His Master*, in translations fully approved by him. Meanwhile he completed *Immortality*, the novel I think of as his masterpiece, in 1990. Thanks to another outbreak of translator-itis, I found myself sitting in Milan's secret Paris office in January 1991 working through an English translation line by line ('Please tell me, Robert, what is the true meaning of this word 'weird'?') as the US launched Operation Desert Storm in the first Gulf War, and the Soviet empire began to disintegrate with the collapse of oil prices. In the climax to a wonderful decade of being Kundera's English publisher, Faber produced hardback editions of *Immortality* and *The Joke* in successive years, 1991 and 1992, to great acclaim.

These were heady times, but Milan always had the pessimism of the exile. I remember sitting under the eaves in his apartment on the rue Littré in the summer of 1989. The Soviet Union was falling apart, refugees were fleeing to the West, and I was excited by what looked like a moment of history. Perhaps, I ventured, liberation could follow in Czechoslovakia, too? Milan shook his head. 'Not in my lifetime, no.' By November, the Berlin Wall was down, and the Velvet Revolution underway. In my experience of books and politics, cock-up usually comes before conspiracy. That's history's joke.

Robert McCrum, 2016

PART ONE

Ludvik

So HERE I WAS, home again after all those years. Standing in the main square (which I had crossed countless times as a child, as a boy, as a young man), I felt no emotion whatsoever; all I could think was that the flat space, with the spire of the town hall (like a soldier in an ancient helmet) rising above the rooftops, looked like a huge parade ground and that the military past of the Moravian town, once a bastion against Magyar and Turk invaders, had engraved an irrevocable ugliness on its face.

During those years, there was nothing to attract me to my hometown; I told myself that I had grown indifferent to it, which seemed natural: I had been away for fifteen years, had almost no friends or acquaintances left here (and wished to avoid the ones I did have), my mother was buried among strangers in a grave I had never tended. But I had been deceiving myself: what I had called indifference was in fact rancor; the reasons for it had escaped me, because here as elsewhere I had had both good and bad experiences, but the rancor was there, and it was this journey that had made me conscious of it: the mission that had brought me here could easily have been accomplished in Prague, after all, but I had suddenly begun to feel an irresistible attraction to the prospect of carrying it out here in my hometown precisely because this was a mission so cynical and low as to mock any suspicion that I was returning out of some maudlin attachment to things past.

I gave the unsightly square a final knowing look and, turning my back on it, set off for the hotel where I had booked a room for the night. The porter handed me a key hanging from a wooden pear and said, "Third floor." The room was not attractive: a bed along one wall, a small table and chair in the middle, an ostentatious mahogany

3

chest of drawers with mirror next to the bed, and a tiny cracked sink by the door. I put my briefcase down on the table and opened the window: it looked out onto a courtyard and the bare grubby backs of neighboring buildings. I closed the window, drew the curtains, and went over to the sink, which had two faucets—one blue, the other red; I turned them on; cold water trickled out of both. I looked over at the table, which at least had room for a bottle and two glasses; the trouble was, only one person could sit at it: there was only one chair. I pushed the table up to the bed and tried sitting at it, but the bed was too low and the table too high; besides, the bed sank so much under my weight that it was obviously not only unsatisfactory as a seat but equally unlikely to perform its function as a bed. I pushed it with my fists, then lay down on it, carefully lifting my legs so as not to dirty the blanket. The bed sagged so badly I felt I was in a hammock; it was impossible to imagine anyone else in that bed with me.

I sat down on the chair, stared at the translucent curtains, and began to think. Just then the sound of steps and voices penetrated the room from the corridor; two people, a man and a woman, were having a conversation, and I could understand their every word: it was about a boy named Petr, who had run away from home, and his Aunt Klara, who was a fool and spoiled the boy. Then a key turned in a lock, a door opened, and the voices went on talking in the next room; I heard the woman sighing (yes, even sighs were audible!) and the man resolving to have a few words with Klara.

I stood up, my decision firm; I washed my hands in the sink, dried them on the towel, and left the hotel, though I had no clear idea of where to go. All I knew was that if I didn't wish to jeopardize the success of my journey (my long, arduous journey) with this unsuitable hotel room, I would have no choice, much as I disliked it, but to ask a discreet favor of some local acquaintance. I ran through all the old faces from my youth, rejecting each in turn, if only because the confidential nature of the service to be rendered would require me laboriously to bridge the gap, account for my long years of absence—something I had no desire to do. But then I remembered a man here whom I'd helped to find a job and who would be only too glad, if I knew him at all, to repay one good turn with another. He was a strange character, at once scrupulously moral and oddly unsettled and unstable, whose wife, as far as I could tell, had divorced him years before for living anywhere and everywhere but with her and their son. I was a little nervous: if he had remarried, it would complicate my request; I walked as fast as I could in the direction of the hospital.

The local hospital is a complex of buildings and pavilions scattered over a large landscaped area; I went into the booth at the gate and asked the guard to connect me with Virology; he shoved the telephone over to the edge of his desk and said, "o2." I dialed o2, only to learn that Mr. Kostka had just left and was on his way out. I sat down on a bench near the gate so as not to miss him, and watched men wandering here and there in blue-and-white-striped hospital gowns. Then I saw him: he was walking along deep in thought, tall, thin, likeably unattractive, yes, it was clearly he. I stood up and headed straight towards him, as if meaning to bump into him; first he gave me an irritated look, but then he recognized me and opened his arms. I had the feeling he was pleasantly surprised, and the spontaneity of his welcome delighted me.

I explained that I'd arrived less than an hour before and was here on some unimportant business that would last two or three days; he immediately told me how surprised and gratified he was that my first thought had been to see him. Suddenly I felt bad that I had not come to him disinterestedly, for himself alone, and that my question (I asked him lightly if he had remarried) only appeared to be sincere, though it was actually based on a low calculation. He told me (to my relief) that he was still on his own. I said we had a lot to talk about. He agreed and regretted that he had only a little over an hour before he was due back at the hospital and in the evening he was leaving town. "You mean you don't live here?" I asked in dismay. He assured me that he did, that he had a one-room flat in a new building, but that "it's no good living alone." It turned out that Kostka had a fiancée in another town fifteen miles away, a schoolteacher with a two-room flat of her own. "So you'll be moving in with her eventually?" I asked. He said he was unlikely to find as interesting a job there as the one I had helped him to find and his fiancée would have trouble finding a job here. I began (quite sincerely) to curse the ineptitude of a bureaucracy unable to arrange for a man and a woman to live together. "Calm down, Ludvik," he said with gentle indulgence. "It's not as bad as all that. Traveling back and forth does cost time and money, but my solitude remains intact and I am free." "Why is your freedom so important to you?" I asked him. "And why is it so important to you?" he countered. "I'm a skirt chaser," I replied. "I don't need freedom for women, I need it for myself," he said, and went on: "Say, how about coming to my place for a while, until I have to leave?" I could not have wished for anything better.

Soon after leaving the hospital grounds, we came to a group of new buildings jutting up fitfully one after the next from an unleveled, dust-laden plot of land (without lawns, paths, or roads) and forming a pitiful scene at the town's edge, where it bordered on the empty flatness of farflung fields. We went in one of the doors and climbed a narrow staircase (the elevator was out of order) to the fourth floor, where I saw Kostka's card. As we walked from the entrance hall into the room, I was greatly pleased: in the corner stood a wide, comfortable divan; the room also had a table, an easy chair, a large collection of books, a record player, and a radio.

I praised the setup and asked about the bathroom. "Nothing luxurious," said Kostka, pleased by my interest. He took me back to the entrance hall and opened the door to a small but pleasant bathroom complete with tub, shower, and sink. "Seeing this nice place of yours gives me an idea," I said. "What are you doing tomorrow afternoon and evening?" "Unfortunately I have to work late tomorrow," he answered apologetically. "I won't be back until seven or so. Are you free in the evening?" "Possibly," I answered, "but do you think you could lend me the place for the afternoon?"

My question surprised him, but he replied immediately (as if worried I might think him unwilling), "I'd be only too glad to share it with you." Then, deliberately trying not to pry into my plans, he added, "And if you need a place to sleep tonight, you're welcome to stay here. I won't be back until morning. No, not even then. I'll be going straight to the hospital." "No, there's no need. I have a room at the hotel. The thing is, it isn't very pleasant, and tomorrow afternoon I need a pleas-

ant atmosphere. Not just for myself, of course." "Of course," said
Kostka, lowering his eyes, "I thought as much." He paused, then
added, "I'm glad to be able to do you a favor." And after another pause:
"Providing it really is a favor."

Then we sat down at the table (Kostka had made coffee) and had a
short chat (I tested the divan and found to my delight that it was firm
and neither sagged nor creaked). Before long Kostka announced that it
was time for him to be getting back to the hospital and quickly initiated
me into the major mysteries of the household: the faucets in the
bathtub needed extra tightening, contrary to generally accepted pro-
cedure hot water was available exclusively from the one marked C, the
socket for the record player was hidden under the divan, and there was
a newly opened bottle of vodka in the cupboard. He gave me two keys
on a ring and showed me which was for the door of the building and
which for the flat. During a lifetime of sleeping in various beds I had
developed a personal cult of keys, and I slipped Kostka's into my pocket
with silent glee.

On our way out Kostka expressed the hope that his flat would bring
me "something really beautiful." "Yes," I said, "it will help me to
achieve a beautiful demolition." "Do you think demolition can be
beautiful?" said Kostka, and I smiled inwardly, recognizing in his
response (delivered mildly, but conceived as a challenge) the Kostka (at
once likeable and ridiculous) I had first met more than fifteen years
before. I replied, "I know you're a quiet workman on God's eternal
construction site and don't like hearing about demolition, but what can
I do? Myself, I'm not one of God's bricklayers. Besides, if God's
bricklayers built real walls, I doubt we'd be able to demolish them. But
instead of walls all I see is stage sets. And stage sets are made to be
demolished."

Which brought us back to where (some nine years before) we had
parted ways; this time our dispute had a swiftly metaphorical pace: we
were well aware of its fundamentals and did not feel the need to
reiterate them; all we needed to repeat was that we had not changed,
that we were as different as ever. (I must say that it was our differences
that endeared Kostka to me and made me enjoy our arguments; I used

them as a touchstone of who I was and what I thought.) To leave me in no doubt about himself, he replied, "What you've just said sounds good. But tell me: How can a skeptic like you be so sure he knows how to tell a stage set from a wall? Haven't you ever doubted that the illusions you ridicule are really nothing but illusions? What if you're wrong? What if they were genuine values and you were a demolisher of values?" And then: "A value debased and an illusion unmasked have the same pitiful form; they resemble each other and there is nothing easier than to mistake one for the other."

I walked with Kostka back through town to the hospital, playing with the keys in my pocket and feeling good to be with an old friend willing to argue me over to his truth anytime, anyplace, even here and now on our way across the bumpy ground of a new housing complex. Of course Kostka knew we had all the following evening to look forward to, so he allowed himself to turn from philosophizing to more mundane affairs, wanting to make sure I would wait for him until he came back at seven the next day (he didn't have another set of keys) and asking me whether there was really nothing else I needed. I put my hand up to my face and said, "Just a trip to the barber's," because it felt disagreeably stubbly. "Leave it to me," said Kostka. "I'll see that you get a special shave."

I accepted Kostka's patronage and let him take me to a small barbershop with three large revolving chairs towering before three mirrors. Two of the chairs were occupied by men with heads bent back and faces covered with soap. Two women in white smocks were leaning over them. Kostka went up to one and whispered something in her ear; the woman wiped her razor on a cloth and called to the back of the shop; out came a girl in a white coat who took over the abandoned man, while the woman Kostka had talked to nodded to me and motioned me to the remaining chair. Kostka and I shook hands, and as he left I took my place in the chair, leaning back against the headrest, and since for many years now I had not liked to look at my own face, I avoided the mirror directly opposite me and raised my eyes, letting them wander over the blotchy white ceiling.

I kept my eyes on the ceiling even after I felt the barber's fingers tucking the white cloth into my shirt collar. Then she stepped back, and all I could hear was the sound of the razor sliding up and down the leather strap. I settled into a kind of immobility of agreeable indifference. I felt her wet, slippery fingers smearing soap over my skin, and I mused on how strange and ridiculous it was to be caressed so tenderly by an unknown woman who meant nothing to me and to whom I meant nothing. The barber started to spread the soap with a brush, and it was as if I were no longer sitting there, as if I had sunk into the blotchy white expanse on which my eyes were fixed. Then I imagined (since the mind, even when at rest, never stops playing its games) that I was a defenseless victim entirely at the mercy of the woman who had sharpened the razor. And because my body had dissolved in space and all I could feel was the touch of her fingers on my face, I imagined that the gentle hands holding (turning, stroking) my head did so as if it were unattached to my body, as if it existed independently and the sharp razor waiting on the nearby table were there merely to consummate that beautiful independence.

Then the touching stopped, and when I heard the barber step back and actually pick up the razor, I said to myself (since the mind had not stopped playing its games) that I had to see what she looked like, this keeper (uplifter) of my head, my tender assassin. I looked down from the ceiling into the mirror. I was astounded: the game I was playing had suddenly, uncannily taken a turn towards reality; the woman leaning over me in the mirror—it seemed to me that I knew her.

She was holding my earlobe with one hand and carefully scraping the soap off my face with the other; I watched her, and the likeness that had so astonished me a minute before began slowly to dissolve and disappear. She leaned down over the basin, slid two fingers along the razor to remove the foam, straightened up again, and gave the chair a gentle turn; again our eyes met for an instant, and again it seemed to me that it was she! True, the face was somewhat different, an older sister's face: grayed, faded, slightly sunken; but then, I hadn't seen her for fifteen years! During that period, time had superimposed a mask on her true face, but fortunately the mask came with two holes that allowed her real eyes, her true eyes, to shine through, and they were just as I had known them.

Then the trail became muddied again: a new customer came in and sat down behind me to wait his turn; he struck up a conversation with my barber, going on about the fine summer we were having and the swimming pool they were building outside of town; when she responded (I paid more attention to her intonation than to her words, which were of no significance), I was certain that I didn't recognize the voice; it sounded detached, devoid of anxiety, almost coarse; it was the voice of a stranger.

By that time she was washing off my face, pressing it between her palms, and (in spite of the voice) I began to believe once more that this was she, that after fifteen years I was once more feeling her hands on my face caressing me with long gentle strokes (I had completely forgotten she was washing, not caressing me). Her stranger's voice babbled away to the talkative customer, but I refused to believe it; I wanted to believe her hands, to recognize her by her hands; I wanted the degree of kindness in her touch to determine whether it was she and whether she recognized me.

She took a towel and dried my face. The talkative customer was laughing loudly at one of his own jokes, and I noticed that my barber was not laughing, that she probably hadn't been listening to what he'd said. That disturbed me because I took it as proof that she had recognized me and was secretly shaken. I decided to speak to her as soon as I got out of the chair. She pulled the cloth from my neck. I stood up. I dug into my breast pocket for a five-crown note. I waited for our eyes to meet so I could call her by her name (the customer was still going on about something), but she kept her head turned indifferently away from me, taking the money so briskly and impersonally that I suddenly felt like a madman fallen prey to his own hallucinations and could not find the courage to say anything to her.

I left the barbershop feeling oddly frustrated; all I knew was that I knew nothing and that it was a great *callousness* to be uncertain of recognizing a face I had once so dearly loved.

I hurried back to the hotel (on the way I caught a glimpse of an old friend, Jaroslav, first fiddle of a local cimbalom band, but avoided his eyes as if fleeing his loud, insistent music) and phoned Kostka; he was still at the hospital.

"That barber you got to shave me—is her name Lucie Sebetka?"

"She goes under a different name now, but that's who she is. Where do you know her from?" asked Kostka.

"Oh, it's been a very long time," I answered, and not even thinking about dinner, I left the hotel again (it was getting dark) and set off to wander through the town.

PART TWO

Helena

I

T ONIGHT I'M GOING to bed early, I may not fall asleep, but I'm
going to bed early, Pavel left for Bratislava this afternoon, I'll fly to
Brno early tomorrow morning and go the rest of the way by bus, little
Zdena will have to be on her own for two days, she won't mind, she
doesn't care much for our company anyway, at least not mine, she
worships Pavel, Pavel is the first man in her life, he knows how to
handle her, he knows how to handle all women, knew how to handle
me, still does, this week he was his old self again, stroking my face and
promising to stop off for me in Moravia on his way back from
Bratislava, he said it was time we started talking things over, he must
have realized we couldn't go on like this, I hope he wants it to be the
way it was before, but why did he have to wait until now, now that I've
met Ludvik? Oh, the pain of it all, but no, I mustn't give in to sadness,
let sadness never be linked with my name, these words from Fucik are my
motto, even when they tortured him, even in the shadow of the gallows
Fucik was never sad, and what do I care if joy is out of fashion
nowadays, maybe I'm just an idiot, but they're idiots too with their
fashionable skepticism, why shouldn't I trade my idiocy for theirs, I
don't want to split my life down the middle, I want it to be one from
beginning to end, that's why I like Ludvik so much, because when I'm
with him I don't have to alter my ideals and tastes, he's so normal,
straightforward, cheerful, definite about everything, that's what I love,
that's what I've always loved.

I'm not ashamed of the way I am, I can't be anything but what I've
always been, until I was eighteen all I knew was the well-ordered flat of
a well-ordered bourgeois clan and schoolwork, schoolwork, I was as
isolated from real life as I could be, and when I arrived in Prague in

forty-nine it was like a miracle, I was so happy, I'll never forget it, and that's why I can never erase Pavel from my heart, even though I don't love him anymore, even though he's hurt me, no, I can't, Pavel is my youth, Prague, the university, the dormitory, and most of all the Fucik Song and Dance Ensemble, nowadays no one knows what it meant to us, that's where I met Pavel, he sang tenor, I sang alto, we gave hundreds of concerts and demonstrations, we sang Soviet songs and our own socialist-construction songs and of course folk songs, we liked those the best, I fell so in love with Moravian folk songs they became the leitmotif of my existence.

As for how I fell in love with Pavel, I could never tell anyone today, it was like a fairy tale, the anniversary of the Liberation, a big demonstration in Old Town Square, our ensemble was there too, we went everywhere together, a handful of people among tens of thousands, and up on the rostrum sat all kinds of important statesmen, Czech and foreign, and there were all kinds of speeches and applause, and then Togliatti himself went up to the microphone and said a few words in Italian, and the whole square responded as usual by shouting and clapping and chanting slogans. Pavel happened to be standing next to me in the crush, and I heard him shouting something of his own into the general hubbub, something different, and when I looked over at his lips, I realized he was singing, or rather screaming, a song, he was trying to get us to hear him and join him, he was singing an Italian revolutionary song that was in our repertory and very popular at the time: *Avanti popolo, a la riscossa, bandiera rossa, bandiera rossa . . .*

That was Pavel all over, he was never satisfied with reaching the mind alone, he had to get at the emotions, wasn't it wonderful, I thought, saluting the leader of the Italian workers' movement in a Prague square with an Italian revolutionary song, I wanted more than anything for Togliatti to be moved the way I was, so I joined in with Pavel as loud as I could, and others joined us and others and others, until finally the whole ensemble was singing, but the shouting was terribly loud and we were no more than a handful, there were fifty of us to at least fifty thousand of them, the odds were overwhelming, but we fought a desperate fight, for the whole first stanza we thought we wouldn't make it and our singing would go unheard, but then a miracle occurred, little by little more voices broke into song, people began to realize what was going on, and the song rose up slowly out of the pandemonium in the square like a butterfly emerging from an enormous rumbling chrysalis. And finally that butterfly, that song, or at least the last few bars, flew up to the rostrum, and we gazed eagerly at the face of the graying Italian, and we were happy when we thought we saw him respond to the song with a wave of the hand, and I was certain, even though I was too far away to tell, I was certain I saw tears in his eyes.

And in the midst of all the enthusiasm and emotion, I don't know how it happened, I suddenly seized Pavel's hand, and he seized mine, and when the square was quiet again and another speaker stepped up to the microphone, I was afraid he'd let go, but he didn't, we held hands all the way to the end of the demonstration and didn't let go even afterwards, the crowds broke up, and we spent several hours together roaming through Prague in all its spring finery.

Seven years later, when little Zdena was five, I'll never forget it, he told me *we didn't marry for love, we married out of Party discipline*, I know he said it in the heat of an argument, I know it was a lie, Pavel married me for love, he didn't change until later, but still what a terrible thing to say, wasn't he the one who was always telling everybody that love was different nowadays, a support in battle rather than an escape from the world, that was how it was for us anyway, we didn't even take the time to eat, after two dry rolls at the Youth League office we might not meet again all day, I'd wait up for Pavel until midnight when he came home from those endless, six-hour, eight-hour meetings, in my free time I copied out the talks he gave at all sorts of conferences and political training sessions, he attached a great deal of importance to them, only I know how much the success of his political appearances meant to him, he never tired of repeating that the new man differed from the old insofar as he had abolished the distinction between public and private life, and now, years later, he complains about how back then the Comrades never left his private life alone.

We went together for nearly two years, and I was getting a little impatient, and no wonder, no woman can be content forever with puppy love, Pavel was perfectly content, he enjoyed the convenient lack of commitment, every man has a selfish streak in him, it's up to the woman to stand up for herself and her mission as a woman, unfortunately Pavel was less attuned to the problem than the rest of our ensemble, especially a few of the girls I was close to, and they had a talk with the others, and the upshot of it all was that they called Pavel before the committee, I have no idea what they said to him there, we've never discussed the matter, but they must have been tough on him, morals were pretty strict in those days, people really overdid it, but maybe it's better to overdo morality than immorality the way we do now. Pavel kept out of my way for a long time, I thought I'd ruined everything, I was desperate, I was ready to commit suicide, but then he came back, oh, how my knees trembled, he asked me to forgive him and gave me a locket with a picture of the Kremlin on it, his most treasured possession, I never take it off, it's more than just a reminder of Pavel, much more, and I cried tears of joy, and two weeks later we were married, and the whole ensemble came to the wedding, sang and danced for almost twenty-four hours, and I told Pavel that if we ever betrayed each other it would be tantamount to betraying everyone at the wedding, betraying everyone at the demonstration in Old Town Square, betraying Togliatti, it makes me laugh when I look back on everything we ultimately *did* betray. . . .

2

LET'S SEE, what shall I wear tomorrow, the pink sweater, the blue raincoat, they show off my figure best, I'm not as slim as I used to be, but then again I've got something to make up for the wrinkles, something none of the young girls have, the charm of a life lived to the hilt, that's what draws Jindra to me, the poor boy, I can still see the disappointment in his face when I told him I'd be taking the plane and he'd have to go by himself, he's happy for every minute he can spend with me and show off his nineteen-year-old virility, he'd have broken all speed records just to impress me, oh, he's not much to look at, but he's good with the equipment and an excellent driver, the reporters like taking him along on minor assignments, and why not, it's nice to know there's someone around who likes me, I haven't been particularly popular at the radio station these past few years, people call me a bitch, a fanatic, a dogmatist, a Party bloodhound, and I don't know what else, but they'll never make me ashamed of loving the Party and sacrificing all my spare time to it. What else do I have to live for? Pavel has other women, I don't even bother to check on them anymore, little Zdena worships him, for ten years now my work has been hopelessly routine, features, interviews, broadcasts about fulfilled plans and model barns and milkmaids, that and the equally hopeless situation at home, it's only the Party that's never done me any harm, and I've never harmed the Party, not even in the days when almost everyone was ready to desert it, in fifty-six when there was all that talk about Stalin's crimes, and people went wild and began rejecting everything, saying our papers were a pack of lies, nationalized stores didn't work, culture was in decline, farms should never have been collectivized, the Soviet Union had no freedom, and the worst part of it all was that even

Communists went around talking like that, and at their own meetings, Pavel too, and again they all applauded him, Pavel was always being applauded, it began when he was a child, he was an only child, his mother took his picture to bed with her, her prodigy, child prodigy but adult mediocrity, he doesn't smoke, doesn't drink, but he can't live without applause, it's his alcohol and nicotine, how thrilled he was at the new chance to pull at people's heartstrings, he spoke about those awful judicial murders with such emotion that people all but wept, I could tell how much he enjoyed his indignation, and I hated him.

Luckily the Party gave the squawkers a good rap on the knuckles, and when they calmed down Pavel calmed down too, he didn't want to risk his cushy lectureship in Marxism at the university, but something did remain behind, a germ of apathy, mistrust, misgiving, a germ that reproduced in silence, in secret, I didn't know how to counter it, I just clung to the Party more tightly than ever, the Party is almost like a living being, I can tell it all my most intimate thoughts now that I have nothing to say to Pavel, or anyone else for that matter, the others don't like me either, it all came out when we had to take care of that awful business, one of my colleagues at the station, a married man, was having an affair with a girl in the technical department, single, irresponsible, and cynical, and in desperation his wife turned to our Party committee for help, we spent hours going over the case, we interviewed the wife, the girl, various witnesses from work, we tried to get a clear, well-rounded picture of things and be scrupulously fair, the man was given a reprimand by the Party, the girl a warning, and both had to promise the committee to stop seeing each other. Unfortunately, words are merely words, they agreed to split up only to keep us quiet and in fact went on seeing each other on the sly, but the truth will out, we soon found out about it, and I took a firm stand, I proposed that the man be expelled from the Party for having deliberately deceived and misled it, after all, what kind of Communist could he be if he lied to the Party, I hate lies, but my proposal was defeated, and the man got off with another reprimand, at least the girl had to leave the station.

And did they take it out on me for that, they made me look like a monster, a beast, it was a regular smear campaign, they started poking about in my private life, and that was my Achilles' heel, no woman can live without feelings, she wouldn't be a woman if she did, so why deny it? Since I didn't have love at home, I sought it elsewhere, not that I found any, but they laid into me at a public meeting, called me a hypocrite, trying to pillory others for breaking up marriages, trying to expel, dismiss, destroy, when I myself was unfaithful to my husband at every opportunity, that was how they put it at the meeting, but behind my back they were even more vicious, they said I was a nun in public and a whore in private, as if they couldn't see that the only reason I was so hard on others was that I knew what an unhappy marriage meant, it wasn't hate that made me do what I did, it was love, love of love, love of their house and home, love of their children, I wanted to help them, I too have a child, a home, and I tremble for them!

Though maybe they're right, maybe I am just a bitter old witch and people should be free to do as they please and no one has the right to go sticking his nose into their private lives, maybe this world we've thought up is wrong and I really am a dirty commissar and won't mind my own business, but that's what I'm like and I can only act as I feel, it's too late now, I've always believed that man is one and indivisible and that only the petty bourgeois divides him hypocritically into public self and private self, such is my credo, I've always lived by it, and that time was no exception.

As for my being bitter, I'm willing to admit I hate those young girls, those little bitches, so sure of themselves and their youth and so lacking in solidarity with older women, they'll be thirty some day, too, and thirty-five, and forty, and don't try to tell me she loved him, what does she know about love, she'll sleep with any man the first night, no inhibitions, no sense of shame, I'm mortified when they compare me to girls like her just because I, a married woman, have had a few affairs with other men, the difference is I was always looking for love, and if I made a mistake, if I didn't find it, I'd turn away in horror and look elsewhere, even though it would have been much simpler to forget my girlish dreams of love, forget them and cross the border into the realm of that monstrous freedom where shame, inhibitions, and morals have ceased to exist, that vile, monstrous freedom where everything is permitted, where deep inside all you need to understand is the throb of sex, that beast.

And I know, too, that if I crossed that border, I would stop being myself, I'd be somebody else, I don't know who, and I'm terrified of that awful transformation, so I keep looking for love, desperately looking for love, a love I can embrace just as I am, with all my old dreams and ideals, because I don't want my life to split down the middle, I want it to remain whole from beginning to end, that's why I was so fascinated when I met you, Ludvik, oh Ludvik . . .

3

IT WAS really awfully funny the first time I went to his office, he didn't even make much of an impression on me, I got right down to business, telling him about my concept of the radio broadcast and explaining what information I needed from him for it, but when he started talking to me I suddenly felt confused, tongue-tied, inarticulate, and when he noticed how uncomfortable I was he immediately switched to more general topics, asked whether I was married, whether I had any children, where I spent my vacation, and he also told me how young I looked, how pretty, it was nice of him, he wanted to get me over my stage fright, when I think of all the braggarts I meet, never let you get a word in edgeways and can't hold a candle to Ludvik, Pavel would have talked about himself the whole time, but it was really funny, I spent a full hour with him and didn't know any more about his institute than when I came, back home I quickly put something down on paper, but it just wasn't right, maybe I was glad, it gave me an excuse to phone him and ask if he wouldn't mind reading over what I'd written. We met at a café, my pitiful story was four pages long, he read it through, gave me a gallant smile, and said it was excellent, he'd made it clear from the start he was interested in me more as a woman than as a reporter, I wasn't sure whether to feel flattered or insulted, but he was so nice to me, and we understood each other, he wasn't one of those intellectual types I dislike, he had a rich life behind him, he'd even worked in the mines, that's the kind of person I really liked, I told him, but the thing that excited me most was he was from Moravia, he'd even played in a cimbalom band, I couldn't believe my ears, it was like hearing the leitmotiv of my life again, seeing my youth return from the shadows, my heart and soul went out to him.

He asked me what I did all day, and when I told him he said, I can still hear his voice, half joking, half sympathetic, that's no kind of life for someone like you, it's time for a change, he said I should turn over a new leaf, devote more time to the *joys of life*. I told him that was fine with me, joy had always been part of my credo and there was nothing I hated more than today's fashionable cynicism, and he said credos don't mean a thing, people who shout joy from the rooftops are often the saddest of all, oh, how true, I felt like shouting, and then he told me point-blank, no beating around the bush with him, that he'd be by to pick me up the next day at four in front of the radio station, we'd take a drive out into the country. But I'm a married woman, I protested, I can't just run off into the woods with a strange man, and Ludvik responded jokingly that he wasn't a man, he was a scholar, but how sad he looked when he said it, how sad! Seeing him that way made me hot all over, what joy, he wanted me, he wanted me all the more after I reminded him I was married, because it made me more inaccessible, and men desire most what they consider inaccessible, and I drank in all the sadness from his face and realized he was in love with me.

The next day we heard the Vltava murmuring on one side of us, saw the forest rising abruptly on the other, it was all so romantic, I love life to be romantic, I'm sure I behaved like a silly young thing, which may not have been becoming to the mother of a twelve-year-old, but I couldn't help it, I laughed and skipped, pulling him along with me, and when we stopped my heart was pounding, there we stood face to face, and Ludvik bent over slightly and gave me a gentle kiss, I tore myself away from him but then took him by the hand and started running again, I have a little trouble with my heart now and then, it starts beating wildly after the slightest bit of exertion, all I have to do is run up a flight of stairs, so I slowed down a little and got my breath back, and suddenly I heard myself humming the opening two bars of my favorite song, *Oh, brightly shines the sun on our garden* . . . , and sensing he recognized it, I began to sing it out loud, without shame, and I felt years, cares, sorrows, thousands of gray scales peeling off me, and then we found a little inn and had some bread and sausage, everything was perfectly ordinary and simple, the surly waiter, the stained tablecloth, and yet what a wonderful adventure, I said to Ludvik, did you know I was going to Moravia for three days to do a feature on the Ride of the Kings? He asked me where in Moravia, and when I told him he said that was his hometown, another coincidence, it took my breath away, I'll take some time off and go with you, he said.

I was afraid, I thought of Pavel, of the spark of hope he'd kindled in me, I'm not cynical about my marriage, I'm ready to do anything to save it, if only for little Zdena's sake, no, that's not true, mostly for my own sake, for the sake of the past, in memory of my youth, but I didn't have the strength to say no to Ludvik, I just didn't have the strength, and now the die is cast, Zdena is asleep, I'm frightened, at this very moment Ludvik is in Moravia, and tomorrow he'll be waiting for me when my bus pulls in.

PART THREE

Ludvik

I

Y ES; I WENT wandering. I stopped for a moment on the bridge that spanned the Morava and gazed downstream. How ugly, this Morava (a river so brown it seems to run liquid mud instead of water) and how depressing its bank: a street of five two-story middle-class houses, each standing separately like a freakish orphan; apparently they were the beginnings of a grandiose embankment that never came to anything; two of them were ornamented with ceramic angels and small stucco bas-reliefs now chipped and cracked: the angels had lost their wings, and the bas-reliefs, worn down in places to bare brick, had lost their meaning. Beyond the orphan houses the street petered out into a row of iron pylons and high-tension wires, then grass with a few straggling geese, and finally fields, horizonless fields, fields stretching out into nowhere, fields in which the liquid mud of the Morava is lost to sight.

Towns have a propensity to produce mirror images of each other, and this view (I had known it from childhood, and it had no significance for me at all) suddenly reminded me of Ostrava, that temporary dormitory of a mining town, full of deserted buildings and dirty streets leading into the void. I had walked into an ambush; I stood there on the bridge like a man exposed to machine-gun fire. I couldn't bear to go on looking at that woebegone street of five solitary houses because I couldn't bear to think about Ostrava. So I turned my back on it and started walking upstream.

I walked along the bank on a narrow path flanked on one side by a thick row of poplars. To the right of the path a mixture of grass and weeds sloped down to water level, and across the river, on the opposite bank, stood the warehouses, workshops, and courtyards of several small factories; to the left of the path beyond the trees there was a sprawling rubbish heap and, farther on, open fields punctuated by more metal pylons and high-tension wires. I walked that narrow path as though crossing a long footbridge over the waters—and I compare that landscape to a broad expanse of water because I felt the cold go through me; and because I walked the path as if at some point I might plunge off it. I was aware that the ghostly atmosphere of the landscape was merely a metaphor for everything I had tried not to recall after my encounter with Lucie; I seemed to be projecting suppressed memories onto everything I saw around me: onto the desolation of the fields and courtyards and warehouses, onto the murk of the river, and onto the pervasive chill that gave unity to the whole scene. I understood that there was no escaping the memories, that I was surrounded by them.

2

THE EVENTS LEADING to my first major disaster (and, as a direct result of its uncharitable intervention, to Lucie) might well be recounted in a lighthearted and even amusing tone: it all goes back to my fatal predilection for silly jokes and Marketa's fatal inability to understand them. Marketa was the type of woman who takes everything seriously (which made her totally at one with the spirit of the era); her major gift from the fates was an aptitude for credulity. This is not a euphemistic way of saying that she was stupid; no: she was gifted and bright and in any case young enough (nineteen) that her naïve trustfulness seemed more charm than defect, accompanied as it was by undeniable physical charms. Everyone at the university liked her, and we all made more or less serious passes at her, which didn't stop us (at least some of us) from poking gentle, nonmalicious fun at her.

Of course, fun went over badly with Marketa, and even worse with the spirit of the age. It was the first year after February 1948; a new life had begun, a genuinely new and different life, and its features, as I remember them, were rigidly serious. The odd thing was that the seriousness took the form not of a frown but of a smile, yes, what those years said of themselves was that they were the most joyous of years, and anyone who failed to rejoice was immediately suspected of lamenting the victory of the working class or (what was equally sinful) giving way *individualistically* to inner sorrows.

I had few inner sorrows at that time, and moreover, I had a considerable sense of fun; even so it can't be said that I fully succeeded with regard to the joyousness of the era: my jokes were not serious enough as long as contemporary joy could tolerate neither pranks nor irony, being, as I said, a grave joy that proudly called itself *"the historical optimism of the victorious class*," a solemn and ascetic joy, in short, Joy with a capital J.

I remember how we were all organized into "study groups" that met for frequent criticism and self-criticism sessions culminating in formal evaluations of each member. Like every Communist at the time, I had a number of functions (I held an important post in the Students Union), and since I was also quite a good student, I could pretty well count on receiving a positive evaluation. If the public testimonials to my loyalty to the State, my hard work, and my knowledge of Marxism tended to be followed by a phrase along the lines of "harbors traces of individualism," I had no reason to be alarmed: it was customary to include some critical remark in even the most positive evaluations, to censure one person for "lack of interest in revolutionary theory," another for "lack of warmth in personal relations," a third for "lack of caution and vigilance," a fourth for "lack of respect for women." But the moment a remark like that was not the only factor under consideration (when it was joined by another or when someone came into conflict with a colleague or was under suspicion or attack), those "traces of individualism," that "lack of respect for women," could sow the seeds of destruction. And each of us carried the first fatal seed with him in the form of his Party record; yes, every one of us.

Sometimes (more in sport than from real concern) I defended myself against the charge of individualism and demanded from the others proof that I was an individualist. For want of concrete evidence they would say, "It's the way you behave." "How do I behave?" "You have a strange kind of smile." "And if I do? That's how I express my joy." "No, you smile as though you were thinking to yourself."

When the Comrades classified my conduct and my smile as *intellectual* (another notorious pejorative of the times), I actually came to believe them because I couldn't imagine (I wasn't bold enough to imagine) that everyone else might be wrong, that the Revolution itself, the spirit of the times, might be wrong and I, an individual, might be right. I began to keep tabs on my smiles, and soon I felt a tiny crack opening up between the person I had been and the person I should be (according to the spirit of the times) and tried to be.

But which was the real me? Let me be perfectly honest: I was a man of many faces.

And the faces kept multiplying. About a month before summer I began to get close to Marketa (she was finishing her first year, I my second), and like all twenty-year-olds I tried to impress her by donning a mask and pretending to be older (in spirit and experience) than I was: I assumed an air of detachment, of aloofness; I made believe I had an extra layer of skin, invisible and impenetrable. I thought (quite rightly) that by joking I would establish my detachment, and though I had always been good at it, the line I used on Marketa always seemed forced, artificial, and tedious.

Who was the real me? I can only repeat: I was a man of many faces.

At meetings I was earnest, enthusiastic, and committed; among friends, unconstrained and given to teasing; with Marketa, cynical and fitfully witty; and alone (and thinking of Marketa), unsure of myself and as agitated as a schoolboy.

Was that last face the real one?

No. They were all real: I was not a hypocrite, with one real face and several false ones. I had several faces because I was young and didn't know who I was or wanted to be. (I was frightened by the differences between one face and the next; none of them seemed to fit me properly, and I groped my way clumsily among them.)

The psychological and physiological mechanism of love is so complex that at a certain period in his life a young man must concentrate all his energy on coming to grips with it, and in this way he misses the actual content of the love: the woman he loves. (In this he is much like a young violinist who cannot concentrate on the emotional content of a piece until the technique required to play it comes automatically.) Since I have spoken of my schoolboyish agitation over Marketa, I should point out that it stemmed not so much from my being in love as from my awkward lack of self-assurance, which weighed on me and came to rule my thoughts and feelings much more than Marketa herself.

To ease the burden of my embarrassment and awkwardness, I showed off in front of Marketa, disagreeing with her at every opportunity or just poking fun at her opinions, which was not hard to do because despite her brains (and beauty, which, like all beauty, suggested to those in its presence an illusory inaccessibility) she was a girl of trusting simplicity; she was unable to look behind anything; she could only see the thing itself; she had a remarkable mind for botany, but would often fail to understand a joke told by a fellow student; she let herself be carried away by the enthusiasm of the times, but when confronted with a political deed based on the principle that the end justifies the means, she would be as bewildered as she was by a joke; that was why the Comrades decided she needed to fortify her zeal with concrete knowledge of the strategy and tactics of the revolutionary movement, and sent her during the summer to a two-week Party training course.

That training course did not suit me at all, because those were the two weeks I had planned to spend alone with Marketa in Prague, with an eye to putting our relationship (which until then had consisted of walks, talks, and a few kisses) on a more concrete footing; and since they were the only weeks I had (I was required to spend the next four in a student agricultural brigade and had promised the last two to my mother in Moravia), I reacted with pained jealousy when Marketa, far from sharing my feeling, failed to show the slightest chagrin and even told me she was looking forward to it.

From the training course (it took place at one of the castles of central Bohemia) she sent me a letter that was pure Marketa: full of earnest enthusiasm for everything around her; she liked everything: the early-morning calisthenics, the talks, the discussions, even the songs they sang; she praised the "healthy atmosphere" that reigned there; and diligently she added a few words to the effect that the revolution in the West would not be long in coming.

As far as that goes, I quite agreed with what she said; I too believed in the imminence of a revolution in Western Europe; there was only one thing I could not accept: that she should be so happy when I was missing her so much. So I bought a postcard and (to hurt, shock, and confuse her) wrote: Optimism is the opium of the people! A healthy atmosphere stinks of stupidity! Long live Trotsky! Ludvik.

3

MARKETA RESPONDED to my provocative postcard with a brief and banal note and left the rest of the letters I sent her during the summer unanswered. I was up in the mountains pitching hay with my student brigade, and Marketa's silence overwhelmed me with heavy sadness. I wrote her almost daily letters overflowing with prayerful, mournful infatuation: couldn't we at least see something of each other the last two weeks of the summer? I begged her; I was willing to give up the trip home, the visit to my poor deserted mother; I was willing to go anywhere just to be with Marketa; and it was not merely because I loved her but because she was the only woman on my horizon and the state of boy without girl was intolerable. But Marketa never answered.

I couldn't understand what had happened. I arrived back in Prague in August and managed to catch her at home. We took our usual walk along the Vltava and over to Imperial Meadow (that melancholy island of poplars and deserted playgrounds), and Marketa claimed that nothing had changed between us; she behaved, in fact, as she had before, but precisely that rigidly unwavering *sameness* of everything (sameness of kiss, sameness of conversation, sameness of smile) depressed me. When I asked if I could see her the next day, she told me to phone and we would set a time.

I did phone; an unfamiliar woman's voice informed me that Marketa had left Prague.

I was unhappy as only a womanless twenty-year-old can be, a rather shy young man who has known few encounters with physical love, few and fleeting and gauche, and who is constantly preoccupied with it. The days were unbearably long and futile; I was unable to read, I was unable to work, I went to three different films a day, one showing after another, just to kill time, to drown out the screech of the hoot owl issuing from deep inside me. I, whom Marketa regarded (thanks to my own laborious attempts to show off) as a man almost totally blasé about women, could not get up the courage to talk to girls walking along the street, girls whose beautiful legs made my heart ache.

And so I was very glad when September came at last, bringing classes and (several days before classes began) my work at the Students Union, where I had an office to myself and all kinds of things to keep me busy. The day after I got back, however, I received a phone call summoning me to the District Party Secretariat. From that moment I remember everything in perfect detail. It was a sunny day, and as I came out of the Students Union building I felt the grief that had plagued me all summer slowly dissipating. I set off with an agreeable feeling of curiosity. I rang the bell and was let in by the chairman of the Party University Committee, a tall thin-faced youth with fair hair and ice-blue eyes. I gave him the standard greeting, "Honor to Labor," but instead of responding he said, "Go straight back. They're waiting for you." In the last room of the Secretariat, three members of the committee awaited me. They told me to sit down. I did, and understood that this was out of the ordinary. These three Comrades, whom I knew well and had always bantered with, wore severe expressions.

Their first question was whether I knew Marketa. I said I did. They asked me whether I had corresponded with her. I said I had. They asked me whether I remembered what I wrote. I said I did not, but immediately the postcard with the provocative text materialized before my eyes and I began to have an inkling of what was going on. Can't you recall anything? they asked. No, I said. Well, then, what did Marketa write to you? I shrugged my shoulders to give the impression that she had written about intimate matters I couldn't possibly discuss in public. Didn't she write anything about the training course? they asked. Yes, I said. What did she say? That she liked it there, I answered. And? That the talks were good, I answered, and the group spirit. Did she mention that a healthy atmosphere prevailed? Yes, I said, I think she did say something like that. Did she mention that she was discovering the power of optimism? Yes, I said. And you, what do you think of optimism? they asked. Optimism? I asked. What should I think of it? Do you consider yourself an optimist? they went on. I do, I said timidly. I like a good time, a good laugh, I said, trying to lighten the tone of the interrogation. Even a nihilist can like a good laugh, said one of them. He can laugh at people who suffer. A cynic also can like a good laugh, he went on. Do you think socialism can be built without optimism? asked another of them. No, I said. Then you're opposed to our building socialism, said the third. What do you mean? I protested. Because you think optimism is the opium of the people, they said, pressing their attack. The opium of the people? I protested again. Don't try to dodge the issue. That's what you wrote. Marx called religion the opium of the people, and you think our optimism is opium! That's what you wrote to Marketa. I wonder what our workers, our shock workers, would say if they were to learn that the optimism spurring them on to overfulfill the plan was opium, another added. And the third: For a Trotskyite the optimism that builds socialism can never be more than opium. And you are a Trotskyite. For heaven's sake, what ever gave you that idea? I protested. Did you write it or did you not? I may have written something of the kind as a joke, but that was two months ago, I don't remember. We'll be glad to refresh your memory, they said, and read me my postcard aloud: Optimism is the opium of the people! A healthy atmosphere stinks of stupidity! Long live Trotsky! Ludvik. The words sounded so terrifying in the small Party Secretariat office that they frightened me and I felt they had a destructive force I was powerless to counter. Comrades, it was meant to be funny, I said, feeling they couldn't possibly believe me. Do you consider it funny? one of the Comrades asked the other two. Both shook their heads. You have to know Marketa, I said. We do, they replied. Then don't you see? Marketa takes everything seriously. We've always poked a little fun at her, tried to shock her. Interesting, replied one of the Comrades. Your other letters give no sign that you fail to take Marketa seriously. You mean you've read all my letters to Marketa? So the reason you make fun of Marketa, said another one, is that she takes everything seriously. Tell us now, what is it she takes seriously? Things like the Party, optimism, discipline, right? Are those the things that make you laugh? Try to understand, Comrades, I said, I don't even remember writing it, I must have dashed it off, it was just a few sentences, a joke, I didn't give it a second thought. If I'd meant anything bad by it, I wouldn't have sent it to a Party training course! How you wrote it is immaterial. Whether you wrote it quickly or slowly, in your lap or at a desk, you could only have written what was inside you. That and nothing else. Perhaps if you'd thought things through, you might not have written it. As it is, you wrote what you really felt. As it is, we know who you are. We know you have two faces—one for the Party, another for everyone else. I had run out of arguments and kept reiterating the old ones: that it was all in fun, that the words were meaningless and that there was nothing behind them but the state of my emotions, and so on. I failed completely. They said I had written my sentences on an open postcard, there for everyone to see, that my words had an *objective* significance that could not be explained away by the state of my emotions. Then they asked me how much Trotsky I had read. None, I said. They asked me who had lent me the books. No one, I said. They asked me what Trotskyites I had met with. None, I said. They told me they were relieving me of my post in the Students Union, effective immediately, and asked me to give them the keys to my office. I took them out of my pocket and handed them over. Then they said that the Party level at which my case would be handled was that of my own Organization at the university's Natural Sciences Division. They stood up and looked past me. I said "Honor to Labor" and left.

Later I remembered I had a lot of things at the Students Union office. My desk drawer had socks in it as well as personal papers, and in a cabinet, alongside the files, was a half-eaten rum cake from my mother's oven. I had just given up my keys at the Party Secretariat, but the downstairs porter knew me and gave me the house key, which hung with all the others on a wooden board; I remember everything down to the last detail: the key was attached by strong cord to a small wood tag with the number of my office painted on it in white; I unlocked the door and sat down at my desk; I opened the drawer and took out my things; I was slow and absentminded; in that short period of relative calm I was trying to come to grips with what had happened to me and what I ought to do about it.

It wasn't long before the door opened and in came the three Comrades from the Secretariat. This time they were far from cold and reserved. This time their voices were loud and agitated. Especially that of the shortest of the three, the official in charge of Party cadres. How did I get there? he snapped at me. What right did I have to be there? Did I want him to have the police haul me off? What was I doing rummaging around in the desk? I told him I'd come for the rum cake and the socks. He said I had no right whatsoever to be there even if I had a whole file cabinet full of socks. Then he went to the desk and looked through the contents paper by paper, notebook by notebook. Since these were in fact my personal belongings, he finally allowed me to put them into a suitcase while he looked on. I stuck them in with my dirty, crumpled socks, and managed to squeeze in the rum cake, by wrapping it in the greasy paper that had caught the crumbs during its stay in the cabinet. He followed my every move. I left the room with my bag, and he told me not to show my face there again.

As soon as I was away from the Comrades of the District Secretariat and from the invincible logic of their interrogation, I felt I was innocent, that there was nothing so terrible in what I had written on the postcard, and that the best thing to do would be to talk to someone well acquainted with Marketa, someone I could confide in, someone who would tell me the whole business was ridiculous. I looked up a fellow student, a Communist, and when I'd told him the story from beginning to end, he said that the Secretariat was bigoted and humorless and that he, knowing Marketa, had a clear idea of what it was all about. In any case, the man for me to see was Zemanek, who was going to become Party Chairman at Natural Sciences and knew both Marketa and me very well.

4

I HAD no idea Zemanek had been chosen Party Chairman, and it seemed a stroke of luck: not only did I in fact know him well, I was confident he would be sympathetic if for no other reason than my Moravian origins. For Zemanek loved singing Moravian folk songs; at the time it was very fashionable to sing folk songs, and to do so not like schoolchildren but in a rough voice with arm thrust upwards, that is, in the guise of a *man of the people* whose mother had brought him into the world under a cimbalom during a village dance.

Being the only genuine Moravian in the Natural Sciences Division had won me certain privileges: on every special occasion, at meetings, celebrations, on the First of May, I was always asked to take up my clarinet and join two or three other amateurs from among my fellow students in a makeshift Moravian band. So we had marched (clarinet, fiddle, and bass) in the May Day parade for the past two years, and Zemanek, who was good-looking and liked to be the center of attention, put on a borrowed folk costume and joined us, dancing, waving his arms in the air, and singing. Though he was born and bred in Prague and had never set foot in Moravia, he enjoyed playing the village swain, and I couldn't help liking him. I was glad that the music of my small homeland, from time immemorial a paradise of folk art, was so popular, so loved.

Another advantage was that Zemanek knew Marketa. The three of us were often together on various occasions during our student days; once (there was a large group of us) I made up a story about some dwarf tribes living in the Czech mountains, documenting it with quotes from an alleged scholarly paper devoted to the subject. Marketa was astonished that she had never heard of them. That was no surprise,

I said. Bourgeois scholarship had deliberately concealed their existence, because they were bought and sold as slaves by capitalists.

But somebody ought to bring it out into the open! cried Marketa. Why doesn't somebody write about it? It would make a really strong case against capitalism!

Perhaps the reason no one writes about it, I said pensively, is that the whole thing is rather delicate: the male dwarfs had extraordinary sexual capacities, which was why they were so much in demand and why our Republic secretly exported them for hard currency, especially to France, where they were hired by aging capitalist ladies as servants, though obviously used for different purposes altogether.

The others stifled their laughter, which was prompted not so much by the wittiness of my invention as by Marketa's attentive expression, her passion for supporting (or opposing) the issue at hand; they bit their lips to keep from spoiling Marketa's pleasure at learning something new, and some of them (Zemanek, in particular) joined in and endorsed my account of the dwarfs.

When Marketa asked what they looked like, I remember Zemanek telling her with a straight face that Professor Cechura, whom Marketa and the assembled company had the honor of seeing regularly on the lecture hall podium, was of dwarf descent, possibly on both sides, but certainly on one. Zemanek claimed to have it from Cechura's assistant, who had once spent a summer in the same hotel as the professor and his wife and could vouch for the fact that between them they were not quite ten feet tall. One morning he had gone into their room not realizing they were still asleep, and he was amazed to find them lying not side by side but head to foot: Professor Cechura curled up in the lower half of the bed and Mrs. Cechura in the upper.

Yes, I confirmed: it is absolutely clear that both Cechura and his wife are of dwarf extraction. Sleeping head to foot is an atavistic custom of all dwarfs of that region, and in olden days they built their huts on long rectangular plots rather than circular or square ones, because not only husband and wife but entire clans slept in long chains, one below the other.

Recalling our fabrication, I felt a faint glimmer of hope even on that black day. Zemanek, who would have the main say in my case, knew both Marketa and my style of comedy and would understand that the postcard was nothing but a bit of provocation aimed at a girl we all admired and (probably for that very reason) liked to pull down a peg. So at the first opportunity I gave him a full account of my misfortune; he listened attentively, frowning all the while, then said he would see what he could do.

In the meantime, I lived in a state of suspended animation, attending lectures as usual and waiting. I was called before numerous Party commissions, whose job it was to establish whether or not I belonged to a Trotskyite group; I tried to prove that I had no idea what Trotsky stood for; I met my interrogators' glances head-on; I was looking for trust, and the few times I found it, I would carry that glance with me for a long time, nurture it, try patiently to kindle a spark of hope from it.

Marketa continued to avoid me. I realized it was on account of the postcard, and I was too proud and sensitive to ask her for anything. Then one day she herself stopped me in a corridor at the university and said, "There's something I'd like to talk to you about."

So once again, after a few months' break, we took one of our walks; it was autumn by then, we were both wearing long trench coats, yes, very long, down below the knee, as was the style in that time of extreme inelegance; it was drizzling, and the trees on the embankment were leafless and black. Marketa told me how the whole thing had come about: while still at the training course, she had been called in by the Comrades in charge and asked whether she had received any letters there; she said she had. From whom? they asked. She said her mother had written to her. Anyone else? Oh, a friend now and then, she said. Can you tell us his name? they asked. She gave them my name. And what did Comrade Jahn write about? She shrugged her shoulders, not wanting to quote my card. Did you write to him? they asked. I did, she said. What did you write? they asked. Oh, nothing much, about the training course, that kind of thing. Are you enjoying the course? they asked her. Oh, yes. I love it, she answered. And did you write that to him? Yes, I did, she answered. And what was his response? they went on. His response? Marketa said, hesitating, he's a little odd, you have to know him. We do know him, they said, and we would like to know what he wrote. Can you show us his postcard?

"You're not angry with me, are you?" said Marketa. "I had to show it to them."

"You don't have to apologize," I said. "They knew all about it before talking to you; otherwise they wouldn't have called you in."

"I'm not apologizing," she protested, "and I'm not ashamed of having given them the card. That's not what I meant at all. You're a Party member, and the Party has a right to know exactly who you are and what you think." She had been shocked by what I had written, she told me. After all, everybody knew that Trotsky was the archenemy of everything we stood for, everything we were fighting for.

What could I say? I asked her to tell me what had happened after that.

After that, they read the card and were horrified. They asked her what she thought of it. She said it was disgraceful. They asked her why she hadn't brought it to them of her own accord. She shrugged her shoulders. They asked her if she knew what it meant to be vigilant, on guard. She hung her head. They asked her if she knew how many enemies the Party had. She said yes, she knew, but she would never have believed that Comrade Jahn . . . They asked her how well she knew me. They asked her what I was like. She said I was a bit odd, I was a staunch Communist all right, but there were times I would come out with things a Communist had no business saying. They asked her to give an example. She said she couldn't remember anything specific, but that nothing was sacred to me. They said that was obvious from my postcard. She told them we often argued about things. And she told them again that I said one thing at meetings and another when I was with her. At meetings I was all enthusiasm, while with her I made a joke of everything, made everything seem ridiculous. They asked her if she thought a man like that should be a Party member. She shrugged. They asked her if the Party could build socialism when its members went around proclaiming that optimism was the opium of the people. She said the Party would never build socialism that way. They told her that was enough. And that she not tell me anything for the moment, because they wanted to see what else I would write. She told them she never wanted to see me again. They replied that would be a mistake on her part, and she should keep writing so they could find out more about me.

"And then you showed them my letters?" I asked Marketa, turning bright red at the thought of my sentimental effusions.

"What else could I do?" said Marketa. "But I couldn't go on writing after what had happened. I couldn't write just to trap you. So I sent you one more card and quit. The reason I didn't want to see you is I was forbidden to tell you anything, and I was afraid you'd ask me and I'd have to lie to your face, and I don't like telling lies."

I asked Marketa what had inspired her to see me today.

She told me it was Comrade Zemanek. He had met her in a university corridor the day after the fall term began and taken her into the small office of the Natural Sciences Party Organization. He told her he had heard that I had written her a postcard with some anti-Party statements. He asked her what they were. She told him. He asked her what she thought of them. She said she condemned them. He approved and asked if she was still seeing me. She was embarrassed and tried to evade the question. He told her they had received a highly favorable report on her from the training course and that the Party Organization was counting on her. She said she was glad to hear it. He told her he did not intend to interfere in her private affairs but that as far as he was concerned, people were judged by the company they kept and that I was not the most promising company for her.

For weeks thereafter, she told me, his words kept running around in her head. She had not seen me for several months, so Zemanek's admonition was superfluous; yet it was that very admonition that started her thinking about whether it was not cruel and morally inadmissible to encourage a person to break up a friendship merely because the friend had made a mistake, and therefore whether it had not also been unjust on her part to break up with me in the first place. She went to see the Comrade who had run the training course and asked him whether she was still forbidden to talk to me about the postcard incident, and learning that there was no longer reason for secrecy, she had stopped me and asked for a chance to talk.

She then confided to me all the things that had been worrying, torturing her: yes, she had acted badly in deciding not to see me any-more; no man is completely lost, however great his mistakes. She recalled the Soviet film *Court of Honor* (at that time very popular in Party circles), in which a Soviet medical researcher places his discovery at the disposal of other countries before his own, an act bordering on treason. She had been especially touched by the film's conclusion: though the scientist is in the end condemned by a court of honor consisting of his colleagues, his wife does not desert him; she does her best to infuse in him the strength to atone for his egregious error.

"So you've decided not to leave me," I said.

"Yes," said Marketa, taking my hand.

"But tell me, Marketa, do you really think I've committed a great crime?"

"Yes, I do," said Marketa.

"And do you think I have the right to remain in the Party? Yes or no?"

"No, Ludvik, I don't."

I knew that if I joined the game Marketa had thrown herself into, and which she appeared to be living wholeheartedly on the emotional side, I would gain everything that I had sought in vain for months: powered by a salvationist passion as a steamboat is powered by steam, she was all ready to give herself to me. On one condition, of course: that her salvationist urge be fully satisfied; for that to happen, it was necessary that the object of salvation (alas, I in person) would have to agree to acknowledge his deep, his very deep guilt. And that I could not do. I was minutes away from the long-desired goal of her body, but I could not take it at that price; I could not agree to my guilt and accept an intolerable verdict; I could not stand to hear anyone supposedly close to me acknowledge that guilt and that verdict.

I did not give in to Marketa, I refused her help, and I lost her; but is it true that I felt innocent? Of course, I kept assuring myself of the farcical nature of the whole affair, but even as I did so (and here we come to what now, with hindsight, I find most upsetting and most revealing) I began to see the three sentences on the postcard through the eyes of my interrogators; I myself began to feel outraged by my words and to fear that something serious did in fact lurk behind their comedy, to know that I never really had been one with the body of the Party, that I had never been a true proletarian revolutionary, that I had "gone over to the revolutionaries" on the basis of a *simple* (!) decision (we felt participation in the proletarian revolutionary movement to be, so to speak, not a matter of *choice* but a matter of *essence*, a man either was a revolutionary, in which case he completely merged with the movement into one collective entity, or he was not, and could only *want* to be one; in that case, he would always consider himself guilty of not being one).

Looking back on my state of mind at the time, I am reminded by analogy of the enormous power of Christianity to convince the believer of his fundamental and never-ending guilt; I also stood (we all stood) before the Revolution and its Party with permanently bowed head, and so I gradually became reconciled to the idea that my words, though genuinely intended as a joke, were still a matter of guilt, and a self-critical investigation started up in my head: I told myself that it was no accident those thoughts had occurred to me, that the Comrades had long been reproaching me (undoubtedly with reason) for "traces of individualism" and "intellectual tendencies"; I told myself that I had taken to preening myself on my education, my university status, and my future as a member of the intelligentsia, that my father, a worker who died during the war in a concentration camp, would never have understood my cynicism; I reproached myself for letting his working-man's mentality die in me; I reproached myself on every possible score and in the end came to accept the necessity for some kind of punishment; I resisted one thing and one thing only: expulsion from the Party and the concomitant designation of *enemy*; to live as the branded enemy of everything I had stood for since early childhood and still clung to seemed to me a cause for despair.

Such was the self-criticism, and at the same time suppliant plea, I recited a hundred times to myself and at least ten times to various committees and commissions and finally to the plenary meeting in the lecture hall of the Natural Sciences Division, at which Zemanek delivered the opening address on me and my errors (effective, brilliant, unforgettable), recommending in the name of the Organization that I be expelled from the Party. The discussion following my self-critical statement went against me: no one spoke on my behalf, and finally everyone present (and there were about a hundred of them, including my teachers and my closest friends), yes, every last one of them raised his hand to approve my expulsion not only from the Party but (and this I had not expected) from the university as well.

That night, I took the train home, but home brought me no comfort, because for days I was unable to work up the courage to tell my mother, who took great pride in my studies, what had happened. But the day after my arrival, Jaroslav, a school friend who had played in the cimbalom band with me, dropped by and was delighted to find me at home: it turned out he was getting married in two days and immediately asked me to be his best man. I couldn't refuse an old friend, and so I found myself celebrating my downfall with a wedding ceremony.

On top of it all, Jaroslav was a dyed-in-the-wool Moravian patriot and a folklore expert, and he availed himself of his own wedding to satisfy his ethnographic passions by arranging the festivities around a structure of old popular customs: regional dress, a cimbalom band, a "patriarch" and his flowery speeches, the rite of carrying the bride over the threshold, songs, and any number of details to fill up the day, all reconstructed more from textbooks of ethnography than from living memory. But one curious thing caught my attention: friend Jaroslav, the new head of a flourishing song and dance ensemble, clung to all the old customs but (presumably mindful of his career and obedient to atheist slogans) gave the church a wide berth, even though a traditional wedding was unthinkable without a priest and God's blessing; he had the "patriarch" give all the ritual speeches, but purged them of all biblical motifs, even though it was precisely on these motifs that the imagery of the old nuptial speeches was based. The sorrow that kept me from joining the drunken wedding party had sensitized me to the chloroform seeping into the clear waters of these folk rituals, and when Jaroslav asked me (as a sentimental reminder of the days when I had played in the band with him) to grab a clarinet and sit in with the other players, I refused. I suddenly saw myself playing in the last two May Day parades with Prague-born Zemanek at my side singing and dancing and waving his arms. I was unable to take the clarinet, and all this folkloric din filled me with disgust, disgust, disgust. . . .

5

HAVING LOST the right to continue my studies, I also lost the right to defer military service and was certain to be called up that coming autumn. To fill the time, I signed up for two long work brigades: one, repairing roads near Gottwaldov; the other, towards the end of summer, helping with seasonal labor at a fruit-processing plant; but autumn finally came, and one morning (after a sleepless night on the train) I reported to a camp in an ugly, unfamiliar suburb of Ostrava.

I stood in a courtyard with the other conscripts of my unit, strangers all; in the gloom of initial mutual unfamiliarity, the harshness and the strangeness of others comes sharply to the fore; that is how it was for us; the only human bond we had was our uncertain future, and conjecture was rampant. Some claimed we were to be given black insignia, others denied it, still others didn't know what it meant. I did know, and that possibility horrified me.

Then a sergeant came and took us to an outbuilding; we poured into a corridor and along the corridor into a large room hung all around with enormous posters, photographs, and clumsy drawings; pinned to the far wall, the large letters cut out of red paper, was the inscription WE ARE BUILDING SOCIALISM, and under that inscription stood a chair, and beside the chair a little old man. The sergeant pointed at one of us and told him to go sit in the chair. The old man tied a white cloth around the young fellow's neck, dug into the briefcase that was leaning against a chair leg, pulled out an electric haircutter, and plunged it into his hair.

The barber's chair inaugurated a production line designed to turn us into soldiers: after being deprived of our hair, we were hustled into the next room, where we were made to strip to the skin, wrap our clothes in a paper bag, tie them up with string, and pass them in at a window;

then, naked and shorn, we proceeded across the hall to another room, where we were issued nightshirts; in our nightshirts we went on to the next door, where we received our army boots; in boots and nightshirts we marched across the courtyard to another building, where we got shirts, underpants, socks, a belt, a uniform (there were the black insignia!); and finally we came to the last building, where a noncommissioned officer read out our names, divided us into squads, and assigned us rooms and bunks.

That same day still, we formed ranks again, went to supper, then to bed; in the morning we were wakened, taken out to the mines, and, at the pit head, divided by squads into work gangs and presented with tools (drill, shovel, and safety lamp) that almost none of us knew how to use; then the cage took us below ground. When we surfaced again with aching bodies, the waiting noncoms assembled us and marched us to the barracks; after the midday meal we went out to drill, and after drill we cleaned up and had political instruction and compulsory singing; and for private life, a room with twenty bunks. And so it went, day after day.

During those first days the depersonalization that had overwhelmed us seemed utterly opaque to me; the impersonal prescribed functions we carried out took the place of all manifestations of humanity; the opacity was, of course, merely relative; it stemmed not only from the situation itself, but also from the difficulty we had in adjusting our sight (it was like entering a dark room from broad daylight); with time our sight improved, and even in this *penumbra of depersonalization* we began to see the human in human beings. I must admit, however, that I was one of the last to adjust his vision to the altered light.

The reason was that my entire being refused to accept its lot. The soldiers with black insignia, the soldiers whose lot I shared, went through only the most perfunctory drills and were given no weapons; their main job was to work in the mines. They were paid for their work (in which respect they were better off than other soldiers), but I found that a poor consolation; after all, they consisted entirely of elements that the young socialist republic was unwilling to entrust with arms and regarded as its enemies. Obviously this led to rougher treatment and the threat that their period of service would be extended beyond the compulsory two years; but what horrified me more than anything was being condemned (once and for all, definitively and by my own Comrades) to the company of men I considered my sworn enemies. I spent the early days among the black insignia as a hardheaded recluse; I refused to associate with my enemies, I refused to accommodate myself to them. Passes were hard to come by at the time (no soldier had a *right* to a pass; he received a pass only as a *reward*, which meant he was allowed out once every two weeks—on Saturday), but even when the soldiers surged out in gangs to the bars and after girls, I preferred to be alone; I would lie on my bunk and try to read or even study, feeding on my unadaptability. I believed I had only one thing to accomplish: fight for my right "not to be an enemy," for my right to get away.

I paid several visits to the unit's political commissar in an attempt to convince him that my presence there was a mistake; that I had been expelled from the Party for intellectualism and cynicism, not as an enemy of socialism; once again (for the umpteenth time) I recounted the ridiculous story of the postcard, a story that now was by no means ridiculous and that in the context of my black insignia sounded more and more suspicious, appearing to harbor something I was suppressing. In all fairness I must note that the commissar heard me out patiently and showed a somewhat unexpected understanding of my desire for justification; he actually did make inquiries about my case somewhere higher up (O inscrutable topography!), but when he finally called me in, it was to say, with unconcealed resentment, "Why did you try to fool me? They told me all about you. A known Trotskyite!"

I came to realize that there was no power capable of changing the image of my person lodged somewhere in the supreme court of human destinies; that this image (even though it bore no resemblance to me) was much more real than my actual self; that I was its shadow and not it mine; that I had no right to accuse it of bearing no resemblance to me, but rather that it was I who was guilty of the non-resemblance; and that the non-resemblance was my cross, which I could not unload on anyone else, which was mine alone to bear.

And yet I didn't want to capitulate. I really wanted to *bear* my non-resemblance; to be the person it was decided I was not.

It took me about two weeks to become more or less accustomed to hard labor in the mines, to the pneumatic drill, whose vibrations I felt pulsating through my body even as I slept. But I worked hard, with a sort of frenzy. I wanted my output to be exceptional, and before long I was on my way.

The trouble was that no one took it as an expression of my political convictions. Since we were all paid piece rates (true, they deducted room and board, but there was still quite a bit left over), many others, no matter what their politics, worked with considerable energy to wrest at least something worthwhile from all those wasted years.

Even though everyone looked on us as sworn enemies of the regime, we were required to maintain all the forms of public life characteristic of socialist collectives: we, the enemy, took part in discussions of current events under the watchful eye of the political commissar, we went to daily political pep talks, we covered the bulletin boards with pictures of socialist statesmen and slogans about the happy future. At first I volunteered almost ostentatiously for these tasks. But nobody saw that as a sign of my political conscientiousness either: the others volunteered too, when they needed to attract the company commander's attention for an evening's leave. None of them thought of this political activity as political; it was an empty gesture that had to be offered up to those in power over us.

I finally understood that my rebellion was illusory, that my non-resemblance was perceptible only to me, that it was invisible to others.

Among the noncoms who had us at their mercy was a dark-haired Slovak, a corporal whose mild manners and utter lack of sadism set him off from the others. He was generally well liked, though there were some who claimed maliciously that his kind heart sprang only from his stupidity. Unlike us, of course, the noncoms carried arms, and from time to time they would go off for target practice. Once the dark-haired corporal came back from practice basking in the glory of a first in marksmanship. A number of us were particularly boisterous in our congratulations (half sympathetic, half mocking); the corporal blushed with pride.

Later that day, finding myself alone with him, I asked him, just for something to say: "How come you're such a good shot?"

The corporal gave me a quizzical glance and said, "It's this trick I've worked out for myself. I pretend the bull's-eye is an imperialist, and I get so mad I never miss."

And before I could ask him what his imperialist looked like, he added in a serious, pensive voice, "I don't know what you're all congratulating me for. If there was a war on, you're the ones I'd be shooting at."

Hearing those words from the mouth of that good-hearted fellow, so incapable of shouting at us that he was later transferred, I realized that the line tying me to the Party and the Comrades had irrevocably slipped through my fingers. I had been thrown off my life's path.

6

Y ES. All the lines were cut.

Broken off, my studies, my participation in the movement, my work, my friendships; broken off, love and the quest for love; in short, everything meaningful in the course of life, broken off. All I had left was time. Time I came to know intimately as never before. It was not the time with which I had previously had dealings, a time metamorphosed into work, love, effort of every kind, a time I had accepted unthinkingly because it so discreetly hid behind my actions. Now it came to me stripped, just as it is, in its true and original form, and it forced me to call it by its true name (for now I was living sheer time, sheer empty time) so as not to forget it for a moment, keep it constantly before me, and feel its weight.

When music plays, we hear the melody, forgetting that it is only one of the modes of time; when the orchestra falls silent, we hear time; time itself. I was living in a pause. Not in an orchestra's general pause (whose length is clearly determined by a specific sign in the musical score), but in a pause without a determined end. We could not (as they did in other units) shave slivers off a tailor's measure to show the two-year stint shrinking day by day: men with black insignia could be kept on indefinitely. Forty-year-old Ambroz from the Second Company was in his fourth year.

Doing military service at that time and having a wife or fiancée at home was bitter: it meant vainly keeping constant long-distance guard over her unguardable existence; it meant living in constant fear that the company commander would cancel the leave he had promised for one of her rare visits and that she would wait at the camp gates in vain. With a humor as black as their insignia, the men would tell stories of officers lying in ambush for those frustrated women and reaping the benefits that should have belonged to the soldiers confined to barracks.

And yet: the men with a woman at home had a thread stretching across that pause in the score; no matter how thin, how agonizingly thin and fragile it might have been, it was still a thread. I had no such thread; I'd broken off all relations with Marketa, and the only letters I received were from my mother. . . . Well, was that not a thread?

No, it was not; if home is only the parental house, it is no thread; it is only the past: letters written by your parents are messages from a shore you are forsaking; worse still, these letters recalling the port you sailed away from incessantly repeat that you strayed, leaving an environment so decently and so laboriously put together; yes, such letters tell you, the port is still there, unchanging, secure and beautiful in its old setting, but *the bearing, the compass bearing is lost!*

Little by little I grew used to the idea that my life had lost its continuity, that it had been taken out of my hands, and that it only remained for me finally to begin to exist, even in my heart of hearts, in the reality in which I inescapably found myself. And so my eyes gradually adjusted to the *penumbra of depersonalization*, and I began to notice the people around me; later than the others, but fortunately not so late as to alienate myself from them altogether.

The first to emerge from the penumbra was Honza from Brno (he spoke the almost incomprehensible patois of that city), who had been issued his black insignia for assaulting a policeman. The beating resulted from a personal argument with the man, an old schoolmate, but the court didn't see it that way, and he had come to us straight from six months in jail. He was a skilled metalworker but it was clearly all the same to him whether he would one day regain his vocation or do something else; he had no attachments, and as for the future, he displayed an indifference that gave him a carefree, insolent feeling of freedom.

The only other one of us with this rare feeling of inner freedom was Bedrich, the most eccentric occupant of our twenty-bunk room. Bedrich came to us two months after the usual September influx, having originally been assigned to an infantry unit where he had stubbornly refused to bear arms on strict religious grounds; then the authorities intercepted letters he'd addressed to Truman and Stalin, passionately appealing for the disbanding of all armies in the name of socialist brotherhood; in their confusion they let him take part in drill, and though he was the only man without a weapon, he went through the manual of arms perfectly, with empty hands. He also took part in political sessions, inveighing enthusiastically against imperialist war-mongers. But when on his own initiative he made a poster calling for total disarmament and hung it in the barracks, he was court-martialed for insubordination. The judges, disconcerted by his pacifist ha-rangues, had ordered him examined by a team of psychiatrists, and after a good deal of temporizing, had withdrawn their charges and trans-ferred him to us. Bedrich was delighted: he was the only one who had deliberately earned his black insignia and took pleasure in wearing it. That was why he felt free—though unlike Honza, he expressed his independence by means of quiet discipline and contented industry.

All the others were plagued by fear and despair: Varga, a thirty-year-old Hungarian from southern Slovakia, who, oblivious of national prejudices, had fought successively in several armies and been in and out of prisoner of war camps on both sides of the front; Petran the carrot top, whose brother had slipped out of the country, shooting a border guard on the way; Stana, a twenty-year-old dandy from a Prague working-class district, on whom the local council had passed a savage sentence for getting drunk in the May Day parade and *deliber-ately* urinating on the curb in full view of the cheering citizens; Pavel Pekny, a law student, who at the time of the February Communist coup had demonstrated against the Communists with a handful of his fellow students (he soon discovered I belonged to the camp of those who had kicked him out of the university after the coup, and he alone showed a malicious satisfaction at the thought that we had both ended up in the same boat).

I could tell about numerous other soldiers who shared my fate then, but I want to stick to essentials: Honza, the one I liked best. I remem-ber one of the first conversations we had together; during a break in a pit gallery where we happened to be sitting (chewing on some bread) side by side, Honza gave me a slap on the knee: "Hey, you there! You deaf and dumb, what makes you tick anyway?" Since I really was deaf and dumb at the time (entirely absorbed by my endless attempts at self-justification), I was hard put to explain (all at once I felt how forced and affected my choice of words must have sounded to him) how I had ended up in the mines and why I actually did not belong there. "Why, you fucking bastard! You mean the rest of us belong here?" I tried to make my position clearer (and choose more natural-sounding words), but Honza, swallowing his last mouthful, interrupted. "You know, if you were as tall as you are stupid, the sun'd burn a hole through your head." Aimed at me, this plebeian mockery suddenly made me ashamed of endlessly dwelling on my lost privileges like a spoiled child, especially since my convictions were based on opposition to privilege.

As time went on, Honza and I became fast friends (Honza respected me for my skill at mental arithmetic; more than once a fast calculation on my part had saved us from being shortchanged on payday). One night he called me an idiot for spending my leaves in camp and dragged me along with the rest of the gang. I'll never forget it. We were a pretty big group, about eight in all, including Stana, Varga, and a former student of applied art by the name of Cenek (Cenek was put in with us because he had insisted on doing cubist paintings at school; now, for an occasional favor, he covered the barracks walls with oversized charcoal drawings of Hussite warriors, complete with flails and maces). We didn't have much choice where to go: the center of Ostrava was off limits, and even in the neighborhoods open to us we were limited to certain places. But that night we were in luck: there was a dance at a nearby hall where none of our restrictions applied. We paid the small entrance fee and surged in. The hall had lots of tables, lots of chairs, but not that many people: ten girls, no more, and about thirty men, half of them soldiers from the local artillery barracks; the minute they saw us, they were on their guard; we could feel their eyes on us, counting heads. We sat down at a long empty table and ordered a bottle of vodka, but the waitress announced sternly that no alcohol was to be served, so Honza ordered eight lemonades; then he collected money from each of us and returned a short while later with three bottles of rum, which we immediately added to our lemonades under the table. We had to act with utmost circumspection because we knew the artillerymen were watching us and wouldn't hesitate to report us for illegal consumption of alcoholic beverages. Members of the normal military, it must be said, were extremely hostile to us: on the one hand, they looked upon us as suspicious elements, criminals, murderers, and enemies (as the propaganda spy novels put it) ready to cut the throats of their poor innocent families; on the other hand (and probably most important), they envied us for having more money and earning hourly five times more than they did.

That was what made our position so unusual: all we knew was drudgery and fatigue, we had our heads shaved clean every two weeks to rid them of all thoughts of self-esteem, we were the disinherited with nothing more to look forward to in life, but we had money. Oh, not much; but for a soldier with only two nights free a month it was a fortune: in those few hours (and in those few places not off limits) he could act like a rich man and make up for the chronic frustration of all the other endless days.

Up on the platform a miserable band oompahpahed its way between polka and waltz for the few couples on the floor while we coolly eyed the girls and sipped our drinks, whose alcoholic content soon lifted us far above anyone else in the hall; we were in a fine mood; I could feel a heady conviviality taking hold of me, a sense of companionship I had not experienced since the last time I played with Jaroslav and the other fellows in the cimbalom band. In the meantime, Honza had come up with a plan to whisk as many girls as possible away from the artillerymen. The plan was admirable in its simplicity, and we lost no time putting it into action. Cenek proved most resolute for the job and undertook to entertain us, braggart and ham that he was, by accomplishing his mission with the greatest ostentation: after dancing with a dark-haired, heavily made-up girl, he brought her over to our table and poured a rum lemonade for himself and another for her, saying to her significantly: "Let's drink to it!" The girl nodded, and they clinked glasses. At that moment a runt wearing the two stripes of an artillery noncom walked up to the girl and said to Cenek in the rudest tone he could muster, "She free?" "Why, of course, dear boy," said Cenek. "She's all yours." And while the girl hopped and skipped with the impassioned corporal to the inane rhythm of a polka, Honza was off phoning for a taxi; as soon as it arrived, Cenek went over and stood by the exit; when the girl finished the dance, she told the corporal she had to go to the ladies' room, and a few seconds later we heard the taxi pull away.

The next to score was old Ambroz from the Second Company, who found himself a woman both too old and shabby (which hadn't prevented four artillerymen from desperately hovering over her); ten minutes later, Ambroz, the woman, and Varga (who was sure no girl would go with him) climbed into a cab and sped off to meet Cenek in a bar at the other end of Ostrava. Before long two more of our group had persuaded another girl to go with them, and that left only Stana, Honza, and me. By now the artillerymen were eyeing us more and more ominously because the connection between our diminishing numbers and the disappearance of the three women from their lair had finally begun to dawn on them. We tried to look innocent, but it was clear a fight was brewing. "How about one more taxi and an honorable retreat," I said, looking wistfully at a blonde I had managed to dance with once early in the evening without plucking up the courage to suggest we leave together; I had hoped to have another chance later on, but the artillerymen had guarded her so zealously that I never got near her again. "Nothing else we can do," said Honza, starting off to the phone. But as he walked across the floor, the artillerymen all stood up from their tables and moved quickly to surround him. The fight now seemed imminent, and Stana and I had no choice but to get up from our table and make our way over to our threatened companion. For a while the group of artillerymen simply stood there in ominous silence, but suddenly one drunken noncom (he probably had his own bottle under the table) launched into a long tirade about how his father had been unemployed under capitalism and it made him sick to stand by and watch these bourgeois brats with their black insignia lord it over them, it made him sick, so if his comrades didn't hold him back, he might just give that bastard (meaning Honza) a good sock in the jaw. At the first pause in the noncom's tirade Honza inquired civilly what the Comrades from the artillery wanted of him. We want you out of here, and on the double, they said, to which Honza replied that that was exactly what we wanted and would they please let him call a taxi. By this point the noncom looked ready to have a fit: the bastards, he screamed in a high-pitched voice, the fucking bastards! We break our asses, we work like slaves for nothing, and these capitalists, these foreign agents, these dirty shitheads ride around in taxis! Not this time! I'll strangle them first with my bare hands!

Soon everyone had joined in, civilians and soldiers alike, along with the employees of the dance hall, who were trying hard to avoid an incident. Then I caught sight of my blonde; she had been left alone at her table and (indifferent to the argument) was making her way to the ladies' room. I detached myself from the crowd as inconspicuously as I could and followed her into the vestibule, where the cloakroom and toilets were; I felt like a beginning swimmer who had been thrown in the deep end, and shy or not, I had to act; I rummaged around in my pocket, pulled out several crumpled hundred-crown notes, and said to her, "How about coming with us? You'll have a better time." She looked down at the money and shrugged her shoulders. I told her I'd wait outside; she nodded, disappeared into the ladies' room, and soon came outside with her coat on; she smiled at me and said she could tell right off I wasn't like the rest of them. It made me feel good; I took her arm and led her across the street and around the corner, where we watched the entrance to the hall (it was lit by a solitary streetlamp) and waited for Honza and Stana to come out. The blonde asked me if I was a student, and when I said I was, she told me she'd had some money stolen from her the day before in the factory cloakroom, and since it belonged to the factory, she was terribly afraid they'd take her to court: could I lend her a hundred crowns? I reached into my pocket and gave her two of the crumpled banknotes.

Before long out came Honza and Stana with their caps and coats on. But the moment I whistled to them, three other soldiers (capless and coatless) rushed out of the hall on their heels. All I could hear was the menacing intonation of their questions, but I didn't need words to guess their meaning: it was my blonde they were after. Then one of them lunged at Honza, and the fight was on. Stana had only one to deal with, Honza two; they were just about to pin him to the ground when I ran up and laid into one of them. The artillerymen had assumed they'd be numerically superior, and as soon as the sides were equal, they lost their momentum; when one of them folded under Stana's fist, we took advantage of their confusion and beat a hasty retreat.

The blonde was waiting obediently for us around the corner. When Honza and Stana saw her, they went wild with joy, saying that I was the greatest, and tried to hug me, and for the first time in as long as I could remember I felt genuinely and hilariously happy. Honza pulled a full bottle of rum from under his coat (how he'd managed to keep it intact through the fight was beyond me) and swung it above his head. We were in uproarious spirits, except we had nowhere to go: we'd been thrown out of one place, the rest were off limits, and our ranting rivals had cut off our taxi supply and might at any moment threaten our very existence with a newly mounted campaign. We set off quickly down a narrow alley between some houses; after a short distance the houses gave way to a wall on one side, a fence on the other; up against the fence stood a hay wagon, and a little farther, a farm machine with a metal seat. "A throne," I said, and Honza sat the blonde on the seat, which was a few feet off the ground. The bottle passed from hand to hand; all four of us drank from it; the blonde soon became voluble and threw a challenge at Honza, "I bet you won't lend me a hundred crowns," whereupon Honza slipped her a hundred-crown note and she opened her coat, hitched up her skirt, and pulled down her panties. She took my hand and pulled me towards her, but I was scared and broke away from her, pushing Stana toward her instead; Stana showed no hesitation whatever and entered resolutely between her legs. They lasted less than twenty seconds together; I wanted to give Honza precedence (partly because I was trying to play the host, partly because I was still scared), but this time the girl was more determined and pulled me against her hard, and when, aroused by her caresses, I was finally ready to oblige her, she whispered tenderly in my ear, "I only came along because of you, silly," and began to sigh, and all at once I genuinely felt she was a nice girl, in love with me and worthy of my love, and she went on sighing, and I went at it with abandon, but suddenly Honza came out with some obscenity, and I realized I wasn't in love with her, so I pulled away from her abruptly, without finishing, and she looked up at me almost frightened and said, "Hey, what's going on?" but by then Honza had taken my place, and the sighs started again.

We didn't get back to camp until nearly two in the morning. At half past four we were up for the voluntary Sunday shift that earned the commander a bonus and us our biweekly Saturday passes. We were sleepy, the alcohol was still in us, and although we moved like zombies through the semi-darkness of the pit gallery, I recalled our evening with pleasure.

Our next leave two weeks later didn't measure up at all; Honza had his pass revoked for some incident, and I went out with two men from another company whom I knew only slightly. We immediately set our sights on a sure thing—a woman whose monstrous height had earned her the nickname Lamp-post. She was ugly, but what could we do? The circle of women at our disposal was severely limited, especially by constraints of time. The necessity of taking full advantage of every leave (so short and so hard to come by) invariably made the men prefer the accessible to the tolerable. By comparing notes, they gradually put together a pool (a pitiful pool) of more or less accessible (and, of course, barely tolerable) women and made it available for general use.

Lamp-post was part of this pool; not that I minded; when the other two joked on and on about how unbelievably tall she was, about how we'd have to find some bricks to stand on when the time came, I found myself in a curious way enjoying this gross and tedious humor: it intensified my raging lust for a woman; any woman; the less individualized, the less personalized, the better; any woman *whatsoever*.

But even though I'd had quite a bit to drink, my burning desire subsided the moment I laid eyes on her. It all seemed disgusting and pointless, and because neither Honza nor Stana nor anyone I liked had been there, I woke up the next morning with a hangover so fierce that the doubts it spawned retroactively included the events of the previous leave.

Had I perhaps felt the stirrings of some moral principle? Nonsense; it was revulsion, pure and simple. But why revulsion, when a few short hours before I had been consumed by desire for a woman and the fury of that desire was intimately bound up with my indifference about who the woman would be? Was I perhaps more delicate than the others? Did I have an aversion to prostitutes? Nonsense: I was gripped by sadness.

Sadness over the sudden realization that there was nothing exceptional about what I had been through, that I had not chosen it out of excess or caprice or an obsessive desire to know and experience everything (the sublime and the despicable), that it had simply become the fundamental and *customary* condition of my existence. That it precisely defined the range of my opportunities, that it accurately depicted the horizon of my love life from then on. That it was an expression not of my freedom (as I might have seen it, say, a year earlier), but of my submission, my limitation, my *condemnation*. And I felt fear. Fear of that bleak horizon, fear of that destiny. I felt my soul shriveling, I felt it retreating, and I was frightened by the thought that it could not escape its encirclement.

7

SADNESS OVER our bleak erotic horizons was something nearly all of us went through. Bedrich (the author of the peace manifestos) resisted it by withdrawing into his own depths to commune with his mystic God, the erotic complement to this religious turn inward being ritual masturbation. Others exhibited a much greater degree of self-deception, supplementing their cynical whoring expeditions with the most maudlin romanticism: many had their own loves at home and burnished their memory to a brilliant sheen; many believed in Enduring faithfulness and faithful Expectation; many tried to convince themselves in secret that girls they had picked up drunk in some bar burned for them with a holy fire. Stana had two visits from a girl he'd gone with in Prague before he was drafted (but had never taken seriously), and suddenly he turned tender and (true to his impetuous nature) determined on an immediate wedding. He claimed to have thought this plan up just to get the two-day marriage leave, but I could see through his cynical façade. It was early March when the commander actually gave him the forty-eight hours, and Stana went off to Prague for the weekend to get married. I remember this perfectly because the day of Stana's wedding turned out to be a very important day for me as well.

I had been granted a pass, and still upset over the last one, squandered on Lamp-post, I avoided my fellow soldiers and went off on my own. I climbed aboard an ancient narrow-gauge tram that linked outlying neighborhoods of Ostrava and let it carry me away. I got off randomly and changed just as randomly to a tram on a different line; the endless outskirts with their curious mixture of factories and nature, fields and garbage dumps, woods and slag heaps, apartment houses and farmhouses, both attracted and disturbed me in a strange way; again I got off the tram, but this time I took a long walk, drinking in the peculiar landscape with something akin to passion and trying to grasp what made it what it was, trying to put into words what gave its multiplicity of disparate elements their unity and order; I walked past an idyllic little house covered with ivy and it occurred to me that it belonged there precisely *because* it was so different from the shabby buildings all around it, from the silhouettes of pit headframes and chimneys and furnaces that served as its backdrop; I walked past low-grade temporary housing and saw a house not too far off, a dirty, gray old house, but with its own garden and iron fence and large weeping willow, a real freak in such surroundings—and yet, I said to myself, it belongs there exactly *because* of this. I was disturbed by all these minor *incompatibilities* not only because they struck me as the common denominator of the surrounding area, but because they provided me with an image of my own fate, my own exile in this city; and of course: the projection of my personal history onto the sheer objectiveness of an entire city offered me a certain relief; I understood that I no more belonged there than did the weeping willow and the little ivy-covered house, than did the short streets leading nowhere, streets lined with houses that seemed to come from a different place; I no more belonged there, in that once pleasantly rustic countryside, than did the hideous temporary housing, and I realized that it was *because* I did not belong there that it was my true place, in this appalling city of incompatibilities, this city whose relentless grip chained together things foreign to each other.

I ended up walking down the long street of an ancient village, now one of the nearer suburbs of Ostrava. I stopped in front of a large two-story building with a vertical CINEMA sign attached to one corner. I speculated idly, as chance passersby are wont to do, on why the sign said only CINEMA, with no name. I searched all over the outside of the building (which looked singularly unlike a cinema) but found no other sign. What I did find was an alley about five feet wide separating the building from the one next door, and after following it into a courtyard, I saw a one-story wing attached to the back with showcases along the wall for film posters. I went up to them but still found no name; I looked around and saw a little girl behind a wire fence in the neighboring backyard. I asked her what the cinema was called; she gave me a surprised look and said she didn't know. I resigned myself to its anonymity; in this Ostrava exile even cinemas had no names.

I drifted back (for no particular reason) to the showcases and noticed only then that the day's feature, that the show of the day, as announced by a poster and two stills, was the Soviet film *Court of Honor,* whose heroine Marketa had alluded to when she took it upon herself to play the angel of mercy in my life, the film whose harsher aspects the Comrades had alluded to during the Party proceedings against me; it had caused me enough grief, and I had hoped never to hear of it again; but no, not even here in Ostrava could I escape its pointing finger. . . . Still, if we don't like a pointing finger, we can turn our back on it. I did, and headed for the alleyway to the street.

And it was then I first set eyes on Lucie.

She was coming in my direction, in the direction of the courtyard; why didn't I simply walk past her? was it because I was merely drifting aimlessly? or because the unusual late-afternoon lighting in the courtyard held me back? or was it something in the way she looked? But her appearance was utterly ordinary. True, later it was this very *ordinariness* that touched and attracted me, but how was it she caught my eye and stopped me in my tracks the first time I saw her? hadn't I seen enough ordinary girls in the streets of Ostrava? or was her ordinariness so extraordinary? I don't know. I only know I stood and looked at her: she took her time, walking slowly to the showcases, stopped in front of the *Court of Honor* stills, then turned towards the entrance and went through the open door into the lobby. Yes, it must have been Lucie's singular slowness that fascinated me, a slowness radiating a resigned consciousness that there was nowhere to hurry to and that it was useless to reach impatiently toward anything. Yes, maybe it really was that melancholy slowness that made me follow her as she went up to the box office, took out some change, bought a ticket, glanced into the auditorium, then turned around and came back out into the courtyard.

I couldn't take my eyes off her. She stood with her back to me, looking out past the courtyard to where a group of cottages and gardens, each enclosed by its own picket fence, crept up a hill until the edge of a quarry cut them off. (I'll never forget that courtyard; I remember its every detail, I remember the wire fence separating it from the backyard where the little girl sat staring out into space, I remember that the steps where she sat were flanked by a low wall with two empty flowerpots and a gray washtub on it, I remember the smoky sun edging its way down over the quarry.)

It was ten to six, which meant the show wouldn't begin for ten minutes. Lucie turned and walked slowly across the courtyard and out into the street; I followed her, the scene of ravaged rural Ostrava behind me gave way to an urban setting. Fifty steps away was a pleasant little square, neatly kept up, with a tiny park and benches in front of a redbrick building with a pseudo-Gothic clock tower. I followed Lucie: she sat down on a bench; her slowness never left her for an instant; she seemed almost to be *sitting slowly;* she didn't look around, didn't let her eyes wander; she sat the way we sit when waiting for the outcome of a surgical operation, waiting for something that so engages us it drives us inwards, away from our surroundings; it must have been that inward concentration that allowed me to hover over her, look her up and down, without her noticing me.

A great deal has been said about love at first sight; I am perfectly aware of love's retrospective tendency to make a legend of itself, turn its beginnings into myth; so I don't want to assert that it was *love;* but I have no doubt there was a kind of clairvoyance at work: I immediately felt, sensed, grasped the essence of Lucie's being or, to be more precise, the essence of what she was later to become for me; Lucie had revealed herself to me the way *religious truth* reveals itself.

I looked at her; I saw a slipshod permanent crumpling her hair into a shapeless mass of curls; I saw a brown overcoat, pitifully threadbare and a bit too short; I saw a face both unobtrusively attractive and attractively unobtrusive; I sensed in this young woman tranquillity, simplicity, and modesty, and I felt that these were qualities I needed; moreover, it seemed to me that we were very much akin: all I had to do was to go up and start talking to her and she would smile as if a long-lost brother had suddenly appeared before her.

Then Lucie raised her head; she looked at the clock tower (even this slight movement is fixed in my memory, the movement of a girl who has no watch and instinctively sits facing a clock). She stood up and started back to the cinema; I wanted to go up to her; I lacked not the courage but the words; my heart was full, but my head was empty of even a single syllable; so I merely followed her into the small lobby. All at once a handful of people rushed in and made a beeline for the box office. I stepped ahead of them and bought a ticket for the detested film.

Meanwhile she had gone in; in the nearly empty auditorium numbered tickets lost all significance, and we sat where we pleased; I turned into Lucie's row and took the seat next to her. At that moment a fanfare from a worn record blared out into the hall, the lights dimmed, and the advertisements appeared on the screen.

Lucie must have realized that the soldier with black insignia had not sat next to her by chance; she must have been aware of me the whole time, must have felt my proximity, all the more, perhaps, because I concentrated entirely on her; to what was happening on the screen, I paid no attention (what a ridiculous revenge: I enjoyed letting the film so often quoted at me by my moral guardians unreel before me unheeded).

Finally the film was over, the lights came on, and the tiny audience stood up and stretched. Lucie stood up too; she took the folded brown overcoat from her lap and put one arm in the sleeve. I quickly put on my cap to hide my clean-shaven skull, and without a word helped her into the other sleeve. She looked up at me briefly, mutely, and gave me a slight nod, but I couldn't tell whether to interpret it as a sign of thanks or as a purely instinctive gesture. Then she inched her way out of the row. I immediately threw on my green coat (it was too long on me and probably not very becoming) and went after her. We were still inside the auditorium when I first spoke to her.

Those two hours of sitting next to her, thinking of her, must have put me on her wavelength: suddenly I was able to talk to her as if I knew her well; I did not begin the conversation with a joke or a paradox, as had been my custom, I was entirely natural—surprising myself, since in the presence of young women, I had always staggered under the weight of my masks.

I asked her where she lived, what she did, whether she went to the movies a lot. I told her that I worked in the mines, that it was hard work, that I didn't have much time off. She said that she worked in a factory and lived in a dormitory, that she had to be in by eleven, that she went to the movies a lot because she didn't like going to dances. I told her I'd be glad to go to the movies with her anytime she was free. She said she'd rather go alone. I asked her if it was because she felt sad. She said it was. I told her I wasn't particularly cheerful either.

Nothing brings people together more quickly (though often spuriously and deceitfully) than shared melancholy; this atmosphere of quiet understanding, which puts all manner of fears and inhibitions to sleep and is easily comprehended by the refined and vulgar, the erudite and unlettered, is the most simple route to rapport, yet extremely rare: for one has to lay aside cultivated restraints, cultivated gestures and facial expressions, and be simple; how I managed to do it (suddenly, with no preparation), I who'd always fumbled blindly behind my false faces, I do not know; I do not know, but it was like an unexpected gift, a miraculous liberation.

We told each other the most ordinary things about ourselves; our confessions were short and to the point. When we reached the dormitory, we stood outside for a while under a streetlamp that bathed Lucie in light, and I looked at her brown coat and stroked her, not her cheeks or her hair, but the ragged material of this touching garment.

I still remember the streetlamp swaying and the girls laughing raucously as they passed us on their way into the dormitory; I remember looking up at Lucie's building, at the bare gray wall and windows without ledges; and I remember Lucie's face, which (unlike the faces of other girls I'd known in similar situations) was calm, almost blank, rather like the face of a schoolgirl standing at the blackboard humbly (without artifice or guile) reciting what she knows, seeking neither high marks nor high praise.

We agreed I'd send a postcard to let her know when I had my next leave and could see her. We said good night (without kissing or touching), and I walked away. After a few steps I turned and saw her standing in the doorway, not unlocking the door, just standing there

68

watching me; only then, when I was a little way off, did she drop her reserve and allow her eyes (so timid before) to fix me in a long stare. Then she lifted her arm like someone who has never waved, who doesn't know how to wave, who only knows that when one person leaves, the other person waves, and did her awkward best to make the gesture. I stopped and waved back, and we stood there looking at each other. Then I started off again, stopped once more (Lucie's hand was still going), and went on, starting and stopping, until finally I turned the corner and we vanished from each other's sight.

8

F<small>ROM THAT EVENING</small> I was different inside; I was inhabited again; housekeeping had suddenly been set up within me as in a room, and someone was living there. The clock that for months had hung silent on the wall had suddenly begun to tick. This was significant: time, which until then had flowed like an indifferent stream from nothingness to nothingness (for I had been living in the pause!), without articulation, without measure, had begun to wear its human face again; to mark itself off, measure itself out. I came to live for my passes, and each day was a rung on the ladder to Lucie.

Never in my life have I devoted such thought, such slow concentration, to a woman (though, of course, I've never had so much time for it either). To no other woman have I felt such gratitude.

Gratitude? For what? First and foremost for releasing me from the pathetically limited erotic horizons that surrounded us. True: Stana the newlywed had also found a way out: he had a beloved wife at home in Prague. But Stana was not to be envied. By marrying, he had set his destiny in motion, and the minute he boarded the train back to Ostrava, he lost all control over it.

By establishing an acquaintance with Lucie, I too had set my destiny in motion; but I did not lose sight of it. Though we didn't meet very often, at least our meetings were fairly regular, and I knew she was capable of waiting several weeks and then greeting me as if we'd seen each other the day before.

But Lucie did more than free me from the overall nausea I felt after our bleak erotic adventures. Even if by that time I knew I'd lost my fight and would never be able to do anything about my black insignia, even if I knew it was senseless to alienate myself from people I'd be living with for two years or more, senseless to trumpet my right to the career I'd chosen for myself (it took me a while to realize how privileged a career it was), my change of attitude was brought about only by reason and will, and therefore could not dry the internal tears I shed over my *lost destiny*. These internal tears Lucie stilled as if by magic. All I needed was to feel her close to me, feel the warm circumference of her life, a life in which there was no room for questions of cosmopolitanism and internationalism, political vigilance and the class struggle, controversies over the definition of the dictatorship of the proletariat, politics with its strategy and tactics.

These were the concerns (so much a part of the times that their vocabulary will soon be incomprehensible) which had led to my downfall, and yet I could not let go of them. I had all kinds of answers ready for the commissions that called me in and asked me what had made me become a Communist, but what had attracted me to the movement more than anything, dazzled me, was the feeling (real or apparent) of standing near the *wheel of history*. For in those days we actually did decide the fate of men and events, especially at the universities; in those early years there were very few Communists on the faculty, and the Communists in the student body ran the universities almost single-handed, making decisions on academic staffing, teaching reform, and the curriculum. The intoxication we experienced is commonly known as the intoxication of power, but (with a bit of good will) I could choose less severe words: we were bewitched by history; we were drunk with the thought of jumping on its back and feeling it beneath us; admittedly, in most cases the result was an ugly lust for power, but (as all human affairs are ambiguous) there was still (and especially, perhaps, in us, the young), an altogether idealistic illusion that we were inaugurating a human era in which man (all men) would be neither *outside* history, nor *under the heel of history*, but would create and direct it.

I was convinced that far from the wheel of history there was no life, only vegetation, boredom, exile, Siberia. And suddenly (after six months of Siberia) I'd found a completely new and unexpected opportunity for life: I saw spread before me, hidden beneath history's soaring wings, a forgotten meadow of everyday life, where a poor, pitiful, but lovable woman was waiting for me—Lucie.

What did Lucie know of the great wings of history? When could she have heard their sound? She knew nothing of history, she lived *beneath* it; it held no attraction for her, it was alien to her; she knew nothing of the *great* and *contemporary* concerns; she lived for her *small* and *eternal* concerns. And suddenly I'd been liberated; Lucie had come to take me off to her *gray paradise,* and the step that such a short time before had seemed so formidable, the one I would take in getting out of history, was suddenly a step toward release. Lucie held me shyly by the elbow, and I let myself be led. . . .

Lucie was my gray usherette. But who was she in more concrete terms?

She was nineteen, though in fact much older, as women tend to be when they've led a hard life and been catapulted headfirst from childhood to adulthood. She said she was from western Bohemia and had finished school before becoming an apprentice. She didn't enjoy talking about home and wouldn't have said anything if I hadn't pressed her. She had been unhappy there. "My parents never liked me," she said, and as proof she told me about how her mother had remarried and her stepfather drank and was cruel to her and how once they'd accused her of hiding some money from them and how they always beat her. When their disagreements reached a certain pitch, Lucie took the first opportunity and left for Ostrava; she had been there a whole year; she had some girlfriends there, but she preferred keeping to herself; her friends went out dancing and brought boys back to the dormitory, and Lucie was against that; she was serious: she preferred going to the movies.

Yes, she thought of herself as "serious" and associated this quality with going to the movies. Her favorites were the war films so prevalent at the time, perhaps because they were exciting, but more likely because the unmitigated suffering in them filled her with feelings of pity and sadness she found uplifting and indicative of the "serious" part of herself she prized so highly.

But it would not be accurate to say that I was attracted to Lucie only by the exoticism of her simplicity. Her simplicity, the gaps in her education, did not prevent her from understanding me. This understanding consisted not in experience or knowledge, or in the ability to argue and advise, but in the receptiveness with which she listened to me.

I remember one summer day: my leave happened to begin before Lucie's shift was over; I had taken a book along, and I sat down on a garden wall to read; I'd been having trouble keeping up with my reading: there was so little time, and communications with my Prague friends were poor; but I'd packed three small books of poetry into my bag, and I read them over and over for the comfort they brought me: they were poems by Frantisek Halas.

Those three books played a strange role in my life, strange if only because I am not a great poetry-lover and they were the only books of poetry I ever really cared for. I discovered them just after I'd been expelled from the Party, during the period when Halas's name was coming back into the public eye: the leading ideologue of the time accused the recently deceased poet of morbidity, skepticism, existentialism, of everything that smacked of political anathema in those days. (The book in which he set forth his views on Czech poetry in general and Halas in particular came out in an enormous printing and was required reading in all Czech schools.)

In times of distress man seeks comfort by linking his grief with the grief of others; laughable as it may sound, I confess that the reason I sought out Halas's verse was that I wanted to commune with someone else who had been *excommunicated*; I wanted to find out whether my own mentality had any similarity to the mentality of a recognized apostate; and I wanted to test whether the grief the powerful ideologue had proclaimed pernicious and cankered might not, in consonance with my own, procure for me a kind of joy (for in my situation, I could scarcely have been expected to find joy in joy). Before leaving for Ostrava, I borrowed the three books from a former fellow student, a lover of literature, and then begged until he agreed not to ask for them back.

When Lucie found me at the appointed place with a book in my hand, she asked me what I was reading. I showed her the pages it was open to. "Poetry!" she said in amazement. "Do you find it strange for me to be reading poetry?" She shrugged her shoulders and said, "No, why should it be?" But I think she did, because in all probability she identified poetry with children's books. We wandered through Ostrava's odd sooty summer, a black summer of coal cars rumbling along overhead cables instead of fleecy clouds scudding across the sky. I noticed that Lucie still seemed drawn to the book, and when we found a small grove and sat down, I opened it and asked, "Are you interested?" She nodded.

I'd never recited poetry to anyone before; I've never done it since. I have a highly sensitive mechanism, a circuit breaker of reticence, that keeps me from opening up too far, from revealing my feelings; and reciting verse seems to me more than just talking about my feelings, it is as if I were standing on one leg at the same time; a certain unnaturalness in the very principle of rhythm and rhyme embarrasses me when I think of indulging in it in anything but solitude.

But Lucie had the magical power (no one after her has ever had it) to bypass the circuit breaker and rid me of the burden of my shyness. In her presence I could dare everything: sincerity, emotion, pathos. And so I recited:

> *Your body is a slender ear of corn*
> *From which the grain has dropped and won't take root*
> *Your body's like a slender ear of corn*
>
> *Your body is a skein of silk*
> *With longing written into every fold*
> *Your body's like a skein of silk*
>
> *Your body is a burnt-out sky*
> *And death dreams under cover in its weave*
> *Your body's like a burnt-out sky*
>
> *Your body is so silent*
> *Its tears quiver beneath my lids*
> *Your body is so silent*

I had my arm on Lucie's shoulder (covered only by the thin material of her flowered dress), I felt it under my fingers, and succumbed to the suggestion that the lines I was reading (a slow-moving litany) referred to the sorrow of Lucie's body, a quiet, resigned body, condemned to death. Then I read her some more poems, including the one that to this day calls forth her image to me; it ends with the lines:

> *Fatuous words I don't trust you I trust silence*
> *More than beauty more than anything*
> *A festival of understanding*

Suddenly I felt Lucie's shoulder shaking under my fingers; she was crying.

What had made her cry? The meaning of the words? The ineffable sadness flowing from the melody of the verse and the timbre of my voice? Had she perhaps been elevated by the hermetic solemnity of the poems and moved to tears by that *elevation*? Or had the lines simply broken through a secret barrier within her and lifted a weight long accumulating there?

I do not know. Lucie held me round the neck like a child, her head pressed against the cloth of the green uniform stretched across my chest, and she cried and cried and cried.

9

MANY TIMES in recent years women of all kinds have reproached me (because I was unable to reciprocate their feelings) with being conceited. This is nonsense, I'm not in the least conceited, but to be frank, it does pain me to think that not since reaching maturity have I been able to establish a true relationship with a woman, that I have never, as they say, been in love with a woman. I'm not sure I know the reasons for this failure, whether they lie in some innate emotional deficiency or in my life history; I don't mean to sound pompous, but the truth remains: the image of that lecture hall with a hundred people raising their hands, giving the order to destroy my life, comes back to me again and again. Those hundred people had no idea that things would one day begin to change, they counted on my being an outcast for life. Not out of a desire for martyrdom but rather out of the malicious obstinacy characteristic of reflection, I have often composed imaginary variations; I have imagined, for example, what it would have been like if instead of expulsion from the Party the verdict had been hanging by the neck. No matter how I construe it, I can't see them doing anything but raising their hands again, especially if the utility of my hanging had been movingly argued in the opening address. Since then, whenever I make new acquaintances, men or women with the potential of becoming friends or lovers, I project them back into that time, that hall, and ask myself whether they would have raised their hands; no one has ever passed the test: every one of them has raised his hand in the same way my former friends and colleagues (willingly or not, out of conviction or fear) raised theirs. You must admit: it's hard to live with people willing to send you to exile or death, it's hard to become intimate with them, it's hard to love them.

Perhaps it was cruel of me to submit the people I met to such merciless scrutiny when it was highly likely they would have led a more or less quiet everyday life in my proximity, beyond good and evil, and never passed through that hall where hands are raised. Say I did it for one purpose only: to elevate myself above everyone else in my moral complacency. But to accuse me of conceit would be quite unjust; I have never voted for anyone's downfall, but I am perfectly aware that this is of questionable merit, since I was deprived of the right to raise my hand. It's true that I've long tried to convince myself that if I had been in their position I wouldn't have acted as they did, but I'm honest enough to laugh at myself: why would I have been the only one not to raise his hand? Am I the one just man? Alas, I found no guarantee I would have acted any better; but how has that affected my relationship with others? The consciousness of my own baseness has done nothing to reconcile me to the baseness of others. Nothing is more repugnant to me than brotherly feelings grounded in the common baseness people see in one another. I have no desire for that slimy brotherhood.

Then how is it I was able to love Lucie? Fortunately, the observations I have just made date from a later period, and so (a mere adolescent and more prone to sorrow than reflection) I was still able to accept Lucie with open arms and a trusting heart, accept her as a gift, a gift from heaven (a heaven of benevolent gray skies). That was a happy time for me, the happiest in my life, perhaps: I was run down, worn out, harassed half to death, but day by day I felt a growing sense of inner peace. It's funny: if the women who now hold my conceit against me and suspect me of considering everybody a fool—if those women knew about Lucie, they'd call *her* a fool and completely fail to understand how I loved her. And I loved her so much I couldn't conceive of ever parting from her; true, we never talked about marriage, but I at least was absolutely serious about marrying her one day. And if it did enter my mind that the match was an unequal one, the inequality of it attracted more than repelled me.

For those few happy months I can be grateful to my commanding officer as well; the noncoms pushed us around as much as they could, searching for specks of dirt in the folds of our uniforms, tearing apart our beds if they found the slightest crease in them; but the commanding officer was a good man. He was beginning to show his age and had been transferred to us from an infantry regiment—a step down, it was rumored. In other words, the fact that he too had been through the mill may have disposed him in our favor. Not that he didn't require order, discipline, and an occasional voluntary Sunday shift (to give his superiors evidence of his political activism), but he never assigned us backbreaking busy work, and he issued our biweekly Saturday passes without reluctance; I even believe I managed to see Lucie as often as three times a month that summer.

When I wasn't with her, I wrote to her; I wrote her innumerable letters and cards. Looking back, I can't quite picture what I put in them. But that's not the point, what my letters were like; the point is that I wrote Lucie any number of letters and Lucie never wrote me one.

I could not get her to write to me; perhaps I intimidated her with my own letters; perhaps she felt she had nothing to write about or would make spelling mistakes; perhaps she was ashamed of the awkward penmanship I knew only from the signature on her identity card. It was not within my power to make her see that it was precisely her awkwardness, her ignorance, that made me so fond of her, not that I valued primitiveness for its own sake, but because it bore witness to Lucie's purity and gave me the hope of imprinting myself in her more deeply, more inextricably.

At first, Lucie merely thanked me shyly for my letters; soon she found a way to repay me: since she did not write, she chose to give me flowers. It all began like this: we were strolling through a wooded area when Lucie suddenly bent down, picked a flower, and handed it to me. I was touched; it didn't surprise me in the least. But when she stood waiting with a whole bunch of them the next time we met, I began to feel a little embarrassed.

I was twenty-two and painstakingly careful to avoid anything liable to cast doubts on my virility or maturity; I was ashamed of having to walk along the street carrying flowers; I did not like buying them, still less receiving them. In my embarrassment I pointed out to Lucie that it was men who gave flowers to women, not women to men, but when I saw the tears well up in her eyes, I hastened to add how beautiful they were, and accepted them.

There was nothing to be done. From then on, there were flowers waiting for me every time we met, and in the end I gave in, because I was disarmed by the spontaneity of giving and understood that Lucie cared for it; perhaps her tongue-tied state, her lack of verbal eloquence, made her think of flowers as a form of speech; not in the sense of heavy-handed conventional flower symbolism, but in a sense still more archaic, more nebulous, more instinctive, prelinguistic; perhaps, having always been sparing of words, she longed for that mute stage of evolution when there were no words and people communicated by simple gestures, pointing at trees, laughing, touching one another. . . .

Whether or not I grasped the essence of Lucie's flower-giving, I was finally moved by it and wanted to give her something, too. Lucie had exactly three dresses, which she wore in regular alternation, so that our rendezvous followed one another in three-four time. I liked all her clothes, precisely because they were worn and not very tasteful; I liked her brown overcoat too (short and threadbare at the cuffs), which, after all, I'd stroked before stroking her face. Yet I took it into my head to buy Lucie a dress, a beautiful dress, many dresses. And one day I suggested we go to a department store.

At first, she thought it was just for fun, to watch the people streaming up and down the stairs. On the second floor I stopped at a long rack of tightly packed dresses, and Lucie, seeing me eye them with interest, came closer and began to comment on some of them. "That's a nice one," she said, pointing at a dress with a busy red floral pattern. There were very few good-looking dresses, but some were a bit more present-able than others; I pulled one out and called over to the salesman, "Could the young lady try this one on?" Lucie may have wanted to resist but didn't dare in front of the salesman, a stranger, and so, before she knew what had happened, she found herself behind the curtain.

I gave her some time, then pulled open the curtain slightly to see how she looked; although the dress she was trying on was not particularly attractive, I was flabbergasted: its more or less modern cut had completely transformed her. "May I have a look?" I heard the salesman asking behind me, whereupon he went into an extended paean to Lucie and the dress. Then he turned, looked straight at my insignia, and (knowing full well the answer in advance) asked if I was a political. I nodded. He gave me a wink and said with a smile, "I may have a few things in a better line to show you. Would you care to see them?" and he immediately produced an assortment of stylish summer dresses and a dazzling evening gown. Lucie tried on one after the other; they all looked good on her, and she looked different in each; in the evening gown I didn't recognize her at all.

Turning points in the evolution of love are not always the result of dramatic events; they often stem from something that at first seems completely inconsequential. In the evolution of my love for Lucie the dresses were just that. Until that day at the dress department Lucie had been many things to me: a child, a source of comfort, a balm, an escape from myself; she was literally *everything* for me but a woman. Our love in the physical sense of the word had proceeded no further than the kissing stage. And even the way she kissed was childish (I'd fallen in love with those kisses, long but chaste, with dry closed lips counting each other's fine striations as they touched in emotion).

In short, until then I had felt tenderness for Lucie, but no sensual desire; I'd grown so accustomed to its absence that I wasn't even conscious of it; my relationship with Lucie seemed so beautiful that I could never have dreamed anything was missing. Everything fit so harmoniously together: Lucie, her monastically gray clothes, and my monastically chaste relation with her. The moment she put on another dress, the equation failed to balance; all at once Lucie departed from my images of Lucie; I realized that possibilities and forms other than the touchingly rustic were available to her. I suddenly saw her as an attractive woman with a graceful, well-proportioned figure and legs alluringly outlined under the well-cut skirt, a woman whose dull modesty dissolved instantly in the bright, elegant clothes. I was bowled over by the *revelation of her body*.

Lucie shared her room at the dormitory with three other young women. Visitors were permitted two days a week for three hours only, from five to eight; they were required to sign in when they arrived, hand over their identity cards, and sign out when they left. In addition, each of Lucie's roommates had her own boyfriend (or boyfriends), and each of them needed the intimacy of the room for trysts, which meant they were involved in constant bickering and backbiting and kept careful record of every minute one stole from the others. It was all so unpleasant that I'd never once tried to visit Lucie there. But I happened to know that in about a month's time all three were going off on an obligatory agricultural brigade. I told Lucie I wanted to take advantage of the situation and see her in her room. She was far from overjoyed; she told me sadly that she preferred meeting me out of doors. I told her I was longing to spend some time with her where no one and nothing could disturb us and we could concentrate entirely on each other; and that I wanted to see how she lived. She was powerless to refuse, and I remember to this day how excited I was when she finally agreed.

10

B<small>Y THAT TIME</small> I had been in Ostrava nearly a year, and military service, so unbearable at first, had become habitual and ordinary; it was still unpleasant and exhausting, of course, but I had found a way to live with it, make a few friends, and even be happy; for me the summer was radiant (the trees were coated with soot, but they seemed a rich, deep green when I gazed on them with my coal-mine eyes); yet as is so often the case, the seed of misfortune lay hidden at good fortune's core. The sad events of autumn were conceived in this green-black summer.

It all started with Stana. Within several months of his March marriage he'd begun to hear rumors that his wife was hanging around the bars; he was terribly upset and wrote her letter after letter; her replies calmed him down for a while, but then (about the time it started getting warm) he had a visit from his mother; he spent an entire Saturday with her and came back to the barracks pale and tight-lipped; at first he was too ashamed to tell anyone anything, but the next day he opened up to Honza, then to others, and soon we all knew; and when Stana saw that we all knew, he talked about it even more, all the time; it became an obsession: his wife had been sleeping around, and he was going to go and wring her neck. He tried to get a two-day pass from the company commander, but found him none too willing: he had been getting nothing but complaints about Stana from both the mines and the barracks, complaints about his absentmindedness and irritability. So Stana asked for a twenty-four-hour pass. The commander took pity on him and granted it. Stana left and we never saw him again. All I know about what happened I know from hearsay:

As soon as he got to Prague, he pounced on his wife (I call her his wife, but she was actually just another nineteen-year-old girl), and she admitted everything brazenly (perhaps even eagerly); he started beating her; she fought back; he started choking her and smashed a bottle over her head; she fell to the floor and lay there motionless. He panicked and fled; somehow or other he found an empty summer cottage in the mountains and holed up there in terrified anticipation of being caught and hanged for murder. They found him two months later and put him on trial, not for murder but for desertion. His wife, it turned out, had regained consciousness shortly after he ran off and had nothing to show for the adventure but a bump on the head. While he was in the military prison, she divorced him, and today she is the wife of a famous Prague actor whose shows I see now and then just to remind myself of Stana and his sad end: after he completed his army service, he stayed on in the mines; an accident cost him a leg, and then the botched amputation cost him his life.

That woman, who continues to glitter in artistic circles, it's said, was the downfall of more than Stana; she was the downfall of us all. At least that's the way it seemed to us, though, of course, we can never be certain whether (as everyone assumed) there was a causal connection between the scandal surrounding Stana's disappearance and the ministerial commission's visit to our barracks shortly thereafter. Nonetheless, our commander was given his walking papers and replaced by a young officer (he couldn't have been more than twenty-five); from the day he arrived, everything changed.

I say he was about twenty-five, but he looked younger, he looked like a boy; and he was all the more determined to make an impression. We used to say among ourselves that he rehearsed his speeches in front of the mirror, that he learned them by heart. He didn't like to shout, he spoke drily, and with the utmost composure he let us know that he regarded us all as criminals. "I know you'd be happy to see me strung up," the boy commander told us the first time he addressed us, "but if anybody is hanged around here, it's going to be you, not me."

The first clashes were not long in coming. The incident with Cenek has stuck in my memory most, perhaps because we found it so amusing. During his first year of military service Cenek had done a large number of murals, which under the previous commanding officer had always received their due. As I've said before, Cenek was partial to the Hussite warriors and their leader Jan Zizka; to please his friends he always liked to throw in a few naked women, justifying them to the commander as symbols of liberty or the motherland. The new commander, also wishing to make use of Cenek's services, called him in and asked him to do something for the room where political instruction classes were given. He took the opportunity to tell him to forget about all those Zizkas and "pay more attention to the present," to show the Red Army and its alliance with our working class and also its role in the victory of socialism in February 1948. Cenek said "Will do!" and set to work; after several afternoons spent on the floor painting, he tacked up the large sheets of paper along the far wall of the room. When we first saw the finished picture (it was a good five feet high and twenty-five feet long), we were dumbstruck: in the center stood a heroically posed, warmly clad Soviet soldier with a submachine gun slung over his shoulder, a shaggy fur cap pulled down over his ears, and about eight naked women crowding round him. The two standing on either side were gazing up at him coquettishly; he had an arm around the shoulders of each and was laughing a jubilant laugh; the other women paid court to him, extending their arms to him or simply standing there (one was lying down), showing off their pretty figures.

Cenek took up a position in front of the picture (we were waiting for the political officer to arrive and had the room to ourselves) and gave us a talk that went something like this: Now, here to the right of the sergeant, that's Alena, the first woman I ever had. I was sixteen at the time, and she was the wife of an officer, so she should feel right at home here. I've painted her the way she looked at the time, you can be sure she's gone downhill since, but even then she was on the plump side, right here (he pointed his finger) around the thighs. Because she was much more attractive from the rear, I've done another one of her here (he walked over to one end of the picture and pointed to a woman who, showing her bare behind to the audience, seemed to be leaving). You see that her royal rump is just a little oversized, but that's the way we like them, isn't it? And this one (he pointed to the girl on the sergeant's left), this one is Lojzka, I was much more experienced by the time I got to her, she had small breasts (he pointed to them), long legs (he pointed to them), and very pretty features (he pointed to them too), and she was in my year at school. And this is our model from live drawing class, I knew her by heart and so did all twenty of us guys, because she always used to stand in the middle of the classroom while we learned how to paint the human body, but none of us ever touched her, her mother was always there waiting at the end of the class to whisk her off, so she showed herself off to us, God bless her, with all due propriety. Now, this one (he pointed to a woman lolling on a stylized divan), this one was a whore from the word go, come up a little closer (we did), see that little mark on her belly? It's a cigarette burn they say she got from a jealous woman she was having an affair with because, yes, gentlemen, she liked it both ways, her sexuality was a real accordion, gentlemen, where you could find just about anything, we'd all be able to cram ourselves in there, just as we are, with our wives, our girlfriends, our kids, and our great-grandparents to boot.

Cenek was obviously approaching the climax of his statement when the political commissar entered the room and told us to sit down. The commissar was used to Cenek's murals from the days of the old commander; he paid no attention to the new picture and began reading aloud from some pamphlet elucidating the differences between socialist and capitalist armies. Just as Cenek's commentary was fading away in our minds and we were settling down to our own quiet reveries, the boy commander appeared in the room. He had come to check up on the commissar's talk, but before he could receive the commissar's report, he was transfixed by what he saw on the far wall; he did not even permit the commissar to go on with his talk but barked at Cenek, What is the meaning of this? Cenek broke ranks and planted himself in front of the picture and began: Here we have an allegorical representation of the significance of the Red Army for the struggle of our nation; here (he pointed to the sergeant) is the Red Army; at his side (he pointed to the officer's wife) is symbolized the working class, and here on the other side (he pointed to his schoolmate) is the symbol of the month of February. These (he pointed to the other ladies) are the symbols of liberty, of victory, here is the symbol of equality; and here (he pointed to the officer's wife displaying her behind) we see the bourgeoisie making its exit from the stage of history.

Cenek fell silent and the commander declared that the mural was an insult to the Red Army and must be removed at once; and that Cenek would have to take the consequences. I asked (under my breath) why. The commander heard me and asked if I had any objections. I said I liked the picture. The commander said he wasn't surprised; it was perfect for masturbators. I reminded him that Myslbek had sculpted liberty as a nude, that Ales had a famous painting of the Jizera River as three nudes; that painters had done this forever.

The boy commander gave me a dubious look and repeated his order that the mural be taken down. Nevertheless, we may have managed to confuse him, because Cenek was not punished; but the commander had taken a dislike to him and to me as well. Cenek was soon up on charges, and a little later so was I.

This is how it happened: One day our company was working with picks and shovels in an out-of-the-way section of camp; under the none too watchful eye of a lethargic corporal, we spent most of the time leaning on our shovels discussing this and that, and failed to notice the boy commander observing us from a distance. We only discovered him when we heard his stern voice say: "Private Jahn, come here!" I grabbed my shovel energetically and went and stood at attention before him. "Is that your idea of work?" he asked. I can't quite remember how I responded, but I know I wasn't insolent, because I had no intention of making life in the barracks any harder for myself or needlessly antagonizing a man who had complete power over me. But after my innocent, even embarrassed reply, his eyes hardened, he stepped up close to me, grabbed hold of my arm, and flipped me over his shoulder in a perfectly executed jujitsu move. Then he squatted down beside me and pinned me to the ground (I had made no attempt to defend myself, I was simply astonished). "Had enough?" he asked in a loud voice (so everyone could hear). I told him I had. He ordered me on my feet and announced to the assembled company, "I am giving Private Jahn two days' detention. Not because he was insolent. His insolence, as you saw, I took care of with my own hands. No, I am giving him two days for lying down on the job. And next time the rest of you can expect the same." Then, turning on his heel, he strode off in style.

At the time, I felt nothing but hatred for him, and hatred shines too bright a light on things, depriving them of relief. I saw him merely as a vindictive, wily rat. Now I see him above all as a young man playing a role. The young can't help playacting; themselves incomplete, they are thrust by life into a completed world where they are compelled to act *fully grown*. They therefore adopt forms, patterns, models—those that are in fashion, that suit, that please—and enact them.

Our boy commander too was incomplete, and he suddenly found himself at the head of a group of soldiers he couldn't possibly understand; if he was able to come to grips with the situation, it was only because so much of what he had read and heard offered him a ready-made mask: the cold-blooded hero of the cheap thrillers, the young man with nerves of steel who outwits the criminal gang, the man of few words, calm, cool, with a dry wit and confidence in himself and the might of his own muscles. The more conscious he was of his boyish appearance, the more fanatical his devotion to the role of superman, the more forced his performance.

But was this the first time I encountered adolescent actors? At the time of the postcard interrogation I had just turned twenty, and my interrogators couldn't have been more than a year or two older. They too were above all boys covering their incomplete faces with the mask they admired most, the mask of the hard, ascetic revolutionary. And what about Marketa? Hadn't she modeled herself after the female savior in some B movie? And Zemanek, suddenly seized by the sentimental pathos of morality? Wasn't that a role as well? And myself? Didn't I run back and forth among several roles until I was tripped up and lost my balance?

Youth is terrible: it is a stage trod by children in buskins and a variety of costumes mouthing speeches they've memorized and fanatically believe but only half understand. And history is terrible because it so often ends up a playground for the immature; a playground for the young Nero, a playground for the young Bonaparte, a playground for easily roused mobs of children whose simulated passions and simplistic poses suddenly metamorphose into a catastrophically real reality.

When I think of all this, my whole set of values goes awry and I feel a deep hatred towards youth, coupled with a certain paradoxical indulgence towards the criminals of history, whose crimes I suddenly see as no more than a frightful agitation of the immature.

And when I think of the immature, I think also of Alexej; he too played his great role, one that went beyond both his reason and his experience. He had something in common with our commander: he too looked younger than his age; but (in contrast with the commander) there was nothing attractive about his boyishness: he had a puny build, shortsighted eyes behind thick glasses, skin covered with the pimples of eternal puberty. He'd begun his service at an infantry officers candidate school but was suddenly transferred to us. The notorious political trials were brewing, and in many halls (of the Party, of justice, of the police) hands were unceasingly raised to strip the accused of confidence, honor, and freedom; Alexej was the son of a highly placed Communist official who had recently been arrested.

He appeared one day in our company and was given Stana's orphaned bunk. He showed us the same reserve I had shown my new companions at first; and when it became known that he was a member of the Party (he hadn't yet been expelled), the others began watching what they said in his presence.

As soon as he found out I had been a Party member myself, he opened up to me a bit; he confided that come what might, he was determined to pass the supreme test life had placed before him and never betray the Party. Then he read me a poem he wrote (the first he had ever written) when he heard he was to be transferred to our regiment. It included this quatrain:

> Do as you please, Comrades,
> Make a dog of me, spit on me too.
> But in my dog's mask, under your spittle, Comrades,
> I'll remain faithfully in the ranks with you.

I understood what he meant, because I had felt just the same a year before. But by now I felt it much less painfully: Lucie, my usherette into the everyday world, had removed me from the regions where the Alexejs live in desperate torment.

II

WHILE THE BOY commander was busy setting up his new regime, I was concerned mainly with getting myself a pass; Lucie's roommates had gone off to work in the fields, and I hadn't been let out of camp for a month; the commander had taken careful note of my face and name, and in the army that's the worst thing that can happen. He lost no opportunity to make it clear that every hour of my life depended on his fancy. As for passes, the outlook was grim; at the very beginning he'd announced that leave would be granted only once a month, and then only to those who regularly volunteered for Sunday shifts; this being so, we all volunteered; but it was a miserable existence, working all month without any time away from the mines, and when one or another of us actually did get a Saturday off and staggered back at two in the morning, he went to work the next day dead tired and looked like a sleepwalker for a long time thereafter.

I started working Sunday shifts too, although that in itself was no guarantee of a pass: the credit earned by a Sunday shift could easily be offset by a badly made bed or some other such infraction of the rules. Nevertheless, the vanity of power manifests itself not only in cruelty but also (though less often) in gentleness. And so, some weeks having passed, it pleased the boy commander to be generous, and at the last moment, he granted me an evening pass, two days before Lucie's roommates were due back.

I was trembling with excitement when the old woman at the desk signed me in and told me to go up to the fifth floor, where I knocked on a door at the far end of a long hallway. The door opened, but Lucie stood hidden behind it, and all I could see was the room itself, which at first glance bore no resemblance whatever to a dormitory room; I seemed to have entered a room made ready for some religious celebration: the table was decorated with a bunch of bright gold dahlias, the window flanked by two enormous rubber plants, and everything (the vase, the bed, the floor, even the pictures) was festooned with green sprays (asparagus ferns, I recognized them immediately), as if Jesus Christ were expected to ride in on a donkey.

I took Lucie in my arms (she was still hiding behind the door) and kissed her. She was wearing the black evening gown and high heels I had bought for her the day we went shopping for clothes. She stood there like a priestess amidst all the solemn greenery.

We closed the door behind us, and only then did I become aware that I was in an ordinary room and that the verdant decor overlay four iron beds, four scratched night tables, a larger table, and three chairs. But nothing could dampen the delight that had overcome me the minute Lucie opened the door: for the first time in a month, I was out of camp for a few hours. Not only that: for the first time in a year I was in a *small room;* the intoxicating breath of intimacy that enveloped me was nearly overwhelming.

Until then, whenever I went walking with Lucie, the open spaces kept me tied to the barracks and my lot there; the ever-present air currents were like an invisible chain binding me to the camp gate and its inscription WE SERVE THE PEOPLE; I felt there was nowhere I could ever stop "serving the people"; I hadn't been inside a small private room for an entire year.

It was a completely new situation: I had the feeling that for three hours I would be totally free; I could fearlessly (and against all military regulations) throw off not only my cap and belt but also my shirt, trousers, boots, everything, and I could even jump up and down on them if I so desired; I could do whatever I pleased and never worry about being observed; besides, the room was nice and warm, and the warmth and freedom went to my head like piping hot wine; I put my arms around Lucie, kissed her, and took her over to the green-bedecked bed. The sprays on the bed (it was covered by a cheap gray blanket) moved me deeply; the only way I could interpret them was as symbols of wedlock; I was struck (and touched) by the idea that the most ancient customs unconsciously resonated in Lucie's simplicity, that she wished to bid her virginity farewell with all due ceremony.

It was some time before I realized that although Lucie was responding to my kisses and embraces, she was also holding back. Her lips kissed me hungrily but remained closed; she pressed her whole body up against mine, but when I slipped my hand under her skirt to feel the skin of her legs, she pulled away. I realized that the blind, giddy spontaneity with which I wanted to abandon myself with her remained one-sided; I remember at that point (no more than five minutes after I'd entered the room) feeling my eyes well up with tears of disappointment.

We sat down side by side (crushing the poor sprays under our buttocks) and began to make conversation. After a few minutes (the conversation languished) I tried again to take Lucie in my arms, but she resisted; I began struggling with her but soon realized that this was not a playful amorous tussle but a real fight, that it was turning our loving relationship into something ugly, that Lucie was resisting in earnest, furiously, almost desperately. I soon gave up the battle.

I tried to persuade her with words; I began to talk; I suppose I told her that I loved her and that loving meant giving yourselves to each other, fully; I didn't say anything original, of course (my goal wasn't particularly original either); but if it was unoriginal, my argument was irrefutable; nor did Lucie try to refute it. Instead, she remained silent or said, "Don't, please, no," or "Not now, not today . . ." and tried (with rather touching ineptitude) to change the subject.

I began again: Are you one of those girls who excite a man only to make fun of him? Are you so callous, so spiteful? . . . and again I put my arms around her, again we had a brief, depressing struggle, harsh and without an ounce of love to it, and again it left an aftertaste of ugliness.

I stopped; suddenly it came to me, the reason why she was putting up such resistance; God, why hadn't I thought of it before? She was just a child, afraid of love, a virgin, frightened, frightened of the unknown; I determined to camouflage my urgency, which must have terrified her, to be gentle, delicate, and make the act of love no more than an extension of the gentle, delicate caresses we had known together. So I stopped insisting and began to coax. I kissed her (so terribly long that I found no pleasure in it), fondled her (insincerely), and tried as surreptitiously as possible to work her into a reclining position. I finally succeeded; I stroked her breasts (Lucie never resisted this); I told her I wanted to be tender to her whole body, because her body was she and I wanted to be tender to all of her; I even managed to raise her skirt a little and kiss her eight or nine inches above the knee; but I didn't get any farther; when I tried to put my head in her lap, she jerked away from me in terror and jumped off the bed. Her face had a convulsive look about it I'd never seen before.

Lucie, Lucie, is it the light that makes you so ashamed? Would you rather it was dark? She clutched at my question as if it were a life preserver. Yes, she was ashamed of the light. I went over to the window to pull the blinds, but Lucie shouted out, "No, don't do it! Don't draw the blinds!" "Why not?" I asked. "Because I'm afraid," she said. "What are you afraid of, the light or the dark?" Instead of answering, she burst into tears.

Her resistance aroused no pity in me whatsoever; it seemed senseless, unmerited, unjust; it tortured me, I couldn't comprehend it. I asked her whether she was resisting because she was a virgin, whether she was afraid of the pain. She answered all of my questions with an obedient nod of the head, seeing in each a reason for her refusal. I told her how wonderful it was that she was a virgin and would find out everything with me, the man who loved her. "Aren't you looking forward to being mine and all that goes with it?" Yes, she was, she said. I put my arms around her again, and again she resisted. I could hardly control my anger. "Why do you keep fighting me?" She said: "Please, next time, I do want it, but next time, please, some other time, not this evening." "And why not?" She answered: "Not this evening." "But why?" She answered: "Please, not now!" "But when? You know very well this is our last chance to be alone together. Tomorrow your roommates are coming back. Where else can we be alone?" "You'll find a place," she said. "All right," I said, "I'll find a place. But promise you'll come with me. It's not likely to be as nice a room as this one." "That doesn't matter," she said. "That doesn't matter. It can be wherever you like." "All right then, but promise you'll become my woman there, promise you won't put up a fight." "All right," she said. "Promise?" "Yes."

I realized that this promise was the most I would get out of Lucie that evening. It wasn't much, but it was something. I suppressed my indignation, and we spent the rest of the time talking. When I left, I shook my uniform free of asparagus fern, stroked Lucie's face, and told her I'd be thinking of nothing but our next time together (and I wasn't lying).

12

A FEW DAYS after that meeting with Lucie (it was a rainy autumn afternoon), we were marching in a column from the mines to the barracks; the road was rutted with deep puddles; we were muddy, drenched, and yearning for a rest. Most of us hadn't had a single Sunday off all month. But as soon as lunch was over we were called out by the boy commander and informed that during the inspection of our quarters he had uncovered certain irregularities. He then handed us over to the noncoms and ordered them to drill us for an extra two hours as punishment.

Since we had no weapons, our military exercises were particularly nonsensical; their only purpose was to waste our time. I remember that under the boy commander we once spent a whole afternoon hauling heavy boards from one end of the camp to the other; the next afternoon we hauled them back; and we went on alternating for ten more days. Everything we did in camp after a day in the mines was a sort of board-hauling. This time, instead of boards, we were hauling our bodies back and forth; we turned them about face and right face, we flung them to the ground and picked them up again, we ran here and there with them and dragged them through the mud. Three hours later the commander showed up and motioned to the noncoms to take us off for physical training.

Behind the barracks was a small field that could be used for soccer or drill or running. The noncoms decided to stage a relay race; our company was made up of nine squads of ten men each, so we formed nine ten-man teams. The noncoms needed no excuse to run us into the ground, but because they were mostly between eighteen and twenty and had the ambitions of their age, they wanted to run too, in order to prove that we were worthless; they decided to pit themselves against us and put together their own team.

It took a long time for them to explain what they had in mind and for us to understand it: the first ten men would sprint from one end of the field to the other, where each would find a man waiting for him, and those men would sprint back to where the first men had started off from, by which time another ten men would be waiting for them, and so on. Then they counted us off laboriously and dispatched us to opposite ends of the field.

We were dead tired after the mines and the drills, and furious at the thought of having to run a race besides; and then I confided a primitive idea to one or two friends: let's all run very slowly! The idea caught on at once and was passed from mouth to mouth, until the weary mass of soldiers began to stir with stifled laughter.

At last we were in place and ready for a race whose entire concept was a pure absurdity: although we would be racing in our uniforms and heavy boots, we had to kneel down at the starting line; although we would be passing the baton in a most unorthodox manner (the runner we handed it to would be facing us), we had real batons to do it with and a real pistol shot to start us off. The corporal in the tenth position (the first runner for the noncoms) shot out at breakneck speed, while we (I was in the first heat) straightened up slowly and started off in a slow jog; after twenty yards we were hard put to keep from laughing, because the corporal had nearly reached the other end while we jogged along improbably abreast, not far from the starting line, huffing and puffing in a simulated excess of effort; the crowd of soldiers at each end of the field began egging us on: "Faster, faster, faster . . ." At the midpoint we met the second runner for the noncom team tearing towards the line we had left. At last we reached the other end and handed on our batons as the third noncom darted out with his baton behind us.

Today I look back on that relay race as the last great parade of my companions of the black insignia. Their ingenuity knew no bounds: Honza limped terribly, but we cheered him on with all our might, and he scored a hero's victory (to great applause) by coming in two steps before the others; Matlos the Gypsy fell to the ground eight or nine times; Cenek lifted his knees to his chin with each step (which must have tired him much more than running at top speed). No one spoiled the game: not Bedrich, the disciplined (and resigned) drafter of peace manifestos, who trotted along at the same pace as the others but with great dignity; nor Pavel Pekny, who disliked me; nor old Ambroz, who ran bolt upright, his hands clasped behind his back; nor redheaded Petran, who gave out a high-pitched screech; nor Varga the Hungarian, who shouted "Hurrah!" as he ran—not one of them spoiled this admirable and simple stage production that had us all holding our sides.

Then we saw the boy commander walking towards the field from the barracks. One of the corporals saw him too and went over to report. The commander heard him out, then went up to the edge of the field to watch the race for himself. The noncoms (whose anchorman had long since crossed the finish line) started getting nervous and shouting, "Get a move on! Faster! Hurry it up!" but our cheers completely drowned them out. The noncoms didn't know whether to stop the race or not; they ran back and forth to confer, keeping an eye on the commander, but the commander never even glanced in their direction; he was watching the race with an icy stare.

The time had finally come for our last group of runners; Alexej was one of them; I was very curious to see how he would run; I was not mistaken: he wanted to spoil the game; he ran ahead full force, he gained five meters in the first twenty. But then something peculiar happened: his pace slowed and he ceased to gain on the others; I realized in a flash that Alexej couldn't spoil the game even if he wanted to: he was such a puny young man that after two days they had to assign him to light work, like it or not, because he had neither muscles nor wind! And so it seemed to me that his run was the highlight of the entire farce; however hard Alexej flogged himself, he was indistinguishable from the boys idling along five steps behind him at the same speed. The noncoms and the commander must have been convinced that Alexej's brisk start was as much a part of the comedy as Honza's feigned limp, Matlos's tumbles, and our cheering. Alexej's fists were clenched as hard as those of the runners behind him; they strained and wheezed every bit as much as Alexej. The difference was that Alexej felt *real* pain and his efforts to overcome it sent *real* sweat pouring down his face; in mid-course Alexej slowed down even more, and a row of clowning runners gradually overtook him; thirty yards from the end, they passed him; at twenty yards, he stopped running altogether and hobbled his way to the finish line, one hand clutching his left side.

Then the commander ordered us to fall in. He asked why we'd run so slowly. "We were tired, Comrade Captain." He told everyone who was tired to raise his hand. We raised our hands. I looked over at Alexej (who was standing in the row in front of me); he was the only one who didn't raise his hand. But the commander didn't notice him. He said, "I see, all of you." "No," came the reply. "Who wasn't tired?" Alexej said: "I wasn't." "You weren't?" asked the commander, staring at him. "How is it you weren't tired?" "Because I'm a Communist," answered Alexej. The company half grumbled, half laughed. "Are you the one who finished last?" asked the commander. "I am," said Alexej. "And you weren't tired," said the commander. "No," answered Alexej. "If you weren't tired, then you sabotaged the training exercise on purpose. That's two weeks for attempted mutiny. The rest of you were tired, you have an excuse. But since your output in the mines is so low, you must be using up all your energy on your days off. In the interest of your health, there will be no leaves in the company for two months."

Before he went to the guardhouse, Alexej had a talk with me. He reproached me for not behaving like a Communist and asked me with a stern look whether I was for socialism or not. I replied that I was for socialism, but that in the black-insignia camp, it made no difference, because here there was another line of demarcation: on one side, those who had lost their own destinies, and on the other side, those who had taken them away and could do with them as they pleased. But Alexej did not agree: according to him, the line between socialism and reaction held everywhere and our barracks were simply a means of defending socialism against its enemies. I asked him how the boy commander was defending socialism against its enemies by sending him, Alexej, to the guardhouse for two weeks and by treating all the men in such a way as to make them socialism's most confirmed enemies. Alexej admitted that he disliked the commander. But when I said that if our barracks were a means of defending socialism against its enemies, he, Alexej, should not have been sent here, he replied brusquely that this was exactly where he should be. "My father was arrested for espionage. Do you understand what that means? How can the Party trust me? It is the Party's *duty* not to trust me."

A few days later I had a talk with Honza; I was bemoaning (with Lucie in mind) our two months without leave. "Don't you worry, Ludvik old boy," he said. "We'll be out more than ever."

Among my companions, the good-natured sabotage of the relay race strengthened our feeling of solidarity and led to a flurry of activity. Honza put together a small council to make a rapid review of the possibilities of going absent without leave. Within two days everything was ready; a bribery fund had been set up; the two noncoms in charge of our bunkrooms had been bought off; several strands of wire had been unobtrusively cut at a well-chosen point in the fence, where the camp ended near the infirmary, only five yards from the nearest cottages. The closest cottage was occupied by a miner we knew from the pit; it didn't take long for the boys to get him to leave his gate unlocked; the escaping soldier had only to make his way unnoticed to the fence, crawl quickly under, and sprint the fifteen feet to the cottage gate; once inside, he was safe: he walked through the house and emerged on the suburban street on the other side.

Thus, the exit route was relatively secure, but we had to be careful not to abuse it; if too many men sneaked out of camp on the same day, their absence would easily be spotted, so Honza's council had to regulate the escapes and establish a long-term schedule.

But before I ever had my turn, the whole enterprise came to grief. One night the commander made a personal inspection of our quarters and discovered three men missing. He cornered the noncom in charge, who hadn't reported the men's absence, and asked him, as if he knew everything, how much we had paid him. The corporal, assuming the commander knew the whole story, made no attempt to hide it. When the commander confronted him with Honza, he confirmed that Honza was the one who had given him the money.

The boy commander had checkmated us. The corporal, Honza, and the three soldiers who had left that night were sent away for court-martial. (I didn't even have time to say good-bye to my best friend; it happened during a single morning, while we were in the mines; not until years later did I learn they'd all been convicted and Honza got a year in prison.) The commander announced to the assembled men that the ban on leaves was extended for a further two months and that the entire company would come under a special disciplinary regime. He had also requested the construction of two watchtowers, searchlights, and two characters with wolfhounds to guard the barracks.

The commander's attack was so sudden and successful that we all believed someone had squealed on Honza's operation. Not that informing particularly flourished among the black insignia; we all had contempt for it, but we knew the possibility was always there; it was the most effective means at our disposal for improving our conditions, getting discharged without delay, receiving good character references, and ensuring ourselves some sort of future. We had succeeded (the great majority of us) in not falling into that ultimate baseness, but we couldn't resist suspecting others of it.

On this occasion suspicion spread rapidly, turned into collective conviction (though other explanations of the commander's attack were possible), and settled unconditionally on Alexej. He was in the guardhouse serving out his sentence; he still had to put in his time down in the mines and spent a good part of the day with us, so everyone asserted he'd had ample opportunity ("with those cop's ears of his") to pick up something of Honza's scheme.

Poor bespectacled Alexej went through the mill: the foreman (one of us) started giving him the toughest jobs; his tools suddenly began vanishing, and he had to pay for replacements out of his wages; he was the constant butt of insults and insinuations, had to put up with hundreds of minor inconveniences; and the day he returned to the barracks someone had written on the wooden wall above his bunk, in big, black, greasy letters, BEWARE OF THE RAT.

Several days after Honza and the other four delinquents were led off under escort, I looked into our platoon bunkroom late in the afternoon; it was empty except for Alexej, who was bent over making his bunk. I asked him why he had to remake it. He told me the boys messed up his bunk several times a day. I told him they were all convinced he'd informed on Honza. He protested almost tearfully that he knew nothing about it and would never inform on anybody. "How can you say you wouldn't inform?" I said. "You regard yourself as an ally of the commander. It's only logical that you would give him information." "I'm not the commander's ally! The commander is a saboteur!" he said, his voice breaking. Then he told me the conclusions he'd come to while thinking things over during his solitary confinement: Black insignia were created by the Party for men it could not trust with arms, but whom it wanted to re-educate. But the class enemy never sleeps, and it wants at all costs to prevent the re-education process from being successful; it wants the black-insignia soldiers sustained in their violent hatred for Communism, as a reserve force for the counterrevolution. The way the commander treated the men, the way he kept provoking them, it was all clearly part of the enemy's plan. You never knew where the enemy might be lurking. The commander was definitely an enemy agent. Alexej knew his duty and had drafted a detailed account of the commander's activities. I was stunned. "What's that? You've written what? And who have you sent it to?" He replied that he'd sent a complaint about the commander to the Party.

We went outside. He asked me if I wasn't afraid of being seen with him. I told him he was a fool for asking and a bigger fool if he thought his letter was going to reach its destination. He replied that he was a Communist and was required to act at all times in a manner he need not be ashamed of. And again he reminded me that *I* was a Communist (even though I'd been expelled from the Party) and should behave accordingly. "As Communists we are responsible for everything that goes on here." I thought this laughable; I told him that responsibility was unthinkable without freedom. He replied that he felt free enough to act like a Communist; that he must and would prove that he was a Communist. As he said this his jaw trembled; today, after all these years, I can still remember that moment clearly and am more aware now than I was then that Alexej was not much more than twenty at the time, that he was an adolescent, a boy, and that his destiny hung on him like a giant's clothes on a tiny body.

I remember that not long after my conversation with Alexej, Cenek asked me (just as Alexej had feared) what I was doing talking to that rat. I told him Alexej might be a fool but he was no rat; and I told him about Alexej's complaint about the commander. Cenek was unimpressed. "I don't know if he's a fool or not," he said, "but I'm absolutely positive he's a rat. Anyone who can publicly renounce his father is a rat." I didn't understand at first; he was surprised I hadn't heard; after all, the political commissar himself had shown us the newspapers from a few months back in which Alexej's statement had appeared: he had renounced his father for betraying and defiling the most sacred things his son knew.

That evening the searchlights on the watchtowers (constructed during the last few days) made their debut and illuminated the darkened camp; a guard with a dog patrolled the barbed wire. I felt terribly alone: I was without Lucie and knew I would not see her for two whole months. The same evening I wrote her a long letter; I wrote that I wouldn't be seeing her for a long time, that we weren't allowed out of camp, and that I was sorry she'd denied me what I desired, the memory of which would have helped me to live through these gloomy weeks.

The day after I sent the letter off, we were doing our endless attentions, forward marches, hit-the-dirts. I was following the prescribed movements automatically and hardly noticed the corporal giving his orders or my companions marching or throwing themselves onto the ground; I was no longer aware of my surroundings: the barracks on three sides, barbed wire on the fourth, and beyond it the road. Now and then someone would walk past outside the wire; now and then someone would stop (mainly children, alone or with their parents, who would explain that the men behind the wire were soldiers and that they were drilling). All that was lifeless scenery to me, a painted backdrop (everything on the other side of the barbed wire was a painted backdrop); so I was scarcely conscious of the fence until someone called softly in that direction, "Hey there, girl, what're you staring at?"

Then I saw her. It was Lucie. She was standing by the fence, wearing her shabby brown overcoat (it occurred to me that when we were buying clothes in the summer we had forgotten that summer would end and cold weather come) and the fashionable black high-heeled shoes (my gift). She was standing motionless by the wire, watching us. The soldiers commented on her strangely patient air with rising interest, loading their remarks with the desperation of men kept in forced celibacy. The corporal noticed that the men's attention was wandering, and soon realized the cause; he was evidently enraged by his powerlessness; he couldn't order the girl away from the fence; outside the wire was a realm of relative freedom to which his jurisdiction did not extend. He therefore ordered the men to keep their comments to themselves, then stepped up the volume of his voice and the pace of the drill.

She began walking back and forth, and for a while I would lose sight of her, but she always returned to the spot where we could see each other. Then the drill was over, but I couldn't go up to her, as we were marched off to an hour of political instruction; we listened to sentences about the camp of peace and imperialist warmongers, and only after the lesson was I able to slip out (it was almost dark by then) and see whether Lucie was still by the fence; she was, and I ran over to her.

She told me not to be angry with her, that she loved me, and that she was sorry if she'd made me sad. I told her I didn't know when I could see her again. She said it didn't matter, she'd come and see me here. (At this point a few of the men walked past and yelled something obscene at us.) I asked her whether she would mind having soldiers shout at her like that. She said that she wouldn't, that she loved me. She handed me a rose through the wire (the bugle sounded, calling us to assembly); we kissed through a gap in the barbed wire.

13

Lucie came to the fence almost every day when I was on the morning shift in the mines and spent the afternoons in camp; every day I received a small bunch of flowers (once during inspection the ser-geant threw them on the floor) and exchanged a few words with her (always the same, because we actually had nothing to say to each other; we didn't exchange news or ideas; we simply wished to reassure each other of a single constantly reiterated truth); at that time, I wrote her almost daily; it was the most intensive period of our love. The searchlights on the watchtowers, the dogs barking at the approach of evening, the cocky boy reigning over it all took up very little room in my mind, which was concentrated only on Lucie's visits.

I was actually very happy in those barracks, surrounded by dogs, and in the mines, wielding my pneumatic drill. I was happy and proud, for in Lucie I possessed a prize vouchsafed neither to my fellow soldiers nor to our officers: I was loved, I was loved publicly and demon-stratively. Even if Lucie wasn't my companions' idea of the perfect woman, even if the way she showed her love was—from their point of view—rather odd, it was still the love of a woman and it aroused wonder, nostalgia, and envy.

The longer we were cut off from the world and women, the more women dominated our talk with their every particular, every detail. We recalled birthmarks, outlined (pencil on paper, pick in clay, finger in sand) breasts and backsides; we argued over which absent buttock had the most perfect curves; we gave exact renditions of words and sighs uttered during intercourse; this was all discussed again and again, always with new details. I too was interrogated, and my companions were all the more curious about my girl as they saw her every day and so were easily able to tie her actual appearance into my narrative. I couldn't disappoint my friends; I couldn't not tell them; so I described Lucie's nakedness, which I'd never seen, our lovemaking, which I'd never known, and as I spoke, a precise, detailed picture of her quiet passion rose before my eyes.

What was it like, the first time I made love to her?

It was in her room at the dormitory; she undressed in front of me, docile, devoted, but unwilling, as she was after all a country girl and I was the first man to see her naked. And it was this obedience mingled with shyness that drove me wild; when I approached her, she shrank back and covered her crotch with her hands. . . .

Why does she always wear those black high heels?

I said I'd bought them for her to wear when she was naked; she was shy about it but did everything I asked of her; I kept my clothes on till the last possible moment, and she would walk up and down in front of me naked in those heels (how I enjoyed seeing her naked when I was dressed!) and then go over to the cupboard, where she kept the wine, and naked, fill my glass. . . .

So when Lucie came up to the fence, I wasn't the only one looking at her; I was joined by ten or so of my fellow soldiers, who knew precisely what she was like when she made love, what she said, how she moaned, and who would make all kinds of innuendos about the black heels she had on again, and picture her walking naked in them around her tiny room.

Each of my friends could conjure up one or another woman and share her with the rest of us, but I was the only one who could offer a *look* at this woman; only my woman was real, alive, and present. The feeling of comradely solidarity that had led me to paint so detailed a picture of Lucie's nakedness and erotic behavior had the effect of painfully intensifying my desire for her. I was not upset by the obscenities my companions used each time she appeared; they could never take her away (the barbed wire and dogs protected her from all of us, myself included); on the contrary, they gave her to me: they *brought into focus* a stirring image of her, painted a picture of her and me together in a frenzied seduction; I succumbed to my companions, and all of us succumbed to desire for Lucie. Whenever I went up to her at the fence, I could feel myself tremble; I was tongue-tied with desire; I couldn't understand how for six months, like a timid student, I had failed to see the woman in her; I was willing to give anything for a single act of copulation with her.

I do not say that my attitude towards her had become coarse or superficial or that it had lost its tenderness. I would even say that it was the only time in my life I experienced *total desire for a woman* in which everything was involved: body and soul, lust and tenderness, grief and frenzied vitality, desire for vulgarity and desire for consolation, desire for the moment of pleasure as well as for eternal possession. I was totally involved, totally intense, totally concentrated, and I now think of those days as a paradise lost (an odd paradise guarded by a dog patrol and echoing with a corporal's commands).

I resolved to arrange a meeting with Lucie at all costs; I had her promise that she wouldn't put up a fight and would meet me anywhere I chose. She'd confirmed this promise many times during our brief talks through the fence. All I had to do was to dare a dangerous act.

It wasn't long before I came up with a scheme. Honza's escape plan had never been discovered by the commander. The fence still had an imperceptible gap in it, and the arrangement with the miner who lived in the cottage nearby merely needed renewing. Of course, the camp was heavily guarded, and escape by day was impossible. Even at night there were the searchlights and the dog patrol, but it was all more for effect and the commander's gratification than from suspicion of a break on our part; attempted escape meant the possibility of court-martial, and that was much too risky. Precisely for this reason I told myself that my scheme had a good chance of succeeding.

It only remained to find a suitable hideaway for Lucie and myself, preferably not too far from camp. Most of the men living in the area worked in the same mine as we did, and it wasn't long before I found someone (a fifty-year-old widower) who was willing to lend me his place (for three hundred crowns). The two-story gray house was visible from camp; I pointed it out to Lucie through the fence and told her my plan; she was not delighted; she begged me not to take any risks for her sake, and she agreed in the end only because she didn't know how to say no.

The appointed day arrived. It began rather oddly. Right after we got back from our shift, the boy commander had us fall in for one of his frequent talks. Usually he tried to scare us with the war about to break out and the hard days ahead for all reactionaries (by which he mainly meant us). This time he introduced some new ideas: the class enemy had wormed its way into the Communist Party itself; but let spies and traitors take note that enemies who hid behind masks would be dealt with a hundred times more severely than those who said what they thought, because an enemy who hid behind a mask was no better than a mangy dog. "And we have one such mangy dog here in our ranks," said the boy commander and ordered the boy Alexej to step forward. Then he pulled a piece of paper out of his pocket and thrust it in his face. "Have you seen this letter before?" "I have," said Alexej. "You're a mangy dog. And also an informer and a sneak. But a dog's yelp can't reach heaven." And before his eyes, he tore the letter to shreds.

"I have another letter for you," he added, handing Alexej an unsealed envelope. "Read it out loud." Alexej took a sheet of paper out of the envelope, skimmed it—and remained silent. "Read it out loud!" repeated the commander. Alexej remained silent. "Are you going to read it or aren't you?" asked the commander, and when Alexej still remained silent, he barked out, "Hit the dirt!" and Alexej flung himself into the mud. The boy commander stood over him for a moment, and we knew what was coming: up! down! up! down! Alexej would have to pick himself up, fling himself down, pick himself up, fling himself down. The commander, however, did not proceed with his orders but turned away from Alexej and started walking slowly along the front rank; he carefully inspected the men's equipment, reached the end of the rank (it took him several minutes), and then walked slowly back towards the soldier lying flat on the ground. "Now read it," he said, and Alexej lifted his muddy chin, stretched out his right hand (it was still clutching the letter), and, lying there on his stomach, read out loud, "This is to inform you that on September 15, 1951, you were expelled from the Communist Party of Czechoslovakia. Signed on behalf of the Regional

Committee by . . ." Then the commander ordered Alexej to retake his place in the ranks and handed us over to a corporal for drill.

After drill there was political instruction. At about six-thirty (it was dark by then), Lucie was standing by the wire; when I went up to her, she indicated with a nod that all was well, and left. Then came supper, cleanup, and finally lights out; I waited in bed until the corporal in charge of our bunkroom was asleep. Then I pulled on my boots and slipped out just as I was, in white longjohns and nightshirt; I walked down the hall and into the yard, feeling quite chilly in my nocturnal attire. The opening in the fence was just behind the infirmary; it couldn't have been better placed: if anyone stopped me, I could say I was feeling sick and on my way to wake the medical officer. But no one stopped me; I skirted the infirmary and crouched down in its shadow; the searchlight idled on one spot (clearly the sentry in the tower no longer took his job very seriously), and the space I had yet to cross lay in darkness; my only problem now was keeping clear of the dog patrol; it was quiet (dangerously quiet: I was unable to perceive any source of danger); I had been standing there for about ten minutes when finally I heard a dog's bark; it came from behind, from the other side of camp; I jumped up and dashed across to the fence (a distance of no more than five yards), to where, thanks to Honza's handiwork, the wire didn't quite touch the ground; I dropped on my stomach, crawled under, and ran the last five steps to the wooden fence of the miner's house; everything was just as we'd planned it: the gate was open, and across the tiny courtyard a light was burning in a window behind a curtain. I tapped at the window, and a few seconds later a giant of a man opened the door and noisily invited me in. (I was terrified at the volume of his voice; I couldn't forget I was a mere five yards away from camp.)

The door led straight into the room; I stopped for a moment in the doorway, disoriented by what I found: sitting around a table (with an open bottle on it) were five other men; when they saw me, they burst out laughing at my outfit; they said I must be cold in that nightshirt and poured me a glass; I took a taste: it was ethyl alcohol, scarcely diluted; they told me to toss it right down; I did, and had a coughing fit; this again provoked a burst of fraternal laughter, and they pulled up a chair for me; they asked how I'd managed to "cross the border," again made fun of my ridiculous getup, and called me Runaway Longjohns. They were all miners in their thirties and probably got together there regularly; they'd been drinking, but they weren't drunk, and after my initial surprise their carefree presence relieved my anxiety. I let them pour me another glass of their unusually strong and pungent drink. Meanwhile the owner of the house had gone into another room and come back carrying a dark suit. "You think it'll fit?" he asked. He was nearly a head taller than I was and considerably broader, but I said, "It'll *have* to." I pulled the trousers on over my longjohns, but I had to hold on to them to keep them from falling. "Anybody got a belt?" asked my benefactor. No one had. "How about a piece of string?" I said. A piece of string was found, and just about kept the trousers up. When I put the jacket on, the men decided (I'm not quite sure why) that I'd look just like Charlie Chaplin if I had a bowler hat and cane. To make them laugh, I put my heels together and pointed my toes out. The dark trousers rippled down over the insteps of my boots; the men loved it and told me no woman would be able to resist what she saw in the twinkle of my eye. They poured me a third glass and accompanied me outside. The owner assured me I could knock on the window at any hour of the night to change clothes again.

I stepped into the dimly lit suburban street. It took me more than ten minutes to get to the house where Lucie was waiting. I had to circle the entire camp and pass directly in front of the brightly illuminated gates; my fears turned out to be completely groundless: the civilian disguise worked perfectly, the guard looked right through me, and I reached my destination safe and sound. I opened the outside door (it was lit by a solitary streetlamp) and made my way by memory (I had never been in the house and knew it only from the miner's description): staircase to the left, up one flight, door straight ahead. I knocked. A key turned in the lock and Lucie opened the door.

I took her in my arms (she'd arrived around six, when the miner had left for the night shift); she asked if I'd been drinking; I said I had, and told her how I'd got there. She said she'd been trembling, afraid something would happen to me. (It was only then I noticed she actually was trembling.) I told her how much I'd looked forward to seeing her; I held her in my arms and felt her trembling more and more. "What's the matter?" I asked her. "Nothing," she answered. "Why are you trembling, then?" "I was afraid for you," she said, and twisted lightly from my embrace.

I looked around. It was a small, austerely appointed room: a table, a chair, a bed (a bed with slightly soiled sheets); over the bed there was a religious picture; against the opposite wall, a cupboard with jars of fruit preserves along the top (the sole more or less intimate detail in the room); above, hanging from the ceiling, a single unshaded light bulb burned, glaring disagreeably and brutally illuminating my body, whose sadly comic appearance instantly pained me: the enormous jacket, the trousers belted with string, the black boot tips, and on top, my clean-shaven skull shining like a pale moon in the bulb's incandescence.

"Forgive me for looking like this, Lucie, please," I said, and explained once again the necessity for my disguise. She assured me it didn't matter, but (carried away by an alcohol-induced impetuosity) I declared that I couldn't possibly stand there in front of her like that, and threw off the jacket and trousers; underneath I was wearing a night-shirt and those awful army-issue longjohns, a much more ridiculous outfit than the one I'd just shed. I went over and switched off the light, but no darkness came to my rescue: the streetlamp shone right into the room. And since I was more ashamed of being ridiculous than I was of being naked, I tore off the rest of my clothes. I put my arms around her. (Once more I felt her trembling.) I told her to undress, to remove everything that stood between us. I caressed her everywhere, repeating my plea again and again, but Lucie told me to wait a little, that she couldn't, that she couldn't right away, that she couldn't so soon.

I took her hand and we sat down on the bed. I laid my head in her lap and rested it there for some time; suddenly I realized the incongruity of my nakedness (faintly luminous in the dirty yellow of the streetlamp); it occurred to me that everything had turned out the opposite of what I'd dreamed: instead of a naked girl serving wine to a fully dressed man, a naked man was lying in the lap of a fully dressed woman. I saw myself as the naked Christ taken down from the cross and placed in the arms of a compassionate Mary, and I was horrified by this vision, because I hadn't come to Lucie for compassion and consolation, I'd come for something entirely different, and again I forced myself on her, kissing her (her face and dress) and trying surreptitiously to undo her buttons.

But I met with no success: once again Lucie twisted away from me; I lost my initial impulse, my confident impatience, I had exhausted my supply of words and caresses. I remained there stretched out on the bed, naked and motionless, while Lucie sat over me stroking my face with her rough fingers. Little by little I was overcome by bitterness and anger: I reminded Lucie, mentally, of the risk I'd taken to meet her; I reminded her (mentally) of the punishment I might yet have to face. But these were only superficial reproaches (which was why I could tell her about them—even if only mentally); the true source of my wrath lay much deeper (and I would have been ashamed to tell her): I was thinking of my own misery, the pitiful misery of a failed youth, the misery of endless weeks of frustration, the humiliating eternity of unfulfilled desire. I was remembering my vain courtship of Marketa, the ugliness of the blonde on the tractor, and again my vain courtship of Lucie. And I felt like crying out: why must I be adult in everything, sentenced as an adult, expelled, branded a Trotskyite, sent to the mines as an adult, why only in love am I forbidden to be adult and forced to swallow the full humiliation of immaturity? I hated Lucie, hated her all the more knowing she loved me, because that made her resistance all the more absurd, incomprehensible, infuriating. And so after half an hour of sullen silence I launched a fresh attack.

I rolled over onto her; using all my strength, I managed to pull up her skirt, tear off her brassiere, and put my hand on her naked breast, but Lucie resisted more furiously and (possessed by the same blind force as I was) finally struggled loose, jumped off the bed, and backed up against the cupboard.

"Why are you fighting me?" I shouted at her. Unable to answer, she told me not to be angry, to forgive her, but said nothing by way of explanation, nothing logical. "Why are you fighting me? Don't you know I love you? You must be crazy!" I shouted. "Then throw me out," she said, still pressing up against the cupboard. "That's what I'll do, I'll throw you out, because you don't love me, because you're making a monkey of me!" I was giving her an ultimatum, I shouted. Either she gave herself to me, or I never wanted to see her again.

Once more I went up to her and put my arms around her. This time she didn't try to stop me, but she was limp, as if all the life had gone out of her. "What's so special about your virginity? Who are you saving it for?" She was silent. "Say something!" "You don't love me," she said. "I don't love you?" "No, you don't. I thought you did, but you don't. . . ." And she burst into tears.

I got down on my knees, I kissed her feet, I begged her. But she went on crying and saying I didn't love her.

Suddenly I was seized by an insane rage. I felt there was a super-natural force standing in my way, constantly tearing out of my hands everything I wanted to live for, everything I desired, everything that was mine; I felt it was the same force that had robbed me of my Party, my Comrades, my studies at the university, of everything, and always senselessly and for no reason. I understood that the same supernatural power was now opposing me in the person of Lucie, and I hated her for having become its instrument; I hit her across the face, because it wasn't Lucie I was slapping, it was that hostile force; I shouted that I hated her, that I didn't want to see her, that I never wanted to see her, that I never wanted to see her again.

I threw her brown coat at her (it had been lying on the chair) and shouted at her to get out.

She put on her coat and left.

Then I lay down on the bed with a void in my heart and I wanted to call her back, because I already missed her the moment I told her to go, because I knew that it was a thousand times better to be with a dressed and recalcitrant Lucie than to be without Lucie; because to be without Lucie meant living in absolute solitude.

All this I knew, and yet I did not call her back.

I lay there naked on the bed in that borrowed room for a long time because I couldn't face going back to the house the way I felt, joking with the miners, answering their cheerfully lewd questions.

Finally (very late in the night) I dressed and went out. The street-lamp still shone opposite the house I was leaving. I circled the camp, tapped on the window (now dark) of the cottage, waited about three minutes, undressed in the presence of the yawning miner, made some noncommittal answer to his inquiry about the success of my venture, and (once more in nightshirt and longjohns) headed for camp. I was in a state of despair and total indifference. I didn't pay a bit of attention to where the dog patrol or the beam of the spotlight might be. I crawled under the wire and started off quietly in the direction of the barracks. I had just reached the wall of the infirmary when I heard: "Halt!" I stopped. A flashlight shone on me. I heard a dog snarling.

"What are you doing there?"

"Puking, Comrade Sergeant," I replied, leaning against the wall with one hand.

"Get on with it, man, get on with it," said the sergeant, and went back to his rounds with the dog.

14

I SOON GOT TO bed without any further complications (the corporal was fast asleep), but I couldn't even shut my eyes, and so I was glad when the noncom's harsh voice (yelling "Rise and shine!") put an end to that bad night. I slipped into my boots and ran to the washroom to splash some cold, refreshing water over myself. When I got back, I found a group of half-dressed men clustered around Alexej's bed trying hard to muffle their laughter. I immediately guessed what was going on: Alexej (lying on his stomach under the blanket) was still sound asleep. It reminded me of Franta Petrasek, from the Third Company, who, to get even with his commander, had simulated a sleep so sound that three consecutive superiors had failed to shake him awake; it wasn't until they'd carried him out into the yard in his bed and turned the fire hose on him that he started lazily rubbing his eyes. But with Alexej insubordination was out of the question, and his heavy sleep could only be a consequence of his physical weakness. While I was thinking a corporal (the one in charge of our room) came in from the hall with a gigantic pail of water in his arms; he was surrounded by a few soldiers who had obviously been egging him on in this imme-morially stupid prank, so dear to the minds of noncoms of all eras and regimes.

I was irritated by this pathetic reconciliation between the men and the corporal (usually so despised); I was irritated that a common hatred for Alexej had suddenly erased all old scores between them. They had obviously interpreted the commander's speech yesterday about Alexej's informing in such a way as to confirm their own suspicions, and felt a sudden surge of solidarity with the commander's cruelty. I was over-come with rage, a blinding rage aimed at the entire lot of them, at their

113

unthinking eagerness to believe every accusation, at their readily available cruelty, and so I quickly interposed myself between the corporal and Alexej's bed and said in a loud voice: "Get up, Alexej! Get up, you idiot!"

At this someone twisted my arm from behind and forced me to my knees. I looked around and saw Pavel Pekny. "Who asked you to butt in, you Commie bastard!" he hissed at me. I wrenched my arm away and smacked him in the face. There would have been a fight then and there if the others hadn't quieted us down: they were afraid we'd wake Alexej prematurely. Meanwhile, the corporal was there with his pail. He stepped up to Alexej, roared out "Rise and shine!" and poured the entire contents of the pail, a good three gallons of water, all over him.

But a strange thing happened: Alexej remained lying exactly as before. For a moment the corporal was at a loss. Then he bawled, "On your feet, soldier!" But the soldier didn't stir. The corporal bent over and shook him (the blanket was soaking wet, the whole bed was soaked through, and pools of water were forming on the floor). He managed to turn Alexej over so that we could see his face: it was sunken, pale, immobile.

The corporal shouted: "Doctor!" No one moved: everybody was staring at Alexej in his sodden nightshirt. "Doctor!" the corporal shouted again, pointing at a soldier who ran out immediately.

(Alexej lay there motionless, he was smaller and frailer than before, he was much younger, he was like a child, only his lips were locked together the way a child's never are, and the drops kept dripping from him. Someone said: "It's raining.")

Then the medical officer arrived, took Alexej's wrist, and said, "I see." He removed the drenched blanket and we could see Alexej lying before us at full (small) length, in his soaking wet longjohns with the bare feet sticking out at the end. The doctor looked around and picked up two vials from the table next to his bed; he peered into them (they were empty) and said, "Enough for two." Then he pulled a sheet off the nearest bed and covered Alexej with it.

All this had put us behind schedule, so that we ate breakfast on the double, and three-quarters of an hour later we were on our way underground. Then came the end of the shift, and drill and political instruction, and compulsory singing, and cleanup, and lights out, and all the time I thought of how Stana had gone, my best friend Honza had gone (I never saw him again, but I did hear that after completing military service, he'd managed to escape across the border into Austria), and now Alexej was gone too; he assumed his mad role blindly and bravely, and it wasn't his fault that he was suddenly unable to go on with it, that he lacked the strength to *remain in the ranks,* in his *dog's mask.* He had never been a friend of mine, the virulence of his faith was alien to me, but his fate made me feel closer to him than to any of the others; I felt that his death concealed a reproach to me, as if he had wished to let me know that the moment the Party banishes a man from its ranks, that man has no reason to live. I suddenly felt guilty for not having liked him, because now he was dead, irrevocably dead, and I'd never done anything for him, although I was the only one here who could have done something for him.

But I had lost more than Alexej and the unique opportunity to save a fellow man. Looking back on it today, from a distance, I see it was then I lost the warm sense of solidarity and companionship I'd had with my fellow black insignias, and with it any chance of resurrecting my trust in men. I began to have doubts about the value of our solidarity, which was based solely on the force of circumstance and an urge for self-preservation that compressed us into a densely packed flock. And I began to think that the black insignia group was as capable of bullying a man (making him an outcast, hounding him to death) as the group raising their hands in the university lecture hall that day in the past, or perhaps as capable as any group.

I felt at the time that I'd been overrun by a desert, I was a desert within a desert, and I wanted to call out to Lucie. Suddenly I could not understand why I'd desired her body so compulsively; now it seemed to me that she was not a corporeal woman but only a transparent pillar of warmth striding through a land of never-ending frost, a pillar of warmth that was receding from me, was driven away by me.

During drill the next day, my eyes never left the fence waiting for her to come. But the entire time the only person who stopped was an old woman, who pointed us out to her snot-nosed little grandchild. That evening I wrote a letter, long and sorrowful, begging Lucie to come back; I said I had to see her, I didn't want anything from her, I just wanted her to be there for me to see and know that she was with me, that she was there at all. . . .

As if to mock me, the weather suddenly turned warm, the sky was blue, and there was a glorious October. The leaves were a blaze of color, and nature (that pitiful Ostrava nature) celebrated autumn's farewell with mad ecstasy. I felt mocked because my desperate letters went unanswered and the people who stopped at the fence (under the alluring sun) were all horribly irrelevant. After about two weeks one of my letters came back; the address had been crossed out, and someone had written in pencil: Moved. Forwarding address unknown.

I was terror-stricken. A thousand times since my last meeting with Lucie I had turned over in my mind everything I'd said to her, everything she'd said to me, a hundred times I had cursed myself, a hundred times justified myself, a hundred times I had convinced myself I'd driven her away for good, a hundred times reassured myself she'd understand and forgive me. But the note on the envelope had the ring of a verdict.

I could not contain my distress, and the very next day I embarked on another of my harebrained schemes. I say "harebrained," but it was no more dangerous than my previous escape, so that the epithet "harebrained" emphasizes in retrospect its lack of success rather than the risks involved. I knew that Honza had carried it off several times during the summer when he was seeing a Bulgarian woman whose husband was away at work in the morning, and I based my scheme on his. I arrived at the pithead with everyone else, picked up my number and safety lamp, smudged my face with coal dust, and made a quiet getaway. I ran straight to Lucie's dormitory and questioned the woman at the desk. All I learned was that Lucie had left about two weeks before with a suitcase containing all her possessions; no one knew where she'd gone, she didn't tell anybody. I was frightened: had anything happened to her? The woman looked at me and said rather airily, "What can you expect? They don't have real jobs. They come and they go. They keep everything to themselves." I went to the place where she'd worked, and asked the personnel department about her; but I didn't find out a thing. I wandered through Ostrava until the shift was almost over and got back in time to mingle with the men as they surfaced. But I must have missed something in Honza's escape technique; the whole thing backfired. In two weeks' time I was hauled before a court-martial and given ten months for desertion.

Yes, it was here, at the moment when I lost Lucie, that the long period of hopelessness and emptiness began, the period evoked by the muddy outskirts of my hometown when I arrived on this short visit. Yes, that was when it all began: my mother died while I was in jail, and I couldn't even go to her funeral. After serving out the ten months, I went back to the black insignia in Ostrava for my final year of military service. Then I signed up for another three years in the mines, because rumor had it that anyone who didn't would have to stay on a year with the battalion. And so I spent the next three years mining coal as a civilian.

I take no pleasure in thinking back on all this or talking about it; in fact, I don't like to hear men cast out like myself from a movement they had trusted boast of their destinies. True, there was a time when I too glorified my outcast destiny as something heroic, but it was false pride. I've had to keep reminding myself that I wasn't assigned to the black insignia for having been courageous or for having fought, for sending my idea out to do battle with the ideas of others; no, my fall was not preceded by any real drama; I was more the object than the subject of my story, and (unless one considers suffering, sadness, or defeat values) I have nothing whatsoever to boast of.

Lucie? Oh, yes: for fifteen years I had not set eyes on her, and it was a long time before I even had news of her. After my discharge I heard she was somewhere in western Bohemia. But by that time I had ceased inquiring after her.

PART FOUR

Jaroslav

I

I SEE a road winding through the fields. I see the dirt in that road rutted by the narrow wheels of peasant carts. And I see verges flanking the road, grassy verges so green I cannot help stroking their smooth slopes.

All around, the fields are small, not the vast agglomerations of our collectives. How can that be? Is this not today's landscape I am passing through? What sort of land is this?

I walk on and a wild rose bush appears before me on the verge. It is covered with tiny roses. I stop and I am happy. I sit down in the grass beneath the bush and in a while I lie down. I can sense my back touching the grassy earth. I feel it with my back. I support it on my back and beg it not to be afraid of being heavy and resting its full weight on me.

Then I hear a clattering of hoofs. In the distance a small cloud of dust appears. It comes nearer, growing more transparent and sparse. Horses emerge from it. Astride the horses sit young men in white uniforms. But the closer they come, the clearer the carelessness of their dress. Some jackets are fastened with gleaming buttons, others hang open, and there are men in shirtsleeves as well. Some wear caps, others are bareheaded. No, this is no army, they are deserters, turncoats, outlaws! They are *our* cavalry! I raise myself from the ground and watch their approach. The first horseman unsheathes his saber and thrusts it in the air. The cavalry comes to a halt.

The man with the drawn saber has leaned down over his horse's neck and is staring at me.

"Yes, it is I," I say.

"The king!" says the man in wonderment. "I recognize you."

I bow my head, happy at being recognized. They have ridden thus for centuries, and still they know me.

"How do you fare, my king?" asks the man.

"I am fearful, my friends."

"Are they pursuing you?"

"No. It is worse than any pursuit. Something is being prepared against me. I do not know the men who surround me. I enter my house and within is a different room, a different wife, and everything is different. I think I am mistaken and rush out, but outside it is indeed my house! Mine without, a stranger's within. And so it is wherever I turn. Something is afoot, my friends, which puts me in fear."

The man asks: "You have not forgotten how to ride?" Only now do I note that by his horse there stands a saddled mount without a rider. The man points to it. I put my foot in the stirrup and hoist myself up. The horse rears, but I am firmly in the saddle, my knees gripping its sides with delight. The man pulls a red veil from his pocket and hands it to me, saying, "Veil your face, that they may not know you!" I wind it round my face and am suddenly blind. "The horse will lead you," I hear the man's voice say.

The entire formation sets off at a trot. I feel the riders jogging along on both sides of me. Their calves touch mine and I hear the snorting of their horses. We ride thus for an hour's time, body close to body. Then we halt. The same man's voice addresses me. "We have arrived, my king!"

"Arrived?" I ask. "Arrived where?"

"Do you not hear the murmur of a mighty river? We stand on the bank of the Danube. Here you are safe, my king."

"Yes, I feel that I am safe. I should like to cast off my veil."

"You may not, my king, not yet. You do not need your eyes. The eyes would but deceive you."

"But I wish to see the Danube. It is my river, my mother river, I wish to see it!"

"You do not need your eyes, my king. Everything there is I shall tell you. It is better thus. Around us are plains, as far as the eye can see. Pasture. Here and there are bushes, here and there a wooden stake, the crossbar of a well. But we are on the grass by the riverbank. Not far from us the grass goes into sand, for the river here has a sandy bed. But now pray dismount, my king."

We dismount and sit upon the ground.

"The men are making a fire," I hear the man's voice say, "the sun is already merging with the distant horizon and it will be cold."

"I should like to see Vlasta," I say suddenly.

"You will see her."

"Where is she?"

"Not far from here. You will go to her. Your horse will take you to her."

I jump up and ask to leave at once. But the man's hand seizes me by the shoulder and forces me to the ground. "Sit here, my king. First you must rest and eat your fill. Meanwhile, I shall tell you about her."

"Where is she?"

"An hour's ride from here is a wooden cottage with a thatched roof. It is encircled by a wooden fence."

"Yes, yes." I nod, and feel a joyous weight upon my heart. "All wood. That is as it should be. In her cottage there must not be a single nail."

"Yes," the voice goes on. "The fence is fashioned of wooden pickets roughly hewn. One still discerns the original shape of the branches in them."

"All things of wood are like cats or dogs," I say. "They are more beings than things. I love the world of wood. Only there am I at home."

"Beyond the fence grow sunflowers, marigolds, dahlias, and there too grows an old apple tree. At this very moment Vlasta stands upon the threshold."

"How is she dressed?"

"In a skirt of linen, slightly stained, for she is on her way back from the cowshed. In her hand she holds a wooden bucket. She is barefoot. But she is beautiful, because she is young."

"She is poor," I say, "a poor servant girl."

"Yes, but nonetheless a queen. And since a queen, she must be hidden. Even you may not go to her, lest she be revealed. Only in your veil may you go to her. Your horse will lead you to her."

So fine was the man's narration that it engulfed me in a sweet languor. I lay upon the grass listening to his voice and when it fell silent, I heard only the murmur of the water and crackle of the fire. So beautiful was it that I dared not open my eyes. But I had no choice. I knew the time had come and my eyes must open.

2

UNDERNEATH ME there was a mattress on the lacquered wood. I don't like lacquered wood. Neither do I like the curved metal legs on which the sofa stands. Above me there is a pink glass globe with three white bands hanging from the ceiling. I don't like this globe either. Nor the buffet facing me, its glass displaying other useless glass. The only wooden object in the room is the black harmonium in the corner. It's the only thing I like in the room. It used to be Papa's. Papa died a year ago.

I stood up from the sofa. I didn't feel rested. It was Friday afternoon, two days before Sunday's Ride of the Kings. Everything was up to me. Everything in our district connected with folklore is up to me. For two weeks now I haven't had a decent night's sleep what with all the errands, the chores, the petty arguments.

Then Vlasta came into the room. I keep telling myself she ought to gain weight. Fat women are usually good-natured. Vlasta is thin, her face already crisscrossed by fine wrinkles. She asked me whether I'd remembered to stop at the laundry on my way home from school. I'd forgotten. "I might have known," she said, and asked if I would stay home for once. I had to tell her no, I had a meeting in town. A district meeting. "You promised to help Vladimir with his homework." I shrugged. "Who's going to be at the meeting?" I gave her some names, and Vlasta interrupted. "Mrs. Hanzlik too?" I nodded. Vlasta looked upset. I knew I was in for it. Mrs. Hanzlik had a bad reputation. It was common knowledge that she slept around. Vlasta didn't suspect me of being involved with her, but she bristled whenever her name came up. She looked down her nose at any meeting Mrs. Hanzlik attended. It was impossible to talk to her about it. I preferred to slip out of the house.

The meeting was devoted to last-minute preparations for the Ride of the Kings. The whole thing was a mess. The District National Committee was starting to cut back on our budget. Only a few years ago it had provided lavish subsidies for folk events. Now we had to support the District Committee. If the Youth League had no way of attracting members anymore, why not let it take over the Ride of the Kings? That would boost its prestige. Gone were the days when profits from the Ride would go to subsidize other, less popular, folk activities. This time the Youth League could have them and do whatever it pleased with them. We asked the police to close off the road for the duration of the Ride. That very day we had received their refusal. It was impossible to disrupt traffic just for the sake of the Ride. But what kind of a Ride would it be with the horses stampeding among the cars? Nothing but worries, worries . . .

I couldn't get away from the meeting before eight. In the square, I saw Ludvik. He was walking in the opposite direction. I almost stopped dead in my tracks. What was he doing here? I caught his glance, which rested on me for a second and shifted quickly away. Pretending he hadn't seen me. Two old friends. Eight years on the same school bench! And he pretends he doesn't see me!

Ludvik was the first crack to appear in my life. By now I'm used to it. My life is a less than sturdy house. I was in Prague not long ago and I went to one of those little theaters, the kind that started springing up in the early sixties and quickly became the rage owing to the student humor of the young players. The show wasn't very interesting, but the songs were clever and the jazz quite good. All of a sudden the musicians donned feathered hats like the ones we wear with our folk costumes, and did a takeoff on a cimbalom ensemble. They screeched and wailed, mimicking our dance steps and the way we throw our arms up in the air. . . . It went on for no more than a few minutes, but it had the audience rolling in the aisles. I couldn't believe my eyes. Five years ago no one would have dared make clowns of us like that. And no one would have cracked a smile. Now we're a laughingstock. How is it we're suddenly a laughingstock?

And Vladimir. I've been having trouble with him these past few weeks. The District Committee proposed him to the Youth League as this year's king. Having a son chosen king has always been a great honor for the father. And this year they were going to honor me. Reward me in the person of my son for everything I'd done for folk culture. But Vladimir bridled. He had all kinds of excuses. First he said he wanted to go to Brno on Sunday for the motorcycle races. Then he claimed he was afraid of horses. Finally he came out and admitted he didn't want to be king if it was arranged from above. He didn't want to pull strings.

The grief it's caused me. He seems to want to block out everything in his life that might remind him of mine. He always balked at taking part in the children's song and dance group I initiated in conjunction with our ensemble. He was quick with the excuses even then. He had no gift for music, he claimed. Yet he did quite well on the guitar and enjoyed getting together with friends to sing the latest American hits.

Of course, he's only fifteen. And he loves me. He's a sensitive boy. We had a heart-to-heart talk a few days ago. Maybe he understood.

3

I REMEMBER it well. I was sitting in the swivel chair, Vladimir across from me on the sofa. I leaned my elbow on the closed lid of the harmonium, my favorite instrument. I'd heard it ever since I was a child. My father played it every day. Folk songs, mainly, with simple harmonies. It was like the bubbling of a far-off spring. If only Vladimir would try to understand it. If only he'd try to understand.

During the seventeenth and eighteenth centuries the Czech nation almost ceased to exist. In the nineteenth century it was virtually reborn. Among the old European nations it was a child. True, it also had its own great past, but it was cut off from that past by a gap of two hundred years, when the Czech language retreated to the countryside, the exclusive property of the illiterate. But even in their midst it never ceased to create its own culture. A modest culture, completely hidden from the eyes of Europe. A culture of songs, fairy tales, ancient rites and customs, proverbs and sayings. The only narrow footbridge across the two-hundred-year gap.

The only bridge, the only link. The only fragile stem of an unbroken tradition. That is why the men who at the turn of the nineteenth century began to create a new Czech literature and music grafted them onto this stem. That is why the first Czech poets and musicians spent so much time collecting tales and songs. And that is why their early attempts were often little more than paraphrases of folk poetry and folk melodies.

If only you'd try to understand, Vladimir. Your papa is not just a crackpot folklore addict. Maybe he is an addict, but he goes deeper than that. He hears in folk art the sap that kept Czech culture from drying up.

My love for it dates back to the war. They tried to make us believe we had no right to exist, we were nothing but Czech-speaking Germans.

We needed to prove to ourselves we'd existed before and still did exist. We all made a pilgrimage to the sources.

I was playing bass at the time in an amateur jazz band. One fine day, we had a visit from some members of the Moravian Society. They said we should resurrect the cimbalom band. That it was our patriotic duty.

Who could have refused under those circumstances? I went and played the violin with them.

We roused old songs from their deathlike slumber. Those nineteenth-century patriots had put folk songs into songbooks in the nick of time. Modern civilization was already pushing folklore into the background. So in the beginning of our century we had folklore societies springing up, taking folk art out of the songbooks and bringing it back to life. First in the towns. Then in the countryside as well. And most of all in Moravia. They worked to revitalize the folk rituals, the Ride of the Kings, they supported folk ensembles. For a while they seemed to be fighting a losing battle. Folklorists couldn't revive traditions as rapidly as civilization could bury them.

The war gave us new impetus. In the last year of the Nazi occupation, the Ride of the Kings was staged in our village. There was an army camp in the town, and German officers jostled the local population in the streets. The Ride turned into a demonstration. A host of colorful young men on horseback, with sabers. An invincible Czech horde. A deputation from the depths of history. That's how all the Czechs saw it, and their eyes lit up. I was fifteen at the time, and they chose me king. I rode between two pages and had my face veiled. I was proud. And my father was proud, knowing they had chosen me king in his honor. He was a village schoolmaster, a patriot, everyone admired him.

I believe things have a meaning, Vladimir. I believe the fates of men are bonded one to the other by the cement of wisdom. I see a sign in the fact that it was you they chose to be king this year. I'm as proud as I was twenty years ago. Prouder. Because in you they wish to honor me. And I appreciate this honor, why deny it? I want to hand my kingdom over to you. And I want you to accept it from me.

Perhaps he did understand me. He promised to accept the offer to be king.

4

IF ONLY HE would try to understand how interesting it all is. I can't imagine anything more interesting. Anything more exciting.

Take this, for example. Prague musicologists have long claimed that the European folk song originated in the Baroque. Village musicians who played and sang in the orchestras of the great houses brought the musical culture of the nobility into the life of the people. From this they conclude that the folk song is not an original artistic form. It is merely a derivative of formal music.

Now, that may have been the case in Bohemia, but the songs we sing in Moravia can't be explained in this way. Look at their tonality. Baroque music was written in major and minor keys. Our songs are sung in modes that court orchestras never dreamed of!

For example, the Lydian. The scale with the raised fourth. It always evokes in me nostalgia for the pastoral idylls of antiquity. I see the pagan Pan and hear his pipes:

Baroque and Classical music paid fanatical homage to the orderliness of the major seventh. It knew no other path to the tonic than through the discipline of the *leading tone*. It was frightened of the minor seventh that stepped up to the tonic from a major second below. And it is precisely this minor seventh that I love in our folk songs, whether it belongs to the Aeolian, Dorian, or Mixolydian. For its melancholy and pensiveness. And because it abjures the foolish scamper toward the key note with which everything ends, both song and life:

But there are also songs in tonalities so curious that it is impossible to designate them by any of the so-called ecclesiastical modes. They take my breath away:

Moravian songs are, in terms of tonality, unimaginably varied. Their musical thought is mysterious. They'll begin in minor, end in major, hesitate among different keys. Often when I have to harmonize them, I just do not know how I am to understand the key.

And they are similarly ambiguous when it comes to rhythm. Especially the long-drawn-out ones that are not used for dancing. Bartok called them *parlando* songs. Their rhythm cannot be written down in our notation system. Or let me put it differently. From the vantage point of our notation all folk singers sing their songs in a rhythm that is imprecise and wrong.

How can that be explained? Janacek maintained that the complexity which makes it impossible for us to do justice to all the nuances of the rhythm is due to the various fleeting moods of the singer. It depended on where they were singing, when they were singing, how they felt when they were singing. The folk singer reacted in his singing to the color of the flowers, to the weather, to the sweep of the country-side.

But isn't that just a bit too poetic an explanation? During my first year at the university a professor told us of an experiment he had conducted. He'd asked several folk artists to interpret the same rhythmically indefinable song independently of one another. Measuring the results on accurate electronic equipment, he ascertained that their singing was exactly the same.

The rhythmical complexity of the songs is therefore not due to any imprecision or imperfection or to the mood of the singer. It has its own mysterious laws. In one kind of Moravian dance song, for example, the second half of the measure is always a fraction of a second longer than the first half. Now, how can such rhythmic complexity be notated? The metrical system used by formal music is based on symmetry. A whole note divides into two halves, a half into two quarters, a measure is divided into two, three, or four equal beats. But what to do with a measure that is divided into two beats of unequal length? For us today, our biggest headache is how to notate the original rhythm of Moravian songs.

One thing at least is clear. Our songs cannot be derived from Baroque music. Bohemian songs, maybe. Perhaps. Bohemia always had a higher level of civilization, and there was greater contact between town and country villagers and court. Moravia had its great houses too. But the world of the peasants was far more remote by reason of its primitiveness. Here, no country folk went to play in court orchestras. These conditions enabled us to preserve folk songs from the oldest of times. This explains why they are so enormously varied. They derive from different phases of their long, slow history.

So when you come face to face with the whole of our folk music culture, it's like having a woman from *The Thousand and One Nights* dancing before you and gradually throwing off veil after veil.

Look! The first veil. The cloth is rough and patterned with trite designs. These are the youngest songs, of the last fifty, seventy years. They came to us from the west, from Bohemia. Brought by the teachers who taught the children to sing them in our schools. For the most part, they are songs in major keys, of a common West European type, only slightly adapted to our rhythms.

And the second veil. Much more colorful. The songs of Hungarian origin. They came with the encroachment of the Magyar language into the Slavic regions of Hungary. Gypsy groups spread them far and wide throughout the nineteenth century. Everyone knew them. Czardases and recruiting songs with that special syncopated rhythm.

As the dancer throws off this veil, there is another one! They are the songs of the native Slav population from the seventeenth and eighteenth centuries.

But the fourth veil is even more beautiful. These are even older songs. They go back as far as the fourteenth century, when the Wallachians made their way to us across the Carpathians from the east and southeast. Their shepherd and brigand songs know nothing of chords and harmony. They are conceived purely in melodic terms, in archaic tonalities. Pipes and fifes lend a special character to the melodies.

Once this veil has fallen away, there is no other beneath it. The dancer is dancing completely naked. These are the oldest songs of all. They stretch back into ancient pagan times. They are based on the oldest system of musical thought. On the system of four tones, on the tetrachord. Mowing songs. Harvest songs. Songs tightly bound up with the rites of the patriarchal village.

Bartok has shown that on this oldest of levels the songs of Slovakia, Moravia, Hungary, and Croatia resemble each other to the point of being indistinguishable. When you imagine this territory, the first grand Slavic dominion from the ninth century rises before your eyes, the Great Moravian Empire. Its borders were swept away a thousand years ago, yet they remain imprinted to this day in this most ancient stratum of folk songs.

The folk song or folk rite is a tunnel beneath history, a tunnel that preserves much of what wars, revolutions, civilization have long since destroyed aboveground. It is a tunnel through which I see far into the past. I see Rostislav and Svatopulk, the first Moravian princes. I see the ancient Slavic world.

But why go on speaking only about the Slavic world? Once we

racked our brains to make sense of an enigmatic folk song text. It mentioned hops in some unclear connection with a cart and a goat. Someone is riding on a goat, someone else in a cart. Then hops are praised for their power of turning maidens into brides. The folk singer who sang it for us had no idea what it meant either. The tenacity of age-old tradition had preserved a combination of words now lacking all trace of intelligibility. In the end there turned out to be only one possible explanation: the ancient Greek Dionysian festival. A satyr on a billy goat and a god grasping his thyrsus wound round with hops.

Classical antiquity! I couldn't believe it. But then, at the university, I studied the history of musical thought. The structure of our oldest folk songs is indeed analogous to that of ancient Greek music. The Lydian, Phrygian, and Dorian tetrachords. The concept of the descending scale, whose final tone is the highest and not the lowest—the latter becoming the key tone only when music began to think harmonically. So our oldest songs belong to the same era of musical thought as the songs sung in ancient Greece. They preserve classical antiquity for us.

5

AT SUPPER tonight I kept seeing Ludvik's eyes turn away from me. And I felt myself clinging all the more to Vladimir. Suddenly I was afraid I'd been neglecting him. That I'd never really succeeded in drawing him into my world. After supper Vlasta stayed in the kitchen, and I went into the living room with Vladimir. I tried to tell him about folk songs. It didn't work. I felt like a schoolteacher. I wondered whether I was boring him. Of course, he sat there silently looking as if he were listening. He's always been a good boy. But how can I tell what's actually going on in that head of his?

I'd been torturing him for quite a while with my lecture when Vlasta stuck her head into the room and said it was time for bed. What could I do? She was the heart and soul of the house, its calendar and clock.

We won't argue. Off to bed, my boy, good night.

I left Vladimir in the room with the harmonium. He sleeps there on the sofa with the metal legs. I sleep next door beside Vlasta in the marriage bed. I won't go to bed yet. I'd twist and turn and worry whether I was waking Vlasta. I'll take a breath of fresh air. It's a warm night. The garden of the old one-story dwelling where we live is full of old-fashioned rural smells. There's a wooden bench under the pear tree.

Damn Ludvik. Why did he show up today of all days? I'm afraid it's a bad omen. My oldest friend! This was where we used to sit as boys, under this very tree. I liked him from the start. When we first went to the same school. He had more brains in his little finger than the rest of us put together, but he never showed off. He couldn't have cared less about either school or teachers, and he enjoyed doing anything that was against the regulations.

Why did the two of us become such close friends? Kismet, most likely. We were both half orphans. Mama died in childbirth. And Ludvik's father, a bricklayer, was hauled off to a concentration camp by the Germans. Ludvik was thirteen at the time. He never saw him again.

Ludvik was the eldest son. And by then, he was also the only one, because his younger brother had died. After his father's arrest, mother and son were left alone. They barely managed to make ends meet. School fees were high. For a while it seemed he would have to quit.

But at the eleventh hour salvation came.

Ludvik's father had a sister who had married a rich local builder well before the war. Afterwards she had lost almost all contact with her bricklayer brother. But when they took him away, her patriotic heart was suddenly inflamed. She told her sister-in-law that she would support Ludvik. She herself had only one somewhat backward daughter, and Ludvik with his talents made her envious. Not only did she and her husband assist him materially, but they invited him to their house daily. They introduced him to the cream of local society. Ludvik had to appear grateful to them, because his studies depended on their support. Well, he couldn't bear them. Their name was Koutecky, and from that time on we used it to refer to anyone pompous and pretentious.

Madame Koutecky looked down her nose at Ludvik's mother. She'd always felt her brother had married beneath him. Her brother's arrest did nothing to change her mind. The heavy artillery of her charity was aimed at Ludvik and Ludvik alone. She saw in him her own flesh and blood and longed to make him over into her son. The existence of her sister-in-law she regarded as a regrettable mistake. She never invited her to her house. Ludvik saw all this, gritting his teeth. He was ripe for rebellion. But his mother would beg him tearfully to be sensible.

That was one reason why he so liked coming to our place. The two of us were like twins. Papa loved him almost more than he loved me. It made him happy to see Ludvik devouring the books in his library one by one. When I started playing in the jazz band, Ludvik wanted to play too. He bought a cheap clarinet at the open market and could hold his own on it in no time. We played jazz together and together joined the cimbalom band.

Towards the end of the war the Kouteckys' daughter got married.

Ludvik's aunt decided to make it a big event. She wanted to have five pairs of bridesmaids and groomsmen behind the bride and groom. She forced on Ludvik the duty of taking one of these roles, giving him the eleven-year-old daughter of the local pharmacist as a partner. Ludvik lost all sense of humor. He was embarrassed to play the fool at a wedding masquerade of provincial snobs. He considered himself an adult and was ashamed to offer his arm to a mere child. He was furious at being displayed as the Kouteckys' charity case. Furious at being forced to kiss the cross during the ceremony after everyone had slobbered over it. That evening he deserted the festivities to join us in our back room at the local inn. We'd been playing music, and now, gathered around the cimbalom, we were drinking and started to tease him. He lost his temper and proclaimed that he hated the bourgeois. Then he cursed the marriage ceremony and said he spat on the Church and was going to leave it.

We didn't take him too seriously, but a few days after the war ended he did what he had promised. Of course, he mortally offended the Kouteckys. He didn't care. He was only too happy to break all ties with them. He went to lectures the Communists sponsored. He bought the books they published. Our region was solidly Catholic, our school particularly so. Yet we were willing to forgive Ludvik his Communist eccentricities. We allowed him his rights.

In 1947 we finished school. That autumn we enrolled at the university, Ludvik in Prague, I in Brno. I didn't see him again until the following year.

6

THE YEAR WAS 1948. Everything was upside-down. When Ludvik came home for the summer, we didn't quite know how to greet him. For us the February Communist coup meant a reign of terror. Ludvik brought his clarinet but never touched it. We spent the whole night in debate.

Was that when the friction between us began? I don't think so. In fact, he nearly won me over that night. He steered clear of political arguments and stuck to our group. He said we had to look at our work in a broader context. What was the point of merely reviving a lost past? If we looked back, we'd end up like Lot's wife.

Well, what do you propose we do? we cried.

Of course, he replied, we must cherish our heritage of folk art, but that wasn't enough. We were in a new age now. Wide horizons were opening. We needed to purge the everyday musical culture of hit-tune clichés, clichéd tunes, of the kitsch that the bourgeois had used to force-feed the people. We needed to replace them with an original and genuine art of the people.

Strange. What Ludvik was calling for was nothing but the old utopia of the most conservative Moravian patriots. They too went on eternally about the godless depravity of urban culture. They heard the pipes of Satan in the strains of the Charleston. But that didn't matter much. It only made his words more comprehensible to us.

At any rate, his next point sounded more original. He was talking about jazz. Jazz had grown out of Negro folk music and conquered the whole Western world. It could serve us as encouraging proof that folk music had miraculous powers. That it could engender the dominant musical style of an entire period.

138

We listened to Ludvik with a mixture of admiration and revulsion. We were irritated by his certainty. He had the look all Communists had at the time. As if he'd made a secret pact with the future and had thereby acquired the right to act in its name. Another reason we found him so offensive was that all of a sudden he was completely different from the Ludvik we had known. With us he'd always been one of the boys, full of mockery. Now he was talking pompously, shamelessly using the most grandiose words. And of course, we were also annoyed at the free and easy way he associated the fate of our band with the fate of the Communist Party even though not one of us was a Communist. Yet his words did have a kind of attraction for us. His ideas corresponded to our innermost dreams. They elevated us to a historic greatness.

In my mind I call him the Pied Piper. A little trill on his flute and we all flocked after him. Where his arguments were too sketchy, we rushed to his aid. I remember my own reflections. I was reviewing the evolution of European music from the Baroque on. After the impressionist era it had grown weary of itself. It had exhausted almost all its sap in its sonatas and symphonies as well as in its clichéd tunes. That was why jazz had had such a miraculous effect on it. Above thousand-year-old roots, fresh sap now began to rise. Jazz captured more than European nightclubs and dance halls. It captured Stravinsky, Honegger, Milhaud, who opened their compositions to its rhythms. But take note. At the same time, or about ten years earlier, European music was infused with new blood, the ancient Old World folklore that had nowhere else remained so alive as here among us in Central Europe. Janacek and Bartok! So the parallel between folk music and jazz derived directly from the evolution of European music. They had each made an equal contribution to the formation of serious modern music in the twentieth century. However, with music for the masses, it was different. The old European folk music had left almost no imprint on it. Here, jazz remained in complete command of the field. And here was where our mission began. *Hic Rhodus, hic salta!*

Yes, right, we said: the same strength was concealed in the roots of our folk music as in the roots of jazz. Jazz had its own melodic specificity, which still bore traces of the basic six-tone scale of early Negro songs. But our folk songs also had their own melodic specificity, and were even more varied in tonality. Jazz had an original rhythm that owed its prodigious intricacies to an African drum culture dating back tens of centuries. But our music was rhythmically original too. Finally, jazz grew from the principle of improvisation. But the remarkable ensemble work of our village fiddlers, who can't read a note, also depends on improvisation.

Yes, but there is one thing, Ludvik added, that differentiates us from jazz. Jazz is quick to develop and change. Its style is in constant motion. It had traveled a precipitous road from early New Orleans counterpoint to swing, bop, and beyond. The New Orleans variety had never dreamed of the harmonies used in today's jazz. Our folk music, in contrast, is a motionless princess from bygone centuries. We have to awaken it. It must merge with the life of today and develop along with it. It must develop like jazz: without ceasing to be itself, without losing its melodic and rhythmic specificity, it must create its own new and newer phases of style. It isn't easy. It is an enormous task. A task that can be carried out only under socialism.

What did it have to do with socialism? we protested.

He explained it to us. The ancient countryside had lived a collective life. Communal rites marked off the village year. Folk art knew no life outside those rites. The romantics imagined that a girl cutting grass was struck by inspiration and immediately a song gushed from her like a stream from a rock. But a folk song is born differently from a formal poem. Poets create in order to express themselves, to say what it is that makes them unique. In the folk song, one does not stand out from others but joins with them. The folk song grew like a stalactite. Drop by drop enveloping itself in new motifs, in new variants. It was passed from generation to generation, and everyone who sang it added something new to it. Every song had many creators, and all of them modestly disappeared behind their creation. No folk song existed purely for its own sake. It had a function. There were songs sung at weddings, songs sung at harvesting, songs sung at Carnival, songs for Christmas, for haymaking, for dancing, for funerals. Even love songs did not exist outside certain customs. The rural evening promenade, the song under the maiden's window, courtship, all were part of a collective rite in which song had its established place.

Capitalism had destroyed this old collective life. And so folk art had lost its foundations, its reason for being, its function. It would be useless to try to resurrect it while social conditions were such that man lived cut off from man, everyone for himself. But socialism would liberate people from the yoke of their isolation. They would live in a new collectivity. United by a common interest. Their private and public lives would merge. They would be connected by a host of rituals. Some they would take from the past: harvest festivals, folk dances, customs bound up with their daily work. Others they would create anew: May Day, meetings, the Liberation anniversary, rallies. In all of these folk art would find its place. Here it would develop, change, and be renewed. Did we finally understand?

And before long it was apparent that the unbelievable was coming true. No one had ever done so much for folk art as the Communist government. It earmarked enormous amounts for setting up new ensembles. Folk music, fiddle and cimbalom, resounded daily from the radio. Moravian folk songs inundated the universities, May Day celebrations, youth festivities, and dances. Jazz not only disappeared from the face of our country but became a symbol of Western capitalism and its decadence. Young people stopped dancing the tango and boogie-woogie. They grabbed one another's shoulders and danced circle dances. The Communist Party went all out to create a new way of life. It based its efforts on Stalin's famous definition of the new art: socialist content in national form. And national form in music, dance, and poetry could come from nowhere but folk art.

Our band rode the exhilarating waves of that policy. It soon gained national fame. It took on singers and dancers and became a great ensemble, performing on hundreds of stages and making annual tours abroad. And we didn't sing only the traditional lays about brigands slitting their beloveds' throats, we wrote new pieces all our own, songs about Stalin or about the plowed fields or the harvest or cooperative farms. No longer was our song just a memory of the past. It was alive. It was part of contemporary history. It accompanied it.

The Communist Party supported us. So our political reservations quickly melted away. I myself joined the Party at the beginning of forty-nine. And the others from the ensemble soon followed me.

7

Bᴜᴛ ɪɴ those days Ludvik and I were still close. When did the first shadow fall between us?

Of course I know. I know very well. It was at my wedding.

I'd been studying violin at the conservatory and musicology at the university. My third year in Brno, I started feeling uneasy. At home Papa was going from bad to worse. He had a stroke. He came out of it, but from then on he had to be very careful. I kept worrying about his being by himself and thinking that if anything happened to him, he couldn't even send me a telegram. Every Saturday I'd come home with my heart in my mouth, and every Monday morning I'd leave for Brno with a new anxiety. One day the anxiety overwhelmed me. It had tortured me on Monday, tortured me more on Tuesday, and on Wednesday I threw all my clothes into my bag, paid off my rent, and told the landlady not to expect me back.

I remember to this day walking home from the station. The way to my village, which borders on the town, lies across the fields. It was autumn, just before twilight. The wind was blowing, and some boys were zigzagging paper kites in the sky from the ends of interminable strings. Papa had once made me a kite. He took me into the field, threw the kite into the air, and ran with it until the wind took hold of the paper and carried it high. I didn't enjoy it much. Papa enjoyed it a lot more. I was touched now by the memory and quickened my pace. The idea crossed my mind that Papa had sent that kite into the air to Mama.

From childhood on I've always pictured Mama in heaven. Oh, it's been years since I believed in God or life eternal or anything like that. I'm not talking about faith. I'm talking about fantasy. And I don't see why I should have to give it up. I'd feel orphaned without it. Vlasta rebukes me for being a dreamer. She says I don't see things as they are. I do see things as they are, but in addition to these visible things I see the invisible. It's not for nothing that fantasy exists. It's what makes homes of our houses.

I never knew my mama. So I never wept for her. I've always been pleased that she was young and beautiful and in heaven. None of the other children had a mama as young as mine.

I like to think of Saint Peter perched on a stool looking down on earth through a tiny window. Mama often visits him there. Peter will do anything for her because she is pretty. He lets her look out too. And Mama sees us. Myself and Papa.

Mama's face was never sad. Quite the opposite. When she looked down at us through the window in Peter's gatehouse, she often used to laugh. Who lives in eternity knows no sorrow. He knows that life on earth lasts but an instant and reunion is imminent. But when I was living in Brno and leaving Papa alone, Mama's face began to look sad and reproachful. And I wanted to live in peace with Mama.

So I hurried home and saw the kites suspended in the heavens. I was happy. I had no regrets about what I'd left behind. Of course I liked my violin and my musicology. But I had no career ambitions. Nothing, not even the most promising success, could replace the joy of coming home.

When I told Papa I wouldn't be going back to Brno, he was terribly angry. He didn't want me to ruin my life for his sake. So I told him that I'd been expelled for poor marks. He finally believed me and got even angrier. But I didn't let it bother me. I hadn't come home to waste my time. I went on playing first fiddle in our band and found a job as violin teacher in the local music school. I could devote myself to the things I loved.

One of them was Vlasta. She lived in the neighboring village, which today, like my own village, has been incorporated into the town. She danced with our ensemble. I met her when I was studying in Brno, and I was glad that I was able to see her almost every day after my return. But I didn't fall in love with her until somewhat later, unexpectedly, when she took such a spill during a rehearsal that she broke her leg. I carried her in my arms to the hastily summoned ambulance. I felt her brittle, frail body in my arms. Suddenly I realized, with astonishment, that I was six feet two and weighed well over two hundred pounds, that I could have been a lumberjack, and that she was weak, so weak.

It was a moment of illumination. In Vlasta's wounded frame I suddenly saw another, more familiar figure. How could I have failed to notice it before? Vlasta was the *poor servant girl*, a figure of so many folk songs! The poor girl who had nothing on earth but her honor, the poor girl who was humiliated, the poor girl in rags, the poor orphan girl.

Literally, of course, that was not the case. She had both her parents, and they were anything but poor. But precisely because they had been well-to-do farmers, the new era was pushing them to the wall. Vlasta would come to rehearsals in tears. Heavy delivery quotas had been levied on the family. The authorities had proclaimed her father a kulak. They had requisitioned his tractor and implements. They had threatened him with arrest. I felt sorry for her and comforted myself with the idea that I would take care of her. Of the poor servant girl.

From the moment I saw her in the light of folk song lyrics, I felt as if I were reliving a love experienced a thousand times over. As if I were playing it from an ancient score. As if the songs were singing me. I gave myself up to the resonant stream, I dreamed of my wedding and looked forward to it.

Two days before the ceremony Ludvik appeared out of nowhere. I greeted him warmly. I immediately told him the great news of my marriage and said that as my best friend he was bound to be my witness. He promised to come. And he did.

My friends from the ensemble staged a real Moravian wedding for me. They came for us early in the morning, playing and singing and wearing folk costumes. A fifty-year-old cimbalom player had taken on the duty of "patriarch," the leader of the celebration. First Papa regaled them all with slivovitz, bread, and fatback. Then the patriarch signaled for silence and recited in a sonorous voice:

Right honored guests, maidens and masters,
Ladies and gentlemen!
I have summoned you all to this abode
Because the youth who here abideth hath made bold
To ask that we with him might wend our way to the father
of Vlasta Netahal,
Which gentle maid he hath now chosen for his bride. . . .

The patriarch is the heart, the soul, the director of the entire cere-mony. That is how it has always been. That is how it has been for a thousand years. The groom was never the subject of the wedding. He was its object. He was not getting married. He was being married. The marriage seized him and carried him as on a giant wave. He was not to act or speak. The patriarch acted and spoke for him. But not even the patriarch. It was age-old tradition that men experienced one after the other, inspiriting them with its comforting flow.

Led by the patriarch, we set off for the neighboring village. We walked across the fields, and my friends played as we went. In front of Vlasta's house a group of people from the bride's side awaited us in folk costume. The patriarch recited:

We are weary travelers
And do beseech you
To grant us entry to this humble abode,
For we are thirsty and hungry.

An elderly man stepped forward from the group standing in front of the gate: "If you are worthy people, you are welcome!" And he invited us to enter. Silently we crowded in. We were only weary travelers, as the patriarch had called us, and so did not at first disclose our true intent. But then the old man, who was spokesman for the bride's family, challenged us: "If you have a burden upon your hearts, speak now!"

The patriarch began to speak, first obliquely and in parables, and the old man answered him in kind. Only after many such detours did the patriarch reveal why we had come.

Whereupon the old man put the following question:

> *I ask you, dear friend,*
> *Why does this honest groom desire to take this honest*
> *   maid to wife?*
> *Is't for the flower or for the fruit?*

And the patriarch replied:

> *To each it is well known that the flower blooms in*
> *   beauty and in grace, causing our joy to flourish.*
> *But the flower fades*
> *And fruits do ripen.*
> *Thus do we take this bride not for the flower, but for the*
> *   fruit, which does our bodies nourish.*

The responses continued until the bride's spokesman brought them to an end: "Let us then call the bride to hear whether she gives her consent." He went into the next room and returned leading a woman. She was tall, thin, bony, and her face was veiled by a scarf. "Here is your bride!"

But the patriarch shook his head, and with loud murmurs we all corroborated his disagreement. The old man tried to talk us into accepting her but finally had to take the masked woman back. Only then did he bring out Vlasta. She was wearing black boots, a red apron, and a multicolored bolero. On her head was a garland of rosemary. She looked beautiful. He placed her hand in mine.

Then the old man turned to the bride's mother and called out to her in a doleful voice: "O mother dear!"

At those words my bride withdrew her hand from mine, knelt on the ground before her mother, and bowed her head. The old man continued:

> *Mother dear, forgive me all the wrongs which I have done you!*
> *Mother dearest, I beg you, forgive me all the wrongs*
> *   which I have done you!*

Mother most beloved, I beg you by the five wounds of
Christ, forgive me all the wrongs which I have done you!

We were no more than mimes for an age-old text. And the text was beautiful, it was exciting, and everything was true. Then the music started up again, and we proceeded to town. The civil ceremony took place at the town hall, but the music didn't stop there either. Then came dinner. After dinner there was dancing.

In the evening, the bridesmaids removed the garland of rosemary from Vlasta's head and ceremonially handed it to me. They made a pigtail of her loose hair, wound it round her head, and clapped a bonnet over it. This was the rite that symbolized the step from virginity to womanhood. Of course, it had been a long time since Vlasta was a virgin. So she wasn't entitled to the symbol of the garland. But that didn't seem to me important. At some higher and more binding level, she was losing her virginity now, and only now, when the bridesmaids handed me her garland.

Lord, why is it that the memory of that garland of rosemary affects me more than our first embrace, more than Vlasta's real virgin blood? I don't know why, but it does. The women sang songs, and in the songs, the garland floated off across the water and the current untied its red ribbons. It made me want to weep. I was drunk. I saw before my eyes the floating garland and the brook passing it on to the stream, the stream to the river, the river to the Danube, and the Danube to the sea. I saw before my eyes the garland going, never to return. Yes, never to return. All the basic situations in life occur only once, never to return. For a man to be a man, he must be fully aware of this never-to-return. Drink it to the dregs. No cheating allowed. No making believe it's not there. Modern man cheats. He tries to get around all the milestones on the road from birth to death. The man of the people is more honest. Singing on his way, he goes to the core of every basic situation. When Vlasta's blood stained the towel I'd placed beneath her, I had no idea I was dealing with never-to-return. But at this moment of the ceremony and the songs, the never-to-return was there. The women were singing songs of farewell. Stay, stay, my gallant swain, and grant me leave to part with my dear mother. Stay, stay, restrain your whip, and grant me leave to part with my dear father. Stay, stay, rein in your horse, for I have yet a sister dear and do not wish to leave her. Farewell, my maiden friends, for they are taking me from you, nor will they suffer my return.

Then it was night, and the guests accompanied us home.

I opened the gate. Vlasta paused on the threshold and turned again to the cluster of friends gathered in front of the house. Suddenly one of them intoned the final song:

> *On the threshold she stood,*
> *Budding fair maidenhood,*
> *The fairest rose of all.*
> *Then the threshold she crossed,*
> *All her beauty she lost,*
> *Lost her beauty beyond recall.*

Then the door closed behind us, and we were alone. Vlasta was twenty, I a bit older. But I was thinking that she'd crossed the threshold and from that magic moment onward her beauty would fall from her like leaves from a tree. I saw in her the imminent fall of the leaves. The fall that had already begun. I was thinking that she was not only a flower, but that at that moment, the future moment of fruition already existed within her. I felt the inexorable order in it, an order I accepted and merged with. I thought in that moment of Vladimir, whom I could not know then and whose features I had not even a premonition of. And yet I did think of him, and past him to his children. Then Vlasta and I climbed into the high-piled bed, and it seemed to me that the wise infinitude of the human species took us into its soft embrace.

8

WHAT DID Ludvik do to me at the wedding? Nothing really. He was tight-lipped and strange. When the dancing began in the afternoon, the boys in the ensemble tried to give him a clarinet. They wanted him to play. He refused. Not long after that he left altogether. Luckily I was pretty far gone by then and didn't pay much attention to the matter. The next day, though, I realized his departure had left a blot on the day before. The alcohol diluting in my blood increased this blot to considerable proportions. And Vlasta even more than the alcohol. She had never liked Ludvik.

When I told her Ludvik would be my witness, she had been less than pleased. The morning after, she was quick to remind me of his behavior. She said he'd gone around all day looking as if we were putting him to great inconvenience. She had never seen anyone so conceited.

But that same day Ludvik came to see us. He brought Vlasta some gifts and made his apologies. Would we forgive him for acting as he had yesterday? He told us what had happened. He'd been kicked out of both the Party and the university. He didn't know what to expect next.

I couldn't believe my ears and hardly knew what to say. Besides, Ludvik didn't want anybody's pity and quickly changed the subject. The ensemble was leaving in two weeks for a major foreign tour. Provincials that we were, we could hardly wait for it to begin. Ludvik understood and started asking me all about it. But I remembered right away that Ludvik had yearned to go abroad since he was a child and now his chances of getting out were very slim. At that time and for many years thereafter, people with political blemishes on their records were not allowed out of the country. I saw how different our lives had become, and I tried to avoid saying so. This meant I couldn't talk openly about our tour, because I would be throwing light on the gulf that had suddenly opened between our destinies. I wanted to shroud that gulf in darkness and was afraid of any word liable to throw the least bit of light on it. But I couldn't find a single one that didn't. Everything I said with the slightest bearing on our lives served to remind us that we'd taken separate paths. That we had different opportunities, different futures. That we were being carried off in opposite directions. I tried to talk about trivial and indifferent matters in an attempt to cover up our mutual estrangement. But that was worse still. The willful insignificance of the conversation became unbearably painful.

Ludvik soon said good-bye and left. He had volunteered for a labor brigade somewhere, and I went abroad with the ensemble. I did not see him for several years. I wrote him a few letters when he was in the army in Ostrava. Each time I mailed one I was left with the same sense of dissatisfaction I'd had after our last talk. I was unable to face Ludvik's fall. I was ashamed of the success I'd made of my life. I found it intolerable to dole out words of encouragement or sympathy to Ludvik from the heights of my contentment. Instead I tried to pretend that nothing had changed between us. I went on about what we were doing, what was new in the ensemble, about the new cimbalom player, about our latest adventures. I tried to make it sound as though my world were still our common world.

Then one day Papa received an obituary announcement. Ludvik's mother had died. None of us had even known she was ill. When Ludvik disappeared from my horizon, she had disappeared with him. Holding the announcement in my hand, I realized how indifferent I had become to people even slightly removed from the path my life had taken. My successful life. I felt guilty without actually having done anything wrong. And then I noticed something that gave me a shock. The announcement had been signed by the Kouteckys. There was no mention at all of Ludvik.

The day of the funeral arrived. From early morning I felt nervous at the prospect of meeting Ludvik again. But Ludvik never came. Only a handful of people followed the coffin. I asked the Kouteckys where Ludvik was. They shrugged their shoulders and said they didn't know.

The procession stopped at a large tomb with a heavy marble stone and the white statue of an angel.

The property of the rich builder's family had been confiscated and they were living on a meager income. All they had left was this large family vault with a white angel. I knew all this, but I couldn't understand why the coffin was being interred there.

Only later did I learn that Ludvik had been in prison at the time. His mother was the only one in town who'd known. When she died, the Kouteckys took over the body of an unloved sister-in-law and proclaimed it their own. At last they were avenged on their ungrateful nephew. They had robbed him of his mother. They had covered her up with a heavy marble stone guarded by a white angel with curly hair and a palm frond. I'll never forget that angel. He was soaring above the ravaged life of a friend from whom even the bodies of his parents had been stolen. The angel of robbery.

9

VLASTA DOESN'T like extravagance. Sitting out in the garden at night is an extravagance. I heard a vigorous tapping at the windowpane. Behind the window loomed the severe shadow of a woman's figure in a nightdress. I am obedient. I can never say no to those weaker than myself. And because I am six feet two and can lift a two-hundred-pound sack with one hand, in all my life I have yet to find anyone I can resist.

So I went in and lay down beside Vlasta. To break the silence, I mentioned seeing Ludvik earlier in the day. "And so?" she said with a display of indifference. There's nothing I can do about it. She can't stomach him. All this time, and she can't stand him. Not that she has anything to complain about. Since our wedding she's seen him exactly once. In fifty-six. By then I could no longer gloss over the gulf dividing us, not even to myself.

Ludvik had been through military service, a prison sentence, and several years in the mines. He was making arrangements in Prague to resume his studies and had come to our town to take care of a few legal formalities. I was nervous about meeting him again. But the man I met wasn't a broken malcontent. Not at all. He was different from the Ludvik I had known. There was a toughness about him, a solidity, and he was perhaps calmer. Nothing calling for pity. It looked as though we'd have no trouble bridging the gulf I had so feared. To renew old ties, I invited him to a rehearsal of our ensemble. I still thought of it as his ensemble too. What did it matter that the cimbalom, second violin, and clarinet had been taken over by different musicians and I was the only one left of the old crowd?

Ludvik sat next to the cimbalom player and followed the rehearsal from there. First we played our favorite songs, the ones we used to play when we were still in school. Then we ran through a few we'd unearthed in remote mountain villages. Finally we did a set of those we consider most important. They are not genuine folk songs, but songs we ourselves have composed in the folk art spirit. We sang about plowing up the old border plots to make one immense collective field out of a multitude of private ones, about the poor who were now masters in their own country, about a tractor driver who now lacks nothing. The music was indistinguishable from the music of authentic folk songs, but the words were more up to date than the newspapers. Our favorite was the one about Julius Fucik, the hero tortured by the Nazis during the Occupation.

Ludvik sat and stared at the cimbalom mallets racing from string to string. Every once in a while he poured himself a small glass of wine. I watched him over the bridge of my violin. He was deep in thought and never once looked at me.

Then wives began tiptoeing into the room, a sign that the rehearsal was coming to an end. I invited Ludvik home. Vlasta made us something to eat and then went to bed, leaving us alone. Ludvik talked about everything under the sun. But I could tell that the real reason he was so talkative was to avoid what I wanted to talk about. And how could I fail to talk to my best friend about our greatest shared possession? So I broke into his idle chatter. What did you think of our songs? He answered that he liked them. But I wasn't going to let him get off with a cheap politeness. I continued to question him. What did he think of the new songs we'd composed ourselves?

Ludvik didn't want to get into a debate. But step by step I drew him on until finally he started talking. Those few old songs we'd found he thought were truly beautiful. Otherwise he didn't care for our repertory. We were pandering too much to prevailing tastes. And no wonder. We performed before the widest possible public and wanted to please. So we stripped our songs of everything original. We stripped them of their inimitable rhythms, imposing conventional rhythmic patterns in their place. We chose our songs from the recent past, the csardas and so on, because they were easier to listen to, more accessible.

I protested. We were barely getting started. We wanted folk music to be as popular as possible. That was why we had to make concessions to popular taste. The most important thing was that we'd created our own *contemporary* folklore, new folk songs with something to say about life as we live it now.

He disagreed. It was precisely these new songs that jarred on his ears most of all. What pitiful imitations! And what fakery!

To this day it pains me to think back on it. Who was it who warned us that if we kept looking backwards we'd end up like Lot's wife? Who was it who told us that folk music would spawn the new style of the age? Who was it who urged us to set folk music in motion and make it march along with the history of our time?

That was all a utopia, said Ludvik.

A utopia? But the songs are there! They exist!

He laughed in my face. You may sing them, you and your ensemble, but show me one other person who does. Show me one collective farmer who sings your collective farm songs for pleasure. The farmer would make a face. The songs are so unnatural and false. The propaganda text sticks out from the pseudo-folk music like a badly sewn-on collar. A pseudo-Moravian song about Fucik! What nonsense! A Prague Communist journalist! What did he have in common with Moravia?

I objected that Fucik belonged to us all and that we had just as much right to sing about him in our own way.

In our own way? You don't sing in our way, you sing the agitprop way! Look at the words. And why a song about Fucik anyway? Was he the only one in the underground? The only one tortured?

But he's the best known!

Of course he is! The propaganda apparatus wants a hierarchy in its gallery of dead heroes. They want a chief hero among heroes.

Why poke fun at that? Every age has its symbols.

True, but it's interesting to know who has been chosen to serve as a symbol! There were hundreds of people just as courageous at the time, and now they are forgotten. Well-known people too. Politicians, writers, scientists, artists. And none of them became symbols. You don't find their pictures hanging in schools and offices. And many left behind important bodies of work. But it's precisely their work that is the difficulty. It can't be touched up, cut down, or reshaped. It's the work that kept them from gaining entrance to the propaganda gallery of heroes.

None of them wrote *Notes from the Gallows!*

That's just it! What about the hero who keeps his mouth shut? What about the hero who doesn't turn his last moments into a spectacle. Into an educational lecture? Fucik, though little known at the time, decided it was of the utmost importance to inform the world of what he thought, felt, and experienced in prison, of what he recommended for mankind. He scribbled it out on tiny scraps of paper, risking the lives of those who smuggled them out of prison and kept them safe. Think of the opinion he must have had of his own thoughts and impressions! Think of the opinion he must have had of himself!

This was more than I could take. So Fucik was nothing but a self-satisfied windbag?

Ludvik was not to be stopped. No, he replied, that wasn't the main thing that compelled him to write. The main thing was his weakness. Because being brave in solitude, without witnesses, without the reward of others' approbation, face to face with himself, that took great pride and strength. Fucik needed an audience. In the solitude of his cell he created at least a fictitious audience for himself. He needed to be seen! To be nourished by applause! Even if only fictitious applause! To turn his cell into a stage and make his lot bearable not only by living it, but by performing it, exhibiting it!

I was prepared for Ludvik's sadness. Even bitterness. But I hadn't anticipated this venom, this ironical hatred. What had tortured Fucik done to him? I see the worth of a man in his beliefs. I know Ludvik was punished unjustly. But that only makes it worse! Because in that case the motivation for his change of views is all too transparent. Can a man abandon everything he's stood for just because he's been insulted?

I said as much to Ludvik's face. But then something unexpected happened. He didn't respond at all. It was as though the fever of his fury had suddenly subsided. He gave me a quizzical look and then, quite calm and collected, told me not to be upset. He might well be wrong. He said it in such a strange, cold voice that I knew very well it was not meant sincerely. I didn't want our talk to end on this insincerity. Despite my annoyance I was still guided by my original intention. I still meant to come to terms with Ludvik and renew our old friendship. Even though we'd clashed head on, I hoped that eventually, once our quarrel had died down, we would be able to find our way back to a bit of the common ground where it was once so pleasant and where we could once more live together. But all my attempts to continue the conversation were in vain. Ludvik apologized, saying that he had a tendency to exaggerate and that he had allowed himself to go on as usual. He asked me to forget everything he'd said.

Forget? Why should we forget a serious discussion? Would it not be preferable to continue it? It wasn't until the next day that I grasped the real meaning behind this request. Ludvik stayed overnight and ate breakfast with us. After breakfast we had a half-hour to talk. He told me what a hard time he'd been having getting permission to complete his last two years at the university. How being expelled from the Party had branded him for life. How wherever he went he was distrusted. That it was only thanks to a few friends from before the February coup that he had any chance of going back to school. He talked about other friends in similar positions. He talked about how they were followed and had their every word taken down. How people in their circles were interrogated and how a zealous or malicious piece of testimony could blight their lives for yet a few more years. Then he abruptly changed the subject to something trivial, and when the time came to say good-bye, he told me he was glad to have seen me, and asked me again to forget what he'd said the day before.

The connection between the request and the reference to his friends' experiences was only too clear. I was stunned. Ludvik had stopped speaking to me because he was afraid! He was afraid our talk might not remain private! He was afraid I would denounce him! He was afraid of me! It was awful. And again, completely unexpected. The gulf between us was much deeper than I had thought. It was so deep that it didn't even permit us to finish a conversation.

IO

V LASTA IS asleep. Poor thing. From time to time, lightly, she snores. They're all asleep. And here I lie, long and big, and I think how powerless I am. That talk with Ludvik had really brought it home to me. Until then I'd confidently supposed that the whole thing was in my hands. Ludvik and I had never done anything to hurt each other. With a little good will why couldn't we be friends again?

As it turned out, nothing was in my hands. Neither our estrangement nor our reunion was in my hands. So I hoped that they were in the hands of time. Time has passed. Nine years since our last meeting. Meanwhile, Ludvik has graduated and found an excellent job as a scientist in a field he enjoys. I follow his destiny from afar. I follow it with affection. I can never regard Ludvik as an enemy or a stranger. He is my friend, but he is enchanted. Like the fairy tale prince's bride when she's changed into a snake or a toad. In fairy tales the prince always saves the day by his faithful patience.

But time hasn't yet wakened my friend from his enchantment. More than once during those years I heard of visits he'd made here. But he never came to see me. Today I saw him and he turned away. Damn Ludvik.

It all began the last time we talked. Year by year I've felt a wasteland growing around me and anguish spreading within. There is more and more fatigue, less and less joy and success. The ensemble used to go on a foreign tour every year, but then the invitations began to dwindle, and now we're hardly invited anywhere. We work all the time, work harder than ever, but we're surrounded by silence. I'm standing in a deserted hall. And I have the feeling it's Ludvik who has ordered me to be alone. Because it's not your enemies who condemn you to solitude, it's your friends.

Since that time I've started taking refuge on a road through the fields. On a road through the fields with a lone wild rose bush on the verge. There I meet the last of the faithful. There is the deserter with his men. There is the wandering minstrel, and beyond the horizon there is a wooden cottage, and in it Vlasta, the poor servant girl.

The deserter calls me king and has promised me that I may take refuge under his protection at any time. All I have to do is go to the rose bush. There we will always meet.

It would be so simple to find peace in the world of fantasy. But I've always tried to live in the two worlds at the same time without giving up one for the other. I must not give up the real world even though I am losing everything in it. Perhaps it will be enough in the end if I manage one thing. One last thing:

To hand over my life as a clear message to the one person able to understand it and carry it on. Until I have done so, I may not go away with the deserter to the Danube.

The one man of whom I think, my ultimate hope after all my defeats, lies asleep a wall away. The day after tomorrow he will mount his horse. He will wear ribbons across his face. They will call him king. Come, my boy. I am falling asleep. They will call you by my title. I will sleep. I want to dream of you on your horse.

PART FIVE

Ludvik

I

I SLEPT long and fairly well. I didn't wake up until after eight, didn't remember any dreams, good or bad, didn't have a headache, but simply didn't want to get up; so I stayed in bed; sleep had erected a sort of wall between myself and my Friday-evening encounter; not that Lucie had dropped that morning out of my consciousness but that she had returned to her former abstract state.

To her abstract state? Yes: When Lucie disappeared from Ostrava so mysteriously and cruelly, I had no practical way of going after her. And as time went on (after my release from military service), I gradually lost the desire to do so. I told myself that however much I'd loved her, however *unique* she was, she was inextricably bound up with the *situation* in which we met and fell in love. It seemed to me an error in reasoning for a man to isolate a woman he loves from all the circumstances in which he met her and in which she lives, to try, with dogged inner concentration, to purify her of everything that is not her *self*, which is to say also of the *story* that they lived through together and that gives their love its shape.

After all, what I love in a woman is not what she is in and for herself, but the side of herself she turns towards me, what she is *for me*. I love her as a character in our common love story. What would Hamlet be without the castle at Elsinore, without Ophelia, without all the concrete situations he goes through, what would he be without the *text* of his part? What would be left but an empty, dumb, illusory essence? Likewise, Lucie without the Ostrava outskirts, without the roses handed through the barbed wire, without the shabby clothes, without my own endless weeks of despair, would probably cease to be the Lucie I'd loved.

163

Yes, that was how I saw it, that was how I explained it, and as year followed year, I was almost afraid of meeting her again, because I knew that we'd meet in a place where Lucie would no longer be Lucie and I would be unable to pick up the thread. Which doesn't mean, of course, that I'd stopped loving her, that I'd forgotten her, or that her image had paled; on the contrary; in the form of a quiet nostalgia she remained constantly within me; I longed for her as one longs for something definitively lost.

And since Lucie had become for me a definitive past (which still lives as past and is dead as present), she gradually lost in my mind her corporeal, material concreteness and became more and more a kind of legend, a myth inscribed on parchment and laid in a metal casket at the very foundation of my life.

Perhaps that was why the incredible could happen. I wasn't sure whether the woman in the barbershop was Lucie. And that was also why the next morning (duped by the interlude of sleep) I felt that yesterday's encounter was not *real;* that it too unfolded on the level of legend, prophecy, or riddle. If on Friday evening I'd been struck by Lucie's real presence and suddenly transported to a far-off time over which she held sway, on this Saturday morning I only asked with a calm (and well-rested) heart: *why* did I meet her? what did the encounter mean and what was it trying to *tell* me?

Do stories, apart from happening, being, have something to say? For all my skepticism, some trace of irrational superstition did survive in me, the strange conviction, for example, that everything in life that happens to me also has a sense, that it *means* something, that life speaks to us about itself through its story, that it gradually reveals a secret, that it takes the form of a rebus whose message must be deciphered, that the stories we live comprise the mythology of our lives and in that mythology lies the key to truth and mystery. Is it an illusion? Possibly, even probably, but I can't rid myself of the need continually to *decipher* my own life.

So I lay on the creaky hotel bed and I thought of Lucie, transformed again into a mere idea, a mere question. The bed began to creak, and as soon as the creaking entered my consciousness, my thoughts turned (abruptly, brutally) to Helena. As if that creaking bed was a voice summoning me to duty, I heaved a sigh, slipped my feet off the bed, sat up, stretched, ran my fingers through my hair, looked out the window at the sky, and stood up. My Friday encounter with Lucie, de-materialized though it was in the morning, had nonetheless dulled and tempered my interest in Helena, an interest so intense only a few days before. All that was left of it now was a mere *awareness* of interest; an interest translated into the language of memory, a sense of obligation to a lost interest that my reason assured me would certainly return in all its former intensity.

I went over to the sink, threw off my pajama top, and turned the faucet on full force; I cupped my hands under the stream of water and immediately started splashing my neck, shoulders, and body; I rubbed myself down with a towel; I wanted to send the blood coursing through my veins. Because I felt alarmed; alarmed by my indifference to Helena's arrival; alarmed that my indifference (my temporary indif-ference) would spoil an opportunity that was hardly likely to come again. I decided to eat a hearty breakfast and wash it down with a shot of vodka.

I went downstairs to the coffee shop, but all I found was an array of chairs mournfully stranded, legs up, on bare tables, and an old woman in a dirty apron puttering around in their midst.

I went to the reception desk and asked the porter, ensconced behind the counter in a deep armchair and deep lethargy, whether I could get breakfast in the hotel. Without moving, he told me that the coffee shop was closed on Saturdays. I went outside. It was a pleasant day, the clouds scudding across the sky and a gentle wind raising dust from the pavement. I hurried towards the square. I passed a crowd of women, young and old, queuing outside the butcher's; they were holding shopping bags and nets, and patiently, lifelessly waiting their turn to get into the shop. Among the pedestrians strolling or hurrying by I was caught by those bearing ice-cream cones in their hands like miniature torches and licking their red caps. Soon I came out into the square. Before me stood a sprawling one-story structure, a cafeteria.

I went in. It was a large room with a tile floor and long-legged tables where people stood eating sandwiches and drinking coffee or beer.

I didn't feel like eating breakfast there. From early morning I'd had my heart set on a good solid breakfast of eggs, bacon, and a shot of alcohol to restore my lost vitality. I remembered a restaurant a short walk away in another square, with a small park and a Baroque monument. That restaurant was not particularly attractive either, but all I needed was a table, a chair, and a single waiter to serve whatever was on hand.

I walked past the monument. The plinth supported a saint, the saint supported a cloud, the cloud supported an angel, the angel supported another cloud, and on this cloud sat another angel, the last. I took a long look at the poignant pyramid of saints, clouds, and angels that simulated in heavy stone the heavens and their heights, whereas the real heavens were pale (morning) blue and hopelessly removed from that dusty stretch of earth.

I crossed the park with its neat lawns and benches (though bare enough not to break the atmosphere of dusty emptiness) and tried the restaurant door. It was locked. I began to realize that my dream breakfast would remain a dream, and this alarmed me because I'd made up my mind with childlike obstinacy that a hearty breakfast was the key to success for the entire day. I realized that provincial towns take no account of eccentrics wishing to eat their breakfasts sitting down and that the restaurants would not open until much later. So rather than set off in search of another place to eat, I turned and walked back through the park.

Again I passed people carrying little red-capped cones, and again I thought that the cones looked like torches, and that there might be some meaning in their shape, because those torches were not torches, but *parodies of torches*, and the pink trace of pleasure they so solemnly displayed was not pleasure but a *parody of pleasure*, which would seem to capture the inescapably parodical nature of all torches and pleasures in this dusty little town. And then I told myself that since I kept meeting these licking torchbearers, I was going in the direction of a pastry shop where I could find that table and chair and perhaps some black coffee and a bite to eat.

Instead of a pastry shop I came to a milk bar; there was a long line of people waiting for cocoa or milk with rolls, the same high tables for eating and drinking, and in the back a few regular tables and chairs, all taken. So I joined the line, and after inching along for a few minutes I was able to buy a glass of cocoa and two rolls and find a table which, though encumbered by a half-dozen more or less empty glasses, offered a spot free of spilled liquid.

I ate with cheerless haste: in no more than three minutes I was back in the street; it was nine o'clock; I had two hours to go: Helena had taken the early flight from Prague and was due in on a bus from Brno just before eleven. I saw that these two hours would be utterly empty, utterly wasted.

Of course, I could have made the rounds of my childhood haunts, pausing in sentimental meditation before the house where I was born and where my mother lived until she died. I often think about her, but here, in the town where her remains lie fraudulently buried under alien marble, it is as if all my thoughts of her are poisoned: they might commingle with the feeling of my powerlessness at that time and my venomous bitterness—and that is what I was defending myself against.

So there was nothing for me to do but sit on a bench in the square, stand up after a while, go over to the shopwindows, glance at the titles of the books in the bookshop, buy *Rude Pravo* at a newsstand, go back to the bench, skim the dull headlines, read a couple of fairly interesting reports in the foreign affairs column, then get up from the bench again, fold the paper, and throw it into a wastebasket in mint condition; next, walk slowly up to the church, stop in front of it, peer up at its two towers, climb its broad steps and enter the vestibule, then the church proper, diffidently, so no one would be shocked when the newcomer failed to cross himself.

When some more people came in, I started feeling like an intruder who doesn't know what to do with himself, how to bend his head or clasp his hands, so I went out again, looked at the clock, and saw that I still had plenty of time left. I tried to focus my mind on Helena, to put the long minutes to some use by thinking of her; but the thoughts remained static, wouldn't evolve; the best I could do was conjure up a visual image of her. It's a well-known phenomenon: when a man waits for a woman, he finds it extremely difficult to think of her and can do little else but pace up and down under her motionless effigy.

And pace I did. Across from the church I noticed ten empty baby carriages standing outside the old town hall (today the town's National Committee building). While I wondered what they were doing there, a breathless young man pushed another carriage up to them, the (quite nervous) woman accompanying him lifted a white lacy bundle (clearly containing a baby) from the carriage, and together they hurried into the hall. Mindful of the hour and a half I had left to kill, I went in after them.

Along the broad staircase there were some idle bystanders, and walking up the stairs, I saw more and more people. The second-floor corridor was crowded, whereas the stairs leading higher were empty. The event they had gathered for was apparently to take place on this floor, most probably in the room off the corridor whose open door was packed with people. I entered and found myself in a modest-sized hall with seven or so rows of chairs occupied by people who seemed to be waiting for some performance to begin. On a dais at the head of the room was a long table covered with red cloth, and on the table, a large bouquet in a vase; the artistically arranged folds of the national flag adorned the wall behind; immediately in front of the dais (about ten feet from the first row of the audience) were eight chairs facing it in a semicircle; at the other side of the hall, in the back, was a small harmonium with a bald old man hunched over its open keyboard.

There were still several free chairs; I took one. For a long time nothing happened, but the people, far from bored, were leaning over and whispering to one another in keen anticipation. Meanwhile the groups that had remained in the corridor filtered in, occupying the few remaining seats and lining the walls.

Finally the long-awaited action got under way: a door behind the dais opened to reveal a woman with a long thin nose, wearing a brown suit and glasses; she looked out into the hall and raised her right hand. The people around me fell silent. Then she turned back towards the room she'd just left, apparently to give a sign to someone there, but instantly she was facing us again, leaning against the wall and flashing a fixed, ceremonial smile. Everything seemed to be perfectly synchronized, for at the very moment her smile came on, the harmonium started up behind my back.

A few seconds later a flaxen-haired young woman appeared in the doorway behind the dais, red in the face, with elaborate hairdo and makeup, a terrified expression in her eyes, and white swaddling clothes in her arms. The woman in brown pressed closer to the wall to let her pass, smiling to encourage the baby carrier. And she advanced, unsure of herself, clutching the baby; then another emerged with the same white swaddling clothes, and after her (in single file) a whole detachment of them. I kept my eye on the first one: she stared up at the ceiling, then her eyes fell and met the glance of someone in the audience; the glance so ruffled her that she tore her eyes away and smiled, but the smile (the *effort* of a smile) quickly vanished, leaving only a rigid configuration of the lips. All this happened on her face within a matter of seconds (the time it took to cover the fifteen or twenty feet from the door); because she was walking too straight a line and failed to turn when she came to the semicircle of chairs, the woman in brown had to detach herself from the wall (frowning slightly), hurry over to her, tap her gently on the shoulder to remind her which way to go. The woman quickly corrected her course and led the other baby carriers around in front of the chairs. There were eight of them in all. Finally, having completed their prescribed routes, they stood with their backs to the audience, each before a chair. The woman in brown pointed to the floor; the women gradually got the message and (their backs still to the audience) sat down (with their bundles) on the chairs.

The shadow of dissatisfaction left the face of the woman in brown, and she was smiling again as she walked over to the half-open door and into the back room. After standing there a few seconds, she stepped briskly back against the wall. A man of about twenty appeared in the doorway; he wore a black suit and a white shirt whose collar, stuffed with a patterned tie, was cutting into his neck. He kept his eyes on the floor and wavered slightly as he walked. Seven more men followed, of varying ages but all in dark suits and white shirts. They walked up behind the women sitting with their babies and stopped, each behind a chair. At that moment a few of them seemed uneasy and started looking around as if searching for something. The woman in brown (whose face shadowed instantly as before) ran up to them and, hearing out a whispered plea, nodded permission, whereupon the men sheepishly changed places.

Resuming her smile, the woman in brown again went to the door. This time she didn't have to nod or make a sign. A new detachment made its entrance, and I must say that it was disciplined, disciplined and skilled, marching without embarrassment and with almost professional elegance: it was composed of ten-year-old children, boys alternating with girls; the boys wore dark-blue trousers, white shirts, and folded red kerchiefs with one point hanging down their backs and the other two tied in a knot around their necks; the girls wore dark-blue skirts, white blouses, and the same red kerchiefs at their necks; each child carried a small bouquet of roses. They moved, as I say, with supreme confidence, and instead of heading toward the semicircle of chairs like their predecessors, they spread out in front of the dais; then they stopped and executed a left turn, so that they stood in a line before the dais, covering the whole of its length and facing the seated women and the audience.

There was another short pause, and a new figure appeared at the door unaccompanied, and advanced directly to the long table covered in red on the dais. He was a middle-aged man without a hair on his head. He walked with dignity, his back straight; he wore a black suit and carried a bright red portfolio; halfway along the table, he stopped and turned to the audience, bowing to them slightly. As he did so he revealed a bloated face and a broad red, white, and blue ribbon around his neck and a large gold medal dangling from it in the vicinity of his stomach and bobbing up and down as he leaned forward.

All of a sudden one of the boys standing in front of the dais began (without formally requesting permission) to speak in a loud voice. He said spring had come and all papas and mamas were rejoicing and the whole earth was rejoicing. He went on in that vein until one of the girls broke in and said something similar, with no clear meaning but with frequent repetitions of the words mama, papa, spring and several times the word rose. Then she was cut short by another of the boys, who was in turn cut short by another of the girls, but one could hardly say that they were at odds, because they were all saying more or less the same thing. One boy, for instance, proclaimed that children were peace. The girl who came after him said that children were flowers. Whereupon all the children were united by this idea, repeated it once more in unison, and stepped forward, stretching out the hand holding the bouquet. Because there were eight of them and eight women sitting in the semicircle, each woman received a bouquet. The children went back to their places in front of the dais and didn't say another word.

Next, the man standing above them on the dais opened his red portfolio and began to read. He too spoke of spring, of flowers, of mamas and papas, he also spoke of love, which according to him bore fruit, but suddenly his vocabulary was transformed and the words duty, responsibility, the State, and citizen appeared; suddenly there was no more papa and mama, but father and mother, and he was enumerating all the blessings the State offered them (the fathers and mothers) and reminding them that it was their duty in return to bring up their children to be model citizens. Then he called on all parents present to affirm this ceremonially with their signatures, and indicated a thick leather-bound volume lying on a corner of the table.

At that point, the woman in brown came up behind the mother sitting at one end of the semicircle and touched her on the shoulder. The mother turned her head, and the woman took her baby. Then the mother stood and walked over to the table. The man with the ribbon around his neck opened the book and handed the mother a pen. The mother signed and returned to her chair, where the woman in brown gave her baby back. The husband went over to the table and signed; then the woman in brown took the next mother's child and sent the mother over to the table; then her husband signed, then the next mother, the next husband, and so on until they were all done. Then the strains of the harmonium wafted through the hall again, and the people around me in the audience rushed up to the mothers and fathers to shake their hands. I too was on my way forward (as if wanting to shake someone's hand) when suddenly the man with the ribbon around his neck called me by name and asked me whether I recognized him.

Of course I hadn't recognized him, even though I'd watched him all through his speech. To avoid answering his vaguely unpleasant question in the negative, I asked him how he was. Not too bad, he said, and all at once I knew him: of course, it was Kovalik, a schoolmate of mine; it had just taken some time to recognize his features, which were blurred by his fleshy new face; in any case, Kovalik had been one of the less memorable students: neither well-behaved nor rowdy, neither sociable nor solitary, mediocre in his studies—in short, he was inconspicuous. In those days he'd had a shock of hair across his brow, and it was now missing: I had an easy excuse for not recognizing him right away.

He asked me what I was doing here, whether I had any relatives among the mothers. I said no, I hadn't, I'd come out of idle curiosity. He gave me a contented smile and began to explain that the National Committee had done a great deal to imbue civil ceremonies with dignity, adding with modest pride that he, as the official in charge of citizen affairs, could take some of the credit and had even been commended at the district level. I asked him whether what I'd seen was a christening. He told me no, it wasn't a christening, it was a *welcoming of new citizens to life*. He was clearly glad to have a chance to expand on the subject. He said there were two great opposing institutions involved: the Catholic Church with its traditional thousand-year-old rites and the civil institutions that must supplant the thousand-year-old rites with their own. He said that people would stop going to church to have their children christened or to get married only when our civil ceremonies had as much dignity and beauty as the church ceremonies.

I told him this was obviously no easy matter. He agreed and said he was glad that citizen affairs officials like himself were finally getting a little support from our artists and it was about time artists saw their duty and gave our people real socialist burials, weddings, and christenings (here he immediately corrected himself and said "welcomings of new citizens to life"). He added that the verses the young Pioneers had just recited were really beautiful. I nodded and asked whether there might not be a more effective way of weaning people away from religious ceremonies, to give them the option of avoiding *any* sort of ceremony whatsoever.

He said that people would never give up their weddings and funerals. And that from our point of view (he emphasized the word "our" as if to make it clear to me that he too had joined the Communist Party) it would be a pity not to use them to bring people closer to our ideology and our State.

I asked my old classmate what he did with people who didn't want to take part in his ceremonies, whether there were any such people. He said of course there were, since not everybody had come round to the new way of thinking yet, but if they didn't attend, they kept receiving invitations, and most of them came in sooner or later, after a week or two. I asked him whether attendance at such ceremonies was compulsory. He replied with a smile that it wasn't, but that the National Committee used attendance as a touchstone for evaluating people's sense of citizenship and their attitude towards the State, and in the end people realized that and came.

In that case, I said, the National Committee was stricter with its believers than the Church was with theirs. Kovalik smiled and said that could not be helped. Then he asked me up to his office. I said that unfortunately I was a little pressed for time because I had to meet someone at the bus station. He asked me whether I'd seen any of the "boys" (meaning our classmates). I said that I hadn't, but I was glad for the chance to see at least him, because as soon as I had a child to christen I'd know where to go. He laughed and gave me a punch on the shoulder. We shook hands, and I went out into the square again, aware that in fifteen minutes the bus would arrive.

Fifteen minutes is not a long time. I crossed the square, walked past the barbershop, peered through the window (although I knew that Lucie wouldn't be there till the afternoon), and then strolled in front of the bus station imagining Helena: her face under pancake makeup, her reddish, obviously dyed hair; her figure, far from slim, though retaining the basic rapport of proportions necessary to perceive a woman as a woman; I imagined everything that placed her on the exciting borderline between the repellent and the attractive, her voice, too loud to be pleasant, her excessive gestures involuntarily betraying an impatient anxiety to *continue* still to please.

I had seen Helena only three times in my life, too little to fix her image exactly in my mind. Whenever I tried to conjure it up, one or another of her features stood out to such an extent that she would turn into a caricature of herself. But no matter how inaccurate my imagination was, precisely by its very distortions it had managed to capture something essential of Helena's existence, something hidden beneath her outward form.

This time I was particularly unable to rid myself of the image of Helena's flabbiness, her flaccidity, signs not only of her age and her motherhood but above all, of her psychic or erotic defenselessness (undisguised by her self-importance), her vocation as sexual prey. Did this image really derive from her essence, or only from my own attitude to her? Who can tell? The bus was due any minute, and I longed to see Helena just as my imagination had interpreted her to me. I hid in a doorway to observe her for a while, to watch her look around *powerlessly*, not seeing me and suddenly wondering whether she'd made the trip in vain.

The large express bus pulled into the square, and Helena was one of the first to alight. She wore a blue raincoat (with turned-up collar and belt pulled tight) that gave her a young, sporty look. Yes, she looked good in it. She surveyed the square, took a few steps forward to check the area obscured by the bus, then, far from standing defenselessly, she turned without hesitation and headed in the direction of my hotel, where she had booked a room for the night.

Once more I verified that my imagination offered me only a deformed Helena. Fortunately she was always more attractive in the flesh than in my mind, something I realized anew looking at her back as she made her way to the hotel in her high heels. I set off after her.

When I entered the lobby, she was leaning against the reception desk, registering with the listless clerk. She was telling him her name: "Helena Zemanek, Ze-ma-nek." I stood behind her, listening to her. As soon as the clerk was through, she asked, "Is there a Comrade Jahn staying here?" The clerk mumbled that there wasn't. I stepped up to her and laid my hand on her shoulder.

2

Everything that had happened between myself and Helena was part of a precise and deliberate plan. No doubt, even at our first meeting, Helena already had some designs of her own, but they did not go far beyond the vagueness of female desire, which wants to preserve its spontaneity and sentimental poetry and therefore doesn't try to arrange and stage-manage the course of events in advance. I, on the other hand, had from the start acted as a meticulous stage manager of the story I was about to experience, and had left nothing to the whims of inspiration, neither choice of words and proposals, nor choice of a room for our time together. I was wary of the slightest risk, afraid to bungle an opportunity that meant so much to me, not because Helena was particularly young, particularly nice, or particularly attractive, but purely and simply because her name was Zemanek and her husband was a man I hated.

That day at the institute when they informed me that a woman named Zemanek from the radio was coming to see me and that I was to give her some information about our research, I did think of my former friend for a moment, but I quickly dismissed this coincidence of names as a mere trick of chance, and if I was annoyed by their sending her to me, it was for entirely different reasons.

I don't like journalists. They are for the most part shallow, verbose, and insolent. The fact that Helena worked for radio rather than a newspaper only increased my aversion. In my view newspapers have one extenuating attribute: they make no noise. Their tediousness is silent; they can be put aside, thrown into the wastebasket. The tediousness of radio lacks that extenuating attribute; it persecutes us in cafés, restaurants, trains, even during our visits to people who have become incapable of living without nonstop feeding of the ears.

But I was irritated even by the way Helena spoke. It was clear to me that before coming to the institute she'd thought her whole report through and that all she needed from me was a few facts and figures, a few examples to prove her hackneyed points. I did my very best to make things tough for her; I deliberately spoke in complex and confusing sentences and tried to upset the preconceived notions she'd brought with her. When at one point she came dangerously close to understanding what I was saying, I put her off the track by becoming familiar; I told her how well red hair suited her (though I thought the exact opposite), asked her how she liked her work at broadcasting and what she liked to read. And in a quiet reflection far below the surface of our conversation, I came to the conclusion that the coincidence in names was not necessarily a coincidence. There seemed to be a family resemblance between this phrase-mongering, loudmouthed, pushy woman and the man I remembered as phrase-mongering, loudmouthed, and pushy. So in the light, almost flirtatious tone the conversation had assumed, I asked her about her husband. I was on the right track; a few further questions identified Zemanek beyond a doubt. I must say that at that moment I didn't as yet want to come to know her as I later did. On the contrary: the revulsion I had felt when she entered the room was only intensified by the discovery. My first reaction was to look for a pretext to cut the interview short and pass her on to another member of the institute; I even had a blissful image of throwing this incessantly smiling woman out the door, and I regretted that it was impossible.

But at the very moment I felt I couldn't stand it anymore, Helena, stirred by my intimate questions and remarks (unaware of their purely investigative function), with some gestures revealed herself as so naturally feminine that my rancor suddenly took on a new complexion: behind the veil of Helena's journalistic playacting I saw a *woman*, a woman capable of functioning as a woman. Just the kind of woman Zemanek deserved, I said to myself with a private little sneer, and quite adequate punishment; but I had to correct myself immediately: I was too quick to make this contemptuous judgment: it was too subjective, too forced; in fact, she must have been rather pretty once, and there was no reason to suppose that Pavel Zemanek no longer enjoyed using her as a woman. I kept up the light tone of the conversation without giving any indication of what was on my mind. Something was forcing me to find out as much as I could about the *feminine* side of the journalist sitting opposite me, and this compulsion automatically governed the direction of the conversation.

The mediation of a woman is capable of imposing on hatred certain qualities characteristic of affection, for example curiosity, carnal interest, the urge to cross the threshold of intimacy. I rose to a kind of exaltation: I imagined Zemanek, Helena, and their world (their alien world) and with an odd pleasure I fondled my rancor (my attentive, almost tender rancor) against Helena's appearance, rancor against her red hair, rancor against her blue eyes, rancor against her short bristly lashes, rancor against her round face, rancor against her sensuous, flared nostrils, rancor against the gap between her two front teeth, rancor against the ripe fleshiness of her body. I observed her the way men observe the women they love; I observed her as if I wanted to embed everything about her in my memory. And to disguise the rancor behind my interest, my remarks became more lighthearted, more and more amiable, so that Helena became more and more feminine. I kept thinking that her mouth, her breasts, her eyes, her hair, all belonged to Zemanek, and I mentally fingered them, held them, weighed them, testing whether they could be crushed in my fist or shattered against the wall, and then I carefully reexamined them, first with Zemanek's eyes, then with my own.

Perhaps I did have a fleeting and utterly impractical Platonic idea that it might be possible to move this woman further and further from the plane of our coquettish conversation towards the target area of the bed. But it was only one of those ideas that flash through the mind like a spark and are quickly extinguished. Helena thanked me for the information I'd given her and announced that she wouldn't take any more of my time. We said good-bye, and I was glad to see her go. The odd exaltation had passed; I felt no more for her than my former antipathy, and I was uncomfortable at having treated her with such intimate concern and kindness (feigned though they were).

Nothing would have come of the meeting if Helena herself hadn't phoned a few days later and asked whether she might see me. Perhaps she really did need me to go over the text of her broadcast, but at the time I had the impression that this was a pretext and that her tone of voice was more in keeping with the intimate, lighthearted side of our last conversation than with its professional aspect. I adopted this tone quickly, without thinking, and stayed with it. We met at a café; provocatively I avoided everything connected with Helena's broadcast; shamelessly I made light of her interests as a journalist; I saw that I'd upset her equilibrium and at the same time that I had begun to dominate her. I invited her to go to the country with me. She protested, reminding me she was a married woman. Nothing could have given me greater pleasure. I lingered over her delightful objection, so dear to me; I played with it; I kept returning to it; I joked about it. The only way she could get me off the subject in the end was to accept the invitation. From then on everything went exactly according to plan. I had dreamed this plan up with the power of fifteen years of rancor, and I felt inexplicably certain that it would be successfully accomplished.

Yes, the plan was being accomplished. I picked up Helena's small overnight case at the reception desk, and we went upstairs to her room, which was just as hideous as my own. Even Helena, who had a peculiar tendency to describe things as better than they were, had to admit as much. I told her not to be upset, that we'd manage somehow. She gave me a glance dripping with meaning. Then she said she wanted to wash up, and I said that was a good idea and that I would wait for her in the lobby.

When she came downstairs (wearing a skirt and pink sweater under her unbuttoned raincoat), I noticed again how elegant she looked. I told her we'd have lunch at the People's House, that the food there was far from good but the best there was. She said that since I was a native she would put herself entirely in my hands, offer no resistance. (She seemed to be choosing her words with their double entendre value in mind, a laughable and gratifying effort on her part.) We followed the route I'd taken that morning in my vain quest for a decent breakfast, and Helena kept reiterating how glad she was to get to know my hometown, but although she was in fact here for the first time, she never once looked around, never asked what this or that building was, never in any way behaved like a visitor who is seeing an unfamiliar town for the first time. I wondered whether her lack of interest came from a shriveled soul that no longer was able to feel ordinary curiosity, or from the fact that she'd concentrated all her attention on me and had none left for anything else; I wanted to believe the second hypothesis.

Again we walked past the Baroque monument: the saint supporting a cloud, the cloud an angel, the angel another cloud, that cloud another angel; the sky was bluer than it had been earlier; Helena took off her raincoat, tossed it over her arm, and said that it was warm; the warmth intensified the persistent sensation of a dusty void; the monument jutted up in the middle of the square like a piece broken off from the heavens that couldn't find its way back; I thought to myself that we too had been *cast out* into this oddly deserted square with its park and restaurant, cast out irrevocably, that we too had been broken off from something; that we imitated the heavens and the heights in vain, that no one believed in us; that our thoughts and our words scaled the heights in vain when our deeds were as low as the earth itself.

Yes. I was struck by an acute awareness of my own *lowness;* it had taken me by surprise; but what surprised me even more was that it didn't horrify me, that I accepted it with a certain feeling of pleasure, if not joy or relief; and the pleasure I felt was enhanced by the certainty that the woman walking by my side was driven to these dubious hours of afternoon adventure by motives not much higher than my own.

The People's House was already open, but because it was only eleven forty-five, the restaurant was still empty. The tables were laid, in front of every chair was a soup bowl containing a knife, fork, and spoon on a paper napkin. We sat down, set the utensils and napkins next to our plates, and waited. Several minutes later a waiter appeared in the kitchen door. He surveyed the dining hall with a weary eye and started to go back to the kitchen.

"Waiter!" I called.

He turned around and took a few steps in the direction of our table. "Did you want anything?" he asked, still fifteen or twenty feet away. "We'd like to have lunch," I said. "No food until twelve," he replied, heading for the kitchen. "Waiter!" I called again. He turned around again. "Tell me," I had to shout because he was quite a distance away, "have you got any vodka?" "Vodka? No, there's no vodka." "Well, then, what have you got?" "Rye," he called out over the distance, "or rum." "That's pathetic!" I shouted, and then: "All right, two ryes!"

"I haven't even asked if you drink rye," I said to Helena.

Helena laughed. "I can't say I'm used to rye."

"No matter," I said. "You'll get used to it. You're in Moravia now, and rye is the most popular drink among the people here."

"Marvelous!" said Helena with delight. "That's what I like best, just an ordinary little restaurant where truck drivers and mechanics go, with just ordinary things to eat and drink."

"So you like lacing your beer with rum."

"Well, not quite," she said.

"But you like being among the people."

"Oh, yes," she said. "I can't stand those chic places with a dozen waiters hovering over you and serving you one dish after another. . . ."

"That's right. There's nothing better than a hole in the wall where the waiter refuses to look at you and you can't breathe for the smoke and the stink. And there's nothing better than rye. I never touched anything else when I was a student."

"I like simple food too, like potato fritters or sausages with onions, I can't think of anything better."

My mistrust is so entrenched that when someone starts listing his likes and dislikes I am unable to take it seriously, or to put it more precisely, I can accept it only as an indication of the person's self-image. I didn't for a moment believe that Helena breathed more easily in filthy, badly ventilated dives than in clean, well-ventilated restaurants or that she preferred cheap alcohol and food to haute cuisine. However, this declaration of faith wasn't without value for me, because it revealed her predilection for a special pose, a pose long since outdated and out of style, a pose going back to the years when revolutionary enthusiasm delighted in anything that was "common," "plebeian," "ordinary," or "rustic," just as it loved to despise everything that was "refined" or "elegant," anything connected with good manners. In Helena's pose I recognized the period of my youth, and in Helena's person Zemanek's wife. My early-morning concerns quickly dissolved, and I began to concentrate.

The waiter brought us two glasses of rye on a tray, placed them in front of us, and left behind a sheet of paper (the last carbon copy, no doubt) with an all but illegible blur of the day's dishes on it.

I raised my glass and said, "Let's drink to rye, to ordinary rye!"

She laughed, touched her glass to mine, and said, "I've always yearned for a man who was . . . simple and direct. Unaffected. Straight-forward."

We took a swig and I said, "There aren't many like that."

"But they do exist," said Helena. "You're one."

"I wouldn't say that," I said.

"You are."

Once more I was amazed by the incredible human capacity for transforming reality into a likeness of desires or ideals, but I was quick to accept Helena's interpretation of my personality.

"Who knows? Perhaps," I said. "Simple and straightforward. But what does simple and straightforward mean? It means being what you are, wanting what you want and going after it without a sense of shame. People are slaves to rules. Someone tells them to be this or that, and they try so hard that to the day they die they have no idea who they were and who they are. They are nobody and they are nothing. First and foremost a man must have the courage to be himself. So let me tell you right away: I'm attracted to you, Helena, and I desire you, even though you're a married woman. I can't put it any other way, and I can't let it go unsaid."

To say this was embarrassing, but it was necessary. The management of a woman's mind has its own inexorable rules; anyone who decides to persuade a woman or to refute her point of view with rational argu-ments is hardly likely to get anywhere. It is much wiser to grasp her basic self-image (her basic principles, ideals, convictions) and contrive to establish (with the aid of sophistry, illogical demagoguery, and the like) a harmonious relation between that self-image and the desired conduct on her part. For example, Helena dreamed of "simplicity," "unaffectedness," "straightforwardness." These ideals of hers had their origin in the revolutionary puritanism of an earlier time and were associated with the idea of a "pure," "unsullied," highly principled, and strictly moral man. But because the world of Helena's principles was based not on reflection but (as with most people) on illogical imperatives, nothing was simpler than to associate the idea of the "straightforward man" with behavior altogether unpuritanical, immoral, adulterous, and thereby prevent the desired behavior (that is, adultery) from entering into neurotic conflict with her inner ideals. A man may ask anything of a woman, but unless he wishes to behave like a brute, he must make it possible for her to act in harmony with her deepest self-deceptions.

Meanwhile, people had been trickling into the restaurant, and soon most of the tables were occupied. The waiter now reappeared and was going from table to table taking orders. I handed Helena the menu. She said I knew more about Moravian food and handed it back.

There was of course no need to know anything about Moravian food since the menu was exactly the same as in all restaurants of its category and consisted of a narrow selection of standard dishes, all equally unalluring and therefore difficult to choose among. I was (dolefully) contemplating the smeary page when the waiter came up and asked me impatiently for our order.

"Just a second," I said.

"You wanted to order fifteen minutes ago, and you still haven't made up your minds," he reminded me, and left.

Fortunately he came back fairly soon, and we ventured to order roulade of beef and another round of rye, this time with soda. Helena (chewing the beef) remarked how marvelous it was ("marvelous" was her favorite adjective) to be sitting with me in a strange place, a place she'd dreamed of so often during her days in the ensemble when she sang the songs that originated in this region. Then she said that it was probably wrong of her to feel so happy with me, but that she couldn't help it, she hadn't the will power, and that was that. I told her there was nothing more reprehensible than being ashamed of one's own feelings. Soon I called the waiter and asked for the check.

Outside, there was the Baroque monument jutting up in front of us again. It looked laughable. I pointed to it: "Look, Helena, look at those saints climb! Look at them fighting their way up! How they'd love to get to heaven! And heaven couldn't care less about them! Heaven doesn't know they exist, the winged yokels!"

"How true," said Helena, in whom the fresh air had reinforced the effect of the alcohol. "Why do they keep them anyway, those holy statues? Why don't they build something to celebrate life instead of all that mysticism?" Yet she still had enough self-control to add, "Or am I just full of hot air? Am I? Well, am I?"

"No, you're not, Helena. You're absolutely right. Life is beautiful, and we can never celebrate it enough."

"Yes," said Helena. "No matter what people say, life is marvelous, if you want to know who gets my goat, it's those killjoy pessimists, even if I have plenty to complain about, you don't hear a peep out of me, what for, I ask you, what for, when life can bring me a day like today; oh, how marvelous it all is: a strange town, and me here with you. . . ."

I let her talk, inserting a word of encouragement whenever she paused. Before long we were standing in front of Kostka's building.

"Where are we?" asked Helena.

"There's no decent public place to get a drink in this town," I said. "But I have a small private bar here. Come on in."

"Where are you taking me?" Helena protested, following me into the building.

"It's a genuine Moravian wine bar; haven't you ever been in one?"

"No," said Helena.

On the fourth floor, I unlocked the door to the flat, and we went in.

3

HELENA WAS not in the least taken aback by my leading her into a strange flat, nor did she require any commentary. On the contrary, from the moment she crossed the threshold she seemed determined to proceed from the game of flirtation (which speaks in double entendre and pretends to be a game) to the act that has only a single meaning and believes in the illusion that it is not a game but life itself. She stopped in the middle of Kostka's room to look back at me, and I could read in her eyes that she was waiting for me to go to her, kiss her, and take her in my arms. In that moment she was the Helena I had imagined: defenseless and available.

I went to her; she lifted her face to mine; instead of kissing her, I smiled and rested my fingers on the shoulders of her blue raincoat. She understood and unbuttoned it. I took it out to the entrance hall and hung it up. No, now that everything was ready (my desire and her surrender), I had no intention to rush and in my haste risk missing the slightest nuance of *all* that I wanted to appropriate. I started a trivial conversation; I asked her to sit down, I pointed out all kinds of domestic details, I opened the cupboard containing the bottle of vodka Kostka had shown me, and pretended to be surprised; I twisted off the cap, put two small glasses on the coffee table, and poured some out.

"I'll be drunk," she said.

"We'll both be drunk," I said (knowing very well that I wouldn't get drunk, that I would be careful not to get drunk, because I wanted to keep my memory intact).

She didn't smile; she remained serious; she took a drink and said, "You know, Ludvik, I'd be terribly unhappy if you thought I was just another one of those bored wives longing for adventure. I'm not naïve and I know that you've had many women and that women themselves have taught you not to take them seriously. But I'd be so unhappy . . ."

"I'd be unhappy too," I said, "if you were just another bored wife casually pursuing adventure to escape from her husband. If that's all you were, our meeting here would have no meaning for me."

"Really?" said Helena.

"Really, Helena. You're right that I have had many women and that they have taught me to think nothing of trading one for the next, but meeting you is something different."

"You're not just saying that?"

"No, I'm not. When I first met you, I knew right away that you were the one I'd been waiting for all these years."

"You're not a phrase-monger. You wouldn't talk like that if you didn't mean it."

"Of course not. I don't know how to simulate feelings for women, that's the only thing they've never taught me. So I'm not lying to you, Helena, no matter how incredible it may seem: the first time I met you, I realized I had been waiting for you for years. That I was waiting for you without knowing you. And I knew that now I must have you. That it was inevitable as fate."

"God," said Helena, closing her eyes; her face was flecked with red, perhaps from the alcohol, perhaps from the excitement, and she was now even more the Helena of my dreams: defenseless and at my mercy.

"If only you knew, Ludvik. That's just what I felt too. Right from the start I knew this was no flirtation, that's what frightened me so, because I'm a married woman and I knew that all this with you was truth, that you are my truth and there is nothing I can do about it."

"And you are my truth, Helena," I said.

She sat alone on the divan, her big eyes looking at me unseeingly while I observed her greedily from my chair. I put my hands on her knees and slowly turned up her skirt until her stocking tops and garters appeared on her already ample thighs, evoking something sad and pathetic. Helena sat there, reacting to my touch with neither gesture nor look.

"If only you knew . . ."

"Knew what?"

"About me. The way I live. The way I have been living."

"How have you been living?"

She smiled bitterly.

Suddenly I was afraid she was going to have recourse to the banal expedient of all unfaithful wives and begin to denigrate her marriage, thus robbing me of its value at the very moment it was about to become my prey. "For God's sake, don't tell me that you have an unhappy marriage, that your husband doesn't understand you."

"That wasn't what I wanted to say," said Helena, confused by my attack, "though . . ."

"Though that's just what you're thinking. Every woman starts to think that way when she's alone with another man, but that's where all the untruthfulness begins, and you want to stay truthful, Helena, don't you? You certainly must have loved your husband; your not a woman who gives herself without love."

"No," said Helena softly.

"What is your husband like, anyway?" I asked.

She shrugged her shoulders and smiled. "Just a husband."

"How long have you known each other?"

"Thirteen years as man and wife and a few years before that."

"You must have been a student then."

"Yes. It was my first year."

She tried to pull her skirt down, but I caught her hand and stopped her. I asked again: "What about him? Where did you meet him?"

"In a folk ensemble."

"A folk ensemble? So your husband sang?"

"Yes, we all did."

"And you met in a folk ensemble. . . . A beautiful backdrop for love."

"Yes."

"That whole period was beautiful."

"You have good memories of it too?"

"It was the most beautiful period of my life. Was your husband your first love?"

"I don't want to think of my husband just now," she said.

"I want to know you, Helena. I want to know everything about you. The more I know you, the more you'll be mine. Did you have anyone before him?"

She nodded: "Yes."

I felt almost disappointed that Helena had had another man, because the significance of her attachment to Pavel Zemanek was thus diminished. "A true love?" I asked.

She shook her head. "Just silly curiosity."

"So your first real love was your husband?"

She nodded. "But that was long ago."

"What did he look like?" I asked quietly.

"Why do you want to know?"

"I want you to be mine with everything in you, everything in this head . . ." I stroked her hair.

If there is anything that prevents a woman from telling a lover about her husband, it is rarely nobility, tact, or genuine modesty, but simply the fear of irritating the lover. Once the lover dispels that fear, the woman is grateful to him, feels freer, but above all: she has something to talk about, because topics of conversation are not infinite, and for a woman her husband is the most gratifying topic, since it is the only one on which she feels sure of herself, the only one on which she is an *expert*, and we know that everyone is happy to seem an expert and takes pride in it. So as soon as I assured Helena it wouldn't upset me, she started talking with complete freedom about Pavel Zemanek and got so carried away by her memories that she didn't add a single shadow to her portrait, telling me how she'd fallen in love with him (the straight-backed fair-haired youth), how she'd looked up to him when he became the ensemble's political officer, how she and all the girls she knew admired him (he had a marvelous way with words!), and how their love story had merged harmoniously with the whole period, in defense of which she made some remarks (how were we to know that Stalin had ordered loyal Communists to be shot?), not, perhaps, because she wished to *divert* the conversation to the political theme, but because she felt herself personally involved in this theme. The way she defended the period of her youth and the way she identified herself with it (as if it had been her *home*, a home she'd since lost) seemed almost like a brief manifesto, as if she were saying: take me, and without any conditions save one: that you let me remain as I am, even with my *conviction*. Making so much of conviction in a situation where body, not conviction, is the real issue is abnormal enough to reveal that it is precisely conviction that makes the woman in question neurotic: either she fears being suspected of having no conviction whatsoever and so hastily exhibits one, or (as is more likely in Helena's case) she harbors secret doubts about her conviction and hopes to regain her certainty by staking something of indisputable value in her eyes: the act of love (perhaps in the cowardly unconscious confidence that her lover will be more concerned with making love than arguing about conviction). I did not find Helena's manifesto disagreeable; it brought me closer to the crux of my passion.

"Do you see this?" She pointed to a small silver pendant attached to her watch by a short chain. I leaned over to have a look, and Helena explained that the carving was meant to represent the Kremlin. "I got it from Pavel," and then she told me the whole story, that many years ago a lovesick Russian girl had given it to a Russian boy named Sasha, who had gone off to the big war, and that the end of the war had brought him all the way to Prague, which he protected from destruction, but which brought destruction down on him. The Red Army had set up a small hospital on the top floor of the spacious villa where Pavel lived with his parents, and there the mortally wounded Lieutenant Sasha spent the last days of his life. Pavel became friends with him and stayed by his side for days on end. Just before he died, Sasha gave Pavel as a keepsake the Kremlin pendant, which he had worn on a string around his neck throughout the war. Pavel kept this gift as his most cherished memento. Once, when they were engaged, Helena and Pavel had quarreled and were thinking of breaking up, but then Pavel had come over and given her that cheap ornament (and most cherished keepsake) as a peace offering, and from then on Helena had never taken it off, seeing in it a kind of message (I asked her what kind of message, and she answered, "a message of joy"), a baton to be carried all the way to the finish line.

She sat across from me (with her skirt turned up and her garters attached to fashionable black stretch panties), her face still flushed (with alcohol and perhaps the emotion of the moment), but in that instant her features faded behind the image of someone else: Helena's tale of the thrice-tendered pendant had abruptly brought before me, in its entirety, the person of Pavel Zemanek.

Not for a second did I believe in Sasha, the Red Army man; and even if he had existed, his real existence would have vanished behind the grand gesture by which Pavel Zemanek had transformed him into a character in his own personal legend, a sacred statue, a tool to induce emotion, a sentimental argument, a religious artifact that his wife (clearly more constant than he) would venerate (zealously, defiantly) as long as she lived. I had the feeling that Pavel Zemanek's heart (his viciously exhibitionistic heart) was here, was present; and all at once I was in the midst of that scene of fifteen years ago: the lecture hall of the Natural Sciences Division; Zemanek is sitting at a long table on a dais in the front of the hall, flanked by a fat, round-faced, pigtailed girl in an ugly sweater and a young man representing the District Committee. Behind the dais there is a large blackboard and to its left a framed portrait of Julius Fucik. Opposite the long table rise the benches where, like everyone else, I have taken a seat, I who now, fifteen years later, am looking at Zemanek through the eyes of that time, watching him as he announces that "the case of Comrade Jahn" is open for discussion, I see him as he says: "I shall read the letters of two Communists." After these words he had paused slightly, picked up a slim volume, run his fingers through his long, wavy hair, and begun to read in an ingratiating, almost tender voice.

" 'Death, you have been long in coming. And yet it was my hope to postpone our meeting until many years hence. To go on living the life of a free man, to work more, love more, sing more, and wander the world over . . .' " I recognized Fucik's *Notes from the Gallows*. " 'I loved life, and for the sake of its beauty I went to war. I loved you, good people, rejoicing when you returned my love, suffering when you failed to understand me. . . .' " That text, written clandestinely in prison, then published after the war in a million copies, broadcast over the radio, studied in schools as required reading, was the sacred book of the era. Zemanek read out the most famous passages, the ones everyone knew by heart. " 'Let sadness never be linked with my name. That is my testament to you, Papa, Mama, and sisters, to you, my Gustina, to you, Comrades, to everyone I have loved. . . .' " The drawing of Fucik on the wall was a reproduction of the famous sketch by Max Svabinsky, the old Jugendstil painter, the virtuoso of allegories, plump women, butterflies, and everything delightful; after the war, or so the story goes, Svabinsky had a visit from the Comrades, who asked him to do a portrait of Fucik from a photograph, and Svabinsky had drawn him (in profile) in graceful lines in accord with his own taste: almost girlish, fervent, pure, and so handsome that people who had known him personally preferred Svabinsky's sublime drawing to their memories of the living face. Meanwhile Zemanek read on, everyone in the hall silent and attentive and the fat girl at the table unable to tear her eyes away from him; suddenly his voice grew firm, almost menacing; he had come to the passage about Mirek the traitor: " 'And to think that he was no coward, a man who did not take flight when bullets rained down on him at the Spanish front, who did not knuckle under when he ran the gauntlet of cruelties in a concentration camp in France. Now he pales under the club of a Gestapo agent and turns informer to save his skin. How superficial was his bravery if so few blows could shake it. As superficial as his convictions. . . . He lost everything the moment he began to think of himself. To save his own life, he sacrificed the lives of his friends. He succumbed to cowardice and through cowardice betrayed them. . . .' " Fucik's handsome face hung on the wall as it hung in a thousand other public places in our country, and it was so handsome, with the radiant expression of a young girl in love, that when I looked at it I felt inferior not just because of my guilt, but because of my appearance as well. And Zemanek read on: " 'They can take our lives, can't they, Gustina, but they cannot take our honor and love. Can you imagine, good people, the life we might have led if we had met again after all this suffering, met again in a free life, a life made beautiful by freedom and creation? The life we shall lead when we finally achieve everything we've longed for and fought for and I now die for?' " After the pathos of these last sentences Zemanek was silent.

Then he said: "That was a letter written by a Communist in the shadow of the gallows. Now I shall read you another letter." And he read out the three brief, laughable, horrible lines from my postcard. Then he fell silent, everyone was silent, and I knew I was lost. The silence was long, and Zemanek, that prodigious stage manager, deliberately allowed it to continue. Only after some moments did he call on me to explain myself. I knew that I would be unable to salvage anything: if none of my arguments had had any effect up to now, how could they possibly have any today, when Zemanek had measured my postcard against the absolute standard of Fucik's torments. Of course, I had no option but to stand up and speak. Once more I explained that the message was meant to be a joke, but I condemned the incongruity and coarseness of this joke, talked about my individualism and intellectualism, about my isolation from the people, even uncovered in myself complacency, skepticism, and cynicism, but vowed that in spite of it all, I was still devoted to the Party and was not its enemy. Then there was discussion, and the Comrades accused me of contradicting myself; they asked me how a man who admitted to being a cynic could be devoted to the Party: a fellow student, a woman, reminded me of certain obscene expressions I had used and asked me whether that was the way a Communist spoke; others made abstract remarks on the petty bourgeois mentality and then cited me as a concrete example; and they all agreed that my self-criticism had been superficial and insincere. Then the pigtailed girl sitting at the table next to Zemanek said, "Tell me, how do you think the Comrades tortured by the Gestapo, tortured to death, would have reacted to your words?" (I thought of my father and realized they were all pretending not to know how he had died.) I said nothing. She repeated the question. She forced me to answer. I said: "I don't know." "Think a little harder," she insisted. "You know the answer." What she wanted was for me to pass a harsh sentence on myself through the dead Comrades' imaginary lips, but instead I felt a wave of fury rush through me, a wave of unforeseen and unexpected fury, and rebelling against the many weeks of self-criticism, I answered, "They stood between life and death. They weren't petty. If they had read my postcard, they might have laughed."

The girl with the pigtail had offered me a chance to salvage at least something. It was my last opportunity to *understand* the extent of the Comrades' criticism, identify with it, accept it, and on the basis of this identification exact some understanding on their part. But my unprecedented reply had abruptly excluded me from the sphere of their thinking, I had refused to play the role played at hundreds of meetings, hundreds of disciplinary proceedings, and, before long, at hundreds of court cases: the role of the accused who accuses himself and by the very ardor of his self-accusation (his complete identification with the accusers) begs for mercy.

Again there was silence. Then Zemanek spoke. He said he was unable to find anything humorous in my anti-Party pronouncements. He referred again to Fucik's words and said that in critical situations wavering and skepticism inevitably turned into treachery and the Party was a stronghold which tolerated no traitors within its walls. He said that my response clearly proved I had failed to understand a thing and that not only did I not belong in the Party, but I did not deserve continued expenditure of working-class funds on my studies. He proposed that I be excluded from the Party and expelled from the university. The people in the room all raised their hands, and Zemanek told me I was to surrender my Party card and leave.

I stood up and placed my card on the table in front of Zemanek. Zemanek didn't look at me; he no longer saw me. But I see her now: she is sitting in front of me, drunk, with her face red and her skirt pushed up to her waist. Her heavy legs are bordered at the top by the black of her stretch panties; these are the legs whose opening and closing provide the rhythm that has pulsated through more than a decade of Zemanek's life. On these legs I now placed my palms, and it was as if I had Zemanek's very life in my grasp. I looked at Helena's face, into her eyes, which reacted to my touch by closing slightly.

4

G ET UNDRESSED, Helena," I said quietly.

As she stood up from the divan, the hem of her skirt slipped back down to her knees. She gazed fixedly into my eyes, and without saying a word (or taking her eyes off me), she began to unbutton her skirt along the side. Thus released, it slid down her legs onto the floor; she stepped out of it with her left foot, with her right passed it up to her hand, and laid it on the chair. She was now standing in her sweater and slip. Then she pulled the sweater over her head and tossed it onto the skirt.

"Don't watch," she said.

"I want to see you," I said.

"I don't want you to see me undressing."

I went to her. I took her under the armpits, and as I let my hands move down to her hips I felt her soft full body under the silk of her slip, slightly damp with sweat. She leaned up, her lips half open from longtime habit (bad habit) for a kiss. But I didn't want to kiss her, I wanted to look at her and go on looking as long as possible.

"Get undressed, Helena," I said again, and moved away myself to take off my jacket.

"There's too much light," she said.

"That's all right," I said, and hung my jacket over the back of the chair.

She pulled the slip up over her head and threw it on top of the sweater and skirt; she unfastened the stockings and slid them down her legs one after the other; she didn't throw them; she stepped over to the chair and carefully laid them out; then she thrust out her chest and reached behind her back, and after a few seconds her tightly braced shoulders relaxed and fell forward, and with them fell her brassiere, sliding off her breasts, which, pressed together by her arms, were huddled against each other, big, full, pale, and obviously somewhat heavy.

"Get undressed, Helena," I repeated for the last time. Looking me straight in the eyes, she pulled off the tightly fitting black stretch panties, throwing them on top of the pile. She was naked.

I took careful note of every detail of the scene: I had no interest in finding instant pleasure with a woman (*any* woman); what I wanted was to take possession of one *particular* alien intimate world, and to do so within the course of a single afternoon, within the course of a single act of love in which I was to be not just a man in the throes of lovemaking, but at the same time a man who is guarding and ravaging his fugitive prey and so must be absolutely alert.

Until then I had possessed Helena only with my eyes. Now I still remained at some distance from her while she longed for the warmth of the caresses that would shield her exposed body from the coldness of these eyes. Even from a few steps away I could almost feel the moisture of her lips, the sensual impatience of her tongue. Another second, two, and I went to her. Standing in the middle of the room between two chairs piled with our clothes, we held each other.

She whispered: "Ludvik, Ludvik, Ludvik . . ." I led her to the divan. And onto it. "Come, come," she said. "Come to me, come to me."

Physical love only rarely merges with the soul's love. What does the soul actually do when the body unites (in that age-old, universal, immutable motion) with another body? What a wealth of invention it finds in those moments, thus reaffirming its superiority over the monotony of the corporeal life! How it scorns the body, and uses it (together with its partner) as pretext for insane fantasies a thousand times more carnal than the two coupled bodies! Or conversely: how it belittles the body by leaving it to its pendular to-and-fro while the soul (already wearied by the caprices of the body) turns its thoughts entirely elsewhere: to a game of chess, to recollections of dinner, to a book. . . .

There is nothing rare about the merging of the bodies of two strangers. Even the union of souls may occasionally take place. What is a thousand times more rare is the union of the body with its own soul in shared passion. . . .

What, then, was my soul doing while my body was making love to Helena?

My soul had seen a female body. It was indifferent to this body. It knew that the body had meaning for it only as a body that had been seen and loved in just the same way by someone who was not now present; that was why it tried to look at this body through the eyes of the third, the absent one; that was why it tried to become the third one's medium; it saw the naked female body, the bent leg, the curve of belly and breast, but it all took on meaning only when my eyes became the eyes of the absent one; then, suddenly, my soul entered his *alien* gaze and merged with him; not only did it take possession of the bent leg and the curve of belly and breast, it took possession of them in the way they were seen by the absent third.

And not only did my soul become the medium of this absent third, but it ordered my body to become the medium of his body, and then stood back and watched the writhing struggle of two bodies, two connubial bodies, until all at once it commanded my body to be itself again, to intervene in the connubial coitus and destroy it brutally.

A blue vein bulged on Helena's neck, and a convulsion ran through her body; she turned her head to one side, her teeth bit into the pillow.

Then she whispered my name, and her eyes pleaded for a few moments' respite.

But my soul commanded me to persevere; to drive her from pleasure to pleasure; to change her body's position so that nothing should remain hidden or concealed from the glance of the absent third; no, to grant her no respite, to repeat the convulsion again and again, the convulsion in which she is real and exact, in which she feigns nothing, by which she is engraved in the memory of the absent third like a stamp, a seal, a cipher, a sign. And thus to steal the secret cipher! to steal the royal seal! To rob Pavel Zemanek's secret chamber; to ransack it, make a shambles of it!

I watched Helena's face, flushed and disfigured by a grimace; I put my hand on this face; I put my hand on it as one puts one's hand on an object that can be turned this way or that, crushed or kneaded, and I felt her face accepting my hand on precisely those terms: like a thing eager to be turned and crushed. I turned her head to one side; then to the other; I turned it back and forth several times, and suddenly the motion became a slap; and a second; and a third. Helena began to sob and scream, but it wasn't a scream of pain, it was a scream of excitement, her chin strained up to find me, and I hit her and hit her and hit her; then I saw not only her chin but her breasts straining upward to me, and (arching up over her) I hit her all over her arms and flanks and breasts. . . .

Everything comes to an end; even this beautiful act of demolition was over at last. She lay diagonally across the divan on her stomach, tired, exhausted. I could see the brown birthmark on her back, and beneath, on her buttocks, the red dappling from my blows.

I stood up and staggered across the room; I opened the door to the bathroom and went in; I turned on the cold water and washed my face, hands, and body. I raised my head and saw myself in the mirror; my face was smiling; when I surprised it thus (smiling), the smile seemed funny to me and I burst out laughing. Then I dried myself off with a towel and sat on the edge of the bathtub. I wanted to be alone for a few seconds, savor the rare delight of sudden solitude, rejoice in my joy.

Yes, I was satisfied; perhaps I was even completely happy. I felt victorious, and as for the ensuing minutes and hours, they were super-fluous and had no interest for me.

Then I went back into the room.

Helena was no longer lying on her belly; she had turned onto her side and was looking up at me. "Come to me, darling," she said. Ignoring her invitation, I went over to the chair where my clothes were lying and picked up my shirt.

"Don't get dressed," begged Helena, and stretching an arm out in my direction, she repeated, "Come to me."

I had only one desire: that those ensuing moments should not take place at all, and if they had to, that they should be totally anodyne, insignificant, weightless, lighter than a speck of dust; I wanted to avoid touching her body again, I was horrified at the thought of any show of tenderness, but I was just as horrified at the thought of any tension or dramatics; so I unwillingly renounced my shirt and sat down next to her on the divan. It was horrible: she pushed against me and laid her head on my leg; she kissed me, and soon my leg was wet, but not from her kisses: when she raised her head, I saw her face was covered with tears. Wiping them away, she said, "Don't be angry, darling. Don't be angry if I cry," and she pushed even closer, put her arms around me, and burst into sobs.

"What's the matter?" I said.

She shook her head, saying, "Nothing, silly, nothing at all," and began ardently kissing my face and whole body. "I'm in love," she said, and when I failed to respond, she went on. "Laugh at me if you like, I don't care, I'm in love, in love!" When I still said nothing, she added, "I'm happy." Then she pointed at the table and the unfinished bottle of vodka. "Pour me a drop of that!"

I didn't feel like pouring any, either for myself or for Helena; I feared that any further consumption of alcohol would lead to a dangerous prolongation of the session (which was splendid, but only if it was finished, behind me).

"Please, darling." She was still pointing at the table. "Don't be angry," she added apologetically. "I'm just happy. I want to be happy. . . ."

"You don't need vodka for that," I said.

"Don't be angry. I just feel like it."

There was nothing to do but pour her a glass. "Don't you want any more?" she asked. I shook my head. She tossed it down and said, "Leave it there." I set the bottle and glass down on the floor by the divan.

She was very quick to recover from her fatigue; suddenly she was a little girl wanting to be happy and gay and to let everybody know about it. She obviously felt completely free and natural in her nakedness (all she had on was her wristwatch with the Kremlin miniature dangling from it on its chain) and tried out a number of positions for comfort: crossing her legs under her and sitting Turkish style, then straightening them out again and leaning on an elbow; finally rolling over onto her belly and pressing her face into my lap. She told me in every possible way how happy she was; in between she kept kissing me, which I endured with considerable self-restraint, as her mouth was too wet and she was not satisfied with my shoulders or cheeks but tried to touch my lips as well (and unless blinded by desire, I loathe wet kisses).

Then she told me she'd never known anything like this before; I told her (just to say something) that she was exaggerating. She swore that she never lied in love, that I had no reason to doubt her. Expanding on her thought, she asserted that she had a premonition of it all, that she had a premonition from our very first meeting; that the body has its own foolproof instinct; that naturally I'd impressed her with my intelligence and my élan (yes, élan; I wonder how she discovered that in me), but she also knew (though she would never have dared bring it up until now) that our two bodies had immediately entered into that secret pact which the human body signs perhaps only once in a lifetime. "And that's why I'm so happy, you see?" She swung her legs down from the divan, leaned over for the bottle, and poured herself another glass. She drank it and said, laughing: "What can I do? If you won't join me, I'll have to drink by myself!"

Although I considered the story finished, I must confess that Helena's words didn't displease me; they confirmed the success of my enterprise and my satisfaction with it. And mostly because I didn't know what to say and didn't want to seem too taciturn, I objected again that she was exaggerating when she talked about a once-in-a-lifetime experience; hadn't she herself told me her husband had been the great love of her life?

Helena thought seriously about this (she was sitting on the divan, her feet resting on the floor, her legs spread slightly apart, her elbows propped on her legs, and her right hand holding the empty glass) and said quietly, "Yes."

No doubt she calculated that the grand emotion she had just experienced bound her to an equally grand sincerity. "Yes," she repeated, adding that it was probably wrong of her to denigrate something that once had been in the name of today's miracle. She drank another glass and said that it was the most powerful experiences that were the hardest to compare; and that for a woman love at twenty and love at thirty were completely different; she hoped I understood what she meant: not only from the psychological point of view but also physically.

And then (somewhat illogically and inconsistently) she announced that actually there was a certain resemblance between me and her husband! She was not quite sure where it lay; I didn't look like him, but she couldn't be wrong, she had a foolproof instinct enabling her to look deep into people, behind their outward appearance.

"I'd really like to know what it is that makes me resemble your husband," I said.

She begged my pardon, but after all, I had been the one who wanted to hear about him, and that was the only reason she'd dared to speak of him. But if I wanted to hear the whole truth, she must tell me: only twice in her life had she been attracted to anyone so strongly, so unconditionally—to her husband and to me. The thing we had in common, she said, was a mysterious élan vital; the joy that emanated from us; eternal youth; strength.

Helena may have used a rather vague vocabulary in her attempt to clarify my resemblance to Pavel Zemanek, but there was no denying that she saw and felt the resemblance and clung to it tenaciously. I can't say she hurt or offended me, I was merely stunned by the immense absurdity of her words. I went over to the chair with my clothes on it and slowly started to dress.

"Have I said something wrong, darling?" Helena had sensed my displeasure, and she got up and came over to me; she began stroking my face and begging me not to be angry with her. She tried to stop me from dressing. (For some strange reason she regarded my trousers and shirt as her enemies.) She began trying to convince me that she really loved me, that she wasn't using this word in vain; that perhaps she might have an opportunity to prove it; that she knew right away when I'd asked about her husband that it was foolish to talk about him, that she didn't want any man, any stranger, coming between us;

yes, stranger, because her husband had long been a stranger to her. "I haven't been living with him for three years now, silly. The only reason we don't get a divorce is little Zdena. He has his life, I have mine. We're actually strangers. He is no more than my past, my very ancient past."

"Is that true?" I asked.

"Indeed it is," she said.

"You're lying. I don't believe you," I said.

"I'm not lying. We live in the same flat, but not as man and wife. It's been years since we lived together as man and wife."

The beseeching face of a distressed woman in love was looking at me. Again and again she assured me that she was telling the truth, that she wasn't trying to deceive me; that I had no cause to be jealous of her husband; that her husband was merely the past; that she hadn't even been unfaithful today, because she didn't have anyone to be unfaithful to; and I didn't need to worry: our lovemaking had been not only beautiful but *pure*.

Suddenly I realized, with sheer horror, that there was no reason for me not to believe her. When she saw that, she relaxed a bit and begged me several times to tell her out loud that I believed her; then she poured herself a glass of vodka and wanted us to drink a toast (I refused); she kissed me; it made my flesh creep but I couldn't turn my gaze away from her; I was fascinated by her idiotic blue eyes and by her (animated, quivering) naked body.

But now I saw her nudity in a new light; it was nudity *denuded*, denuded of the power to excite that until now had eliminated all the faults of age in which the whole history and present of Helena's marriage seemed to be concentrated and that had therefore fascinated me. Now that she stood before me bare, without a husband or any bonds to him, utterly herself, her physical unloveliness lost all its power to excite and it too became only itself: a simple unloveliness.

Helena no longer had any idea how I saw her; she was getting more and more drunk and more and more contented; she was happy that I believed in her love but didn't know how to give vent to her happiness. For no apparent reason she decided to switch on the radio, squatting in front of it with her back to me and playing with the dial; she found some jazz; she stood up, her eyes gleaming; she did a clumsy imitation of the undulating movements of the twist (I stared aghast at her breasts flying from side to side). She laughed: "Is that right? You know, I've never tried these dances." She laughed again, very loudly, and came towards me with her arms outstretched; she asked me to dance with her; she was angry when I refused, she said she didn't know the new dances but that she wanted to learn them and I must teach her; she wanted me to teach her a lot of things, she wanted to be young again with me. She begged me to assure her that she was still young (I did). She realized that I was dressed and she was naked; she laughed; it struck her as particularly odd; she asked whether the man who lived here had a big mirror so that she could see us. There was no mirror, only a glass-fronted bookcase; she tried to see us in the glass, but the image was indistinct; she went close to the bookcase and laughed at the titles on the spines of the books: the Bible, Calvin's *Institutes,* Pascal's *Provincial Letters Against the Jesuits,* the works of Jan Hus; she took out the Bible, struck a solemn pose, opened the book at random, and began to read in a clerical voice. She asked me whether she would have made a good priest. I said that reading from the Bible became her but it was time to get dressed because Mr. Kostka would be arriving any moment. "What time is it?" she asked. "Half past six," I said. She seized my left wrist, looked at my watch, and shouted: "Liar! It's only a quarter to six! You want to get rid of me!"

I longed for her to be gone; for her body (so hopelessly material) to dematerialize, melt, turn into a stream and flow away, or evaporate and vanish out the window—but the body was here, a body I had stolen from no one, in which I'd vanquished no one, destroyed no one, a body abandoned, deserted by its spouse, a body I had intended to use but which had used me and was now insolently enjoying its triumph, exulting, jumping for joy.

There was no way to cut short my bizarre torment. It was almost half past six when she started to dress. As she did so she noticed a red mark on her arm where I had hit her; she stroked it, saying she'd wear it as a memento until she saw me again; then she quickly corrected herself:

she would certainly see me long before the memento on her body had disappeared; she stood facing me just as she was (one stocking on and the other in hand), she made me promise we'd see each other before then; I nodded; that wasn't good enough: I had to promise we'd see each other *many times* before then.

She took a long time getting dressed. She left a few minutes before seven.

5

I OPENED the window, because I yearned for a wind to waft away all memory of my ill-starred afternoon, every residue of odor and emotion. Then I put the bottle away, straightened up the cushions on the divan, and when I felt all traces had been removed, I sank into the armchair near the window and looked forward (almost imploringly) to Kostka: to his masculine voice (I had a great need for a deep male voice), to his long, skinny frame and *flat* chest, to his quiet way of talking, eccentric and wise; I looked forward to him telling me about Lucie, who in contrast to Helena was so sweetly incorporeal, abstract, so far removed from conflicts, tensions, and dramas, and yet not without influence on my life: the thought crossed my mind that she'd influenced it in the way astrologers think the movements of the stars influence human life; as I sat there snugly in the armchair (under the open window still expelling Helena's odor), I thought that I had hit on the solution of my superstitious riddle, that now I knew why Lucie had flashed across the sky these past two days: it was to reduce my vengeance to nothing, to turn everything I'd come here for to mist; for Lucie, whom I'd loved so much and who had inexplicably run from me at the last moment, was the goddess of escape, the goddess of vain pursuit, the goddess of mists; and she still held my head in her hands.

PART SIX

Kostka

I

WE HAD not seen each other in many years, and actually we had met only a few times in our lives. This is rather strange, because in my imagination I meet Ludvik Jahn very frequently, and I turn to him in my soliloquies as to my chief adversary. I have grown so accustomed to his incorporeal presence that I found myself in some confusion yesterday when suddenly, after all these years, I met him as a real man of flesh and blood.

I called Ludvik my adversary. Have I the right to do so? Each time I meet him I seem by coincidence to be in a helpless situation, and each time he is the one who helps me out of it. Yet beneath this outward alliance lies an abyss of inward disagreement. I don't know whether Ludvik is as fully aware of it as I am. He has clearly attached greater significance to our outward bond than to our inward difference. He has been merciless to outward adversaries and tolerant of inward discords. Not I. I am the complete opposite. Which is not to say that I don't like Ludvik. I love him, as we love our adversaries.

2

I FIRST MET him in 1947 at one of those turbulent meetings that racked all institutions of higher learning in those days. The fate of the nation was at stake. We all sensed it, myself included, and in all the discussions, debates, and balloting I stood with the Communist minority.

Many Christians, both Catholics and Protestants, held it against me. They considered me a traitor for allying myself with a movement that inscribed godlessness on its shield. When I see these people today, they imagine that after fifteen years I have at last seen the error of my ways. But I have to disappoint them. To this day I have not changed my position at all.

Of course the Communist movement is godless. Though only those Christians who refuse to cast out the beam in their own eye can blame Communism itself for that. I say Christians. Yet where are they? Looking around me, I see nothing but pseudo-Christians living exactly like unbelievers. But being a Christian means living differently. It means taking the path Christ took, *imitating* Christ. It means giving up private interests, comforts, and power, and turning toward the poor, the humiliated, and the suffering. But is that what the churches were doing? My father was a working man, chronically unemployed, with a humble faith in God. He turned his pious face to Him, but the Church never turned its face to my father. And so he remained forsaken amidst his neighbors, forsaken within the church, alone with his God until he fell ill and died.

The churches failed to realize that the working-class movement was the movement of the humiliated and oppressed supplicating for justice. They did not choose to work with and for them to create the kingdom of God on earth. By siding with the oppressors, they deprived the working-class movement of God. And now they reproach it for being godless. The Pharisees! Yes, the socialist movement is godless, but I see in this a casting of divine blame on us, on Christians. Blame for our hardheartedness toward the poor and suffering.

And what am I to do in this situation? Should I be shocked at the drop in church membership? Should I be shocked that the schools are bringing the children up in an antireligious frame of mind? How silly! True religion does not need the favor of secular power. Secular disfavor only strengthens faith.

Or should I fight socialism because we made it godless? Sillier still! I can only lament the tragic error that led socialism away from God. All I can do is to explain this error and work to rectify it.

In any case, why this anxiety, brother Christians? Everything that happens happens according to God's will, and I often wonder whether it isn't God's design to let mankind know that man cannot sit on His throne with impunity and that without His participation even the most equitable order of worldly affairs is doomed to failure and corruption.

I remember those years when people here thought they were but a few steps from paradise. How proud they were: it was their paradise, they were on their way to it with no need of anyone in heaven above. And suddenly it melted away before their eyes.

3

U NTIL the February 1948 coup, my being a Christian suited the Communists quite well. They enjoyed hearing me expound on the social content of the Gospel, inveigh against the rot of the old world of property and war, and argue the affinity between Christianity and Communism. Their concern, after all, was to attract all major levels of the populace, and they therefore tried to win over believers as well. Soon after February, however, things began to change. As a lecturer at the university I took the side of several students about to be expelled for their parents' political stance. By protesting, I came into conflict with the university administration. And suddenly doubts began to be raised about whether a man of such firm Christian convictions was capable of educating socialist youth. It seemed that I'd have to fight for my very livelihood. Then I heard that the student Ludvik Jahn had stood up for me at a plenary meeting of the Party. He had said that it would be base ingratitude to forget what I'd meant to the Party before February. And when they brought up my Christian beliefs, he said they were just a passing phase in my life, one I would surely outgrow, considering my youth.

I went to see him and thanked him for coming to my defense. I told him, however, that not wishing to deceive him, I wanted to remind him that I was older than he and that there was no hope at all of my "outgrowing" my faith. Soon we were debating the existence of God, the finite and the infinite, Descartes's position on religion, whether Spinoza was a materialist, and many other matters. We came to no agreement. I finally asked Ludvik whether he didn't regret standing up for me now that he saw how incorrigible I was. He told me that religious faith was my private affair and that all in all it was of no concern to anyone else.

I never saw him at the university again. Our destinies turned out to be all the more similar. About three months after our talk Jahn was expelled from the Party and the university, and six months later I too had to leave the university. Was I thrown out? Driven out? I can't quite say. All I can say for certain is that doubts about me and my convictions started up again. It is true that some of my colleagues hinted I would do well to make a public statement along atheist lines. And it is true that I had some unpleasant scenes in class when aggressive Communist students tried to insult my faith. My proposed departure was indeed in the air. But I must also say that I had a number of friends among the Communists on the faculty and that they still respected me for my pre-February stance. It would probably have taken very little: a move to defend myself. They would certainly have stood up for me. But I did nothing.

4

"FOLLOW ME," said Jesus to His disciples, and without demur they left their nets, their boats, their homes and families, and followed him. "No man having put his hand to the plow and looking back is fit for the kingdom of God."

If we hear the voice of Christ's appeal, we must follow it unconditionally. This is clear from the Gospel, but in modern times it sounds like a fairy tale. What does an appeal mean in our prosaic lives? And where shall we go, whom shall we follow once we do leave our nets?

And yet the voice of the appeal can reach us even in today's world if our hearing is keen. The appeal does not come through the mail like a registered letter. It comes disguised. And rarely dressed up all rosy and alluring. "Not the deed which you choose, but that which befalls you against your will, your mind, and your desire, that is the path you must tread, thither do I call you, there be you His disciple, that is your time, that is the path your Master trod," wrote Luther.

I had many reasons for being attached to my lectureship. It was relatively comfortable, it left me plenty of time for my own research, and it promised a lifetime career as a university teacher. Yet I was alarmed precisely by my attachment to it. I was alarmed all the more by seeing large numbers of valuable people, teachers and students, forced to leave the universities. I was alarmed by my attachment to a comfortable life whose calm security distanced me more and more from the turbulent fates of my fellow men. I realized that the voices raised against me at the university were an *appeal*. I heard someone calling to me. Someone warning me against a comfortable career that would tie down my mind, my faith, and my conscience.

Of course my wife, with whom I had a five-year-old child, did everything in her power to make me defend myself and stand up for my position at the university. She was thinking of our son and of the future of our family. Nothing else existed for her. When I looked into her already aging face, I was afraid of that eternal anxiety about tomorrow and the coming year, that burdensome anxiety about all tomorrows and all the coming years. I was afraid of this burden, and in my mind I heard Jesus' words: "Take therefore no thought for the morrow; for the morrow shall take thought for the things of itself. Sufficient unto the day is the evil thereof."

My enemies expected me to be tormented with worry, but instead I felt an unexpected insouciance. They thought I would find my freedom restrained, but on the contrary I had just discovered the real meaning of freedom. I realized that man had nothing to lose, that his place was everywhere, everywhere that Jesus went, which means: everywhere among men.

After my initial surprise and regret I went forward to meet the malice of my adversaries. I accepted the wrong they inflicted on me as a coded appeal.

5

COMMUNISTS SUPPOSE, in a manner eminently religious, that a man who is guilty in the face of the Party may gain absolution by doing a stint with the working class in agriculture or industry. During the years after February many intellectuals went off this way to the mines, to factories, to building sites and state farms, so that after a mysterious period of purification they might be allowed to return to offices, schools, and political posts.

When I told the administration that I proposed to leave the university without applying for another scientific position, when indeed I requested to go among the ordinary people, preferably as technical adviser to some state farm, my Communist colleagues, friends and foes alike, interpreted this not in light of my own faith but in light of theirs: as an unprecedented expression of self-criticism. They appreciated it and helped me to find a very good position on a state farm in western Bohemia, a position under a good director and in a beautiful part of the country. They sent me on my way with an unusually favorable letter of recommendation.

I was truly happy in my new situation. I felt reborn. The state farm had been set up in a derelict and scantily populated border village from which the Germans had been expelled after the war. It was surrounded by hills, most of them treeless pastureland. The valleys were dotted with the cottages of widely scattered villages. Frequent mists swirling across the countryside served as a screen between me and the settled land, so that the world was as on the fifth day of creation, when God still seemed undecided about whether to hand it over to man.

The people were closer to that primeval state as well. They stood face to face with nature, endless pastures, herds of cows, flocks of sheep. I felt at ease among them. I soon had a number of ideas about how to put the vegetation in the hilly countryside to better use, how to introduce fertilizers, new ways of storing hay, experimental fields for medicinal herbs, a greenhouse. The director was grateful to me for my ideas, and I was grateful to him for enabling me to earn my bread by useful work.

6

IT WAS 1951. September was cool, but in the middle of October the weather suddenly warmed up, and there was a wonderful autumn lasting well into November. The haystacks drying along the hillsides spread their perfume far over the land. Delicate meadow saffrons shimmered in the grass. It was then that word of the runaway girl began to go round in the villages.

A group of boys from a neighboring village had gone out into the freshly mown fields. In the midst of their boisterous talk they noticed a girl crawl out of a stack, tousled and with hay in her hair, a girl none of them had ever seen before. Startled, she looked all around and began running towards the woods. She disappeared before they could gather their wits and run after her.

A peasant woman from the same village said that one afternoon, when she was busy with something in the yard, a girl of about twenty in a threadbare coat had appeared out of nowhere and asked, eyes on the ground, for a crust of bread. "Where are you going, girl?" the woman asked her. The girl replied that she had a long way ahead of her. "On foot?" "I've lost my money," she replied. The woman asked no more and gave her bread and milk.

A shepherd from our farm added his story. One day up in the hills, he'd put a piece of bread and butter and a jug of milk next to a tree stump. He went off for a minute to his flock, and when he returned, the bread and jug had mysteriously vanished.

The children immediately seized on these reports and eagerly multiplied them with their imaginations. Whenever anyone lost anything, they were quick to take it as proof of her existence. They saw her in the evenings bathing in the pond not far from the village, though it was early November and the water was already very cold. Another evening they heard a woman's voice singing somewhere off in the distance. The adults said that one of the cottages on the hill had its radio turned up full blast, but the children knew it was she, the wild girl, wandering along the hilltops singing, her hair flowing free.

One evening the children made a fire of potato tops and threw potatoes into the glowing ash. Then they stared into the woods, and one of the girls called out that she saw the runaway peering back at them from the shadows. A boy picked up a lump of earth and hurled it in the direction the girl had indicated. Oddly enough, no cry rang out, but something else happened. The children shouted at the boy and nearly came to blows with him.

Yes, it was so: the customary cruelty of children never arose in the legend of the runaway girl, despite the thefts that were attributed to her. From the beginning she had their mysterious sympathy. Was it perhaps the innocent insignificance of the thefts that won their hearts? Was it her tender age? Or was she protected by an angel's hand?

Whatever it was, the lump of earth had kindled a feeling of love for the runaway in the children. That very evening they left a small pile of baked potatoes near the remains of the fire, covering them with ashes to keep them warm and sticking a broken fir branch on top. They even found a name for the girl. On a piece of paper torn from a notebook they penciled in large letters VAGABONDELLA, THIS IS FOR YOU. They laid the paper near the pile and weighted it down with a lump of earth. Then they went and hid in the surrounding bushes, waiting for the timid figure to appear. Evening darkened into night, and still no one came. Finally the children had to leave their hiding places and go home. But at the crack of dawn they were back at their posts. It had happened. The potatoes were gone, and with them, the note and the branch.

The girl became the children's own pampered fairy. They left her jugs of milk, bread, potatoes, and messages. And they never put their gifts in the same place twice. They avoided setting out food in a fixed spot, as if it were meant for beggars. They were playing a game with her. A game of hidden treasure. They started from the spot where they had left the first pile of potatoes and moved farther and farther from the village into the countryside. They left their treasures by tree stumps, by a big rock, near a wayside cross, by a wild rosebush. They never betrayed the whereabouts of the hidden gifts to anyone. They never violated the spider-web delicacy of the game, never lay in wait for the girl nor tried to surprise her. They allowed her to maintain her invisibility.

7

THE FAIRY TALE WAS short-lived. One day the director of our farm
went deep into the countryside with the chairman of the District
National Committee to look over some abandoned cottages and decide
whether they could be used as overnight accommodations for farm
laborers working a long way from the village. On the way they were
overtaken by rain, which quickly became torrential. Nearby there was a
low-lying cluster of firs with a gray hut at its edge: a barn. They ran up,
opened the door, which was secured only by a wooden stake, and
crawled inside. Light filtered through the open door and the cracks in
the roof. In the hay they saw an area that had been smoothed over.
Stretching out on it, they listened to the raindrops falling on the roof,
breathed in the intoxicating scent, and talked about this and that.
Suddenly, running his hand through the wall of hay behind him, the
chairman felt something hard among the dry wisps. It was a suitcase.
An old, ugly, cheap suitcase made of vulcanite. I don't know how long
the two men brooded over the mystery. One thing is certain, that they
opened the suitcase and found four girl's dresses in it, all of them new
and pretty. The fineness of the dresses, I am told, contrasted oddly with
the rural drabness of the suitcase and aroused suspicions of theft.
Under the dresses there were a few articles of girl's underwear, and
hidden among these a bundle of letters tied with a blue ribbon. That
was all. To this day I know nothing of these letters, and I don't even
know whether the director and the chairman read them. All I know is
that from the letters they learned the name of the recipient: Lucie
Sebetka.

While they were contemplating their unexpected find, the chairman
discovered something else in the hay. A cracked milk jug. The blue

enamel jug whose mysterious loss the shepherd had been retelling in the tavern every evening for the past two weeks.

After this, the whole thing ran along predictable lines. The chairman hid in the trees to wait for her, while the director went down to the village and sent the local policeman back up after the chairman. At dusk the girl returned to her fragrant bower. They let her go in, let her close the door behind her, waited half a minute, and then went in after her.

8

BOTH THE MEN who trapped Lucie in the barn were decent fellows. The chairman, formerly a poor farmhand, was an honest father of six children. The policeman was naïve, coarse, good-natured, and wore an immense mustache. Neither of them would have hurt a fly.

And yet I felt a strange pain when I heard how Lucie was trapped. Even now I can't suppress a twinge in my heart when I imagine the director and the chairman rummaging through her suitcase, fingering the most intimate articles of her private life, the tender secrets of her dirty linen, looking where it is forbidden to look.

And I have the same agonizing feeling whenever I imagine her haylined lair with no means of escape, with a single door blocked by two hefty men.

Later, when I learned more about Lucie, I realized to my astonishment that in both these agonizing images the very essence of her fate was directly revealed to me. These two images represented *the situation of rape*.

9

THAT NIGHT Lucie did not sleep in the barn but on an iron bed in a former shop the police had set up as an office. The next day, she was interrogated by the District National Committee. They learned that she had previously worked and lived in Ostrava. She'd run away because she couldn't stand it there anymore. When they tried to find out anything more specific, they were met with stubborn silence.

Why had she chosen to come here, to western Bohemia? She said that her parents lived in Cheb. And why hadn't she gone back to them? She'd left the train long before Cheb because on the way she began to be afraid. Her father had done nothing but beat her.

The District National Committee chairman informed her they would have to send her back to Ostrava since she'd left without the proper permit. Lucie told them she would get off the train at the first stop. They shouted at her for a while but soon saw it wasn't helping matters, so they asked her whether they should send her home, to Cheb. She shook her head vehemently. They tried being strict with her again, but finally the chairman succumbed to his own softheartedness. "What do you want, then?" She asked whether she might not be allowed to stay on and work. They shrugged and said they'd ask at the state farm.

The director was fighting a constant battle with the labor shortage. He agreed to the District National Committee's proposal on the spot. Then he informed me I'd be getting the help in the greenhouse I'd requested for so long. And the same day the chairman of the Committee came to introduce me to Lucie.

I remember it well. It was late November, and after weeks of sun autumn had begun to show its windy and rainy face. It was drizzling.

She stood there in a brown overcoat, suitcase in hand, head bowed bowed, an absent look in her eyes. The chairman, standing by her side and holding the blue jug, announced ceremoniously, "If you've done anything wrong, we forgive you and we trust you. We could have sent you back to Ostrava, but we've let you stay. The working class needs honest men and women everywhere. Don't let it down."

He then went to the office to hand over the shepherd's jug, and I took Lucie to the greenhouse, introduced her to the two girls she'd be working with, and explained to her what she would be doing.

IO

IN MY MEMORY, Lucie overshadows everything I experienced at the time. Despite this, the figure of the District National Committee chairman remains rather clearly outlined. When you were sitting across from me yesterday, Ludvik, I didn't want to offend you. Now that you are with me again in the form in which I know you best, as an image and a shadow, I can say it straight out: that former farmhand who hoped to create a paradise for his suffering neighbors, that honest enthusiast saying his naively high-flown words about forgiveness, faith, and the working class, was much closer to my heart and mind than you, even though he never showed me any personal favor.

You used to declare that socialism grew from the stem of European rationalism and skepticism, a stem both nonreligious and antireligious, and that it was otherwise inconceivable. But can you seriously maintain that it is impossible to build a socialist society without faith in the supremacy of matter? Do you really think that people who believe in God are incapable of nationalizing factories?

I am altogether certain that the line of the European spirit which stems from the teachings of Jesus leads far more naturally to social equality and socialism. And when I think of the most passionate Communists from the first period of socialism in my country—the chairman who put Lucie in my care, for example—they seem to me much more like religious zealots than Voltairean doubters. The revolutionary era from 1948 to 1956 had little in common with skepticism and rationalism. It was an era of great collective faith. A man who kept in step with this era experienced feelings that were akin to religious ones: he renounced his ego, his person, his private life in favor of something higher, something suprapersonal. True, the Marxist teachings were purely secular in origin, but the significance assigned them was similar to the significance of the Gospel and the biblical commandments. They have created a range of ideas that are untouchable and therefore, in our terminology, sacred.

This was a cruel religion. It did not elevate you or me among its priests; perhaps it injured both of us. Yet despite this the era that has just passed was a hundred times nearer to my heart than the era that seems to be approaching today: an era of mockery, skepticism, and corrosion, a petty era with the ironic intellectual in the limelight, and behind him the mob of youth, coarse, cynical, and nasty, without enthusiasm, without ideals, ready to mate or to kill on sight.

The era now passing or already past had something of the spirit of the great religious movements. What a pity that it was incapable of taking its religious self-knowledge through to the ultimate conclusion. It had religious gestures and feelings but remained empty and godless within. At the time I still believed that God would have mercy, that He would make Himself known, that at last He would sanctify this great secular faith. I waited in vain.

This era finally betrayed its religious nature, and it has paid dearly for its rationalist heritage, swearing allegiance to it only because it failed to understand itself. This rationalist skepticism has been corroding Christianity for two millennia. Corroding it but not destroying it. But Communist theory, its own creation, it will destroy within a few decades. In you, Ludvik, it has already been killed. As well you know.

I I

As LONG as people can escape to the realm of fairy tales, they are full of nobility, compassion, and poetry. In the realm of everyday life they are, alas, more prone to caution, mistrust, and suspicion. That was how they treated Lucie. As soon as she left the children's fairyland and became a real girl, a fellow worker, a roommate, she was immediately the object of a curiosity not without the malice people reserve for angels cast out from heaven and fairies banished from tales.

Her silent nature didn't help her either. After about a month, her file from Ostrava arrived at the farm. It told us that she'd started off in Cheb as an apprentice hairdresser. As the result of a morals charge she'd spent a year at a reformatory and had then gone to Ostrava. In Ostrava she was known as a good worker. Her behavior in the dormitory was exemplary. Before her flight there had been only one offense, one entirely unusual: she had been caught stealing flowers in a cemetery.

The reports were brief, and instead of unveiling Lucie's mystery, they made it more enigmatic. I promised the director I'd look after her. I found her intriguing. She worked silently and with concentration. She was calm in her timidity. I found in her none of the eccentricities that might be expected in a girl who had lived several weeks alone in the woods. She declared several times that she was happy on the farm and didn't want to leave. Since she was placid and always willing to give way in any argument, she gradually won over the girls who worked with her. Yet there was always something in her taciturnity that betrayed a life of pain and a wounded soul. What I hoped was that she would confide in me, but I also knew she had had enough quizzings and questionings in her life and that she probably associated them with police interrogations. So instead of questioning her, I began talking myself. I talked to her every day. I told her of my plans to cultivate medicinal herbs on the farm. I told her how in the old days country people used decoctions and solutions of various herbs to cure themselves. I told her about burnet, with which they treated cholera and the plague, and about saxifrage, or breakstone, which actually does break up kidney stones and gallstones. Lucie listened. She liked herbs. But what saintlike simplicity! She knew nothing about them and could hardly name one.

Winter was nearly upon us, and Lucie had nothing to wear but her pretty summer things. I helped her to budget her salary. I prevailed upon her to buy a raincoat and sweater, and as time went on, things like boots, pajamas, stockings, a new overcoat . . .

One day I asked her whether she believed in God. She responded in a way I considered peculiar. She said neither yes nor no. She shrugged her shoulders and said, "I don't know." I asked her whether she knew who Jesus Christ was. She said she did. But she didn't know a thing about Him. Only that He was somehow connected with the idea of Christmas, but it was all a haze of some images that made no sense together. Until that time Lucie had known neither belief nor unbelief. I suddenly felt a moment of vertigo, something akin to what a lover must feel when he discovers no male body has preceded his in his beloved. "Do you want me to tell you about Him?" I asked, and she nodded. The hills and pastures already lay under snow. I talked. Lucie listened. . . .

12

SHE'D HAD too much to bear on her slender shoulders. She needed someone to help her, but there was no one capable of it. The help religion offers is simple, Lucie: Give yourself. Give yourself along with the burden you bear. There is a great comfort in giving yourself. I know you've never had anyone to give yourself to, because you've been afraid of people. But there is God. Give yourself to Him. You will feel lighter.

To give yourself means to lay aside your past life. To remove it from your soul. To confess. Tell me, Lucie, why did you run away from Ostrava? Was it because of those flowers in the cemetery?

Partly.

And why did you take the flowers?

She'd been depressed, so she'd put them in a vase in her room at the dormitory. She also picked flowers in nature, but Ostrava is a black town with hardly any nature around it, just dumps, fences, empty lots, and here and there a copse coated with soot. Beautiful flowers were found only in the cemetery. Lofty flowers, majestic flowers. Gladioli, roses, and lilies. Chrysanthemums too, with their voluminous blossoms of fragile petals. . . .

And how did they catch you?

She enjoyed going to the cemetery and went there often. Not only for the flowers she took away with her, but also because it was nice and quiet there and the quiet was comforting to her. Every tomb was like a private little garden, and she liked to spend some time in front of one or another of them, examining the gravestones with their sad inscriptions. So as not to be disturbed, she would imitate the visitors, the elderly ones in particular, and kneel before a stone. Once she took a fancy to a grave nearly fresh. The coffin had been buried there only a few days before. The earth on the grave was loose and still strewn with wreaths, and in front, in a vase, stood a magnificent spray of roses. Lucie kneeled, and a weeping willow inclined over her like an intimate, whispering heaven. She dissolved into ineffable bliss. Just then an elderly gentleman and his wife approached the grave. Perhaps it was the grave of their son or brother, who knows. They saw an unfamiliar girl kneeling by the tomb. They were astonished. Who was this girl? Her appearance seemed to them to hide a secret, a family secret perhaps, an unknown relative or unknown lover of the deceased. . . . They stopped, not venturing to disturb her. They watched her from a distance. Then they saw the girl stand up, take the beautiful spray of roses they had placed there a few days before, turn, and leave. They ran after her. Who are you? they asked. She was mortified and barely able to stammer out a few words. Finally they realized the girl hadn't known the deceased at all. They called an attendant. They demanded to see her identification papers. They shouted at her, told her there was nothing more abominable than robbing the dead. The attendant confirmed that it wasn't the first flower theft in the cemetery. They called a policeman, she was questioned yet again, and she confessed everything.

13

Lᴇᴛ ᴛʜᴇ ᴅᴇᴀᴅ bury their dead," said Jesus. Flowers on graves belong to the living. You didn't know God, Lucie, but you longed for Him. In the beauty of earthly flowers you found the revelation of the unearthly. You didn't need those flowers for anyone. Only for yourself. For the void in your soul. And they caught and humiliated you. But was that the only reason you ran away from the black city?

She was silent. Then she shook her head.

Someone hurt you?

She nodded.

Tell me, Lucie.

It was a very small room. Dangling crookedly from the ceiling was an unshaded, obscenely naked light bulb. A bed was by the wall, a picture hanging over it, and in the picture a handsome man in a blue robe, kneeling. It was the Garden of Gethsemane, but Lucie didn't know it. That was where he had gone with her, and she had fought and screamed. He wanted to rape her, ripped off her clothes, but she eluded him and ran, far away.

Who was he, Lucie?

A soldier.

Did you love him?

No, she didn't love him.

Then why did you follow him into that room with nothing but a bare bulb and a bed?

It was the void in her soul that drew her to him. And all she could find, poor girl, was a raw youth doing his military service.

But there's one thing I still don't understand, Lucie. Since you did go into that room with him, the room with the bed, why then did you run away?

Because he was nasty and brutal, like all the others.

Who are you talking about, Lucie? What others?

She was silent.

Who did you know before the soldier? Speak, Lucie! Tell me!

14

T HERE WERE six of them and she alone. Six of them between sixteen and twenty. She was sixteen. They called themselves a gang and spoke of the gang with awe, as if it were a pagan sect. On that day they were talking about initiation. They had brought along a few bottles of cheap wine. She took part in the drinking with the blind obedience on which she had lavished all the unrequited daughter's love for a mother and a father. She drank when they drank, laughed when they laughed. Then they ordered her to undress. She had never done that in their presence. But since the leader of the gang took his own clothes off when she hesitated, she realized the command was not directed against her, and complied docilely. She trusted them, trusted even their roughness, they were her shelter and shield, she couldn't imagine losing them. They were her father, they were her mother. They drank, laughed, and gave her more commands. She spread her legs. She was afraid, she knew what it meant, but she obeyed. Then she screamed, and the blood flowed out of her. The boys roared, raised their glasses, and poured the raw sparkling wine down their leader's back, over her body and between her legs, and shouted something about Christening and Initiation, and then the leader stood up from her and another went to her, they each took their turn in order of seniority until it came time for the youngest of all, who was sixteen like her, and Lucie couldn't take any more, she couldn't stand the pain any more, she wanted to rest, wanted to be by herself, and because he was the youngest she dared to push him away. But just because he was the youngest he refused to be humiliated. He was one of the gang after all, he belonged fully! And to prove it he slapped her across the face, and no one in the gang stood up for her because they all knew that the youngest was in the right and was merely claiming his due. Lucie shed tears, but she lacked the courage to resist and so she spread her legs for the sixth time. . . .

Where was this, Lucie?

The flat of one of the boys, while his parents were on night shift, there was a kitchen and one room, the room had a table, a couch, and a bed, over the door hung the framed inscription GOD GRANT US HAPPINESS and over the bed in a frame a beautiful lady in a blue robe holding a child to her breast.

The Virgin Mary?

She didn't know.

And then, Lucie, what happened then?

Then it happened over and over, either in the same flat or in other ones, and out in the fields too. It became a habit with the gang.

And did you like it, Lucie?

She didn't. From that time on they treated her worse, more arrogantly and coarsely, but there was no way out, forward, backward, anywhere.

And how did it end, Lucie?

One evening in one of those empty flats. The police came and took them all away. The boys had some thefts on their conscience. Lucie was unaware of this, but it was common knowledge that she went around with the gang, common knowledge too that she gave its members everything a young girl could give. She was the shame of all Cheb, and at home they beat her black and blue. The boys got varying sentences, and she was sent to a reformatory. She spent a year there—until she was seventeen. She wouldn't have returned home for anything on earth. That is how she came to live in the black city.

15

I was surprised and somewhat taken aback when Ludvik revealed to me on the phone the day before yesterday that he knew Lucie. Fortunately, he only knew her by sight. He'd apparently had a superficial friendship with a girl who lived in the dormitory with her. When he asked me about her again yesterday, I told him everything. I had long felt the need to throw off that burden but had never found anyone I could trust with it. Ludvik has some feeling for me and is at the same time sufficiently removed from my life, and even more so from Lucie's. I therefore had no need to fear that I would be putting her secret in jeopardy.

No, I've never repeated a word of what Lucie confided in me to anyone but Ludvik. Though of course everyone on the farm knew from her file that she'd been to a reformatory and had stolen flowers from a cemetery. They were quite nice to her, but they constantly reminded her of her past. The director spoke of her as "the little grave robber." He meant it in fun, but such talk kept Lucie's past perpetually alive. Lucie was ceaselessly, continuously guilty. And at a time when she needed nothing but total forgiveness. Yes, Ludvik, she needed forgiveness, she needed the mysterious purification that to you is unfamiliar and incomprehensible.

For people, by themselves, don't know how to forgive, and it is not even in their power. They lack the power to annihilate a sin that has been committed. This exceeds a man's strength. Divesting a sin of its validity, undoing it, erasing it out of time, in other words making it into nothing, is a mysterious and supernatural feat. Only God, because He is exempt from earthly laws, because He is free, because He can work miracles, may wash away sin, transform it into nothing, forgive it. Man can forgive man only insofar as he founds himself on God's forgiveness.

Nor can you, Ludvik, forgive, because you do not believe in God. You still remember the plenary meeting when everyone raised their hands against you and agreed that your life should be destroyed. You've never forgiven them that. And not only as individuals. There were about a hundred of them there, and that is a quantity which can serve as a sort of miniature model of mankind. You've never forgiven mankind. From that time on you've mistrusted it, you feel rancor against it. I can understand you, but that doesn't alter the fact that such general rancor against people is terrifying and sinful. It has become your curse. *Because to live in a world in which no one is forgiven, where all are irredeemable, is the same as living in hell.* You are living in hell, Ludvik, and I pity you.

16

EVERYTHING on this earth which belongs to God may also belong
to the Devil. Even the motions of lovers in the act of love. For Lucie
these had become a province of the odious. She associated them with
the bestial adolescent faces of the gang and later with the face of the
insistent soldier. Oh, I can see him before me so clearly I feel I know
him. He mixes the banal, syrupy words of love with the rough violence
of a male caged without women behind the camp wire. And Lucie
suddenly discovers that the tender words are nothing but a false mantle
over a coarse, wolfish body. The whole universe of love collapses before
her eyes into a pit of loathing and disgust.

Here was the source of the disease, here was where I had to begin. A
man who walks along the seashore brandishing a lantern in his outstretched hand may well be a madman. But on a night when the waves
have led a ship astray, the same man is a savior. The planet we inhabit is
a borderland between heaven and hell. No act is of itself either good or
bad. Only its place in the order of things makes it good or bad. Even
physical love, Lucie, is not in itself either good or bad. If it is in
accordance with the order created by God, if it is a true love, then your
loving will be good and you will be happy. For God has decreed that "a
man shall leave his father and his mother and shall cleave unto his wife;
and the two shall be one flesh."

I spoke to Lucie day after day, each time reassuring her that she was
forgiven, that she must not writhe in self-torture, that she must undo
the straitjacket of her soul, that she must humbly give herself up to
God's order, where everything, even the love of the body, would find
its place.

And so the weeks went by. . . .

Then came the first days of spring. Apple trees bloomed on the slopes, and in the gentle wind their crowns looked like swinging bells. I closed my eyes to hear their velvet tones. And then I opened them and saw Lucie in her blue smock, hoe in hand. She was looking down into the valley, and she was smiling.

I watched her smile, and I read it eagerly. Was it possible? Until then Lucie's soul had been in eternal flight, a flight from both past and future. She had been afraid of everything. Past and future for her were watery depths. In her distress she clung to the leaky boat of the present as to an uncertain refuge.

And now, today, she was smiling. For no apparent reason. Just like that. And that smile told me she'd begun looking to the future with confidence. And in that instant I felt like a mariner sighting a longed-for land after many months at sea. I was happy. I leaned on the gnarled stem of an apple tree and for a moment again closed my eyes. I heard the breeze and velvet bells in the white treetops, I heard the birds trilling, and before my closed eyes their song was transformed into thousands of lanterns carried by invisible hands to a great ceremony. I did not see those hands, but I heard the high-pitched voices, and it seemed to me they were children, a joyous procession of children. . . . And all at once I felt a hand on my cheek. And a voice. "Mr. Kostka, you are so good to me. . . ." I didn't open my eyes. I didn't move the hand. I still saw the birds' voices transformed into a dance of lanterns, I still heard the ringing of the apple trees. And the voice added, more faintly: "I love you."

Perhaps I should have expected nothing more than that moment and quickly left, knowing I had done my duty. But before I could reflect, I let a giddy weakness take hold of me. We were completely alone in the wide open country among the pitiful little apple trees; I took Lucie in my arms and sank with her into the bower of nature.

17

WHAT SHOULDN'T HAVE happened happened. When I saw Lucie's calmed soul through her smile, I knew I'd reached my aim and I should have left. But I didn't. With bad consequences. We continued to live on the same farm. Lucie was happy, glowing, she was like the spring, which all around us was gradually changing into summer. But instead of being happy, I was horrified by the great female springtime at my side, which I myself had awakened and which turned all its unfolding blossoms toward me, blossoms that I knew were not mine, must not be mine. I had a son and a wife in Prague who waited patiently for my rare visits home.

I did not wish to break off this beginning of intimacies for fear of wounding Lucie, yet I did not dare go on with them, knowing I was beyond my rights. I desired her, yet at the same time I was afraid of her love, unsure of what to do with it. Only with the greatest effort was I able to maintain the natural tone of our former talks. My doubts had come between us. It seemed to me that the spiritual assistance I'd given Lucie had been shown up for what it was. That I had desired her physically from the moment I'd seen her. That I had been a seducer in priest's robe. That all my talk of Jesus and God was no more than a veil for the most base carnal desires. I felt that the moment I yielded to my sexuality I had soiled the purity of my original intention and been stripped of all my merit before God.

Yet no sooner did I arrive at that conclusion than my reflection made a complete about face: what vanity, I mentally shouted at myself, what presumption to want to be worthy, to be pleasing to God! What do man's merits signify before Him? Nothing, nothing, nothing! Lucie loves me and her health depends on my love! Must I throw her back into despair merely to save my own purity? Will God not despise me all the more? And if my love is sinful, what is more important: Lucie's life or my sinlessness? It will be *my* sin, only *I* will be the one to bear it, only I myself will be lost through my sin!

Then one day these doubts and thoughts were disturbed by outside intervention. The central authorities fabricated political charges against my director. When it became clear that he would defend himself tooth and nail, they tried to strengthen their case by claiming he was surrounded by suspicious elements. I was one of them: a man said to have been expelled from the university for views hostile to the State, and pro-clerical to boot. The director did his best to prove I wasn't pro-clerical and hadn't been expelled from the university. The more he protested the more he demonstrated his close ties with me and the more he harmed himself. My situation was well nigh hopeless.

Injustice, Ludvik? Yes, that's the word you use most often when you hear about this or similar incidents. But I don't know what injustice is. If there were nothing above human affairs and if actions had only the significance ascribed to them by those who perform them, then the concept of injustice would be warranted and I could cite the injustice of being more or less thrown off the state farm where I had worked with devotion. It might even have been logical to defend myself against this injustice and fight furiously for my puny human rights.

But events for the most part have a meaning quite different from the one their blind authors ascribe to them; they are often disguised instructions from above, and the people through whom they occur are merely the unwitting messengers of a higher will whose existence they do not even suspect.

I was certain that was the case here too. So I accepted the developments on the farm with relief. I saw in them a clear instruction: Leave Lucie before it is too late. You have accomplished your task. The fruits of your labors do not belong to you. Your path leads elsewhere.

As a result, I did the same thing I'd done two years earlier at the Natural Sciences Division. I said good-bye to a tearfully disconsolate Lucie and went forth to meet apparent disaster. I offered to leave the farm of my own accord. The director did protest a bit, but I knew he was doing it only out of decency and in the depths of his soul he was glad.

Only this time the voluntary nature of my departure made no impression whatever. I had no pre-February Communist friends to strew my path with good advice and flattering recommendations. I left the farm a man who himself admits that he is unfit to carry out work of any significance in this State. And so I became a construction worker.

18

I~~T WAS~~ an autumn day in 1956. I saw Ludvik for the first time in five years, in the dining car of the Prague-Bratislava express. I was on my way to a factory construction site in eastern Moravia. Ludvik had just finished his stint in the Ostrava mines and had gone to Prague for permission to resume his studies. Now he was returning home to Moravia. We scarcely recognized each other. And when we did, we were amazed by the resemblance of our fates.

I still remember the sympathy in your eyes, Ludvik, as you listened to my tale about leaving the university and about the state farm intrigues that led to my becoming a bricklayer. I thank you for that sympathy. You were furious, you spoke of injustice, of stupidity. You blew up at me too: you reproached me for not standing up for myself, for surrendering without a fight. We should never leave anywhere voluntarily, you said. Let our opponents do the dirty work themselves! Why make their consciences any easier?

You a miner, I a bricklayer. Our stories so similar, and the two of us so different. I forgiving, you irreconcilable; I peaceful, you rebellious. How outwardly near we were, how inwardly distant!

You were far less aware of this inward distance between us than I was. When you gave me the full details of why you'd been expelled from the Party, you took it for granted that I was on your side and equally indignant about the bigotry of the Comrades who punished you for making fun of what they held sacred. What was it that made them so angry? you asked, sincerely astonished.

Let me tell you something: In Geneva, at the time when Calvin ruled, there lived a boy not too different from yourself, an intelligent boy always game for a laugh. One day they found a notebook of his filled with jeering at Jesus Christ and the Gospel. What was it that made them so angry? he must have thought, that boy not so different from yourself. He'd done nothing wrong, it was all just a joke. He had very little hatred in him. Only mockery and indifference. He was executed.

Please don't think I approve of such cruelty. All I'm trying to say is that no great movement designed to change the world can bear sarcasm or mockery, because they are a rust that corrodes all it touches.

Only examine your own attitude, Ludvik. They expelled you from the Party, from the university, put you in among the politically dangerous soldiers, then kept you down in the mines for another two or three years. And you? You became bitter to the depths of your soul, convinced of the great injustice done you. That sense of injustice still determines every step you take. I don't understand you! How can you speak of injustice? They sent you to a black insignia battalion among the enemies of Communism. Granted. But was that an injustice? Wasn't it more like a great opportunity? Think of what you could have accomplished among the enemy! Is there any greater mission? Didn't Jesus send His disciples "as sheep in the midst of wolves"? "They that be whole need not a physician, but they that are sick," Jesus said. "For I am not come to call the righteous, but sinners. . . ." But you had no desire to go among the sinners and the sick!

You will argue that my comparison is invalid. That Jesus sent His disciples "in the midst of wolves" with His blessing, whereas you were first excommunicated and damned and only then sent among the enemies as an enemy, among wolves as a wolf, among the sinners as a sinner.

But do you want to deny you were a sinner? Don't you feel any guilt with regard to your community? Where do you get your pride? A man devoted to his faith is humble and must humbly bear even an unjust punishment. The humiliated shall be raised up. The repentant shall be purified. They who are wronged have the opportunity to test their fidelity. If the only reason you turned bitter towards your community was that it placed too great a burden on your shoulders, then your faith was weak and you failed the test that was set you.

I am not on your side in your quarrel with the Party, Ludvik, because

I know that great things on this earth can be created only by a community of infinitely devoted men who humbly give up their lives to a higher design. You are not, Ludvik, infinitely devoted. Your faith is fragile. How can it be otherwise, when you always refer to yourself alone and to your own miserable reason?

I am not ungrateful, Ludvik. I know what you've done for me and for many others who have been hurt in one way or another by today's regime. I know you use your pre-February connections with high-ranking Communists and your present position to intervene, intercede, assist. I like you for it. But I tell you again for the last time: Look deep into your soul! The deepest motive for your good deeds is not love, but hatred! Hatred towards those who once hurt you, towards those who raised their hands against you in that hall! Your soul knows no God, and therefore knows no forgiveness. You long for retribution. You identify those who hurt you then with those who hurt others now, and you take your revenge on them. Yes, revenge! You are full of hatred even when you help people. I feel it oozing from you. I feel it in your every word. But what are the fruits of hatred if not hatred in return, a chain of further hatreds? You are living in hell, Ludvik, I repeat this, you are living in hell, and I pity you.

19

HAD LUDVIK HEARD my soliloquy, he might have said that I was ungrateful. I know he's helped me a great deal. That time in fifty-six when we met on the train he was distressed by the life I was leading and immediately set to thinking of ways to find me work I would enjoy and derive satisfaction from. I was amazed by his speed and efficiency. He had a few words with a friend of his in his hometown. He hoped to find me a job teaching natural science at a local school. This was quite daring. Antireligious propaganda was still going strong, and it was almost impossible to hire a Christian as a schoolteacher. That was the opinion of Ludvik's friend, who did come up with another idea. That's how I came to obtain my position in the virological department of the local hospital, where for the last eight years I've been breeding viruses and bacteria in mice and rabbits.

That's how it is. If it weren't for Ludvik, I wouldn't be living here, and Lucie wouldn't be living here either.

Several years after I left the farm she got married. She couldn't stay on the farm because her husband wanted to work in a city. They didn't quite know where they wanted to settle. In the end she prevailed on him to move here, to the town where I was living.

I have never received a greater gift, a greater reward. My little lamb, my little dove, the child I had healed and nurtured with my soul is returning to me. She wants nothing of me. She has a husband. But she wants to be near me. She needs me. She needs to hear my voice now and then. To see me at Sunday services. To meet me in the street. I was happy, and at that moment I felt I was no longer young, that I was older than I thought, and that Lucie was perhaps the only achievement of my life.

Is that too little, Ludvik? Not at all. It is enough, and I am happy. I am happy. I am happy. . . .

20

O<small>H, HOW I DELUDE</small> myself! How stubbornly I try to convince myself I've taken the right path! How I parade the power of my faith before the unbeliever!

Yes, I did manage to bring Lucie to faith in God. I managed to calm and heal her. I rid her of her disgust for the things of the flesh. In the end I stepped out of her path. Yes, but what good did I do her?

Her marriage hasn't turned out well. Her husband is a brute, he's openly unfaithful to her, and rumor has it he mistreats her. Lucie has never said a word about it to me. She knows the pain it would cause me. She's made her life out to be a model of happiness. But we live in a small town where nothing remains secret.

Oh, how I delude myself! I interpreted the political intrigues against the director of the state farm as a coded sign from God that I should leave. But how to recognize God's voice among so many other voices? What if the voice I heard was only the voice of my own cowardice?

For I had a wife and child in Prague. I wasn't much devoted to them, but I couldn't part from them either. I was afraid of getting into a situation I couldn't get out of. I was afraid of Lucie's love and didn't know what I should do with it. I was afraid of the complications it might bring me.

I set myself up as the angel of her salvation when in fact I was merely another of her seducers. I loved her once, a single time, then turned away. I acted as though I were offering her forgiveness when she actually should have forgiven me. She wept in despair when I left, and several years later she came and settled in my town. She talked to me. Turned to me as to a friend. She has forgiven me. Besides, it's all clear. It hasn't happened often in my life, but that girl loved me. I had her life in my hands. I had her happiness within my power. And I ran away. No one has ever wronged her as I did.

And suddenly the idea comes to me that I invoke supposed divine appeals as mere pretexts to extract myself from my human obligations. I am afraid of women. I am afraid of their warmth, I am afraid of their constant presence. I was terrified of a life with Lucie just as I am terrified by the thought of moving permanently into the teacher's two-room flat in the neighboring town.

And what was the real reason behind my voluntary resignation from the university fifteen years ago? I didn't love my wife, who was six years older than I. I could no longer stand her voice or her face or the monotonous tick-tock of the family clock. I couldn't live with her, but neither could I inflict a divorce on her, because she was good and had never done anything to hurt me. And so all of a sudden I heard the saving voice of an appeal from on high. I heard Jesus calling me to forsake my nets.

O God, is it truly so? Am I so wretchedly laughable? Tell me it is not so! Reassure me! Make yourself heard, God, louder, louder! In this chaos of confused voices I cannot seem to hear You.

PART SEVEN

Ludvik, Jaroslav, Helena

I

WHEN I got back to the hotel from Kostka's place late that evening, I was determined to leave for Prague first thing in the morning, since I had nothing more to do here: my deceitful mission to my hometown was over. Unfortunately, my head was in such a whirl that I spent half the night tossing and turning on my bed (my creaky bed) unable to sleep; when I finally did drop off, I kept waking up, and it wasn't until early morning that I fell into a deep sleep. As a result, I didn't get up until nine, when the morning buses and trains had already gone and there was no way to leave for Prague till two in the afternoon. When I realized that, I was almost in despair. I felt like a man who has been shipwrecked, and suddenly I was nostalgic for Prague, for my work, for the desk in my flat, for my books. But there was nothing I could do; I had to grit my teeth and go down to the dining room for breakfast.

I entered with caution, as I was afraid of meeting Helena. But she wasn't there (evidently she was already scurrying around the neighboring village with a tape recorder over her shoulder, bothering the passersby with a microphone and silly questions); the room was, however, packed with noisy people sitting and smoking over their beers, black coffees, ryes, and cognacs. I saw that once again my hometown would begrudge me a decent breakfast.

I went out into the street; the blue sky, the ragged little clouds, the gathering heaviness of the air, the dust rising slightly, the street opening into the broad, flat square with its spire (yes, the one that looks like a soldier in a helmet), all this washed over me with the gloom of emptiness. In the distance I could hear the drunken plaint of a drawn-out Moravian song (in which it seemed to me were enthralled the nostalgia of the steppe, of the long rides of the mercenary Uhlans), and suddenly Lucie emerged in my mind, the story of long ago that at this moment . resembled the drawn-out song and spoke to my heart, through which (as through the steppe) so many women had passed without leaving a trace, just as the rising dust leaves no trace on that flat, broad square, settles between the cobblestones and rises again to fly off on a gust of wind.

I strode across those dusty cobblestones and felt the oppressive lightness of the void that lay over my life: Lucie, the goddess of mists, had first deprived me of herself, then yesterday turned my carefully calculated revenge to nothing, and soon after transformed even my memories of herself into something hopelessly ridiculous, into a grotesque mistake: what Kostka told me testifies that all those years I had in fact remembered another woman, because I never knew who Lucie was.

I had always liked to tell myself that Lucie was something abstract, a legend and a myth, but now I knew that behind the poetry of these words hid an entirely unpoetic truth: that I didn't know her; that I didn't know her as she really was, as she was in and to herself. I had been able to perceive (in my youthful egocentricity) only those aspects of her being that were turned directly to me (to my loneliness, my captivity, my yearning for tenderness and affection); she had never been anything to me but *a function of my own situation;* everything that went beyond that concrete situation, everything that she was in herself, had escaped me. But if she was really a mere function of my situation, it was logical that when that situation altered (when another situation succeeded it, when I grew older and changed), *my Lucie* vanished with it, because from then on she was only what had escaped me in her, what had not concerned me, what was beyond me. And so it was also logical that after fifteen years I had not recognized her. She had long been to me (and I had never thought of her except as being "to me") a different person, a stranger.

The message of my defeat had been trailing me for fifteen years, and now it had caught up with me. Kostka the eccentric (whom I'd never taken more than half seriously) had meant more to her, had done more for her, known more about her, and loved her *better* (not more, because the strength of my love could scarcely have been greater): to him she had confided everything—to me nothing; he had made her happy—I had made her unhappy; he had known her physically—I had not. And yet all I needed in order to possess the body I so desperately desired was one simple thing: to understand her, to know her, to love her not only for what she was to me but for everything in her that did not immediately concern me, for what she was in and to herself. I had been unable to do that and so had hurt myself and her. A wave of anger washed over me, anger against myself, at my age at the time, that stupid *lyrical age,* when a man is too great a riddle to himself to be interested in the riddles outside himself and when other people (no matter how dear) are mere walking mirrors in which he is amazed to find his own emotions, his own worth. Yes, for fifteen years I'd thought of Lucie only as the mirror that preserved my image of those days!

Again I saw the bleak room with its single bed and the streetlamp shining in through the grimy glass, again I saw Lucie's ferocious resistance. It was all like a bad joke: I had thought she was a virgin, and she had fought me precisely because she was not a virgin and was probably afraid of the moment when I would discover the truth. Or there is another explanation (which corresponds to Kostka's view of Lucie): her initial sexual experiences had marked her deeply and had deprived the act of love of the meanings most people give it; they had emptied it entirely of tenderness and affection; for Lucie, the body was something ugly and love was something incorporeal; the soul engaged the body in a silent, dogged war.

This interpretation (so melodramatic and yet so plausible) reminded me of the painful rupture (I had known it well in many different forms) between the soul and the body, and recalled (because here the painful was continually shouted down by the ridiculous) a story that made me laugh: a good friend of mine, a woman of rather flexible morals (of which I had myself taken advantage), became engaged to a physicist and firmly resolved, this time, really to fall in *love;* but in order to feel it as a *real* love (distinct from the dozens of love affairs she'd had), she refused her fiancé any physical contact until the wedding night, she walked with him under the trees in the evening, she squeezed his hand, she kissed him under the streetlamps, and so allowed her soul (unburdened by the body) to soar into the clouds and give itself up to vertigo. A month after the wedding she divorced him, complaining bitterly that he had failed to match her great emotion because he had turned out to be a bad, nearly impotent lover.

The drunken plaint of the drawn-out Moravian song in the distance now mingled with the grotesque aftertaste of this story, with the dusty emptiness of the town, and with my sadness, to which was joined the hunger clamoring in my entrails. By now I was only a few steps from the milk bar; I tried the door, but it was shut. A passerby told me: "They're all at the festival today." "At the Ride of the Kings?" "Right. They've got a stand there."

I cursed, but there was nothing I could do about it; I set off in the direction of the song. My hunger pangs were leading me to the folklore festival that I had fled like the plague.

2

FATIGUE. Fatigue since early morning. As if I'd been carousing all night. Yet I slept all night. Except that my sleep is only a skimmed milk of sleep. I had to struggle to suppress my yawns at breakfast. Soon people began drifting in. Vladimir's friends and some onlookers. Then a boy from the farm cooperative brought the horse for Vladimir to our yard. In the midst of it all appeared Kalasek, the cultural adviser of the District National Committee. For two years now we've been at loggerheads. He was dressed in black and had a ceremonial air. With him was an elegant-looking woman. A Prague radio reporter. I was going to be their guide, she said. The lady wanted to record interviews for a program about the Ride of the Kings.

Leave me out of it! I'm not going to play the fool. The radio reporter went on about how thrilled she was to meet me in person, and of course Kalasek started in too. He said it was my political duty to go. The buffoon. I almost had my way. I told them my son was to be king today and that I wanted to be there while he got ready. But Vlasta stabbed me in the back. She said it was her job to get him ready. I should go and speak on the radio.

So in the end I went obediently. The radio lady was working out of a room in the local District Committee building. Besides her tape recorder she had brought along a young man to run errands for her. She didn't stop talking for a minute, except to laugh. Finally she put the microphone to her mouth and asked Kalasek the first question.

Kalasek gave a little cough and began. The cultivation of folk art was an integral part of Communist education. The District Committee was fully aware. That was why it fully supported. It wished them every success and fully shared. It thanked all those who took part. The enthusiastic organizers and the enthusiastic schoolchildren, whom it fully.

Fatigue. Fatigue. Always the same words. Fifteen years of hearing the same old words. And now to hear them from Kalasek, who didn't give a damn about folk art. For him folk art is only a means. A means of boasting of a new activity. A means of fulfilling a directive. A means of boosting his prestige. He hadn't lifted a finger for the Ride of the Kings and had cut our budget down to the bone. Yet he is the one who will get the credit. He is the master of District culture. A former shop clerk who doesn't know a violin from a guitar.

The radio lady put the microphone to her lips. Was I satisfied with this year's Ride of the Kings? I felt like laughing in her face: the Ride hadn't even started yet! But she laughed at me instead: I was such an experienced folk expert that surely I knew how it would turn out. That's the way they are, they know everything in advance. The unfolding of things to come is already known to them. The future has already happened, and for them, it will just go on repeating itself.

I had an impulse to tell her exactly what I thought. That the Ride would be worse than in past years. That every year folk art loses more supporters. That the authorities had lost interest as well. That it was nearly dead. The fact that something like folk music was constantly on the radio should not delude us. What all those folk instrument bands and folk song and dance ensembles play is more like opera or operetta or light music, not folk music. A folk instrument band with a conductor, a score, and music stands! Almost symphonic orchestration! What bastardization! The music that serves you, those bands and ensembles, my dear radio reporter, is just old-style romanticism with borrowed folk melodies! Real folk art is dead, dear lady, dead.

That is what I would have liked to disgorge into the microphone, but in the end I said something completely different. The Ride of the Kings was splendid. The vigor of folk art. The blaze of color. I fully share. I thank everyone who has taken part. The enthusiastic organizers and schoolchildren, whom I fully.

I felt ashamed for talking the way they wanted me to. Am I such a coward? Or so well trained? Or so fatigued?

I was glad to be done with it and made a hasty exit. I was anxious to get home. There were a lot of people in the yard, some just standing there, others decorating the horse with bows and ribbons. I wanted to see Vladimir getting ready. I went into the house, but the door to the living room, where they were dressing him, was locked. I knocked and called out. Vlasta answered from inside. You shouldn't be here, the king is being robed. Damn it, I said, why shouldn't I be there? It's against the tradition, Vlasta's voice answered. I don't see how it's against the tradition for a father to be present while the king is being robed, but I didn't say so. I heard the concern in her voice and I was pleased. I was pleased that they were concerned with my world. My poor and orphaned world.

So I went back into the yard and chatted with the people who were decorating the horse. It was a heavy draft horse lent by the cooperative farm. Patient and placid.

Then I heard a hubbub of voices coming over the closed gate from the street. There was shouting and banging. My moment had come. I was excited. I opened the gate and went out. The Ride of the Kings was marshaled in front of our house. Horses adorned with ribbons and streamers. Young riders in colorful costumes. It was just like twenty years ago. Like twenty years ago, when they came for me. When they asked my father to give them his son to be king.

Near the gate were two pages on horseback, disguised as women, with sabers in hand. They were waiting for Vladimir, to accompany and guard him all day. Now a young man rode out from the band of riders, halted his horse right in front of me, and recited:

> *Hear ye, hear ye, one and all!*
> *Noble papa, suffer us in great array*
> *To lead your son as king away!*

Then he promised that their king would be well guarded. That they would conduct him safely through hostile armies. That they would not deliver him up into enemy hands. That they were ready for the fray. Hear ye, hear ye!

I looked back. In the shadow of our gateway sat a figure on a beribboned horse, in woman's costume, with puckered sleeves and colored ribbons across the face. The king. Vladimir. Suddenly I forgot my fatigue and dejection and felt at ease. The old king was sending the young one out into the world. I went over to him. I was standing right by the horse and on tiptoe so that my mouth was as near as possible to his hidden face. "Good luck, Vladimir," I whispered to him. He didn't reply. He didn't move. And Vlasta told me with a smile: He's not allowed to answer you. He must not say a word till evening.

3

I̶T TOOK me barely a quarter of an hour to reach the village (in my
youth it had been separated from the town by a belt of fields, but now
the two were virtually merged); the singing I'd heard from the town
(there it had sounded distant and nostalgic) here resounded in full
force from loudspeakers attached to houses and telephone poles (eternal dupe, I'd allowed myself a short time ago to be saddened by the
melancholy and apparent tipsiness of the distant voice, and it turned
out to be only a recorded singer on the sound equipment and the two
scratchy discs provided by the District Committee!); just outside the
village they had erected a triumphal arch with a large paper banner
bearing the inscription WELCOME in red ornamental letters; the crowd
was quite dense, and while most wore everyday clothes, here and there
a few old men were in folk costume: high boots, white linen trousers,
and embroidered shirts. Here the street widened into the village green:
between the road and the nearest row of houses there was a wide swath
of grass dotted with trees, and among them a few stands had been set
up (for today's festival) to sell beer, soft drinks, peanuts, chocolate,
gingerbread, sausages with mustard, and waffles; the town milk bar's
stand had milk, cheese, butter, yogurt, and sour cream; none of the
stands served hard liquor, but nearly everyone seemed to me drunk;
people were crowding around the stands, getting in each other's way,
gaping vacantly; now and then someone would break into loud song,
but this was always a false start (accompanied by a drunken raising of
the hand), two or three bars of a song immediately drowned out by the
din of the crowd and the invincible blast of the recorded folk song from
the loudspeakers. The green was littered (though it was still early and
the Ride had not yet begun) with paper beer cups and paper plates
smeared with mustard.

With its reek of abstinence, the milk and yogurt stand repelled people; I bought a cup of milk and a roll without having to wait, and moved off to a less crowded spot to sip my milk in peace. Just then I heard a commotion coming from the other end of the green: the Ride of the Kings had arrived.

Small hats with cockerel feathers, white shirts with full pleated sleeves, blue vests with tufts of red wool, and colored paper ribbons fluttering from the horses' bodies filled the entire area; and immediately the buzz of people and the song from the loudspeakers were joined by new sounds: the whinnying of horses and the call of horsemen:

> *Hear ye, hear ye, one and all,*
> *From hill and dale, from near and far,*
> *Hear, hear what comes to be this Whitsun.*
> *Our pauper king, a righteous one,*
> *Has lost to thieves a thousand head,*
> *Cattle from his empty castle led. . . .*

Ear and eye alike were assaulted by confusion, everything clashed: the folklore from the loudspeakers with the folklore on horseback; the colors of the costumes and horses with the ugly browns and grays of the badly cut clothes of the spectators; the laborious spontaneity of the costumed riders with the laborious officiousness of the organizers, running around in their red armbands among the horses and people, trying to keep the chaos within bounds, which was by no means a simple task, not only because of the unruliness of the spectators (luckily not too numerous) but also because the road hadn't been closed to traffic, the organizers were merely standing at either end of the troop of riders and signaling the cars to slow down; so cars and trucks and roaring motorcycles squeezed their way between the horses, making them uneasy and the riders unsure.

To be frank, in trying so stubbornly to avoid this (and any other) folklore event I had dreaded something quite different from what I now saw. I had expected the lack of taste, expected the blend of real folk art and kitsch, expected opening speeches by cretinous orators, yes, I had expected the worst bombast and falsity, but I hadn't expected this sad, almost moving *forlornness*; it pervaded everything: the handful of stands, the scanty but thoroughly unruly and inattentive spectators, the battle between the everyday traffic and the anachronistic festival, the frightened horses, the loudspeakers inertly bellowing their two unchanging folk songs and completely overpowering (along with the roar of the motorcycles) the young horsemen as they shouted their lines, the veins standing out on their necks.

I threw away my paper cup, and the Ride of the Kings, which had now sufficiently displayed itself to the spectators on the green, set off on a several-hour-long peregrination through the village. I knew it all very well: the last year of the war I myself had ridden as a page (dressed in ceremonial woman's garb, with saber in hand) at the side of Jaroslav, who was then the king. I had no desire to let myself be moved by memories, but (as if the forlornness of the festival had disarmed me) I no longer wanted to force myself to turn my back on this scene; I slowly made my way in the wake of the riders, who had now spread out; in the center of the group was a cluster of three riders: in the middle the king, and on each side a page wearing woman's clothes and carrying a saber. Beside them trotted a few others of the king's escort: the so-called *ministers*. The rest of the procession was split into two independent wings riding on either side of the street; here too the riders' roles were precisely defined: there were the *standard-bearers* (with red flags stuck into their boots and fluttering along the horses' flanks), the *heralds* (reciting before each house their rhymed message about the righteous pauper king who had lost to thieves a thousand head of cattle), and finally the *collectors* (who called out for gifts "For the king, my good woman, for the king!" and held out cane baskets for contributions).

4

THANK YOU, Ludvik, I've known you for just eight days and I love you as I've never loved anyone else, I love you and trust you, I can think of nothing else, and I trust you because even if my mind deceived me or my emotions or my soul, the body has no deceit, the body is more honest than the soul, and my body knows that it has never experienced anything like yesterday, sensuality, tenderness, cruelty, pleasure, pain, my body has never dreamed of anything like it, our bodies made their vows yesterday, now our heads have only to go obediently along, I've known you just eight days and I thank you, Ludvik.

I thank you too for coming at just the right moment, for saving me. Today the weather had been lovely since early morning, the sky was radiant, I was radiant, everything went well this morning, we went to the house where the boy and his parents live and recorded the summoning of the king, and then suddenly he came up to me, and I was afraid, I didn't know he was here already from Bratislava, and I didn't expect such cruelty, imagine, Ludvik, he had the coarseness to bring her with him!

Fool that I am, I had believed to the last that my marriage was not yet completely ruined, that it could still be saved, fool that I am, I had nearly sacrificed even you for that rotten marriage, I nearly called off our rendezvous here, fool that I am, I nearly let myself be taken in by that sugary voice when he told me he would stop off for me here on his way from Bratislava and that he had a lot he wanted to say to me, that he wanted a heart-to-heart talk, and now he brings her, that kid, that brat, a girl of twenty-two, thirteen years younger than me, it's so degrading to lose simply because of being born earlier, I felt so helpless I could have screamed, but I couldn't scream, I had to smile and shake hands with her politely, thank you, Ludvik, for giving me the strength.

When she moved away a bit, he told me that now we'd have a chance to talk it all over frankly among the three of us and that this would be the most honorable way, honor, honor, I know his honor, two years now he's been angling for a divorce, and he knows that with just the two of us he won't get anywhere, he's counting on my being embarrassed face to face with his girlfriend, he thinks I'll be ashamed to play the role of the obstinate wife, that I'll break down and give in. I hate him, he slips the knife between my ribs when I'm on a job, when I need to be calm, at least he could have some respect for my work, to give it some consideration, but this is the way it's been for years and years, I've always been pushed around, I always lose, I'm always humiliated, but now I'm fighting back, I've felt you and your love behind me, I've felt you still in me and on me, and those fine colorful horsemen were all around me shouting and cheering as if crying out that you exist, that life exists, that the future exists, and I felt pride arise within me, the pride I had almost lost, and this pride flooded over me, and I managed to smile sweetly and tell him: There's no need for me to go to Prague with you, I don't want to intrude, and anyway I have the broadcasting car, and as for the agreement you wanted to discuss, that can be settled very quickly, I can introduce you to the man I want to live with, and I'm sure that we can come to an amicable arrangement.

Maybe this was a crazy thing to do, well, but if it was, too bad, it was worth it for that moment of sweet pride, it was worth it, he immediately became five times more friendly, was obviously glad but afraid I might not really mean it, he asked me to repeat it all and then finally I told him your full name, Ludvik Jahn, Ludvik Jahn, and at the end I said to him explicitly, don't worry, honestly, I'm not going to stand in the way of our divorce, don't worry, I wouldn't want you, even if you wanted me. He replied that he was sure we would remain good friends, and I smiled and said I didn't doubt it.

5

Y EARS AGO, when I was still playing the clarinet in the band, we used to wonder just what the Ride of the Kings meant. When the defeated Hungarian king Matthias was fleeing from Bohemia to Hungary, he and his cavalry were forced to hide from their Czech pursuers here in the Moravian countryside and beg their daily bread. The Ride of the Kings is said to be a reminder of that historic event of the fifteenth century, but even a brief perusal of old documents shows that the tradition of the Ride is much older than this. Where, then, did it come from and what does it mean? Does it perhaps date from pagan times, and is it a survival of the rites in which boys were accepted as men? And why are the king and his pages dressed as women? Is it meant to reflect how an armed band (either Matthias' or a much more ancient one) took its leader through enemy country in disguise, or is it a survival of some old pagan superstition according to which transvestism offers protection from evil spirits? And why is the king forbidden to utter a word throughout? And why is it called the Ride of the Kings when there is only one king involved? What does it all mean? No one knows. There are a number of hypotheses, none of them has been proved. The Ride of the Kings is a mysterious rite; no one knows what it means, what it wants to say, but just as Egyptian hieroglyphs are more beautiful to those who cannot read them (and perceive them as mere fanciful sketches), so too, perhaps, the Ride of the Kings is beautiful because the content of its communication has long since been lost and gestures, colors, words come more and more into the foreground, drawing attention to themselves and to their own aspect and shape.

And so, to my astonishment, the initial mistrust with which I watched the straggly departure of the Ride soon vanished, and all at once I was completely enthralled by the colorful cavalcade as it slowly moved from house to house; the loudspeakers had at last fallen silent, and all I could hear (apart from the occasional clatter of vehicles, which I had long been in the habit of filtering out) was the strange music of the heralds' rhymed calls.

I wanted to stand there, to close my eyes and just listen: I realized that here, in the middle of a Moravian village, I was hearing *verse*, verse in the primeval meaning of the word, verse unlike any I could ever hear on the radio or on television or on the stage, verse like a ceremonial rhythmic call on the border between speech and song, verse that moved me solely by the pathos of its meter, as it probably moved the audience when it resounded from the floor of the ancient amphitheaters. It was a music sublime and *polyphonic:* each of the heralds declaimed in a mono-tone, on the same note throughout, but each on a different pitch, so that the voices combined unwittingly into a chord; moreover, they did not all declaim at once; each started his call at a different moment, at a different house, so that the voices came to the ear from here and there, like a canon for several voices: one would be finishing, another halfway through, a third just beginning its invocation at its own different pitch.

The Ride of the Kings straggled down the main street (continually startled by the traffic), and then, at a corner, it split up, one wing continuing straight ahead while the other turned off into a little street; the first house was a small yellow cottage with a fence and a small garden of colorful flowers. The herald broke into humorous improvisa-tions: the cottage had a pretty *fountain,* and its mistress had a son like a *mountain;* there was in fact only a pump at the entrance, and the heavy-set woman of forty, obviously flattered by the title bestowed on her son, laughed and handed a banknote to the rider (the collector) calling out "For the king, my good woman, for the king!" No sooner had the collector dropped it in the basket fastened to his saddle than another herald called out to the woman that she was *fine and dandy* but he preferred her *wine and brandy;* making a cup of one hand, he bent his head back and pretended to drink. Everyone laughed, and the woman, both embarrassed and pleased, ran into the house; she must have foreseen it all, for she returned almost at once with a bottle and a glass for the horsemen.

While the king's retinue was drinking and joking, the king himself sat motionless and grave with his two pages a short distance away, as it is a king's lot to be draped in his gravity, to stand aloof in the midst of his clamorous troops. The pages' horses stood on either side of the king's, so close that the boots of all three nearly touched (the horses had large gingerbread hearts on their breasts, studded with tiny mirrors and trimmed with colored sugar; their brows were decked with paper roses and their manes woven with colored crepe paper ribbons). All three mute horsemen were in their women's clothes: wide skirts, starched puckered sleeves, and on the pages' heads richly ornamented bonnets; only the king had, instead of a bonnet, a silver diadem from which hung three long, wide ribbons, blue at the edges and red in the middle, which completely covered his face and gave him a solemn and mysterious appearance.

I was enchanted by this immobile trinity; twenty years ago I myself had sat on a garlanded horse just like them, but because I was seeing the Ride of the Kings *from within,* I hadn't seen a thing; only now did I really see it, and I couldn't tear my eyes away: the king (a few yards off) sat so straight he looked like a statue under guard, veiled in a flag; maybe, it suddenly occurred to me, maybe it wasn't a king at all, maybe it was a queen; maybe it was Queen Lucie who had come to reveal herself to me in her real form, because her *real* form was actually her *hidden* form.

And at the same moment it occurred to me that Kostka, who combined the obstinacy of reflection with the obstinacy of delusion, was an eccentric, that everything he had told me was possible but not certain; he knew Lucie, of course, he might even know a lot about her, but the main thing had escaped him: that soldier who wanted to have her in the borrowed miner's flat—Lucie really loved him; I could hardly take seriously the story of Lucie gathering those flowers out of some vague religious longing when I remember that she gathered them for me. And if she said not a word of this to Kostka, of this nor of the whole six tender months of our love, then she had kept a secret even from him, and even he did not know her; moreover, it was not clear that she had really moved to this town because of him; it could have been a mere coincidence, but it was also possible that she came here because of me, since she did after all know that it was my hometown. I felt that the account of that original rape was true, but I now had doubts about the precise circumstances: at times the story was colored by the sanguinary view of a man excited by sin, and at times by a blue so radiantly blue as only a man who keeps looking to heaven is capable of seeing; it was clear: in Kostka's narrative, truth and poetry were mixed, and it was nothing more than a new legend (perhaps closer to the truth, perhaps more beautiful, perhaps more profound) that now overlay the old one.

I looked at the veiled king and I saw Lucie riding (unrecognized and unrecognizable) ceremoniously (and mockingly) through my life. Then (in reaction to some odd external compulsion) my gaze slipped to the eyes of a smiling man who had evidently been watching me for some time. "Hello," he said, and came up to me. "Hello," I said. He held out his hand; I shook it. Then he turned and called to a girl I hadn't noticed until then. "What are you waiting for? Come on, I want to introduce you." The girl (tall, good-looking, with dark hair and dark eyes) came up and said: "Broz." She gave me her hand, and I said: "Jahn. Pleased to meet you." Jovially, the man exclaimed: "Well, old boy, it's been years!" It was Zemanek.

6

FATIGUE. Fatigue. I couldn't shake it off. The Ride had set off with the king for the village green and I followed slowly after it. I took deep breaths to overcome the fatigue. I stopped several times with the neighbors who'd come out of their cottages to gape. Suddenly I felt I was just another one of them. That my days of travel and adventure were over. That I was hopelessly bound to the two or three streets where I lived.

By the time I reached the green, the Ride had started down the long main street. I wanted to drag myself after it, but then I saw Ludvik. He was standing by himself on the grassy edge of the road looking thoughtfully at the riders. Damn Ludvik! I wish he'd go to hell! Up to now, he's been avoiding me, well, today I'm going to avoid him! Turning on my heels, I went over to a bench under an apple tree. I would sit and listen to the distant calls of the horsemen.

So there I sat, listening and watching. The Ride of the Kings gradually drifted away. It clung pitifully to the sides of the street, along which cars and motorcycles passed continually. A group of people were walking after it. A pathetically small group. From year to year fewer people come to the Ride. Though this year Ludvik is here. What is he doing here? Damn you, Ludvik! It's too late now. Too late for everything. You come like a bad omen. A dark omen. Seven crosses. Now of all times, when my Vladimir is king.

I looked away. There was only a handful of people left on the green, at the stands and at the tavern door. Most of them were drunk. Drunkards are the most loyal supporters of folk festivals. The last supporters. Once in a while, at least, they have a noble pretext for taking a drink.

Then old man Pechacek sat beside me on the bench. He said it wasn't like old times. I agreed. It wasn't. How beautiful the Rides must have been decades or centuries ago! They weren't as gaudy as they are today. Nowadays they're part kitsch, part fairground masquerade. Gingerbread hearts on the horses' breasts! Loads of paper garlands bought in department stores! The costumes were always colorful, but they used to be simple. The horses were adorned with just one red scarf, tied under the neck across the breast. And the king never had a mask of colored ribbons, just a veil. And he had a rose between his teeth. So he couldn't speak.

Yes, old man, it was better back then. No one had to run after young people who might graciously consent to take part in the Ride. No one had to spend days at meetings arguing over who would organize the Ride and who would receive the proceeds. The Ride of the Kings used to gush forth over the life of a village, like a spring. It would gallop from village to village gathering alms for its masked king. Sometimes it met up with another Ride in another village and there would be a battle. Both sides defended their kings ferociously. Knives and sabers would flash, blood flow. When one Ride captured another's king, they would drink themselves into a stupor at the expense of the king's father.

You're right, old man, you're right. Back when I rode as the king, during the occupation, it was different from today. And after the war too, it was still worth doing. We thought we were about to build a completely new world. That people would return to folk traditions. That even the Ride of the Kings would once again spring forth from the depths of their lives. We wanted to help this springing forth. We sweated to organize folk festivals. But a spring can't be organized. Either it gushes or it doesn't. Look, old man, now we're just wringing it out, our little songs, our Rides, everything. These are the last drops, the droplets, the very last.

Ah, well. The Ride had vanished. It had probably turned into some side street. But we could still hear the heralds. Their calls were magnificent. I closed my eyes and for a moment imagined myself living in another time. In another century. Long ago. And then I opened my eyes and told myself it was good after all that Vladimir was king. He is king of an almost extinct kingdom, but a most magnificent kingdom. A kingdom to which I will remain faithful to the end.

I stood up from the bench. Someone had greeted me. It was old Koutecky. I hadn't seen him in a long time. He had trouble walking and leaned on a cane. I'd never liked him, but his old age aroused my pity. "Where are you off to?" I asked. He said he took a constitutional every Sunday. "How did you like the Ride?" I asked him. He waved his hand. "Didn't even watch it." "Why not?" I asked. Again he waved his hand in annoyance, and it dawned on me then why he hadn't watched: Ludvik was among the spectators. Koutecky didn't want to see him any more than I did.

"Can't say that I blame you," I said. "My son's in the Ride, but even so I don't feel like trailing after it." "Your son? You mean Vladimir?" "Yes," I said, "he's the king." Koutecky said: "That's interesting." "Why?" I asked. "Very interesting," said Koutecky, his eyes lighting up. "Why is that?" I asked again. "Because Vladimir is with our Milos," said Koutecky. I had no idea who Milos was. Milos was his grandson, he told me, his daughter's son. "But that's impossible," I said, "I saw him, I saw him riding off on his horse!" "I saw him too. Milos went off with him from our place on his motorcycle," said the old man. "That doesn't make any sense!" I said, but then I asked: "Where were they going?" "If you don't know, I'm not going to be the one to tell you!" said Koutecky, taking his leave.

7

I HADN'T expected to meet Zemanek (Helena had told me he would be here, but not until the afternoon), and of course I found it extremely unpleasant. But what could I do? There he was, standing in front of me, looking just the way he used to look: his blond hair was as blond as ever, even though he no longer combed it back in long curls but wore it short and brushed fashionably forward over his forehead; he stood as erect as ever and still arched his neck back; he was still jovial and complacent, invulnerable, still enjoyed the favor of the angels and now also of a young girl whose beauty immediately reminded me of the painful imperfection of the body I had been with yesterday afternoon.

Hoping that our encounter would be brief, I tried to answer his banal questions with equally banal responses: he repeated that we hadn't seen each other for years, adding how surprising it was that after so long an interval we should meet "in this godforsaken hole"; I told him I was born here; he apologized and said that in that case it was certainly not all that forsaken; Miss Broz laughed. I didn't react to his jest, saying instead that I wasn't surprised to see him here because, if I remembered correctly, he'd always loved folklore; Miss Broz laughed again and said they hadn't come here for the Ride of the Kings; I asked her whether she had anything against the Ride of the Kings; she said it didn't interest her; I asked her why; she shrugged, and Zemanek said: "Ludvik, times have changed."

Meanwhile, the Ride of the Kings had moved one house farther, and two of the riders were struggling with their horses, which had become agitated. One rider shoved at the other, scolding him for failing to control his horse, and the cries of "idiot" and "moron" mingled rather drolly with the ritual of the festival. Miss Broz said: "Wouldn't it be

269

great if the horse bolted!" Zemanek laughed heartily at this, but by now the riders had managed to calm their horses down, and Hear ye, hear ye again resounded solemnly through the village.

As we followed the sounds of the Ride down a side street lined with gardens full of flowers, I was hunting in vain for some natural pretext for saying good-bye to Zemanek; I had to walk dutifully alongside his pretty companion and continue to trade remarks with her: I learned that in Bratislava, where they had been this morning, the weather was as nice as it was here; I learned that they had driven here in Zemanek's car and that just outside Bratislava they'd had to change the spark plugs; then I learned that Miss Broz was one of Zemanek's students. I knew from Helena that he gave courses in Marxism-Leninism at the university, but even so I asked him what he taught there. He told me he was teaching *philosophy* (his use of this word struck me as revealing; a few years ago he would still have said *Marxism*, but in recent years this subject had so declined in popularity, especially among the young, that Zemanek, for whom popularity had always been of paramount importance, delicately concealed Marxism behind the more general term). I expressed surprise, saying that if I remembered correctly, Zemanek had studied biology; this remark was a malicious allusion to the dilettantism of university teachers of Marxism who entered the field not so much through scholarly research but by serving as propagandists. Miss Broz now entered the conversation to announce that teachers of Marxism had a political pamphlet in their skulls instead of a brain, but that Pavel was entirely different. Pavel welcomed these words; he protested mildly, thereby demonstrating his modesty and at the same time provoking the young woman to further praise. In this way I learned that Zemanek was one of the most popular teachers and that his students worshiped him for not being liked by the university authorities: for always saying what he thought, for being courageous and sticking up for the young. Zemanek continued to protest mildly, and so I learned from his companion further details of the various battles Zemanek had fought in recent years: how the authorities had even wanted to throw him out for not sticking to the rigid, outdated curriculum and for trying to introduce the young people to everything going on in modern philosophy (they

claimed he had wanted to smuggle in "hostile ideology"); how he'd
saved a student from expulsion for some boyish prank (a dispute with a
policeman) that the chancellor (Zemanek's enemy) had characterized as
a *political* misdemeanor; how afterwards the female students had held a
secret poll to determine their favorite teacher, and how he had won it.
Zemanek had by now halted all attempts to stem the flood of praise, and
I said (with an irony, alas, hardly comprehensible to Miss Broz) that I
could see what she meant because, as I remembered it, Zemanek had
been enormously popular back in my own student days. Miss Broz
agreed enthusiastically: she wasn't in the least surprised, since Pavel was
a fabulous speaker and could cut any opponent to pieces in a debate.
"Yes, that's true," Zemanek admitted, laughing, "but even if I cut them
to pieces in a debate, they can cut me to pieces in different and more
effective ways."

In the vanity of this last remark I recognized the Zemanek I had
known; but its *content* staggered me: it was evident that he had completely abandoned his former views, and if he and I were now to frequent the same circles, in any conflict I would, like it or not, find myself
taking his side. This was horrible, it was what I least expected, even
though there was nothing miraculous about such a change in attitude;
on the contrary, it was very common, many others had undergone it, the
whole of society was undergoing it gradually. But it was precisely in
Zemanek that I had not expected this change; he was petrified in my
memory in the form in which I'd last seen him, and now I furiously
denied him the right to be other than the man I'd known.

There are people who claim to love humanity, while others object that
we can love only in the singular, that is, only individuals. I agree and add
that what goes for love also goes for hate. Man, this being pining for
equilibrium, balances the weight of the evil piled on his back with the
weight of his hatred. But try directing your hatred at mere abstract
principles, at injustice, fanaticism, cruelty, or, if you've managed to find
the human principle itself hateful, then try hating mankind! Such hatreds are beyond human capacity, and so man, if he wishes to relieve his
anger (aware as he is of its limited power) concentrates it on a single
individual.

That is why I was staggered. It suddenly occurred to me that any minute now, Zemanek would make use of his metamorphosis (which he had been suspiciously prompt to demonstrate to me) to ask my forgiveness in its name. That is what seemed so horrible. What would I tell him? How would I respond? How would I explain to him that I couldn't make peace with him? How would I explain that if I did I would immediately lose my inner balance? How would I explain that one of the arms of my internal scales would suddenly shoot upward? How would I explain that my hatred of him counterbalanced the weight of evil that had fallen on my youth? How would I explain that he embodied all the evils in my life? How would I explain to him that I *needed* to hate him?

8

HORSES CRAMMED their way into the narrow street. I saw the king from a few yards away. He was sitting on his horse apart from the others. Two other boys on horseback, his pages, were at his side. I was confused. He had Vladimir's slightly stooped back. He was sitting motionless, almost indifferent. Is it he? Maybe. But it might just as well be someone else.

I worked my way closer to him. It would be impossible not to recognize him. Didn't I know by heart the way he held himself, his every gesture? I love him, and love has its own instincts!

Now I was standing right beside him. I could have called to him. That would have been so simple. But it would have been no use. The king must not speak.

Then the Ride swept on to the next house. Now I would know him! The horse's sudden motion would force him to move in some way that would betray him. As the horse stepped forward, the king did in fact straighten up slightly, but the movement gave me no indication of who was behind the veil. The garish ribbons across his face were hopelessly opaque.

9

T HE RIDE of the Kings had advanced past a few more houses, and we
continued to follow behind while our conversation moved on to other
topics: Miss Broz had shifted from Zemanek to herself and was holding
forth on how she loved hitchhiking. She spoke about it with such
emphasis (somewhat affected) that I could see at once that I was hearing
the *manifesto of her generation*. Every generation has its own set of
passions, loves, and interests, which it professes with a certain tenacity,
to differentiate it from older generations and to confirm itself in its
uniqueness. Submitting to a generation mentality (to this pride of the
herd) has always repelled me. After Miss Broz had developed her provocative argument (I've now heard it at least fifty times from people her
age) that all mankind is divided into those who give hitchhikers lifts
(human people who love adventure) and those who don't (inhuman
people who fear life), I jokingly called her a "dogmatist of the hitch."
She answered sharply that she was neither dogmatist nor revisionist nor
sectarian nor deviationist, that those were all words of ours, that we had
invented them, that they belonged to us, and that they were completely
alien to them.

"Yes," said Zemanek, "they're different. Fortunately, they're different! Even their vocabulary is different. They don't care about our suc-
cesses or our failures. You won't believe this, but on the university
entrance exams these young people don't even know what the Moscow
Trials were. Stalin is just a name to them. And imagine, most of them
have no idea that there were political trials in Prague!"

"That's what seems so terrible to me," I said.

"It doesn't reflect well on their education. But for them there's liberation in it. They've simply not admitted our world into their consciousness. They've rejected it altogether."

"Blindness has given way to blindness."

"I wouldn't say that. They impress me. I admire them exactly because they're different. They love their bodies. We neglected ours. They love to travel. We stayed put. They love adventure. We lived our lives at meetings. They love jazz. We insipidly imitated folk music. They're devoted to themselves. We wanted to save the world. With our messianism we nearly destroyed it. Maybe they with their selfishness will save it."

10

How is it possible? The king! That upright figure on his horse, veiled in bright colors! How many times have I seen him, how many times have I imagined him! The most intimate image of all! And now that it's turned into reality, all intimacy is gone. Suddenly it's just a larva daubed with paint, and I don't know what's inside. But what is there of intimacy in the real world other than my king?

My son. The person nearest to me. I stand in front of him, and I don't know whether it is he or not. What, then, do I know if I don't know even that? Of what am I sure in this world if I don't have even that certainty?

I I

W HILE ZEMANEK delivered himself of his eulogy of the younger
generation, I contemplated Miss Broz and found her to my sorrow a
handsome and likable young woman; I felt envious regret that she
wasn't mine. She was walking alongside Zemanek, talking away, taking
his arm every other second, turning confidentially towards him, and I
was reminded (as I am reminded more often every year) that since
Lucie I'd had no girl I loved and respected. Life had mocked me by
sending me a reminder of that failure precisely in the features of the
mistress of the man whom only the day before I thought I'd defeated in
a grotesque sexual combat.

The more I liked Miss Broz, the more I realized how completely she
shared the mentality of her contemporaries, for whom I and my contemporaries merged into a single indistinct mass, all deformed by the
same incomprehensible jargon, the same overpoliticized thinking, the
same anxieties, the same bizarre experiences from some dark and already distant era.

At that moment, I suddenly understood that the similarity between
myself and Zemanek did not lie merely in the fact that Zemanek had
changed his views and thus drawn nearer to mine; the similarity was
deeper and affected our destinies *as a whole:* in the eyes of Miss Broz
and her contemporaries we were alike even when we were at each
other's throats. I suddenly felt that if I were forced to tell Miss Broz the
story of my expulsion from the Party, it would seem to her remote and
too *literary* (yes, the subject has been dealt with in too many bad
novels), and that in this story both I and Zemanek, both my thinking
and his, would seem equally unlikable (equally twisted, equally monstrous). I saw the conciliatory waters of time, which, as we all know,

can efface the differences between entire eras, let alone between two puny individuals, closing over our quarrel, which I had felt was still contemporary and alive. But I fought tooth and nail against the reconciliation offered by time; I do not live in eternity; I am anchored to the thirty-seven years of my own life, and I have no wish to be detached from them (as Zemanek detached himself when he was so quick to embrace the mentality of his juniors), no, I will not shirk my fate, I will not detach myself from my thirty-seven years even if they represent so insignificant and fleeting a fragment of time that it is already being forgotten, has been forgotten.

And were Zemanek to lean over toward me confidentially, start talking about the past, and ask for reconciliation, I would refuse; yes, I would refuse that reconciliation even if Miss Broz interceded, and all her contemporaries, and time itself.

12

FATIGUE. Suddenly I wanted to say good-bye to it all. To go away and stop worrying. I have no wish to remain in this world of material things that I don't understand, that deceive me. There still exists another world. A world where I am at home and with which I am familiar. There is the path, the wild rosebush, the deserter, the wandering minstrel, and Mother.

But in the end I took hold of myself. I must. I must take my quarrel with the world of material things to its conclusion. I must look into the very abyss of all errors and deceptions.

Should I ask someone? The horsemen of the Ride? And make myself a laughingstock? I remembered this morning. The robing of the king. And at once I knew where I must go.

13

OUR PAUPER KING, a righteous one, the horsemen were calling from a few houses farther on, and we followed them. The richly beribboned rumps of the horses, blue, pink, green, and violet, bobbed up and down in front of us. Zemanek suddenly pointed in their direction: "There's Helena." I looked over to where he was pointing, but all I could see was the colorful bodies of the horses. Zemanek pointed again. "There!" Then I saw her, half hidden behind a horse, and I felt myself blush: the way Zemanek had pointed her out (not as "my wife," but as "Helena") showed that he knew I knew her.

Helena was standing on the edge of the sidewalk holding a microphone in her outstretched hand; a wire ran from the microphone to a tape recorder that hung over the shoulder of a youth in a leather jacket and jeans, with earphones over his ears. We stopped not far from them. Zemanek said (abruptly and casually) that Helena was a wonderful woman, that she still looked fabulous and was very capable as well, and that he wasn't surprised we'd hit it off.

I felt my cheeks burn: Zemanek hadn't intended his remark as an attack, on the contrary, he had said it in a most affable tone, and I was also left in no doubt as to the real state of things by the way Miss Broz was looking at me, with significant, smiling glances, as if bent on showing that she was fully informed and perfectly sympathetic, better still, in complicity.

Meanwhile, Zemanek continued his casual references to his wife, making it plain (by hints and innuendos) that he knew everything but didn't object, since he was perfectly liberal when it came to Helena's private life; to give his words an air of nonchalance, he pointed to the youth with the tape recorder and said that the boy there ("Doesn't he look like a gigantic beetle with those earphones?") had been danger-ously in love with Helena for two years and I ought to keep an eye on him. Miss Broz laughed and asked how old he was two years ago. Seventeen, said Zemanek, old enough to fall in love. Then he added jokingly that Helena wasn't a cradle-robber, that she was a virtuous woman, but that a boy like that would grow more furious the less successful he was and would surely put up a fight. Miss Broz added (in the spirit of meaningless banter) that I looked as though I could handle him.

"I'm not so sure about that," said Zemanek with a smile.

"Don't forget that I worked in the mines. I still have some of those muscles left." I wanted to say something insignificant and wasn't aware that this reminder would overstep the bounds of banter.

"You worked in the mines?" asked Miss Broz.

"These twenty-year-olds," Zemanek went on, sticking doggedly to his topic, "are really dangerous in a gang. If they don't like you, you're in for it."

"How long?" asked Miss Broz.

"Five years," I said.

"When was that?"

"I got out nine years ago."

"Oh, that's ancient history, your muscles are all flabby by now," she said, wanting to add her own little quip to the friendly banter. But I was thinking at that moment that my muscles were not flabby, that I was still in excellent shape, and that I could certainly beat up the blond man I was chatting with—but that (most important and most depress-ing) I had nothing but my muscles to rely on in order to settle our old score.

Again I pictured Zemanek turning to me with a smile and asking me to forget everything that had happened between us, and I felt I'd been double-crossed: Zemanek's plea for forgiveness would be supported not only by his change of views, not only by time, not only by Miss Broz and her contemporaries, but by Helena too (yes, now they were all on his side!), because if Zemanek forgave me her adultery, it was merely a bribe for me to forgive him.

When I saw (in my imagination) his face of a blackmailer sure of his powerful allies, I felt such a desire to hit him that I could actually see myself in the act. The riders were shouting, whirling around, the sun was splendidly golden, Miss Broz was making some remark, and before my furious eyes the blood was running down his face.

Yes, this was what I imagined; but what would I really do if he were to ask me to forgive him?

I realized with horror that I would do nothing.

Meanwhile we'd made our way over to Helena and her technician, who was removing his earphones. "Have you already met?" she asked, surprised to see me with Zemanek.

"We've known each other for a long time," he said.

"How?" She was astonished.

"We've known each other since our student days: we were in the same department at the university," Zemanek explained, and I had the impression that he was leading me up the last steps towards that ignominious place (like the scaffold) where he would ask me for my forgiveness.

"Heavens, what a coincidence!" said Helena.

"It happens all the time," said the technician, to remind them of his existence.

"I haven't introduced you," Helena said to me. "This is Jindra."

I shook hands with Jindra (an unattractive freckled youth) and Zemanek said to Helena, "Miss Broz and I had intended to take you back with us, but now I see that wouldn't suit you, that you'd rather go back with Ludvik . . ."

"You're coming with us?" asked the youth in jeans, sounding less than friendly.

"Is your car here?" Zemanek asked me.

"I haven't got a car," I answered.

"Then you can go with them," he said.

"I go eighty!" said the youth in jeans. "If that scares you . . ."

"Jindra!" Helena rebuked him.

"You could come with us," said Zemanek, "but I suspect you prefer your new friend to your old one." As if in passing, he had referred to me as his *friend*, and I was certain that the humiliating reconciliation was only a few steps away; moreover, Zemanek had fallen silent for a moment, as if hesitating, as if he wanted to take me off for a private talk (I hung my head as if to lay it on the block), but I was mistaken: Zemanek looked at his watch and said: "We don't have much time because we have to be in Prague by five. We'll just have to say good-bye! Ciao, Helena!" He shook her hand. "Ciao," he said to me and to the sound technician, and shook our hands too. Miss Broz also shook hands with everyone, and then, arm in arm, they left.

They left. I couldn't tear my eyes off them: Zemanek walking erect, his blond head proudly (victoriously) held high, the brunette at his side; even from the back she was beautiful, she walked lightly, I liked her; I liked her almost painfully, because her departing beauty showed me its icy *indifference*, just like Zemanek (with his affability, garrulity, memory, and conscience), just like my entire past, the past I had made a rendezvous with in my hometown in order to be avenged on it, the past that had strolled by me unseeing, as if it didn't know me.

I was stifled by humiliation and shame. I wanted nothing more than to disappear, go off by myself, wipe out the whole story, the stupid joke, wipe out Helena and Zemanek, wipe out the day before yesterday, yesterday, and today, wipe it all out, so that not a trace remained. "Would you mind if I had a word with Mrs. Zemanek in private?" I asked the sound technician.

I took Helena aside; she wanted to explain something, muttered something about Zemanek and his girl, a confused apology for having had to tell him everything; but nothing interested me at this moment; I was filled with a single desire: to get away, away from here and from the whole of this story; to draw a line through it all. I knew I had no right to deceive Helena any longer; she was innocent with respect to me and I had acted vilely, having turned her into a mere object, into a stone I had tried (and failed) to throw at someone else. I was stifled by the ridiculous failure of my vengeance, and I was determined to put an end to it all, at least now, when it was certainly too late, but nevertheless before it became more than too late. However, it was no use trying to explain everything to her: not only would I have hurt her with the truth, but she would hardly have been able to understand it. So all I could do was to repeat several times that this was our last time together, that I wouldn't be seeing her again, that I didn't love her, and that she must understand this.

It was far worse than I'd foreseen: Helena went pale, started shaking, wouldn't believe me, wouldn't let me go; I went through a minor martyrdom before I could finally get rid of her and leave.

14

A**LL AROUND ME** there were horses and streamers, and I stood
there, stood and stood, and then Jindra came up and took my hand and
squeezed it and asked me what's the matter, what's wrong, and I let
him hold my hand and said, nothing, Jindra, nothing at all, and my
voice sounded like someone else's, strangely high, and then I started
talking very fast about what we still needed to tape, we've got the calls,
we've got two interviews, I still have the commentary to do, so I went
on about things I couldn't possibly keep my mind on, and he stood
there silent beside me, crushing my hand.

He'd never touched me before, he was always too shy, but everyone
knew he was in love with me, and now he was standing beside me and
crushing my hand, and I was babbling on about the program and I
wasn't thinking about it, I was thinking about Ludvik, and then also,
it's funny, I found myself wondering what I looked like to Jindra,
whether the shock had made me look hideous, maybe not, I hope not, I
wasn't crying, I'm just edgy, that's all. . . .

Listen, Jindra, leave me alone for a moment, I'll go write the commentary and then we can tape it, he wouldn't let go and kept asking
gently what's the matter, Helena, what's the matter? but I twisted away
from him and went over to the District Committee building where
we'd borrowed a room, I went there, at last I was alone, an empty
room, I collapsed on the chair and put my head on the table and didn't
move. I had a terrible headache. I opened my bag to see if there was
anything I could take for it, I don't know why I opened it because I
knew I had nothing, but then I remembered that Jindra carries a whole
pharmacy with him, his trenchcoat was hanging on the clothes tree, I
rummaged through his pockets, and sure enough I found a small

bottle of some sort, yes, it was for headaches, toothaches, sciatica, and neuritis, it wasn't for illness of the soul, but at least it would ease my head.

I found a faucet in a corner of the room next door, put some water in an empty mustard jar, and took two tablets. Two, that's enough, that should help, of course Algena can't help me with the illness of my soul, unless I swallow all the tablets in the bottle, because it's poisonous in massive doses, and Jindra's bottle is nearly full, maybe it would be enough.

It was only an idea, a sudden flash, but it kept coming back to me, and I couldn't help thinking, why am I alive, what good is there in going on, but it's not true really, I didn't think anything of the sort, I was hardly thinking at all, I just imagined myself no longer alive and suddenly I felt such bliss, such strange bliss that I wanted to laugh and maybe really did begin to laugh.

I put two more tablets on my tongue, I had no intention of poisoning myself, I merely squeezed the bottle in my palm and said to myself *I'm holding my death in my hand*, and I was enthralled by so much opportunity, it was like going step by step to an abyss, not to jump into it, just to look down. I refilled the glass with water, swallowed the tablets, and went back to our room, the window was open, and the sound of Hear ye, hear ye was still resonating in the distance, but mixed with the racket of the cars, the trucks, and those filthy motorcycles, they drown out everything beautiful, everything I've believed in and lived for, the racket was unbearable, the helpless feebleness of the voices was unbearable, and so I closed the window and again I felt the long, lingering pain in my soul.

Through all our life together, Pavel never hurt me as you, Ludvik, as you did in a single minute, I forgive Pavel, I understand him, his flame is quickly consumed, he has to seek new pastures and a new audience and a new public, he hurt me, but now through this fresh pain I see him without malice, as a mother might, as a bully, a show-off, I smile at his attempts through the years to wriggle out of my embrace, ah! go then, Pavel, go then, you I understand, but you, Ludvik, I don't understand, you came to me in a mask, you came to resurrect me, and once resurrected, to destroy me, you I curse, only you, I curse you and at the same time I ask you to come, to come to me and have mercy.

God, maybe it's just some terrible misunderstanding, maybe Pavel told you something when you were alone together, I don't know, I asked you about it, I begged you to explain why you don't love me anymore, I didn't want to let you go, four times I held you back, but you didn't want to listen, you just said it was all over, finished, finished, definitely, irrevocably, all right, finished, in the end I agreed, in a high soprano voice as if it was somebody else talking, some girl before puberty, and I said in this high-pitched voice, *have a good trip then*, it's funny, I don't know why I wished you a good trip, but it kept tumbling off my tongue: have a good trip, have a good trip then. . . .

Maybe you don't know how much I love you, surely you don't know how much I love you, maybe you think I'm just another married woman looking for an adventure, and you don't understand that you're my destiny, my life, my everything. . . . Maybe you'll find me here lying under a white sheet and then you'll understand you've killed the most precious thing you ever had in your life . . . or you'll come, oh my God, and I'll still be alive, and you'll be able to save me again and you'll be kneeling and crying, and I'll stroke your hands, your hair, and I'll forgive you, I'll forgive you everything. . . .

15

T HERE WAS really nothing else to do, I had to sweep away that bad story, that bad joke which, not content with itself, had gone on monstrously multiplying itself into more and more silly jokes, I not only wanted to wipe out the entire day, which came about by inadvertence, simply because I had overslept and missed my train, but I also wanted to wipe out everything leading up to that day, the whole stupid conquest of Helena, which too was based simply on error.

I hurried away as if I could hear Helena's pursuing footsteps behind me, and I thought: even if I were able to wipe these few pointless days out of my life, what good would that do, when the *entire* story of my life was conceived in error, through the bad joke of the postcard, that accident, that nonsense? And I was horrified at the thought that things conceived in error are just as real as things conceived with good reason and of necessity.

How glad I would be to revoke the whole story of my life! Yet how could I do so by my own exertions when the errors it stemmed from were not only *my own? Who,* in fact, made the error when the silly joke of my postcard was taken seriously? Who made the error when Alexej's father (by now long since rehabilitated, but no less dead for it) was arrested and sentenced? The errors were so common and universal that they didn't represent exceptions or faults in the order of things; on the contrary, they constituted that order. What was it, then, that was mistaken? History itself? History the divine, the rational? But why call them history's *errors?* They seem so to my human reason, but if history really has its own reason, why should that reason care about human understanding, and why should it be as serious as a schoolmarm? What if history plays jokes? And then I realized how powerless I was to revoke my own joke when throughout my life as a whole I was involved in a joke much more vast (all-embracing for me) and utterly irrevocable.

On the deserted village green (now silent because the Ride was making its rounds at the other end of the village), I saw a large sign leaning against a wall and announcing in red letters that today at four in the afternoon a cimbalom band would be giving a concert in the garden of a certain restaurant. Next to the placard was the door to this restaurant, and since it was lunchtime and I had almost two hours before my bus was due to leave, I went inside.

16

I WANTED so much to move just an inch nearer the abyss, I wanted to
lean over the railing and look down into it, as if it could bring me solace
and reconciliation, as if down there, down there at least, if nowhere
else, down there at the bottom of the abyss we might find each other
and be together, without misunderstandings, without malicious people, without aging, without sorrow, forevermore. . . . I went into the
other room again, still with only the four tablets inside me, that's
nothing, I'm still a long way from the abyss, I can't even touch the
railing. I poured the remaining tablets into my palm. Then I heard a
door open in the corridor, I was startled and I stuffed the tablets into
my mouth and gulped them down, it was too much all at once, and I
felt them lumped painfully in my throat, even when I had drunk as
much as I could.

It was Jindra, he asked me how the commentary was coming along
and suddenly I was another person, the confusion had left me, that
high-pitched alien voice was gone, and I was purposeful and decisive.
Please, Jindra, I'm glad you're here, I'd like you to do something for
me. He blushed and said that he'd do anything for me and that he was
glad I felt all right again. Yes, I'm all right now, just wait a minute, I
want to write a few words, and I sat down and took some paper, and
wrote. Ludvik, my dearest, I loved you· body and soul, and now my
body and soul have no reason to live. Farewell, I love you, Helena. I
didn't even reread what I'd written, Jindra sat facing me, watching me,
unaware of what I was writing, I quickly folded the paper and wanted
to put it in an envelope, but there were no envelopes anywhere, Jindra,
do you have an envelope?

Jindra calmly went over to the cabinet by the table, opened it, and began rummaging in it, at any other time I'd have told him off for rummaging through other people's things, but at that moment I wanted an envelope quickly, he gave me one, it had the District Committee letterhead on it, I put my letter inside, sealed it, and wrote Ludvik Jahn on the front, Jindra, do you remember the man who was with us when my husband and that girl were there, yes, that's right, the dark one, I can't leave now and I'd like you to find him and give him this.

Again he took my hand, poor boy, I don't know what he was thinking, how he interpreted my excitement, he could never have guessed what it was about, he just sensed there was something bad happening to me, he crushed my hand again, and all of a sudden I felt terribly pitiful, and he bent down and took me in his arms and pressed his lips against mine, I wanted to resist him, but he held me tight and it went through my mind that this was the last man I would ever kiss in my life, that this was my last kiss, and suddenly I was frantic and I held him too and clasped him and opened my lips and felt his tongue on my tongue and his hands on my body, and in that moment I had a giddy feeling that now I was completely free and that nothing mattered anymore, because I'd been deserted by everyone and my world had crumbled and that's why I was completely free and could do what I liked, I was free like the girl we threw out of the radio station, there was no longer anything distinguishing her from me, my world was in pieces, I could never put it together again, I no longer had any reason to be faithful, or anybody to be faithful to, suddenly I was completely free, just like that girl from the station, that little whore who was in a different bed every night, if I went on living, I too would be in a different bed every night, I felt Jindra's tongue in my mouth, I was free, I knew I could make love to him, I wanted to make love to him, make love to him anywhere, here on the table or on the bare wooden floor, now, at once and without delay, to make love for the last time, to make love before the end, but Jindra had already drawn back, smiling proudly, and said he was off and would soon return.

17

T HE WAITER DASHED around the little room with its five or six tables, thick with smoke and people, bearing on his outstretched arm a large tray heaped with plates, on which I could just make out portions of wiener schnitzel and potato salad (apparently the only Sunday dish), and rudely pushing his way between people and tables, he rushed out of the room and into the corridor. I followed him and found an open door at the end of the corridor leading into the restaurant garden, where people were also eating. At the back, under a linden tree, was an unoccupied table; here I sat down.

The touching Hear ye, hear ye resounded over the village roofs from such a distance now that by the time it reached the garden, surrounded by the walls of the neighboring houses, it sounded only half real. And this seeming unreality made me think that everything around me was not the present but the past, a past fifteen, twenty years old, that Hear ye, hear ye was the past, Lucie was the past, Zemanek was the past, and Helena was just a stone I had wanted to throw at that past; the whole of these three days had been nothing but a theatre of shadows.

What? Just these three days? My entire life, it seemed to me, had always been overpopulated by shadows, and there was little room in it for the present. I imagine a moving walkway (that is, time) and on it a man (that is, myself) who is running in the direction opposite to the direction the walkway takes; the walkway, however, is moving faster than I and is thus slowly taking me farther away from the goal I am heading for; that goal (odd goal, situated in the *back!*) is the past of the political trials, the past of lecture halls where hands are raised, the past of fear, the past of black insignias and of Lucie, the past that bewitches me, that I am trying to decipher, unravel, undo, and that prevents me from living as a man should live, with his head facing forward.

And then there's the bond with which I want to tie myself to the past that hypnotizes me, and this bond is vengeance, but vengeance, as these three days have demonstrated, is just as futile as my running against the moving walkway of time. Yes, it was when Zemanek was reading from Fucik's *Notes from the Gallows* in the lecture hall that I should have gone up to him and punched him in the face, then and only then. When it is postponed, vengeance is transformed into something deceptive, into a personal religion, into a myth that recedes day by day from the people involved, who remain the same in the myth though in reality (the walkway is in constant motion) they long ago became different people: today another Jahn stands before another Zemanek, and the blow that I still owe him can be neither revived nor reconstructed, it is definitely lost.

I cut into the large pancake of schnitzel on my plate, and again the Hear ye, hear ye reached my ears, carrying faintly and nostalgically across the village roofs; I imagined the veiled king and his cavalry, and my heart contracted at the incomprehensibility of human gestures:

For many centuries, just like today, young men have been riding forth in Moravian villages with strange messages in some unknown language that they pronounce with a touching loyalty without understanding it. Some long-dead people certainly had something important to say, and today they are reborn in their descendants like deaf-and-dumb orators speaking to the audience in beautiful and incomprehensible gestures. Their message will never be decoded, not only because there is no key to it, but also because people have no patience to listen to it in an age when the accumulation of messages old and new is such that their voices cancel one another out. Today history is no more than a thin thread of the remembered stretching over an ocean of the forgotten, but time moves on, and an epoch of millennia will come which the inextensible memory of the individual will be unable to encompass; whole centuries and millennia will therefore fall away, centuries of paintings and music, centuries of discoveries, of battles, of books, and this will be dire, because man will lose the notion of his self, and his history, unfathomable, unencompassable, will shrivel into a few schematic signs destitute of all sense. Thousands of deaf-and-dumb Rides of Kings will set out with their piteous and incomprehensible messages, and no one will have the time to hear them out.

I sat in a corner of the garden restaurant over my empty plate, having eaten my schnitzel without realizing it, and I saw that I too (right now, already!) had been included in this inescapable and boundless forgetting. The waiter came, took my plate, stopped to brush a few crumbs off my tablecloth, and hurried to another table. I was seized with regret about this day, not only because it had been futile, but because not even its futility would remain, it would be forgotten along with this table, along with the fly buzzing around my head, along with the yellow pollen scattered on the tablecloth by the flowering linden, along with the slow, indifferent service that is so characteristic of the society I live in, even that society would be forgotten, and even its mistakes and errors and injustices that had hypnotized me, that I had suffered from, that I was consumed by, and that I had vainly attempted to redress, to punish, and to undo—vainly, because what had happened had happened and could never be redressed.

Yes, suddenly I saw it clearly: most people deceive themselves with a pair of faiths: they believe in *eternal memory* (of people, things, deeds, nations) and in *redressibility* (of deeds, mistakes, sins, wrongs). Both are false faiths. In reality the opposite is true: everything will be forgotten and nothing will be redressed. The task of obtaining redress (by vengeance or by forgiveness) will be taken over by forgetting. No one will redress the wrongs that have been done, but all wrongs will be forgotten.

I took another careful look around me, because I knew that the linden tree would be forgotten, and the people at that table, and the waiter (weary after his last stint of running around), and this restaurant, which (uninviting from the street) was on the garden side quite pleasantly overgrown with trellised grapevines. I looked at the open door to the corridor, into which the waiter (the tired heart of the now all but deserted, silent nook) had just vanished, and from which (as soon as the darkness had swallowed him) now emerged a youth in leather jacket and jeans; he stepped into the garden and looked around; then he saw me and headed in my direction; several seconds passed before I recognized him as Helena's sound technician.

I always experience distress when a loving and unloved woman threatens to come back, so when the youth gave me the envelope ("It's from Mrs. Zemanek"), my first wish was somehow to postpone reading it. I told him to take a seat; he complied (leaning on one elbow and squinting contentedly at the sun-drenched linden tree), and I put the envelope on the table and said: "How about a drink?"

He shrugged his shoulders; I suggested vodka, but he refused, saying that he would be driving; he added that if I wanted one, he would be happy to watch. I didn't, but since the envelope was lying on the table in front of me, and I didn't want to open it, any alternative seemed welcome. I asked the waiter as he went past to bring me a vodka.

"You don't happen to know what Helena wants, do you?" I said.

"How should I know? Read the letter," he replied.

"Anything urgent?"

"Do you think she made me memorize it in case I was attacked?"

I picked up the envelope (it had the official letterhead of the District Committee on it); then I put it back on the table in front of me and, not knowing what to say, remarked, "Too bad you're not drinking."

"After all, it's for *your* safety too," he said. The hint was clear: the youth wanted to clarify his return trip and his chances of being alone with Helena. He was not unpleasant; on his face (small, pale, and freckled, with a short, turned-up nose) one could read everything going on inside him; perhaps what made it so transparent was its incorrigible childishness (I say incorrigible because its abnormally tiny features were not the type that age makes any more virile, it only makes an old man's face the face of a child grown old). Such a childish appearance can't please a youth of twenty, because at that age it disqualifies him, so that the only thing he can do is to disguise it in every way possible (just as it was disguised by—oh, that eternal theatre of shadows!—the boy commander): by his dress (his leather jacket was broad-shouldered, well-cut, and well-sewn) and by his behavior (he was self-assured, a trifle rude, at times casually indifferent). Unfortunately for him, he continually betrayed himself in this disguise: he blushed, he couldn't quite control his voice, which at the slightest excitement tended to break (as I'd noticed when we first met), he couldn't even control his eyes and his gestures (he had wanted to indicate his unconcern about whether I was going to Prague with them or not, but when I now assured him I'd be staying here, his eyes too obviously gleamed).

When the waiter brought two vodkas to the table by mistake, the youth waved his hand and said there was no need to take one away. "I wouldn't leave you to drink alone," he said, and raised his glass. "To your health!"

"And to yours!" I said, and we clinked glasses.

We started talking and I learned that the youth was expecting to leave in about two hours, because Helena wanted to go over the material they had taped and add her commentary where necessary, so that the whole thing could be broadcast tomorrow. I asked what it was like working with Helena. Again he blushed and answered that Helena knew what she was doing but was too tough on her crew, since she was always ready to work overtime and disregarded the fact that others might be in a hurry to get home. I asked him if he was in a hurry to get home. He said he wasn't; he was enjoying himself here. Then, taking advantage of the fact that I had started talking about Helena, he asked with a casual air: "How do you know Helena?" I told him and he pressed on. "She's really great, isn't she?"

Particularly when the conversation turned to Helena, he tried to look happy, which I again ascribed to his wish for a disguise, since his hopeless adoration of Helena was evidently common knowledge and he was obliged to do everything he could to avoid wearing the infamous crown of the unrequited lover. So although I didn't take his serenity altogether seriously, it did something to lighten the load of the letter lying before me, and I finally picked it up and opened it: "body and soul . . . no reason to live. Farewell . . ."

I saw the waiter at the other end of the garden and shouted: "The check, please!" The waiter nodded, but refusing to be deflected from his orbit, he vanished into the corridor.

"Come on. There's no time to lose," I told the youth. I stood up and hurried across the garden; he followed me. We went down the corridor and reached the exit, so that the waiter, like it or not, had to run after us.

"A schnitzel, soup, two vodkas," I dictated.

"What's going on?" asked the youth in a subdued voice.

I paid the waiter and told the youth to take me quickly to Helena. We set off at a brisk pace.

"What's happened?" he asked.

"How far is it?" I asked in return.

He pointed some distance ahead of us, and I broke into a run. The District Committee building was a whitewashed one-story structure with a gate and two windows facing the street. We went inside; we found ourselves in an uninviting sort of office: under the window were two desks drawn close together; on one of them lay the tape recorder, open, next to a pad of paper and a woman's handbag (yes, it was Helena's); there were chairs at both desks and a metal clothes tree in a corner. Two coats were hanging on it: Helena's blue raincoat and a man's dirty trenchcoat.

"This is it," said the youth.

"Is this where she gave you the letter?"

"Yes."

But the office was now hopelessly empty; I called out: "Helena!" and was alarmed to hear how uneasy and apprehensive my voice sounded. There was no response. I called out again: "Helena!" and the youth asked:

"Do you think she's . . . ?"

"Looks like it," I said.

"Is that what the letter was about?"

"Yes," I said. "Did they give you any other rooms?"

"No."

"What about the hotel?"

"We checked out this morning."

"She must be here then," I said, and now I heard the youth's voice break as he called anxiously: "Helena!"

I opened the door to the adjacent room; it was another office: desk, wastepaper basket, three chairs, cabinet, and clothes tree (the clothes tree was the same as the one in the first office: a metal pole standing on three legs and spreading upward into three metal branches; because there were no coats hanging on it, it looked human, orphan-like; its metallic nakedness and ridiculously raised arms filled me with anxiety); there was a window over the desk, otherwise just the bare walls; no other door; the two offices were evidently the only rooms in the building.

We went back to the first room; I took the pad off the desk and thumbed through it; there were some almost illegible notes for (judging from the few words I managed to read) a description of the Ride of the Kings; no message, no further parting words. I opened the handbag: there was a handkerchief, a wallet, lipstick, powder, two loose cigarettes, a lighter; no medicine bottle, no poison vial. I tried feverishly to think what Helena could have done, and the likeliest thing seemed to be poison; but in that case there should have been a little bottle somewhere. I went to the clothes tree and rummaged through the pockets of the raincoat: they were empty.

"What about the attic?" the youth said impatiently, having apparently concluded that my search of the room, though it had lasted only a few seconds, was getting us nowhere. We ran into the hallway and saw two doors: one had a glass pane that gave an indistinct view of the back courtyard; we opened the other one, the nearer one, behind which appeared a stone stairway, dark and covered with a layer of dust and soot. We ran up the stairs; we were enveloped in darkness; there was only a single dormer window in the roof (with filthy glass), through which came a dull gray light. All around us we could make out the shapes of every kind of junk (boxes, garden tools, hoes, spades, rakes as well as heaps of documents and an old broken chair); we kept tripping over it.

I wanted to call out "Helena!" but was stopped by fear; I was afraid of the silence that would follow. The youth didn't call out either. We threw the junk around and groped in the dark corners in silence; I could feel how agitated we both were. And the worst source of fear was our silence, by which we were admitting that we no longer expected any answer from Helena, that we were now merely looking for her body, whether hanging or sprawled.

We found nothing, however, and went back down to the office. I checked everything again, desks, chairs, and the clothes tree with her raincoat held by its raised arm, and again in the other room: desk, chairs, the clothes tree with its empty arms raised despairingly. The youth called out (for no reason) "Helena!" and I (for no reason) opened the cabinet, revealing shelves full of documents, writing materials, adhesive tape, and rulers.

"There's got to be somewhere else! A toilet! Or a cellar!" I said, and we went out into the hallway again; the youth opened the door to the courtyard. The courtyard was small; there was a cage of rabbits in one corner; beyond it was an overgrown garden with fruit trees rising from the thick uncut grass (in some remote corner of my mind I was just capable of noticing that the garden was beautiful: bits of blue sky hanging among the green of the branches, the trunks of the trees rough and crooked, and a few bright yellow sunflowers shining between them); at the end of the garden, in the idyllic shade of an apple tree, I saw a wooden shack, a country outhouse. I hurled myself towards it.

The revolving wooden latch, fastened to the narrow frame by a large nail (so that the door could be closed from the outside by turning the latch to the horizontal position), was vertical. I inserted my fingers in the gap between the frame and the door, and, applying gentle pressure, determined that the toilet was locked from inside; this could mean only one thing: Helena was inside. I said quietly: "Helena, Helena!" There was no reply; only the apple tree, stirring in the gentle breeze, rustling its branches against the wooden wall of the shack.

I knew that the silence from the locked shack meant the worst, but I also knew that the only course was to rip the door off and that I was the one who had to do it. Again I inserted my fingers in the gap between the frame and the door and pulled with all my might. The door (fastened not by a hook but, as is often the case in the country, by a mere bit of string) gave way at once and swung wide open. Facing me on the wooden seat, in the stench of the outhouse, sat Helena. She was pale but alive. She looked up at me with terrified eyes and instinctively tugged at her turned-up skirt, which despite her best efforts hardly came halfway down her thighs; she gripped the hem with both hands and pressed her legs tightly together. "For God's sake, go away!" she cried in anguish.

"What's the matter?" I shouted at her. "What have you taken?"

"Go away! Leave me alone!"

At this point the youth appeared behind my back and Helena cried out, "Go away, Jindra! Go away!" She lifted herself off the wooden seat and reached out for the door, but I stepped in between her and the door so that she was forced to totter back onto the round opening of the seat.

In a moment she lifted herself off it again and threw herself at me with a desperate strength (really *desperate,* for she seemed to have little strength left after her last exhausting effort). She gripped the lapels of my jacket with both hands and pushed me out; both of us were now over the threshold. "You beast, beast, beast!" she shouted (if one can call this furious effort to force an enfeebled voice a shout), and tried to shake me; then, suddenly, she let go and started to run across the grass towards the courtyard. She wanted to run away but was betrayed: she had rushed from the outhouse in confusion, without being able to arrange her clothes, so that her panties (the same stretch panties I had seen yesterday, which also served as a garter belt) were twisted around her knees and kept her from advancing (her skirt was down, but the silk stockings on her legs had fallen and their dark, upper fringe with the garters hung below her knees and could be seen beneath her hem); she took a few little steps or jumps (in her high-heeled shoes), but before she had gone even ten feet she fell (fell onto the sunny grass, under the branches of a tree, near the tall, gaudy sunflowers); I took her by the hand and tried to help her up; she tore away from me, and when I bent down over her again, she started flailing wildly so that I caught several blows before I could seize her, using all my strength, pull her to me, pick her up, and hold her in my arms as in a straitjacket. "Beast, beast, beast, beast!" she gasped as she pummeled me on the back with her free hand; and when I said (as gently as possible), "Calm down, Helena," she spat in my face.

Without relaxing my grip, I said: "I'm not letting you go until you tell me what you took."

"Go away, go away!" she repeated frantically, but then she suddenly went quiet, ceased all resistance, and said: "Let me go"; she said it in such a different (weak and weary) voice that I loosened my hold and looked at her; to my horror, her face was lined with some terrible effort, her jaws clamped shut, her eyes unseeing, and her body bending forward, slightly crouched.

"What's the matter?" I asked, and she turned without a word and made her way back to the outhouse; I'll never forget the way she walked: the slow, irregular, jerky steps of her fettered feet; she had only a few yards to cover, but more than once she was forced to stop, and in those intervals I could see (from the way her body cramped) the battle she was waging with her outraged entrails; finally she reached the outhouse, took hold of the door (which had remained wide open), and pulled it shut behind her.

I stayed in the spot where I had picked her up from the grass; and when a loud plaintive moan came from the outhouse, I retreated even farther. Only then did I realize that the youth was standing beside me. "Stay here," I told him. "I'll go find a doctor."

I went into the office; I spotted the telephone right away; it was on the nearest desk. Finding the telephone book was harder, I couldn't see it anywhere. I tried to open the middle drawer of the desk, but it was locked, as were all the smaller side drawers; the second desk was locked as well. I went into the other room; the desk there had only one drawer; it was open, though there was nothing in it but a few photographs and a paper knife. I didn't know what to do, and (now that I knew that Helena was alive and hardly in mortal danger) I was overcome with fatigue; I stood there for a while, staring dumbly at the clothes tree (that lanky metal clothes tree with its arms raised like a soldier ready to surrender); then (not knowing what to do) I opened the cabinet; there on a pile of documents was a blue-green telephone book. I took it over to the telephone and looked up the hospital. I had dialed the number and was listening to the ringing when the youth burst into the room.

"Don't phone anybody! There's no need to!" he shouted. I didn't understand.

He tore the receiver from my hand and put it back on the hook. "I told you, don't bother!"

I asked him to explain what was happening.

"It's not poison at all!" he said, and went over to the clothes tree; he put his hand into the pocket of the trenchcoat and took out a small bottle, which he opened and turned upside down; it was empty.

"Is that what she took?" I asked.

He nodded.

"How do you know?"

"She told me."

"Is it yours?"

He nodded. I took it from him. It had ALGENA printed on the label.

"Don't you know that analgesics are harmful in large doses like that?" I shouted at him.

"There were no analgesics in it," he said.

"What was, then?"

"Laxative tablets," he snapped.

I yelled at him, told him to stop trying to make a monkey of me, that I had to know what had happened and that I wouldn't stand for any more of his insolence. I wanted a straight answer immediately.

Hearing me shout, he shouted back: "I've told you. There were laxatives in the bottle. Does everybody have to know my guts are messed up?" And I understood then that what I'd taken for a stupid joke was the truth.

I looked at him, at his ruddy face and snub nose (small, but large enough to accommodate a considerable quantity of freckles), and the meaning of the whole thing became clear to me: the Algena bottle was a disguise for the ludicrousness of his ailment, just as the jeans and leather jacket were a disguise for the ludicrousness of his childish features; he was ashamed of himself, and he carried his adolescent's lot through life with great difficulty; in that moment I loved him; with his bashfulness (that nobility of adolescence) he had saved Helena's life and spared me years of sleepless nights. In dazed gratitude I looked at his protruding ears. Yes, he had saved Helena's life; but at the price of her immense humiliation; I knew that, and I also knew that it was a humiliation without purpose, a humiliation without meaning, utterly unjust; I knew that it was only another irredressible link in the chain of irredressible links; I felt a guilty and urgent (if vague) need to run after her, to raise her up out of this humiliation, to humiliate myself before her, to assume all the blame and all the responsibility for the senselessly cruel incident.

"What are you staring at?" barked the youth. I walked past him into the hallway without answering; I turned towards the door into the courtyard.

"What are you going out there for?" He caught me from behind by the shoulder of my jacket and tried to pull me towards him; for a second we looked into each other's eyes; then I gripped his wrist and removed his hand from my shoulder. He shoved past me and stood blocking my way. When I went up to him, intending to push him aside, he swung and punched me in the chest.

It was a feeble blow, but he jumped away and stood in front of me in a naïve boxer's stance; his expression was a blend of apprehension and rash courage.

"She doesn't need you out there!" he shouted. I stayed where I was. I thought that maybe he was right: there was nothing I could do to redress the irredressible. And the youth, seeing me standing there not putting up any defense, went on shouting: "She detests you! She doesn't give a shit what happens to you! She said so! She doesn't give a shit what happens to you!"

Nervous tension makes one defenseless not only against tears, but also against laughter; the literal sense of the youth's last words made the corners of my mouth twitch. That maddened him: this time he hit me in the mouth. Then he stood back and again put his fists in front of his face like a boxer, so that only his protruding pink ears were visible behind them.

"That's enough!" I said. "I'm going now."

He shouted after me: "You bastard! You bastard! I know you had something to do with this! I'll get you! You swine!"

I went out into the street. By now it was empty as streets are empty after a festival. A gentle breeze raised the dust, driving it over the flat ground that was as vacant as my own empty, stunned head, in which not a single thought occurred for quite a while.

It was only later that I suddenly found I had the empty Algena bottle still in my hand; I looked at it; it was badly scratched; evidently it had served for a long time as a disguise for laxatives.

After still another long moment, the bottle reminded me of two other bottles, the two bottles of Alexej's barbiturates; they made me realize that the youth had not really saved Helena's life after all: even if there had been analgesics in the bottle, they could hardly have given her more than an upset stomach, especially with the youth and myself so close at hand; Helena's desperation had settled its account with life at a safe distance from the threshold of death.

18

SHE WAS standing in the kitchen over the stove. Standing with her back to me. As if nothing had happened. "Vladimir?" she replied without turning. "You saw him yourself, didn't you? Why ask?" "You're lying," I said. "Vladimir went off this morning with Koutecky's grandson on his motorcycle. I've come to tell you that I know it. I know why you were pleased when that silly radio lady came this morning. I know why I wasn't supposed to be there for the robing of the king. I know why the king kept silent even before the Ride began. It was all very well thought out."

My certainty confused Vlasta. But she soon regained her presence of mind and tried to defend herself by attacking. It was a strange attack. Strange because the opponents didn't stand face to face. She was standing with her back to me, her face turned towards the gurgling soup. Her voice was not raised. It was almost indifferent. As if what she was saying were some ancient self-evident truth that only my eccentricity and lack of understanding obliged her to repeat. If I wanted to hear it, then this was it. From the beginning, Vladimir had not wanted to be king. And Vlasta was not surprised. There was a time when the boys used to do the Ride of the Kings by themselves. Now it was run by a dozen organizations and even the Party District Committee had a meeting about it. Nowadays people couldn't move a finger on their own. Everything was arranged from above. Before, the boys used to elect the king themselves. Now, Vladimir had been suggested to them from above to please his father, and everyone had to obey. Vladimir was ashamed to be a privileged child. Nobody likes people who rely on pull.

"Do you mean Vladimir is ashamed of me?" "He doesn't want to rely on your pull," Vlasta repeated. "Is that why he made friends with those narrow-minded Kouteckys? Those petty bourgeois?" I asked. "Yes, that's why," said Vlasta. "Milos isn't allowed to go to the university because of his grandfather. Just because his grandfather owned a construction company. Vladimir had his way paved with roses. Just because you're his father. Vladimir finds it hard to take. Can't you see that?"

For the first time in my life I was angry with her. They'd tricked me. All the time they'd been coolly observing how I looked forward to the Ride of the Kings. How sentimental, how excited I was. They had calmly deceived me and calmly watched me being deceived. "Was there really any need to deceive me like that?"

Vlasta salted the noodles and said I made things difficult. I was living in another world. I was a dreamer. They didn't want to take my ideals from me, but Vladimir was different. He had no use for my singing and whooping. He got no pleasure from it. He was bored by it. I'd just have to accept it. Vladimir was a modern person. He took after her father. Her father was always a great one for progress. He was the first farmer in the village to have a tractor before the war. Then he had everything taken from him. But from the time the fields went to the cooperative they'd never yielded half as much.

"I'm not interested in your fields. What I want to know is where Vladimir went. He went to the motorcycle races in Brno. Admit it."

She had her back to me, stirring the noodles, and calmly went on talking. Vladimir took after his grandfather. He had his chin and eyes. Vladimir isn't interested in the Ride of the Kings. Yes, if I really wanted to know, he did go to the races. He went to watch the races. Why shouldn't he? He's more interested in motorcycles than in horses in streamers. What of it? Vladimir is a modern person.

Motorcycles, guitars, motorcycles, guitars. A stupid, alien world. I asked: "Just tell me, what does it mean, a modern person?"

She had her back to me, stirring the noodles, and said that even our home couldn't be furnished in a modern way. What a fuss I'd made about that modern floor lamp! Even the modern chandelier I hadn't liked. And yet anyone could see that the modern floor lamp was beautiful. Lamps like that were being bought everywhere these days.

"Shut up," I said. But there was no stopping her. She was all wound up. With her back to me. With her small, spiteful, bony back. This was what irritated me most of all. Her back. That back without eyes. That back so stupidly sure of itself. The back I couldn't come to terms with. I wanted to make her shut up. Turn her around to face me. But I felt such distaste for her that I didn't even want to touch her. I'll make her turn around some other way. I opened the cabinet and took out a plate. I dropped it on the floor. She was silent for a moment. But she didn't turn around. Another plate, more plates. She still had her back to me. Huddled up within herself. I could see from her back that she was afraid. Yes, she was afraid, but she was defiant and wouldn't give in. She stopped stirring and stood motionless, gripping the wooden spoon in her hand. She was hanging on to it as if it could save her. I hated her and she hated me. She didn't move and I never took my eyes off her as I threw more and more china from the shelves onto the floor. I hated her and I hated the whole of her kitchen. Her modern standard kitchen with its modern cabinets, modern plates, and modern glasses.

I felt no excitement. I looked calmly, sadly, almost wearily at the floor covered with fragments of broken china, with pots and pans strewn over it. I was throwing my home on the floor. The home that I'd loved, the home, my refuge. The home in which I'd felt the gentle domination of my poor servant girl. The home I'd peopled with fairy tales and songs about guardian spirits. Over there on those three chairs we'd sat and eaten our dinners. Oh, those peaceful dinners when the silly trusting breadwinner was appeased and bamboozled. I picked up one chair after another and broke their legs off. I put the crippled chairs down on the floor with the pots and broken china. I turned the kitchen table upside down. Vlasta was still standing motionless by the stove with her back to me.

I went out of the kitchen into my own room. There was a red globe hanging from the ceiling, a modern floor lamp, and a hideous modern couch. My violin lay in its black case on the harmonium. I picked it up. At four o'clock we had our concert in the restaurant garden. It was still only one. Where could I go?

I heard sobbing from the kitchen. Vlasta was crying. Her sobs were heartrending, and somewhere deep inside me I felt a painful regret.

Why hadn't she started crying ten minutes ago? I could have let myself be taken in by the old self-delusion and seen her again as the poor servant girl. But it was too late now.

I left the house. The calls could still be heard across the village roofs. We have a pauper king, a righteous one. Where could I go? The streets belonged to the Ride of the Kings, home belonged to Vlasta, the taverns belonged to the drunks. Where do I belong? I am the old king, abandoned and banished. A righteous pauper king without heirs. The last king.

Luckily there are fields beyond the village. A road. And ten minutes away the river Morava. I lay down on the bank. I put the violin case under my head. I lay there for a long time. An hour, maybe two. And I thought of how I'd come to the end. So suddenly and unexpectedly. And it was here. I could not imagine any continuation. I had always lived in two worlds at once. I believed in their mutual harmony. It had been a delusion. Now I had been ousted from one of those worlds. From the real world. Only the other one, the imaginary world, is left to me now. But I can't live only in the imaginary world. Even though I am expected there. Even though the deserter is calling for me and has a horse ready and a red veil for my face. Now I knew! Now I understood why he forbade me to take off the veil and wanted me to know only what he related to me! Now I understood why the king's face must be veiled! Not that he should not be seen, but that he should not see!

I couldn't imagine myself getting up and leaving. I couldn't imagine myself taking a single step. I was expected at four. But I wouldn't have the strength to get up and leave. I only like it here. Here by the river. Here there is water flowing, slowly, and for millennia. It flows slowly and I will lie here, slowly and long.

Then someone spoke to me. It was Ludvik. I expected another blow. But I was not afraid now. Nothing could shake me now.

He sat down and asked if I would be at the performance that afternoon. "You're not going, are you?" I asked him. "I am." "Is that why you came from Prague?" "No, that's not why I came. But things turn out differently from the way we expect." "Yes," I said, "completely differently." "I've been wandering through the fields for an hour. I didn't expect to find you here." "Neither did I." "I have something to ask of you," he said, without looking me in the eye. Just like Vlasta. But I didn't mind it from him. I liked it from him when he didn't look me in the eye. I had the impression that it was his decency. And this decency warmed and restored me. "I want to ask you," he said, "whether you might let me sit in with the band this afternoon."

19

T HERE WERE still a few hours before the next bus was due to leave, so I set off, impelled by the disquiet within me, out of the village and into the fields, trying as I went to drive from my mind all thoughts of that day. It wasn't easy: my lip stung where the youth's fist had connected with it, and again the figure of Lucie emerged to remind me that every attempt to right the wrongs done me had ended with my wronging others. I was driving the thoughts away because everything they kept repeating to me I knew very well now; I tried to keep my mind empty and to admit into it only the distant (and now scarcely audible) calls of the horsemen, which carried me away somewhere beyond myself, beyond my painful story, and thus offered me relief.

I circled the entire village along the field paths until I reached the bank of the Morava and set off along it downstream; on the opposite bank there were a few geese and in the distance woodland, otherwise just fields and fields. Then ahead of me I saw a figure lying on the grassy bank. As I got nearer, I recognized him: he was lying on his back with his face turned up to the sky, and under his head he had a violin case (all around were fields, flat and endless, just as they had been for centuries, only marred by steel pylons supporting the heavy cables of high-tension lines). Nothing would have been easier than to avoid him: his eyes were fixed on the sky and didn't see me. But on this occasion I didn't want to avoid him. I wanted instead to avoid myself and the thoughts that were thrusting in on me. I went up to him and spoke. He looked up at me and his eyes struck me as timid and apprehensive, and I noticed (this was the first time I'd seen him at close range for a number of years) that only a sparse fringe remained of the thick hair which had once added an inch or two to his already lofty stature, and that on the crown of his head there were only a few sad strands covering the bare skin; his departed hair reminded me of the long years in which I'd not seen him, and I suddenly regretted those years of separation (the calls of the horsemen, scarcely audible, came from the distance), and I felt a sudden guilty love for him. He lay before me, raised on one elbow; he was big and clumsy, while his violin case was small and black like a baby's coffin. I knew that his band (once also *my* band) would be playing that afternoon in the village, and I asked if I might be allowed to sit in with them.

I made this request before I had had time to think it through (as if the words came before the thought), so I expressed it abruptly yet completely in accord with my heart; for at that moment I was filled with a sorrowful love; love for this world I had abandoned years ago, for this world, distant and ancient, in which horsemen ride around a village with a masked king, in which people walk around in white frilled shirts and sing songs, for a world that for me is merged with images of my hometown and of my mother (my poor mother, confiscated from me) and of my youth; all day long that love had been quietly growing in me, and now it had burst out almost tearfully; I loved that ancient world and begged it to offer me sanctuary and to save me.

But how and by what right? Hadn't I avoided Jaroslav two days ago precisely because his appearance evoked that irritating folk music? Hadn't I that very morning approached the folk festival with distaste? What had suddenly destroyed the old barriers that for fifteen years had stopped me from looking back happily on my young days in the cimbalom band, stopped me from returning to my hometown with affection? Could it be because a few hours ago Zemanek had sneered at the Ride of the Kings? Was *he* perhaps the one who had made me dislike folk song, was it *he* who had now purified it again? Was I really only the other end of the compass needle of which he was the pointer? Was I really so degradingly dependent on him? No, it was not only Zemanek's mockery that had made it possible for me to regain my love for the world of folk costumes, songs, and cimbalom bands; I could love it because this morning I had found it (unexpectedly) in its forlornness; in its forlornness and in its *abandonment;* it was abandoned by pomposity and publicity, abandoned by political propaganda, abandoned by social utopias, abandoned by the swarms of cultural officials, abandoned by the affected adherence of my contemporaries, abandoned (even) by Zemanek; this abandonment had purified it; purified it like someone with not long to live; illuminated it with an irresistible *ultimate beauty;* that abandonment was giving it back to me.

The band's performance was to take place in the restaurant garden where I had recently eaten and had read Helena's letter; when Jaroslav and I arrived, there were already a few elderly people (waiting patiently for their musical afternoon) and about the same number of drunks staggering from table to table; at the back, around the wide-branched linden tree, were a few chairs, and a double bass leaned against the trunk in its gray canvas shroud; not far from it a man in a white frilled shirt was quietly running the mallets over the strings of the cimbalom; the other members of the band stood nearby, and Jaroslav introduced them to me: the second fiddle (a tall, dark young man in folk costume) was a doctor at the local hospital; the bespectacled bass player was the inspector of cultural affairs for the District Committee; the clarinetist (who agreed to lend me his instrument and alternate with me) was a schoolteacher; the cimbalom player, the only one besides Jaroslav that I remembered, was an economic planner at the factory. After Jaroslav ceremoniously introduced me to them as a founding member of the band, and thus as the clarinet of honor, we took our seats under the tree and began to play.

I hadn't held a clarinet in my hands for a long time, but I knew the first tune well, and I soon lost my initial stage fright, especially when the others voiced their approval at the end of the piece and refused to believe it was such a long time since I had played; then the waiter (the same one I'd paid in such desperate haste a few hours before) pulled up a small table, set it under the branches of our tree, and put a wickerwork demijohn of wine and six glasses out for us; gradually, we began to drink. After we played a few more pieces, I nodded to the teacher; he took back his clarinet and told me again that my playing was excellent; pleased by the praise, I leaned against the trunk of the tree, and while I watched the band, now playing without me, a long-forgotten feeling of warm companionship washed over me, and I was grateful for its coming to my assistance at the end of this bitter day. And once again Lucie emerged before my eyes, and I thought I now knew why she had appeared at the barbershop and then the next day in Kostka's tale, which was both truth and legend: perhaps she had wanted to tell me that her destiny (the destiny of the tarnished young girl) was close to mine; that although we'd passed each other by and failed to find understanding, our life stories were kindred and coupled, because they were both *stories of devastation;* just as physical love had been devastated for Lucie, thus depriving her life of a basic value, so my life had been robbed of values that were to have provided its foundations, and that were in origin pure and innocent; yes, innocent: physical love, however devastated in Lucie's life, is innocent, just as the songs of my region are innocent, just as the cimbalom band is innocent, just as the hometown I hated is innocent, just as Fucik, whose portrait I couldn't look at without loathing, is innocent, just as the word comrade, though for me it had a menacing ring, is as innocent as the word future and many other words. The fault lay elsewhere and was so great that its shadow had fallen far and wide, on the whole world of innocent things (and words), and was devastating them. We lived, I and Lucie, in a devastated world; and because we did not know how to commiserate with the devastated things, we turned away from them and so injured them, and ourselves as well. Lucie, so much loved, so badly loved, is that what you have come to tell me after all these years? Have you come to intercede for the devastated world?

The song came to an end and the teacher handed me the clarinet, saying that he was done for the day, that I played better than he did and deserved to play all the more since nobody knew when I would be coming back. I caught Jaroslav's eye and said I'd be very glad for a chance to come back as soon as possible. Jaroslav asked me if I really meant it. I said I did and we started playing. Jaroslav had long since abandoned his chair, and with his head bent back and his violin, despite all the rules, far down against his chest, he was walking up and down as he played; the second fiddle and I also stood up now and then, mainly when we wanted more space for our flights of inspiration. And exactly in those moments when we devoted ourselves to improvisations that demanded inventiveness, precision, and subtle interplay, Jaroslav became the soul of us all, and I was amazed at what an excellent musician this big fellow was, belonging as he did (he especially) to the devastated values of my life; he had been taken from me, and I (to my detriment and to my shame) had let him go, although he had been perhaps my most faithful, guileless, and innocent friend.

Meanwhile, the character of the audience gathered in the garden was slowly being transformed: to the handful of mostly elderly people who had initially followed our playing with warm interest was now added a growing crowd of young people who occupied the remaining tables, ordered (very loudly) beer and wine, and soon (as the alcohol level rose) began demonstrating their wild need to be seen, heard, and recognized. And so the atmosphere changed completely, the place grew noisier and more agitated (the boys were staggering from table to table, yelling at each other and at their girls), until I caught myself ceasing to concentrate on the music and looking too frequently at the tables in the garden, watching the adolescent faces with undisguised hatred. When I saw those long-haired heads spitting out saliva and words, my old hatred for the age of immaturity flooded back and it seemed to me that I could see nothing but actors, their faces covered by masks of cretinous virility and arrogant brutishness; I found no extenuation in the thought that the masks hid another (more human) face, since the real horror seemed to lie in the fact that the faces beneath the masks were fiercely devoted to the inhumanity and coarseness of the masks.

Jaroslav obviously felt the same, for he suddenly lowered his violin and said that he was in no mood to play for this audience. He suggested that we leave; that we take the roundabout path through the fields, the one we used to take in the old days; it was a fine day, dusk would soon be coming, it would be a warm starlit evening, at some point we would stop by a wild rosebush in the fields, and there we would play, just for ourselves, for our own pleasure, as we used to do; we'd fallen into the habit (the stupid habit) of playing only on prearranged occasions, and he had had enough of it.

At first the others all agreed, rather enthusiastically, because evidently they too felt that their love for folk music should be expressed in more intimate surroundings, but then the bass player (the inspector of cultural affairs) reminded us that we had agreed to play until nine, that this was what the District Committee and the restaurant manager expected, that it had all been planned; that we had to fulfill our obligation, that otherwise the whole organization of the festival would fall apart, and that we could play in the fields some other time.

Just then the lights on the long wires strung from tree to tree all came on; since it was not yet dark and barely even dusk, they spread no light around them but just hung there in the graying space like large motionless teardrops, white teardrops that could not be wiped away and could not flow; there was a sudden and inexplicable melancholy that was impossible to resist. Jaroslav repeated (almost imploringly) that he didn't want to stay here, that he wanted to go out into the fields, to the wild rosebush, and play there for his own pleasure, but then he made a gesture of resignation, pressed the violin to his chest, and began to play.

This time we didn't allow ourselves to be distracted by the audience and played with an even greater concentration than before; the more inattentive and rude the atmosphere in the restaurant garden, the more closely we were ringed (like a desert island) by its tumultuous indifference, the more melancholy we felt, the more we turned in towards one another, playing for ourselves rather than for the audience, forgiving the audience, so that we managed to create through the music a protective enclosure in the midst of the rowdy drunks, like a glass cabin suspended in the cold depths of the sea.

"If the mountains were paper and the oceans ink, / If the stars were scribes, and all the world could think, / Not all their words upon words, in the event, / Could come to the end of my love's testament," sang Jaroslav with the violin still at his chest, and I felt happy inside these songs (inside the glass cabin of these songs) where sorrow is not lightness, laughter is not grimace, love is not laughable, and hatred is not timid, where people love with body and soul (yes, Lucie, with body and soul), where they dance in joy, jump into the Danube in despair, where love is still love and pain is pain, where values are not yet devastated; and it seemed to me that inside these songs I was *at home*, that I derive from them, and if I had betrayed this home, I had only made it *all the more* my home (because what voice is more plaintive than the voice of the home we have wronged?); but I was equally aware that this home was not of this world (though what kind of home was it if it wasn't of this world?), that what we were singing and playing were only memories, recollections, an imaginary preservation of something that no longer was, and I felt the ground of this home sinking under my feet, felt myself falling, clarinet in mouth, falling down into the depths of years, the depths of centuries, into the fathomless depths (where love is love and pain is pain), and I told myself with astonishment that my only home was this descent, this searching, eager fall, and I abandoned myself to it and to my sweet vertigo.

Then I looked at Jaroslav to see whether I was alone in my exaltation, and I noticed (his face was illuminated by a light hanging from the linden tree) that he was very pale; he was no longer singing as he played; his lips were tightly clenched; his timorous eyes had become still more fearful; he was playing wrong notes; the hand holding the violin was slowly slipping downward. Suddenly he stopped playing and sat down. "What's wrong?" I asked; the sweat was running down his brow, and he clutched his left arm near the shoulder. "It hurts," he said. The others hadn't realized that Jaroslav was ill and were still caught up in the spell of the music, now without the first fiddle and clarinet, whose silence gave the cimbalom player a chance to excel, accompanied only by the second fiddle and bass. I immediately went up to the second fiddle (remembering that Jaroslav had introduced him to me as a doctor) and called him over to Jaroslav. Only the cimbalom and bass were playing now, while the second fiddle took Jaroslav's left wrist and held it for a long time, a very long time; then he lifted his eyelids and looked at his eyes; he touched his sweating brow. "The heart?" he asked. "Arm and heart," said Jaroslav, who looked green. By now even the bass had noticed us, propped his instrument against the linden tree, and come over to us, so that the cimbalom player was on his own, entirely unaware of what was going on and thoroughly enjoying his solo. "I'm going to phone the hospital," said the second fiddle. "What is it?" I asked him. "Very faint pulse. Cold sweat. Certainly a heart attack." "Damn!" I said. "Don't worry, he'll make it," he consoled me, and hurried into the restaurant. The people he had to push his way through were too drunk to notice anything; they were only absorbed in themselves, in their beer, in their boasting, and in their insults, which in the far corner of the garden were leading to a brawl.

Finally the cimbalom fell silent too, and we all stood in a circle around Jaroslav, who looked at me and said it was all because we'd stayed there, that he hadn't wanted to stay, he'd wanted to go out in the fields, especially now that I'd come, especially now that I'd come back to them, how beautiful it would have sounded under the stars. "Don't talk so much," I told him. "What you need now is to be calm." I was thinking that although he probably would make it, as the second fiddle had predicted, it would be a completely different life, a life without passionate devotion, without the strain of playing in the band, a life under the aegis of death, a second half, but a second half played after the game is lost, and I suddenly had the feeling that one's destiny is often complete long before death, and that Jaroslav's destiny had come to its end. Overwhelmed with sorrow, I gently stroked the top of his bald head and the long strands of hair sadly trying to cover it, and I realized with a shock that my trip home, made in the hope of striking at the hated Zemanek, had ended with me holding my stricken friend in my arms (yes, at that moment I saw myself holding him in my arms, holding him and carrying him, big and heavy, as if I were carrying my own obscure guilt, carrying him through the indifferent mob and weeping as I went).

We had stood there with him like this for about ten minutes when the second fiddle reappeared and signaled us to help Jaroslav to his feet; supporting him under the arms, we slowly led him through the noisy, drunken adolescents out into the street, where an ambulance stood waiting, all its lights ablaze.

Completed December 5, 1965

AUTHOR'S NOTE

If it didn't concern me, it would certainly make me laugh: this is the fifth English-language version of *The Joke*.

The first version was published in London in 1969 by Macdonald, in a translation by David Hamblyn and Oliver Stallybrass. I remember my amazement when I received the book in Prague; I didn't recognize it at all: the novel was entirely reconstructed; divided into a different number of parts, with chapters shortened or simply omitted. (An odd comparison: between December 1965 and early 1967 the original Czech manuscript was kept from publication in Prague by Communist censorship; I had rejected all the changes they wanted to impose on me, and the novel was finally allowed to appear in April 1967 exactly as I had written it.)

Living in a country occupied by the Russian army, deprived of my passport and so without any possibility of leaving, I found it very difficult to defend myself. I succeeded, nevertheless, in publishing a letter of protest in the *Times Literary Supplement* and even in bringing about the publication in Britain of a revised, complete version, that is, without deletions and with the chapters in their original sequence (Penguin Books, 1970). My satisfaction with this turned out to be only relative: a glance through the book showed me that the translation was still very free; for example, an obviously important matter of punctuation: Helena's monologue, comprising all of Part Two, in which each paragraph is one long "infinite" sentence in my original, had been broken up into many very short sentences. I decided to close the book and to know no more of it.

That Penguin version was actually the third. The second had been published by Coward-McCann in New York a year earlier, not long after the first British edition. It was based on the Hamblyn-Stallybrass translation; in this version the original sequence of parts was respected, but the entire text was systematically curtailed; one need only look at the first two paragraphs: in the complete version of 1970 they consist of twenty-seven lines, in the Coward-McCann edition there are only fifteen. This time all my telegrams of protest from Prague went unanswered. The American publisher was ready to show his sympathy for censored authors in Communist countries, but only on the condition that they submit to his own commercial censorship.

One day I heard that a young American professor of Slavic studies, Michael Henry Heim, had published in a specialized journal a translation of two of the passages that had been deleted from *The Joke*. I was deeply touched by this noble gesture of solidarity with mistreated, humiliated literature. When Knopf, my publisher at the time, refused for reasons obscure to me to work with the translator of my two previous books (who had all my confidence), the translation of my next novel, *The Book of Laughter and Forgetting* (1980), was assigned to Heim. And soon after that, when my new editor, Aaron Asher at Harper & Row, proposed (a dozen years after the first three mutilated versions) that *The Joke* finally appear in a faithful as well as unabridged English-language version, he too approached Heim.

At Aaron's request, I wrote a preface for that new edition of *The Joke*: there I recounted this novel's eventful history in Czechoslovakia and in France, evoked the sad tale of its three earlier English-language versions, and added two paragraphs to convey my exacting concept of the novel and also serve as a message to my new translator:

"When Goethe was working on *Wilhelm Meister*, he allowed his secretary Riemer to read proof for him and strike out a superfluous word or touch up a phrase here or there, though he would never have entrusted his poetry to him. In Goethe's time prose could not make the aesthetic claims of poetry; perhaps not until the work of Flaubert did prose lose the stigma of aesthetic inferiority. Ever since *Madame Bovary*, the art of the novel has been considered equal to the art of poetry, and the novelist (any novelist worthy of the name) endows every word of his prose with the uniqueness of the word in a poem.

"Once prose makes such a claim, the translation of a novel becomes a true art. A novelist whose works are banned in his own country is doubly conscious of the difficulties involved."

When I was sent the manuscript of the new translation, I barely read it; I had a priori confidence in a translator whom I knew as a defender of my novel and thought I could spare myself the laborious job of checking the text in detail. And so in 1982 the fourth English-language version of *The Joke* appeared, first from Harper & Row, then (with identical text) in paperback from Penguin (U.S.) with the words "in a new brilliant translation" on the cover and from King Penguin (U.K.) with "now in the new authorised translation." These words corresponded to what I myself had written in the preface: "now the same professor of literature who ten years ago published the material omitted from the English edition has done the first valid and authentic version of a book that tells of rape and has itself so often been violated."

Nevertheless, I have long been accustomed carefully to review, in manuscript, the translations of my novels, particularly the French but also the Italian, German, and English. I didn't abandon this principle when it came to *The Unbearable Lightness of Being*, on the English-language version of which I spent a great deal of time. When in the autumn of 1990 Aaron proposed the republication of *The Joke* at HarperCollins, I responded, gripped by suspicion: "Yes, of course, but first I want to reread the translation, this time with care."

And so I did. In the beginning there was nothing seriously wrong, and Part Two, "Helena," was quite good, but from the start of Part

Three, I had the increasingly strong impression that what I read was not my text: often the words were remote from what I had written; the syntax differed too; there was inaccuracy in all the reflective passages; irony had been transformed into satire; unusual turns of phrase had been obliterated; the distinctive voices of the characters-narrators had been altered to the extent of altering their personalities (thus Ludvik, that thoughtful, melancholy intellectual, became vulgar and cynical). I was all the more unhappy because I did not believe that it was a matter of incompetence on the translator's part, or of carelessness or ill will: no; in good conscience he produced the kind of translation that one might call *translation-adaptation* (adaptation to the taste of the time and of the country for which it is intended, to the taste, in the final analysis, of the translator). Is this the current, normal practice? It's possible. But unacceptable. Unacceptable to me.

In *The Art of the Novel*, I repeatedly explain my attitude regarding translation and even assert: "I once left a publisher for the sole reason that he tried to change my semicolons to periods." Knowing my attitude, readers should have had no reason to doubt the total fidelity of the fourth English-language version of *The Joke*, which I had so warmly approved in my preface. And so I considered myself guilty of having deceived them and notified Aaron that he might have a difficult time ahead of him.

He and I immediately set to work. On enlarged photocopies of the fourth version, I entered word-for-word translations of my original, either in English or in French, wherever I thought it necessary. The changes grew more numerous, and soon I realized that, based on that fourth version, a new, fifth version was taking shape. In Heim's translation there are, of course, a great many faithful renderings and good formulations; these naturally were retained, along with many fine solutions from the Hamblyn-Stallybrass translation. I sent my work in regular installments to Aaron, who created an English-language version from these disparate elements and sent it to me for final correction and approval. We had begun in the spring of 1991, and working without respite, we finished only toward the end of the year.

What more is there to say? Thanks to Aaron Asher for undertaking, without a moment's hesitation, an arduous task that in our commercialized world must seem rather quixotic. To my readers, a promise: there will not be a sixth English-language version of *The Joke*.

February 1992

Faber Modern Classics was launched in April 2015, and draws upon Faber & Faber's unique and diverse publishing since the company was first established in 1929. With titles from the fiction, non-fiction, poetry and drama lists brought together in one beautiful livery, these are the books and authors who have earned Faber a reputation for publishing the most powerful and original writing of each generation.

Faber & Faber is one of the great independent publishing houses. We were established in 1929 by Geoffrey Faber, with T. S. Eliot as one of our first editors. We are proud to publish award-winning fiction and non-fiction, as well as an unrivalled list of poets and playwrights. Among our writers we have five Booker Prize-winners and twelve Nobel Laureates, and we continue to seek out the most exciting and innovative writers at work today.